D0395553

"You didn't answer my question," Solomon said smoothly. "In case you've forgotten, I'm referring to the one about your feelings for me."

Speechless, Monique's heart sang with delight. Rays of joy pierced her soul and rose to her face like a summer sunrise.

"Say something." His deep voice simmered with barely checked passion.

With a smile trembling on her lips, she said, "You're mighty talkative tonight."

With that, Solomon advanced cautiously. The anticipation was almost unbearable. Monique's feet seemed to be drifting along a cloud until she moved into his approach. His warm strength descending over her, Solomon gathered her in his arms as she wrapped her arms around his neck and lifted her face to his. His mouth pressed against hers and swallowed the soft sigh that escaped her lips.

All hesitation fled. The kiss was everything Monique had wished it would be—and then some.

Slowly, she lifted her eyes to his. They were filled with warmth and a curious deep longing. When she did open her mouth to reply, in slow motion, he lowered his head for a feather-light brush of his lips over hers.

Eyes closed and lips parted invitingly, she hungered for more.

SENSUAL AND HEARTWARMING
ARABESQUE ROMANCES FEATURE
AFRICAN-AMERICAN CHARACTERS!

BEGUILED   (0046, $4.99)
by Eboni Snoe
After Raquel agrees to impersonate a missing heiress for
just one night, a daring abduction makes her the captive of
seductive Nate Bowman. Across the exotic Caribbean seas
to the perilous wilds of Central America . . . and into the
savage heart of desire, Nate and Raquel play a dangerous
game. But soon the masquerade will be over. And will they
then lose the one thing that matters most . . . their love?

WHISPERS OF LOVE   (0055, $4.99)
by Shirley Hailstock
Robyn Richards had to fake her own death, change her
identity, and forever forsake her husband Grant, after testifying against a crime syndicate. But, five years later, the
daughter born after her disappearance is in need of help
only Grant can give. Can Robyn maintain her disguise
from the ever present threat of the syndicate — and can she
keep herself from falling in love all over again?

HAPPILY EVER AFTER   (0064, $4.99)
In a week's time, Lauren Taylor fell madly in love with
famed author Cal Samuels and impulsively agreed to be his
wife. But when she abruptly left him, it was for reasons she
dared not express. Five years later, Cal is back, and the
flames of desire are as hot as ever, but, can they start over
again and make it work this time?

*Available wherever paperbacks are sold, or order direct from the
Publisher. Send cover price plus 50¢ per copy for mailing and
handling to Penguin USA, P.O. Box 999, c/o Dept. 17109,
Bergenfield, NJ 07621. Residents of New York and Tennessee
must include sales tax. DO NOT SEND CASH.*

MARGIE WALKER

BREATHLESS

LIBRARY OF
VAL
VALERIE SHIRLEY

PINNACLE BOOKS
KENSINGTON PUBLISHING CORP.

PINNACLE BOOKS are published by

Kensington Publishing Corp.
850 Third Avenue
New York, NY 10022

Copyright © 1995 by Margie Walker

All rights reserved. No part of this book may be reproduced
in any form or by any means without the prior written consent
of the Publisher, excepting brief quotes used in reviews.

If you purchased this book without a cover, you should be
aware that this book is stolen property. It was reported as "un-
sold and destroyed" to the Publisher and neither the Author
nor the Publisher has received any payment for this "stripped
book."

The P logo Reg. U.S. Pat. & TM Off. Pinnacle is a trademark
of Kensington Publishing Corp.

First Printing: April, 1995

Printed in the United States of America

10 9 8 7 6 5 4 3

Prologue

Twenty-five years ago

A young child, a girl about five years old, cowered in the dark. Her little body trembled with terror. Tiny, soft hands stuffed in her mouth, she stifled the tears as not to reveal her location in the small, dark closet adjacent to the violence.

"What do you mean you didn't have time?"

"Whop!"

A man's voice penetrated her sanctuary as its angry power reverberated against the walls. Though the words were muffled and incomprehensible to the child, the painful lesson wrapped around her five-year-old subconscious with each iron fist that crashed into a soft, pliable body. *A woman must do what a man says. All the time. Or else. He gives her the place she holds in his society, in his house.*

The child bit down on her bottom lip, mindful of the blood she drew. She covered her ears, shaking her head from side to side, trying unsuccessfully to block out the destructive din, now seemingly reaching its crescendo, despite her wish that "daddy stop hitting mama."

Then, there was the crash of a door bursting open, followed by another voice. A man, bigger in sound than the first, even more loud and angry. Voices locked in a verbal combat. A struggle pursued and mingled with a woman's pitiful, dirge-like cry.

Following a sudden screaming silence, the closet door flew open. At the fear of discovery, the girl squeezed her eyes shut tight, drew herself even tighter into a protective knot.

"Come on, Taylor baby."

At the tender tone, the gentle command, the little girl unfolded her tiny frame. Welcoming the promise of safety, she raced into the arms of the big man—her hero.

One

Monique's footprints crisscrossed the thick green carpet in front of the massive oak desk. She was waiting for a damage assessment.

She had called her friends Aurelius and Patricia Redmon, a handsome couple from Barbados who doubled as her attorney and business consultant, with her suspicions the night before. They agreed to meet with her at their office at eight this morning. It was one of the few appointments she'd been on time for, arriving promptly with her books and her heart in her hand.

Monique paused in her pacing to stand before the floor-to-ceiling window. Though staring out, she neither saw the flow of traffic on the freeway below, nor felt the late-May sun basking in clear blue skies and shining through, but not penetrating the thick panes. Noise and heat were both effectively locked out from the quiet, cool, professional decor of the room.

She was largely over the hurt of betrayal she'd suffered at the hands of Adrienne Simpson, who managed *T's Place* until a few days ago. Now, she had to figure out what to do about ensuring the future of her nightclub.

"Will you please sit down; you're making me nervous."

Monique flashed a weak smile at Aurelius. Honey complexioned and of medium height with coal black, wavy hair, he sat tall and straight in the high back leather chair behind his desk, quietly twiddling his thumbs. Possessing the manner of a snobbish nobleman, he was a brilliant strategist in entertainment law. He'd helped many a star-craved artist out of legal jams with unscrupulous managers and greedy record companies.

"What's taking so long?" she asked, moaning impatiently as she sat on the edge of the hard leather chair in front of the desk. Her gaze slid to the closed door adjoining the room. She feared the longer Patricia remained cloistered with the books, the worst the damage.

"I estimated she took about seven thousand dollars," she said as if speaking to herself. Then, slapping her thighs, she got up to resume pacing. "Damn," she exclaimed softly, knuckling her forehead. Had she been more suspicious than worried, she might have been able to prevent the theft, she chided herself.

Monique pulled a handful of braids off her neck, then let them fall back in place down her back. Why did she always seem to pick the wrong people to trust, she wondered. Adrienne was the second manager to betray her.

"Ms. Simpson took eight thousand, seven hundred thirty-three dollars and forty-two cents exactly," Patricia corrected, as she sauntered into the room, waving a balance sheet in her hand.

Disgusted, Monique growled deep in her throat as she dropped in the chair. She slid her hands down her face and held them there, fingers splayed to peek through the hurt showing in her lovely cat eyes.

"She's been siphoning for the past three months," Patricia said, passing the paper to Aurelius. "She started right after the last quarter statement and apparently intended to be gone before the next one."

"I trusted her, you know," Monique said somberly. "I can't believe she did this to me."

"Press charges," Patricia said unflinchingly.

"No," Monique said wearily, shaking her head. She had already slept on that decision. "There's no way I'll be able to get the money back. She hasn't come in or called in three days. I haven't been able to reach her anywhere—her mother's or the baby-sitter's."

"But if you don't press charges, the insurance company . . ."

Monique put a halt to the reminder, holding up her hand like a traffic cop. "I know. But if I report the theft, I can could count on an investigation by the Alcohol & Beverage Commission, in addition to having my insurance rates go up. Both are hassles I can live without right now. I'd rather eat the loss." Pushing herself up slowly, she asked herself rhetorically, "Why didn't I see this coming?"

Aurelius looked up from his reading. "Shall I answer that?"

"No," Monique and Patricia replied simultaneously.

"Well, if she thinks she's gotten away with it, she might return," Patricia said, though she didn't sound hopeful.

"Fool me once, shame on you; but fool me twice? No way," Monique quipped, raising fine, arched eyebrows. "The locks on the doors, as well as the security access code have been changed. The staff has been notified that she's persona non grata."

"That was good thinking," Aurelius commended.

"I guess I'll have to go back to the way it was in the beginning and handle everything myself," Monique said with joyless resignation.

"If I remember correctly, handling everything yourself meant living off No-doze, coffee, cigarettes, and four hours of sleep," Patricia recited on her fingers. "Your doctor could have survived off your business alone."

Monique moaned as she buried her face in her hands, recalling the grueling schedule she'd kept during the first six months of running *T's Place*. She was an energetic, decisive woman and her well of determination was deep, honed by a desperate sense of survival and pride. But just thinking about a future of repeating those days that had her eating antacid pills like candy created a burning sensation in her stomach.

"Unfortunately, I don't see where I have any other choice," Monique said with sad fatalism. "Adrienne has proved conclusively that if you don't do it yourself, then someone's going to do it to you."

"Monique," Aurelius said, looking at her with a fond, paternal look, "marketing, promotions and making people feel at home are things at which you perform exceptionally well. You're a wonderful person, a bundle of energy; you're full of ideas and drive . . ."

Monique interrupted the listing of her better qualities before the 'but' came. "I'm just too gullible and naive," she said, but only because she trusted the Redmons.

"No," he said, shaking his head, "you're neither of those. You just don't want to acknowledge the dark sides of people," he said softly, but with emphasis. "And because of that, coupled with the fact that con artists are very good at what they do, crooked employees can and will take advantage of your kind-hearted, good nature."

Monique exchanged a quiet look of knowing with Patricia, a woman she'd met in college before the accountant married the attorney. Patricia was of the same complexion of her husband, and both spoke in the lyrical accents indicative of their native home, but that's where the similarities ended. Tall, slim and lithe like a dancer, she wore her long raven hair in a twisted braid wrapped around her oval head. Her friend smiled at her sadly, nodding her head with assent.

"Okay," she replied, drawing a deep, resigned breath. "What do you propose I do?"

"Either you manage with a heavier hand, a keener eye and hire someone else to handle the other stuff, which is not my first choice," he said with emphasis. "Or," he paused to gage her reaction, "let me find you a manager this time."

Monique's gaze flew to Patricia who returned her surprised look with a concurring nod of her head. Angling her body to sit sideways in the chair, she took the Redmons in her gaze. Her "other heads" when it came to her business, they, along with her father, Marlon Robbins, were the only people she trusted with her life and livelihood.

"If you can find somebody who's going to cover my back and not put a knife in it, be my guest."

"We propose open interviews," Patricia said, reverting to a businesslike tone. "Aurelius will conduct them here. He's better at reading people than I am, so I'll just weed out the obvious non-qualified applicants based on their resumes."

They had already given the matter considerable thought, as if anticipating the inevitable, Monique mused. She felt a sense of gratitude that they were looking out for her best interest, even though it irritated her that she had failed on her own behalf. Looking at them sidelong, her bright, dual-toned almond eyes narrowed suspiciously, she asked pointedly, "What do you mean by open?"

"That means I'll interview everybody whose credentials are credible." At the frown forming across her face, he said firmly, "Yes, that means men, too. You have systematically eliminated them, which I've warned you about. So," folding his arms on the desk, "if a male applicant shows up possessing all the qualities of a good manager, he will be considered. Do I make myself clear?"

Emitting a keening moan, Monique squirmed uncomfortably in her seat. She'd experienced the suffocating domination of a man once, she thought, and that was one too many times. She gnashed her teeth at the memory.

"Maybe with a man, you'll be more on your guard," he speculated out loud.

"Where are you going to find a man," Monique said in a tone reserved for dreaded things, "who'll take twenty-two thousand a year and not fresh out of college? Who has some managing experience with inventory control, scheduling, and payroll and will treat employees like human beings?" she paused for emphasis, "and who'll work for a woman?"

By the time she finished, one hand and two fingers from the other were taken up with her argument.

"Up the salary, offer full insurance coverage, and don't tell him who the real owner is," Aurelius countered, holding up three fingers. "You never told the others anyway," he reminded her.

Pensive-faced, Monique sat back in the chair and crossed her legs at the knee to wiggle a tennis-shoed foot. Conducting a quick calculation in her head, she figured she could manage the first two suggestions by dipping in the emergency fund. Subjugating her ego as far as withholding the fact that she owned *T's Place* was even easier. Aurelius was right: she had never confessed her ownership since opening the club, giving the illusion that she was a conduit for the owner who trusted her explicitly. The past managers weren't concerned with who paid them as long as they got a regular check.

But a male manager, with the right qualifications wouldn't be satisfied not knowing all. In general, men asked too many questions and wanted too much control, she thought, snorting out loud. No, she decided, before voicing her decision out loud.

"No," she said with an emphatic shake of her head. A man hadn't been allowed within a hundred yards of her heart for years. She certainly didn't want one running her business.

"This must be a business decision," Patricia said with a smile tempering her stern tone. "Remember all the plans and the dreams you have for the club. No one can take those from you. But you've got to stay open to the possibility that maybe a man can help you attain everything you've dreamed of for *T's Place*."

Monique chuckled, but it wasn't a happy sound. She didn't need either Aurelius or Patricia reminding her of the stakes. Years of going without, scrimping, saving and borrowing were invested in *T's Place*, a, long-held dream of owning her own business.

"Let me say it again, so there's no misunderstanding between us," Aurelius reiterated. "If I stumble upon a male applicant who is more qualified than a female, then that's your man."

"Pride goeth before the fall," Patricia said.

Agreeing reluctantly, Monique made a grudging sound before she spoke. "All right. I'll try it. But let's get *several* things straight, up-front . . ."

T's Place was lively inside the old warehouse turned club on the edge of downtown Houston. The line inched forward, and finally, Solomon reached the inner sanctum of the popular nightclub. The lights were dimmed, but bright enough to see your feet without losing the ambiance of adult, nighttime entertainment. As was evidenced by the long wait, the place was packed. An appreciative audience responded enthusiastically to the jazz band on stage, playing a popular, contemporary tune.

Solomon tapped his foot in time to the music, as his gaze passed over the throng of heads. All the uniformed waiting staff were busy. But he was not pleased, forced to endure another wait.

Where the hell was the hostess who was supposed to seat him, he wondered, growing disgruntled. If he got the manager's job, the length of time a customer waited would be the first problem he tackled.

The band struck up a snazzy version of *Mr. Magic.*

Just as he decided to seat himself, he caught a glimpse of the hostess. A jolt shot through him as his head snapped in a double-take.

She was slender and graceful. Under the patch of light she passed, her skin glistened with the reddish-gold undertones of the vibrant quality of her bright, warm brown complexion. Long elegant eyebrows, thickened dramatically over her almond-shaped eyes, the color unclear in the lighting. She was coming his way, a bounce in her step, a smile of apology on her face.

Cinnamon and spice, and everything nice.

Solomon was unable to tear his gaze from her. Her dark colored mane was a mass of cornrows held by a wide gold hair clasp. It was an attractive hair-do. Her throat looked warm at the circular collar of the marigold silk caftan-like gown with white embroidery. The fitted bodice defined the high perch of her full bosom and the smallness of her waist.

A customer caught her hand as she passed his table, and she lowered her head to hear over the din of the music. But she never took her eyes off Solomon. Another jolt went through him.

She was probably a college student, working as a hostess to pay for her education, he thought. Just barely legal to his 36 years. Still, he wondered at the skirmish going on inside his body, though he counted her as another favorable point to the owner.

She begged his indulgence with her piquant look—her eyes sparkling with, warmth and laughter, a finger raised in his direction. He felt generous: waiting wasn't so bad after all.

He'd interviewed for the manager's position two weeks earlier. Though he'd been skeptical about a club as a source of employment, he figured something different might be just what he needed. A bigger bank bought out the small one he'd worked for eight years as document control supervisor, managing a staff of twenty employees. His position was eliminated as the larger bank absorbed his department.

He was not a keeper. It was a point which rubbed him abrasively: a woman had been given the responsibility of handling the larger department. She had definite advantages over him that had nothing to do with job qualification, or even competence.

It was best not to dwell on it, Solomon reminded himself. He could have lived off his unemployment for a while, but he'd worked all his life. Sitting home all day, waiting for the money to run out would have only driven him crazy. Not only did he have child support payments to make, but he was a practical, sensible man who knew that at his age, it was unlikely he'd receive an offer for another peachy job that provided the income, benefits and status he'd once held.

Managing this club had definite possibilities, he mused, his eyes riveted on the hostess. Questions about the identity of the owner were evaded, tagged with an explanation that it was the "client's" wish to remain anonymous, he recalled. The attorney never referred to his "client" by name or pronoun. It shored up his suspicion that Aurelius Redmon was the absent proprietor of *T's Place*.

The young hostess excused herself from the customer and continued towards him. She had a cute little nose, with full lips parted in greeting over even teeth.

"Good evening. Welcome to *T's Place*. I'm so sorry you've had to wait," she said.

An alto voice in a soprano body, he thought. "That's quite all right," Solomon replied.

"I have a couple at a table for four who don't mind sharing if you don't mind sitting with them," she said. "Or, I could seat you upstairs, if you prefer."

"I prefer downstairs," he replied.

"Well," she said, her hands clasped together in front of her, her face smiling, "if you'll follow me."

Anywhere, he thought with uncharacteristic fancy, but followed wordlessly, watching the sway of her hips under the movement of the gown as she sauntered through the aisles with light-footed grace. Skepticism receding, he felt more optimistic about managing *T's Place*. He hoped he got the job.

* * *

Mr. Magic, where have you been?

The unsullied memory of a sultry gaze, not hers, Monique hummed the song she hadn't been able to get out of her mind all weekend long as she hopped on the elevator. The eyes belonged to a customer, she recalled, pressing the button for the fifteenth floor. He had a deep look, spoke with a deeper voice still.

Too bad. She maintained a strict policy of non-involvement with the patrons of *T's Place*. She sighed softly with regret as the elevators doors closed. With a swish, the car ascended.

Ten-thirty Monday morning and she was late for the 10 o'clock appointment with Aurelius. He was going to introduce her to the new manager of *T's Place*.

She was ambivalent about the meeting, still uncomfortable with her decision. For the past several days, she'd walked around with her fingers crossed, hoping and praying that the perfect candidate was of the female persuasion. But they had been such hectic days, she often felt she'd take the first candidate, regardless of gender or animal, Aurelius tossed her way.

But caution ruled, and she carefully reviewed the resumes of the final three candidates he recommended. Without question, the most qualified was a man, she recalled, making a bitter face.

The investigation into his professional experiences and education supported his resume. Simple attrition was cited as the reason for his job lost by his previous boss, who lauded him as a responsible individual who took his work seriously. He had the right qualifications and according to Aurelius, the perfect management temperament.

Although she knew in her head that he was right for the job, it hadn't stopped her from trying to find something wrong with him—from his divorced status to his asking salary. And she'd had that nightmare again. The one she called her "stress dream," from which she'd awakened crying like a frightened little girl. In the end, she authorized Aurelius to hire him, despite the disturbing quake she felt about allowing a man to run her business. The new manager of *T's Place* was a man named Solomon T. Thomas.

Despite all the concessions she had to make, the advantages rested with her, she reminded herself. After all, she controlled the purse. And she who controlled the money, owned the man, she mused, the lyrics of "Mr. Magic" resuming in her head, a smart-alecky expression on her face.

The car stopped, the doors opened, and Monique stepped off the elevator, heading for the office at the end of the corridor. Opening the door into the waiting room, she found it empty. Mrs. Berry, the secretary was nowhere around. Voices coming from the other side of the closed door told her that Aurelius had started the meeting without her.

Squaring her shoulders, she pasted her hostess look on her face and knocked once. At the command of "Come in," she sauntered into the room, an apology on her lips. The words stuck in her mouth, which dropped open as her eyes widened to encompass the familiar-looking man standing by one of the chairs in front of the desk.

For all of a micro-second, she felt at once both breathless and an uncanny reception of senselessness. Her wits renewed vexedly to notice the light of recognition flash across his gaze, then suddenly vanish from his eyes. He returned her astonished look with unflappable poise.

Rising from his seat, Aurelius said, "Good. You're here," as he walked around the desk to meet her.

Aurelius's presence was lost on Monique. "You," she exclaimed in an accusatory rush of breath before she could catch herself. Inexplicably, the questions posed to the unknown *Mr. Magic* popped into her head, and she felt a strange sensation of facing the answer.

He was brown-skinned like a Baby Ruth candy bar, but there was nothing babyish or sweet about him in looks or build. He was easily six feet and weighed roughly 180 pounds, with no fat bulging from the front of his shirt or anywhere else that she could see. Conservatively dressed in a dull brown suit, white shirt and dark tie, he was tall, broad-shouldered with slim hips and bow-legged. He wore laced-up black shoes! Despite the serious, reserved cast to his mouth and jawline, suggesting a persevering character, he had sensitive eyes, deep-set and piercing, creating a certain sensuality about his looks.

But it wasn't his temperament that disturbed her. Some seventh sense warned her the arrangement was not going to work. "Uh, Aurelius, can we talk in private?" she asked in a bright, cutesy voice.

"If what you have to discuss with Aurelius concerns the club, I'd like to hear it," Solomon said.

His voice was just as she remembered, deep, command-ing, and yet, oddly comforting, like a warm bubble bath. It belonged to the night with his eyes, she thought, off-bal-anced by the dynamic force of his quiet personality.

"Have you two already met?" Aurelius asked, looking back and forth between them.

"Uh, no, I mean, yes. Well, sort of," she babbled. "He came to the club last week."

"Oh," Aurelius said, with question in his tone and arched brow.

"Not by name," Solomon corrected.

"Well, permit me to do the introductions," Aurelius said. "Solomon Thomas this is Monique Robbins. Monique, this is Solomon, the new manager of *T's Place.*"

With his Barbadian accent more pronounced than usual, Aurelius sounded as if he were introducing her to her be-trothed, Monique thought, flicking a sidelong, raised brow at him.

"Miss Robbins," Solomon said respectfully.

With the phrase "that's your man" flashing across her mind as if on an electronic billboard, Monique hesitantly accepted the hand proffered to her. She felt her subconscious knew something it wasn't telling her. The touch of his hand answered her befuddled brain, as a stream of warmth ran up through her arm, and she felt branded by the contact.

"Now, what matter did you want to bring up?" Solomon asked, dropping her hand quickly. "I only ask because if it's about *T's Place*, it might affect some decisions we've been discussing."

Decisions? Starting to fume, Monique raised her brow in dismay. *They were making decisions about her club?* She wanted to scream, remind them both that she was paying for this meeting. But Aurelius gave her a keep-your-mouth-shut look, as if he'd guessed the reason behind her request for privacy.

"Yes, what is it?" Aurelius asked, cocking a warning brow at her.

Under the heat of Solomon's expectant gaze, the atmosphere in the room thickened with an unyielding tension. Monique felt out-manned. "Where's Patricia?" she asked, tempering the bite in her tone.

"Patricia had an errand to run," Aurelius replied, returning to his seat. "She won't be in until later today. What did you want to talk about? Maybe I can help," he said, shooting a one-upmanship look at her as he settled comfortably in his chair.

Aurelius no doubt planned this meeting knowing Patricia would be out of the office, Monique thought, irked by his treachery. Entertaining thoughts of revenge, she shot him a saccharine smile before she replied, "No, it's personal."

"Then maybe it will keep for a while," Solomon said.

Monique bristled at his patronizing tone. She stuck out her tongue as he turned his back to pick up something from the desk. Then he faced her guileless, all-business expression, holding a manila folder out to her. Careful not to touch his hand as she accepted the folder, the scent of woodsy cologne crossed the chasm between them.

"You were late, so we started without you," Solomon said before taking his seat.

"Please, have a seat," Aurelius offered grandly, gesturing to the second chair in front of the desk. "Solomon and I were just going over the policy he plans to instate at the club."

Policy? she thought, lifting a decidedly piqued brow at Aurelius. He returned her look with a mischievous grin on his face, and her insides quivered with irritation. She entertained reneging on the deal, but remembering the stakes, she swallowed her objections. Gripping the wooden arm of the chair like a frail, old woman who needed a prop, she eased into the chair.

"Please read through this information," Solomon instructed, "and if you have any questions, I'll be happy to go over them with you. And in the future, Miss Robbins, please try and be on time. Punctuality is a plus in my book."

The indulgent smile on his lips and condescension in his voice grated Monique's nerves. It was all she could do to keep from hitting him upside the head with his stupid folder. A subsequent warning glance from Aurelius, however, rearranged her expression to calm and polite. With her temper held in check, she crossed her legs and opened the folder on her knee.

Less than thirty minutes into the meeting following her arrival, Solomon felt as if the cool air had been sucked from the room: the temperature seemed to match the heat outside. He tugged at his tie, but didn't unloosen it, his gaze straying to Monique.

Her legs were crossed at the knee, stretching the jeans even more taut across her slender thighs. She was bobbing her foot, clad in tennis shoes, up and down like a float on rough waters. The movement was beginning to grate on his nerves. She wasn't even on the same page of the policy they were discussing; the folder opened to the first in her lap. Her disinterest was a tangible thing and irked him even more.

"After thinking about it," Solomon said, reading from the typed pages in his manila folder, "I've decided to hold off on getting the time clock until after I've been able to gage the work habits of the staff."

In the light of day, his previous assumptions were put to rest. She didn't need the make-up she'd worn Friday night; it neither enhanced or improved anything about her delicate features. Clean-faced, except for the light gloss on her generous mouth, her skin was radiant and like powdered brown sugar, smooth all over. With magnificent gray-rimmed, amber eyes, ringed with black lashes, she surpassed even his description of lovely. The sunlight streaked her long, thick braids, coloring her hair a healthy glow of chestnut.

She wasn't as young as he originally believed, and he felt exonerated for his lascivious thoughts. He guessed she was in the late-twenty to early-thirty category. Her behavior compared to a two-year old's, however; she couldn't sit still or be attentive.

"That's a good idea," Aurelius replied.

"Now, on to the next item," Solomon said, flipping to the next page. He noticed Monique's hands never moved from their poise, one arm stretched along the armrest, a delicate hand with reddish-orange painted fingernails hanging over the end. The other limb was used as a prop to rest her chin, foot still tapping the air. In that little get-up she wore—a red halter top under a sporty, yellow jacket and white, tight-fitting jeans hugging her fine hips and shapely thighs—he was tempted to add a dress code to the policy. He admitted such a measure was too petty even for him.

"I hope we're not boring you, Ms. Robbins," he said, being purposefully condescending. He sensed she hated it.

"Oh, no," she replied with an indifferent air, "not at all."

"I'm sure we're all eager to get out of here," Aurelius

said diplomatically. "We're almost done, aren't we, Solomon?"

Solomon nodded, wondering how best to broach the next matter which involved Monique. Never one for procrastinating, he decided to jump right in. "Yes. Now, we come to you, Ms. Robbins."

Clearing his throat, Aurelius said, "Uh, I thought we'd already covered Monique's role."

"Yes, we did discuss it," Solomon said, proceeding tactfully, "but that was before you offered the performance bonus."

"So what does one have to do with the other?" Monique asked, planting both feet squarely on the floor, training a puzzled gaze on him.

Now that the discussion had come to her employment, she was interested, Solomon mused sarcastically. He addressed Aurelius.

"Well, the performance bonus holds me up to a higher level of accountability. And if I'm to be responsible for the management of the club, I don't see how Ms. Robbins can continue with the carte blanche freedom she's enjoyed."

The crux of his real concern ran far deeper than accountability, Solomon mused. He worried that she did not know how to handle the money, or more specifically, the power inherently derived from having access to money. Until Ms. Robbins proved reliable and trustworthy, he thought stubbornly, he wasn't willing to surrender one penny of the finances to her.

"I don't know what you mean by carte blanche," Monique said, "but I handle the entire promotional activities for *T's Place*, as well as those matters that pertain to cleaning and upkeep. Now, if you want to vacuum and dust and change toilet paper in the restrooms, be my guest," she said saucily.

"We'll get around to that, too," Solomon replied with staid calmness, averting his gaze to look at Aurelius. "While I understand that managing and advertising are not the same, the money spent for promoting the club comes from the same operating budget. As the manager, I should decide what advertising is necessary, when it's advantageous to do so, what medium to utilize and how much money will be spent on it."

Risking a glance at Monique, Solomon saw the contentious frown on her face. She was an impertinent young woman who smelled like violets. It was quite obvious she was used to getting her way. Well, that was going to change.

"I thought he understood the duties he's been hired to perform and those I assume responsibilities for, of which I don't need his approval," Monique said heatedly to Aurelius.

"Look Aurelius," Solomon said, "certainly you . . ."

Monique cut him off, grounding out, "Aurelius."

Solomon flashed her an annoyed look, then faced the lawyer. "As I was saying, certainly you can see how unfair it is to hold me solely responsible for the keeping costs and spending on an even keel, if she can run out and spend money at her leisure."

Slapping the folder angrily in her lap, Monique snapped, "I do not spend at my leisure."

Undaunted by her outburst, Solomon said to Aurelius. "I simply don't want the fate of my success dependent on hers or anybody else's."

Monique sprang to her feet. "You wouldn't even have a fate to . . ."

Aurelius was up and around the desk before she could finish. "Settle down. Let me handle this, okay?" he said patiently, taking her by the arm.

"All right," she acquiesced, allowing him to help her back in the chair.

With irritation rising, Solomon watched the paternal handling of Monique. Aurelius was treating her like a recalcitrant child. No wonder *T's Place* was facing a crisis, he thought. Aurelius was much too soft-hearted with the employees.

"Solomon," Aurelius said, "maybe I didn't make myself clear enough. Monique is more than the hostess of *T's Place*."

In an eminently patient tone, similar to the one he'd used to calm Monique, Aurelius remained standing, his hands splayed across the top of the chair as if it were a lectern. Solomon felt the hairs on the back of his neck stand up. He had found the attorney a reasonable enough man. Until now. It abetted a new suspicion in him: Monique Robbins was *indeed* more than an employee.

"She's a valuable asset to the club. Acting in the capacity of an entertainment director, so to speak, her skillful handling of promotions has been a deciding factor in the success *T's Place* has enjoyed thus far."

If she was such a valuable asset, then why didn't Aurelius make her the manager? Solomon wondered sarcastically with an old resentment rising anew. He knew why, having fought that fight before. This time, he wouldn't stand for it. It was either him, or her.

"I see your skills in management complementing hers in advertising," Aurelius continued in his judicious tone. "I'm sure if we put our heads together, we can come up with a compromise that will satisfy everybody."

Two

"Isn't it a little too early to be drinking? You wouldn't want to drink up our profits, would you?"

Standing behind the bar with one hand wrapped around the neck of a bottle of brandy and the other clutching a shot glass, Monique cut a narrowed glance at Solomon. Framing the back doorway of the club, his shoulders filled out the beige sports coat magnificently.

Even monochromatically dressed, he was a spectacular-looking man. She shivered imperceptibly as she stared across the room at him defiantly. His piece spoken, his iron-brown eyes were no longer on her, but scanning the club.

He was to have followed her upon leaving Aurelius's office. She lost him somewhere on the freeway: he drove entirely too slow for her. He'd have gotten here faster on a bus.

Recalling Aurelius's grand idea of a compromise, she filled the glass to brimming. Decisions pertaining to entertainment and promotions were her responsibility, but everything else, from the purchase of toilet paper to hiring and firing rested with Solomon. She was to run her ideas and plans by him, not so much for approval, but to ensure he was fully informed of the club's activities. In a nutshell, she and Solomon were to co-manage *T's Place*.

"It's my profits," she mumbled softly as she belted down a swallow.

The rational part of her knew it was for the best. Still, the arrangement seemed more like a sweetheart deal to her,

an unscrupulous agreement, of which the outcome was det-
rimental to the parties concerned. Only, she had more to
lose. Sharing decisions about her club with a stranger was
like giving him a say-so in how she lived her life. Except
for business and volunteer activities, her life was unencum-
bered, free of romantic entanglements. Though not always
satisfying, she was used to it.

The pop of the glass as she set it on the bar attracted Solomon's attention. He turned his head in her direction, but neither surprise nor annoyance crossed his face. He looked so
serious, she wondered if he ever laughed, or smiled even.
Averting his gaze from her, he resumed his examination and
remained standing in the doorway, as if awaiting an invitation.

The strong, silent type, with sapient eyes. And sneaky,
too, Monique reminded herself. He'd known who she was
as early as last Friday when he came to the club.

She followed his gaze, starting from the front of the room
to the back. The tables and chairs were arranged in a half-
circle at the edge of the stage, then spread out like a fan.
Black and white batik tablecloths of muslin covered each
table and seat cushion. On different levels, knickknacks and
a small candle sat atop shelves protruding from the creamy
pink and wood paneled walls, from which oil and watercolor
paintings hung. The bar spanned the entire east wall downstairs, while upstairs it was barely visible from the railing.

Her gaze returned to his, and she wondered what he
saw . . . whether the decor revealed her attempts to create
a relaxed environment, a place to be entertained and waited
upon while retaining the comforts of home? It was all probably lost on him, she thought with a roll of her eyes. Except
for those things like the state-of-the-art sound system—
needed for the live entertainment—she'd bargain hunted.

"One of the first things I noticed when I came to the club
last week was the sense of welcome that pervaded the atmosphere," he said, disturbing the heavy silence. "It was

like entering a comfortable, oversized family room rather than a club."

Startled by his words, Monique's brow shot up. He seemed to be reading her mind. She perceived the opportunity as an invitation to speak, and she was more than happy to enlighten him: it stung that he believed her spendthrift.

"With few exceptions, the furnishings are second-hand," she said, pointing to the wood tables and chairs repaired, re-stained and polished like new. "If some of the paintings depicting family reunions look as if they were done by artists who'd yet to discover their styles, it's because they were done by students the club co-sponsored in a community art workshop last summer.

"The buffalo figurines on the shelves are origami creations. Leon, our security guard made them." Because it was too revealing, she didn't add that the tablecloths, as were a variety of others, were made on her sewing machine. "The next project is setting up a fish tank. Chris, one of the waiters, suggested it," she said.

Her eyes returning to Solomon, his gaze crossed hers in a flash, like a ray of sun glistening across water. She felt suspended there, in the gentle, contemplative look in his eyes. She knew she was breathing—the erratic beat of her heart confirmed it, but her breath was lodged somewhere between her throat and stomach. He severed contact, lowering his lids down over his ingenious eyes, and the air rushed from her lungs in a long, silent sigh that trembled in her bosom.

Monique back-pedaled to take up refuge behind the bar and reached for the bottle to pour herself another drink. Her hands shook so badly, she decided against it. Here it was just a little past noon and she was drinking, she mused dissatisfied with herself: she needed food, not liquor for lunch.

This arrangement of co-managing was not going to work, she thought for the hundredth time. Solomon T. Thomas was someone from whom she had to keep her distance. Heading in her direction, she noted he walked confidently, cleanly, with a quiet economy of effort.

"The ruby carpet doesn't look too expensive. And it blends nicely with the color schemes," he said.

Monique stared at him intently, wondering if he were mocking her. "It wasn't, and it does," she said, her expression wary.

"Whose idea was it for the decoration?" he asked.

A heartbeat of a second passed before Monique spoke. "Mine," she said clearing her throat of a non-existent obstruction.

Solomon nodded his head approvingly. "Nice touch. I like it."

A compliment? she thought, amazed. She wanted to believe the set-up was going to work out after all, but cautioned her impulsive wish.

He lifted a briefcase to the counter. It was the first time Monique noticed he carried one. She watched curiously as he pulled out a bulging folder and set it on top the bar. He re-locked the briefcase, then straightened the folder as stapled pages slid out. In a bold computer print she saw "Code of Behavior" typed across the top of the page.

"I hope you're not going to paper us to death," she said dryly. The brandy was beginning to free her inhibitions.

Feelings concealed, Solomon merely looked across the bar at her with his dark, unfathomable eyes. She felt inexplicably galled by that look, reading it as a perception of her insignificance.

"Let's get started," he said. "I guess the first thing in order is a tour. I'm especially interested in the location of the alarm system. Aurelius told me about the theft." He pulled a set of keys from his pocket and held them up. "Are these the new ones or the old ones?"

"What do you think?" she replied flippantly. If they were the old set, he wouldn't have been able to let himself in.

Solomon didn't even blink an eye. "Just wanted to be

certain," he replied. "It doesn't pay to assume. Oh," he said like an afterthought, "have you called the staff in for the meeting?"

"Yes," she said, elongating the single syllabled word. "Today is their day off, and they're not pleased by having to come in."

"Today really is the best time for me to meet them since the club is closed on Mondays," he said in his even conciliatory, mesmeric voice. Looking at her pointedly, he asked in a parenthesis, "Don't you agree?"

"I told them to be here by two-thirty," she replied. "Is that okay by you?" she asked aloud, silently adding, *Your majesty.*

Solomon lifted his left arm, and the sleeves of his coat rose to reveal a big, plain brown-banded watch on his wide wrist. *Lord, have mercy,* Monique thought, with a slight shake of her head. She would love a chance to spruce up his wardrobe. There just had to be some color in his closet!

"It's twelve-fifteen now," he said, "so that should be fine."

Readjusting his sleeve, he looked across the bar at her with that familiar look, part command, part matter-of-fact reasonableness that would make her look like an idiot if she refused to obey. Monique saluted, then turned to walk off.

"Wait a minute," he said.

Monique froze in her tracks, her shoulders sagging wearily. "Now what?" she asked as she pivoted about-face to him, arching a brow of inquiry.

"Is there an office we can work from? I really don't like being spread out all over the bar."

"Follow me," she instructed, spinning on her soles.

Briefcase clasped at his side and folder shoved under his arm, Solomon trailed after Monique at a discreet distance. She walked jauntily, leaving her flowery trail, a wild, racy scent that teased his senses. She seemed totally unaware just how appetizing she looked—a spicy, full course meal that aroused a seasoned desire in him.

He'd better get his aggression under control, he warned himself, shaking his head to clear the feasting image in his mind. Pushing through the swinging doors just beyond the bar area, he entered a large open area, with a pine scent in the air.

The room contained two yellow plastic tables with matching chairs, a set-up for coffee drinkers on a butcher's block in one corner, and a lumpy-looking love seat in a flower print fabric in another. The plaster walls were white and clean; the cement floor looked as if it had recently been scrubbed.

"This is the employee area," she said.

Her tone was just the shade of neutral before crossing over into rancor, he thought, scanning the area. Her attitude wasn't much better. "It's an awful lot of space for such a small staff," he said.

"Eventually, we'll open a kitchen," she said.

"Hm," he said thoughtfully. He would commit to no plans until after he'd had a chance to look at the books and gage the profitability of such a venture. "We'll see."

She snorted, cut her eyes at him and walked off. Suppressing a smile, he followed her down a narrow, dark corridor. She stopped at the only door near the end of the hallway and punched a set of numbers on the small square box.

"This is the stockroom," she said, pushing open the door. She turned on the light.

Solomon expected chaotic disorder. But he walked into the room and was surprisingly impressed by its organization—liquor, napkins, glasses, straws. Everything was stacked in its own neat section, either on the floor or in the opened cabinets overhead. "Looks fully stocked," he commented.

"It is," she replied dryly.

"Who has access?"

"From now on, only you and I," she replied, turning off the light.

In the dark, Solomon shook his head from side to side. She was going to be difficult. He pulled the door behind him, double checked that it locked, then retraced his steps to the employee area.

Monique was nowhere in sight. Undaunted by her rude disappearance, he followed the lights brightening the opposite corridor. Not far from the main entrance, he stumbled upon two offices behind a glass wall partition, with pink, metal mini blinds raised to their respective ceilings. Each was set up with a desk, computer work station and rollaway chair. Monique was standing at the desk in one office, her back to him, the phone at her ear.

As if sensing his presence, she turned facing him. At the uptilted comers of her small mouth smiling and her eyes sparkling diamonds of delight, Solomon felt struck by a poignant sense of deja vu. His heart slammed against his ribcage, cutting off his breath. While muttering affirmatively into the receiver, she pointed an index finger to the adjacent office.

Grateful, eager even, for the opportunity to leave, Solomon didn't stop to question if it was his office. Reaching the room, he dropped into the chair behind the desk, and breathed.

Surprise hadn't begun to define what he'd felt when Aurelius introduced her. Sure, they discussed a hostess named Monique Robbins, of whom Aurelius seemed both quite fond and protective. Still, he never expected that Monique Robbins was the woman who had haunted his thoughts in the days and created fantasies for his nights ever since last Friday. So enamored by his memory of her, he never put one and one together.

It was the way that Aurelius talked about her that made it seem impossible that they were both referring to the same woman, he reasoned to himself. The Monique Robbins whom Aurelius spoke of was a confident, seasoned veteran of the nightclub scene. This Monique seemed too young to be called a veteran of anything except a bad attitude, he thought, a frown crossing his forehead and jaw clenching in disapproval.

So far, he'd found her to be spoiled and sassy. Not at all like the kind of woman he was usually attracted to. He preferred quiet, serene woman with simple tastes, he thought fiercely, as if needing to remind himself.

He wondered if either of them, he or Aurelius, knew the real Monique. Everything about her screamed of pomp and daring, from her hairstyle, a red band in her hair today, to her narrow feet in a pair of Reeboks. Her attire, though remarkably flattering to her figure and personality, was totally inappropriate for work.

Disconcerted by his fascination, Solomon swiveled the chair away from her and scanned the office with a cursory glance. The open desk was imitation wood, but sturdy. Opening the drawers, he saw new supplies had been installed. There were no windows, but he had a very clear view of her across the glass, still on the phone. She was bent over the desk, offering a provocative profile of her loveliness.

Dragging his mind back to work, he opened the folder and rifled through the stapled pages. They contained information provided him about the current staff, as well as a set of rules he intended introducing today. He didn't have photographs of the employees, but he knew them by name, social security number and earnings. Their salaries were competitive, the pay slightly better than at other establishments.

Monique, he believed, absently tapping the desk, sold herself short as far as her earning potential was concerned. Recalling the high praise for the way she promoted the club, her salary wasn't compensatory to her hard work and skills.

Unless that sporty little red Camaro she drove like a wild-woman on the freeway coming here was part of her payment. Was she the boss's woman? If so, his reactions to her certainly showed no ethical respect in that regard.

He cocked a brow speculatively, then waved it off. "Nah,"

he mouthed silently, his gaze sliding toward the glass partition. With her delectable body draped over the desk, she was rocking from side to side, her round bottom in rhythm with the rest of her movement.

A shiver coursed through him. Solomon closed his eyes and shook his head, bemused. Perhaps there should be a dress code.

"Leon is our security guard. He couldn't get off from his other job," Monique explained to Solomon at exactly two-thirty. The members of the staff were seated at various tables in the club nearest the stage area, adjacent to the bar. They were whispering among themselves, and she knew they were curious about the stranger in their midst.

Looking every inch the executive, Solomon sat apart from the group, flipping through papers. He was as self-contained as an egg, she thought sarcastically. She could mock him all she wanted, but there was no denying the dynamic force about him, the commanding presence he exuded.

Averting her gaze to scan the youthful faces of her staff, she realized now that she hadn't even thought about how they would react to him. All were in their twenties with diverse interests, some of them in school to enhance their career opportunities. While the average length of employment spanned six to nine months, a few of the employees had been with her since the beginning.

Linking her hands in front of her, she said, "Okay troops," pausing for their attention. "I know you're all wondering what's going on. I've heard the complaints from some of you about giving up your off day, and before I continue, I want you to know that you will be compensated for your presence." The announcement was received with applause, and she bowed, tipping her head slightly to the side with a smile. "You've been assembled here for a briefing about the new developments at the club."

"I hope we haven't had another theft," someone from the back said.

"No, thank goodness," Monique replied dryly. "The owner has decided to have co-managers. You know one already, and that's me." They cheered and applauded. "The other is Mr. Solomon Thomas," she said, a hand spread in his direction.

Solomon half-rose from his seat, nodding his head toward the staff.

"Uh," Monique directed to him, "would you like individual introductions or would you prefer to learn who's who on your own?"

"It's up to you," he replied.

Deciding on individual introductions, Monique walked to the twosome seated nearest where she was standing. She put her hands on the shoulders of an elegant, mocha-faced man in a tall, taut frame. "This is Dennis Hancock. He's a second-year psychology major at Texas Southern University."

Dennis waved at Solomon, and received a nod for his greeting.

"And this is Cynthia Luckett," she said, stepping behind a dark complexioned woman with a short afro. Short and reed-thin, Cynthia was studying to take the GED. She appeared hard on the outside; the marshmallow within was deeply buried under a thick layer of bad luck.

Moving on to the next person, Monique stood by an outdoor-looking type, sun-struck with thick tawny gold hair. "This is Chris Winkler. He's studying to be a marine biologist and commutes back and forth to Galveston for classes."

"Just two days a week this summer," Chris clarified, looking up at her before turning to Solomon. "Hi," he waved. As Monique walked away, he called out, "Don't forget my fish tank."

"I won't," she replied laughingly over her shoulder. She headed for a table of three, a cafe-au-lait-complexioned woman sitting between twin, ruddy-faced males. She stood behind the woman. "This is Francine Charles. She joined us six months ago and is doing very well in the tip department."

"Hi. Welcome to *T's Place,* Mr. Thomas," Francine said in a purposefully seductive low voice, earning laughter from the group accustomed to her coquetry.

Pointing down over the heads of the men, Monique said, "Jake and Jason Webster, our bartenders."

The slim, powerfully built pair stood and bowed obsequiously. "I'm Jake. I have hair," he said, turning his head to reveal a red ponytail in a rubber band at his neck. "And I'm Jason, the smart one," the bald one said, tugging at his the earrings piercing his earlobes. Together, they said, "We're the liquor mixers."

With her light laughter joining the mirth echoing through the room, Monique circled the tables moving back toward the front. She stopped at the table where a young black man with short dreadlocks sat alone. Lanky-framed and below average height, he looked like a high school student. She recalled asking him to show proof of his age.

"This is Michael Barnes, the newest addition to our little family. He's studying to become a hair stylist."

"Hi," Michael said shyly.

"And that's it," Monique said, returning to the table where she was the lone occupant. Sitting, she said, "The floor is yours."

Solomon nodded as he got to his feet, took his position facing the group. "Hello everybody," he said. "I've heard some good things about you, that you're good at what you do and that you work well together. I'm looking forward to joining this outstanding team that Ms. Robbins has put together. As she's already mentioned, she and I will co-manage the club. I'll handle the day-to-day operations, and she will continue to take care of promotions and booking.

"I need you to bear with me over the next week or so. I'll try to learn everything as fast as possible. I've been told that some of you make extraordinary money in tips," he said, impressed, "so I know you won't have time to interrupt your work to answer my questions; you'll be too busy making money, which is exactly what I want you to do, so you won't start asking for a raise."

As chuckles wafted across the room, Monique noticed Solomon smiled and turned it on her. It brightened his arresting face, and the magnitude of it pervaded her senses. The sensation brought a warm tingle to her depths. Then he pulled his mouth in at the corners, and the placid look returned. Back to business as usual.

"There are a few changes we need to go over," he continued. "I've written them down, and we'll discuss each item and answer any of your questions," he said, walking around passing out the stapled sheets of paper. "This policy is carved in stone until the theory of it doesn't match practical applications. But one thing that won't change is the code of behavior expected of each of you, particularly regarding punctuality, absenteeism, breaks and cordiality toward customers."

Monique noticed papers rattling as the employees rifled through the policy. Though she was sitting at the front of the room, she was the last to get her handout. Solomon returned to the front of the group.

"You will notice that the shifts have been staggered," he continued. "This schedule is not carved in stone. We'll try it, and if it doesn't work, we'll change it accordingly."

"What's the reason for the change?" Chris asked.

"It was done to accommodate our peak periods, while not having you stand around when we're not busy," Solomon replied. "You still have the same number of hours."

It was also done to keep them from cheating on overtime, Monique thought with pleased suspicion. She had given them the benefit of the doubt, trusting them to be honest. Solomon was taking no chance.

"I see here we get two days off," Debbie said, tilting her brow pleased.

"Yes," he replied. "Two off-days instead of one. And

when you come, you won't be standing around competing
with each other for customers."

Thumbing through the handout to find her name,
Monique saw he scheduled her to arrive at four-thirty in the
afternoon and leave at two. It was an effective means to
keep her out of the daily decision-making before the club
opened, while also getting rid of her during the nightly cash
counts. *I don't think so,* she thought, a battlefield of wrinkles
altering the expression on her face to a tight grimace.

"Monique," Solomon called.

So intent on going through the handout to see what other
changes he planned to initiate and their effect on her,
Monique didn't hear him.

"Monique," he repeated, almost singing her name.

She looked up into Solomon's face, a smile curving his
mouth and mesmeric eyes staring at her patiently. With excitement stirring the blood that ran through her veins, it took
her a second and the laughter from the others to realize he
had been talking to her. Then, he chuckled, and the rich,
prosaic sound created a flutter in her stomach. She was both
excited and aggravated. Masking both extremes of emotion,
she joined in the chuckles. "I'm sorry," she said. "What
were you saying?"

"I developed this schedule before our meeting this morning, so you and I can sit down later and revise it, okay?"

The attempt of an apologetic look on his face increased
her ire at the rise in her pulse and heartbeat. "Okay," she
replied, her voice toneless. With a shuddering sigh, she
watched him walk back to the center of the group.

"Good," he said to the group, clapping his hands together
with emphasis. "You're expected to arrive on time and stay
until your shift is over. A two-day advance notice is required
for time off. In the event of emergencies, you need to call
me as soon as possible."

As the meeting progressed, Monique could see that Solomon proposed some good ideas. Some she had already tried

to initiate, but had little success. Someone had always managed to get around her, and before she knew it, the idea was forgotten. Maybe her presentation had been too informal. Solomon's, on the other hand, was just the opposite. He was organized, and his plans for improvement seemed well-thought out. She suspected he would enjoy greater results than she had, which suited her just fine.

"I'm really looking forward to working here," Solomon said.

The meeting was winding down, and none was more grateful than Monique. She hated long meetings in which nothing more than listening was required.

"I've been a customer at *T's Place* on several occasions," Solomon continued, "and I've always enjoyed my stay. Thanks to your prompt service with a smile"—tipping his head toward the waiters and waitresses in the group—"and the fruity drinks"—he nodded approvingly to the twins—"and the decor, from the arrangement to the glasses you serve drinks in."

He was really pouring it on thick, she thought, amazed by his metamorphosis. With her, he was staid and stuffy. With the staff, he was animated, witty even. He possessed a magic gift. Though arrogant and self-assured, he also had the ability to draw people in like a magnet. He certainly had her staff eating out of his hands. Traitors, she thought.

"As Ms. Robbins said," Solomon added, "you will be compensated, so as not to have to pay you anymore than . . ."

A faint pounding penetrated the conversational din, and Solomon fell silent. All heads turned toward the noise, coming from the front of the club.

"Some stupid can't find the doorbell," Francine said rising. "I'll get it before they start huffing and puffing and break the door down."

She left a trail of laughter and returned seconds later with a coarse, insolent-looking man of Goliath proportions. He swaggered toward the group. Behind his back, Francine mocked his walk, her shoulders stiffened and raised as she took long, wide steps.

Monique exchanged a curious glance with Solomon, then shrugged as she got to her feet. Warily, she walked into the stranger's approach, wondering who he was and what he wanted. Solomon was on her heels.

He wore black like a badge, in stark contrast to his pale white skin. His thinning black hair lay slicked across his head like a skull cap. A square wall of a forehead with heavy brows for a base, he had an obstinate mouth to go with his surly disposition.

"May we help you?"

The man who towered over Monique looked right over her head into Solomon's face. In the end, he responded to her.

"I'm looking for Adrienne. I was told she work here."

Thick with a country twang, he had a cold, stentorian voice. It sent a chill rocketing up Monique's spine. Instinctively, she took a backwards step, right into Solomon. Braced by his warm male strength, his hands steadying her gently at the shoulders, a wave of desire cascaded through her. A transient want to stay there was doused just as quickly by reason. Gathering her wits, she stood on her own two feet without further propping and cleared her throat before she spoke.

"Who are you?"

"I'm her husband," he replied, looking down at her as if daring her to deny it.

Monique wasn't the only one surprised by that revelation. She felt the staff stirring in their seats, conferring with questioning gazes at each other. She believed that the club's previous manager had been divorced from a common-law marriage. "Do you have a name?" she replied.

"Joseph. Joseph Simpson," he said. Scanning the faces of the staff, he asked, "Where's Adrienne?"

"Well, Joseph, I'd like to know the answer to that myself," Monique replied, wetting her lips with her tongue.

"She work here, don't she?" Less than half a question, it was a demand for confirmation. He swaggered a bulging muscled-shoulder forward to stand in true ruffian intimidation form.

Solomon eyed Simpson guardedly. He had lists of likes and dislikes, but one thing in particular stood out above the rest on the latter list: bullies. He considered them boys in grown-up bodies, masquerading as men. He knew their facade of power was but a paper-thin shield to cover their fears and insecurities.

Not that he was an exceptionally brave man, but he would not tolerate the brand of intimidation practiced by people like Simpson. Even his father, whom some would condemn because he ran away from his responsibilities, never relied on his physical prowess to impress his family with his masculine strength.

And Little Miss Muffin here, he thought amused to himself, keeping Monique in his gaze, his main focus on the aggressor. While he admired her courage, he knew that if Simpson just blew on her, she would go sailing across the room like a mild wind. Knowing her need to control, he hoped she wouldn't fight him for the right to face this bully.

Gently, Solomon pulled Monique aside, partially shielding her. "No. Not any longer," he replied with chilly politeness. He neither balled his fists nor shuffled his feet, giving no hints from where he would launch an attack, only that he *would* meet fire with fire.

The message received, Simpson backed down. Staring from one to the other, he said, "You're lying."

"Somebody forgot to lock the back door."

The voice coming from the opposite side of the room cracked the anxiety-filled atmosphere. Tenor in tone, it held a note of scolding. Except Solomon, who didn't take his eyes off Joseph, heads whipped around, momentarily forgetting the intruder.

"Leon," Monique said, "you made it."

Hearing the relief in her voice, Solomon was slightly miffed that she apparently placed more confidence in whomever it was who just walked in. Without relaxing his guard, he cut a sidelong glance at the man to whom Monique seemed happy to see.

The gray security guard uniform restored his memory of Leon. The guard, he noticed, matched the bully Joseph Simpson muscle for muscle, as well as in height. Toast-brown in complexion, he had a kinder face.

"Yeah," Leon replied, advancing upon the center of activity. "I was finally able to get somebody to cover for me at the last minute. What's going on here?" He stopped at Monique's side, eyeing both Joe and Solomon suspiciously.

"I was just informing Mr. Simpson that Adrienne no longer works here. And he was about to leave," Monique directed to Joseph.

Solomon watched the muscles in Joseph's hard jaw twitch. His gaze slid down Leon's arms to his waist, where his thumbs were crooked inside the belt that held the holster and gun. Power respected only power, he thought, forgiving Monique.

"You tell Adrienne to call me," Joseph said glowering, shaking a finger in the air. "I'll be waiting to hear from her at my mama's house."

Three

Solomon sighed, exasperated.

He hadn't even thought about toilet paper, but did Monique have to order the most expensive brand there was? he wondered, staring at two cases of bathroom tissue stacked taller than he. He pulled a case to the floor and opened the cardboard lids.

It was past quitting time, and instead of preparing to knock off, he was up to his elbows in work, checking inventory in the stockroom. He wanted to do his own counting to make sure that the numbers on paper actually corresponded with supplies on hand. He'd already stumbled on one discrepancy: six bottles of Barcardi rum were missing. He'd have to wait until tomorrow to ask the twin bartenders about it, though he had a sneaking suspicion that laxity was the culprit and they'd simply forgotten to write it down.

As soon as the meeting ended that afternoon, everybody shot out of the club like a cannon. Including Monique, he griped silently. He invited her to join him and now knew that was a mistake. She declined. He should have told her what he wanted her to do, he chided himself, pencil stuck behind his ear as he counted individual rolls of paper.

His management style included giving people some rope. If it was in their disposition, ultimately, they hung themselves without any help from him. Everyone would get his or her share of the rope, he thought, thinking about the employees he had inherited.

He was pleased with how easily the meeting had flowed, and even more so by the questions raised and the staff's willingness to give his ideas a chance. At least on the surface.

Completing the count, he recorded the number on the top sheet of the clipboard. He resealed the lids, then moved on to the next box.

Generally, he was on ready-alert regarding people who didn't ask questions, he mused, recalling Michael contributed nothing but his presence to the meeting. But then again, Michael was fairly new, so that could have accounted for his silence. Still, he wasn't going to relax his guard just yet.

A potential problem existed with Francine the flirt. She was a tease, which could lead to trouble with customers if she got too friendly and signals crossed. Dennis was hard to read. He had laughing eyes, but barely cracked a smile. The twins seemed exactly what they appeared to be, a pair of fun-loving pranksters. Chris and Cynthia both seemed like introverts, trying to fit in. That was not a problem.

Solomon stopped counting and stuck the head of the pen between his teeth. A pleasant muse shone in his eyes. Trouble would come in the hot package of one Monique Robbins. He felt certain of that. Lessons in professional behavior were definitely in order as far as she was concerned. Professionals didn't pout when things didn't go their way.

He shook his head, sighing at length. He knew she was going to try his patience, which was considerably long. But she was not going to get a rise out of him, he told himself with confidence and determination. Not one she could see, a silent cynic surfaced to taunt him.

All right, he wasn't perfect, he laughed at himself softly. But he had experience on his side as the oldest of seven children, five of them females. He had taken a page from his mother's book on tolerance. She used to ignore the incessant whining of her children. Eventually they stopped complaining and got creative to achieve or acquire whatever it was they wanted.

Monique Robbins was a bright woman. She would eventually catch on, too.

But, what if she didn't? a skeptic in the back of his head asked.

The answer to that was not so simple, he squirmed uncomfortably, deep frown lines forming across his forehead. He didn't want to think about it. Let's not borrow trouble, he told himself.

Just then a buzzing din, like a dull doorbell went off. Setting the clipboard atop the box, he headed cautiously to the open area, straining to hear. He heard it again, clearly a doorbell, followed by pounding on the heavy, metal door at the back of the club.

It triggered his memory of the incident earlier when the former manager's husband barged in on the meeting, demanding to see her. But it wasn't the abusive man's intrusion he remembered the most. For a flicker of a second, he held Monique in his hands. She was soft and pliant to his touch, and he had been struck by a hardy wish to hold her forever.

The pounding intensified, jolting him back to the present. Passing the bar area, he walked to the back door, thinking Monique must have left her keys. Served her right for leaving in such a haste.

"Coming," he replied to the pounding. He unlatched the bar across the wide door, then pushed it open to confront the impatient glower of a beefy-faced man chomping on an unlit cigar. "Yes, may I help you?"

The man removed the cigar from his mouth before he spoke. "I got Monique's piano," he said, pointing with a thumb over his shoulder to a white truck in the parking lot, *Macmillan Delivery Service* etched on the side.

Piano? He didn't know anything about a piano, Solomon frowned, puzzled.

"Where's Monique?" the man asked, tiptoeing to look over Solomon's shoulder inside.

"Monique is not here," Solomon replied. "Are you sure

you have the right address?" he asked, wondering if the piano was meant to be delivered to her home. The man pulled a folded receipt from his plaid shirt pocket and placed it in his hands. Reading the instructions, Solomon blew out the air ballooning his cheeks. It was as he expected. He was going to have to have a talk with Monique about spending. "Bring it in," he said.

"We're going to have to do it in pieces," the man replied walking off. "Can you prop that door open?" he asked, and without waiting for a reply, yelled to someone inside the truck, "Come on, Lester, let's get to work."

An hour later, Solomon was sitting at a table near the stage, chewing the insides of his mouth. He was still mulling over how to handle this abuse of privilege as he stared at the piano. He didn't have a problem with the club owning a piano, but not one from the top of the line. He never would have thought she had the power to cause his blood pressure to rise so soon, but she had with this major purchase.

The top of the piano was raised while Lester, Ralph McMillan's partner, fiddled under the hood with a tuning key. He plucked a note, then adjusted the sound. Ralph had gone back out to the truck for another piece.

If he didn't stop it now, Solomon told himself, Monique would only continue this rampage of spending. He wondered how the club managed to stay afloat all this time with such a big-spender at the helm. High-priced toilet paper was one thing, but a baby grand piano! At this rate and expense, the club's profits might as well take a plane to Jamaica.

What made her do it, he wondered, rubbing a hand across his head wearily. Was she so angry because she had to share managing the club that she'd gone out and ordered this expensive toy, thinking this was some way to get even? Or just to flex her autocratic, decision-making muscles?

Acting out in anger was not only childish, but distasteful to him. He didn't want to think of her being so vindictive. With deep lines of concentration etched across his forehead, he sighed pensively, searching his mind for a logical explanation.

The piano had to have been ordered before he came on the scene, he reasoned. Before she would have even known about the management arrangement, so the purchase couldn't have been done in anger. The rationale elevated his mood, but with his former marriage tipping his thoughts, he knew that anger often bred rash decisions.

Particularly when money was involved. If perceived synonymously as power, he thought, his lips pressed together in a sign of pique, the results could be disastrous.

The ruffle of those married days renewed his memory of the vow he made following his divorce: beware of women who enjoyed manipulating money. The potential for abuse was great as the application sometimes did not stop at manipulating money, but extended to people.

It was just easier to stay away from women who earned more money in the first place. Money and love mixed about as well as vinegar and Kool-Aid.

Ralph walked in carrying a padded piano bench. He exchanged it for the clipboard on the stage floor. "I need you to sign for this," he said.

"Sure thing," Solomon replied, rising to take the board. "How much did this thing cost, Ralph?" he asked, pointing his pen toward the piano.

"Twenty-two-five," Ralph replied. "Considering what they're running even used these days, that's next to nothing. It was a steal."

If she got such a good deal, maybe the piano was stolen, Solomon thought. He held onto the clipboard tightly. "It's not hot is it?" he asked anxiously.

"Nah," Ralph waved off, tugging the clipboard from his possession. "Every three years or so, the university gets new pianos, so they auction off the old stuff. I put in a bid for Monique and voilá, *T's Place* has a barely used, newly tuned baby grand."

"That's a relief," Solomon sighed the emotion. "How do you know Monique?" he asked just out of curiosity.

"She used to be a volunteer at the Houston Area Women's Center where my wife works," Ralph replied. "Now she does a lot of work with another shelter that was recently opened. Uh, Haven House, I believe it's called." Sticking the cigar back in his mouth, he called over his shoulder, "Hey Lester, you 'bout done?"

"All finished," Lester replied, gathering his instruments in the pouch.

Exchanging banal talk, Solomon walked them out and watched as they drove off.

Summer beckoned. Even in the impending dark, it was as hot as the midday heat. Only his car, a navy Cutlass Olds, remained in the parking lot. After tidying up, he decided he was going to leave for home. It had been a long first day of work.

Just as he was about to lock the door, he saw a pearl gray Cherokee Jeep vehicle pull onto the graveled parking lot and stop with a jolt. It was an old model and bore the signs of wear-and-tear. Seconds later, a woman emerged, tugging a briefcase across the seat. She wore a pencil-slim suit in lavender, high-heeled shoes, with a wide-rimmed straw hat covering her face.

As she sauntered toward the club, Solomon noticed the split in the side of the skirt, showing off a fine, straight leg. Watching the seductive sway of her body, a smile of appreciation formed on his lips. He would have whistled if he had been one for public display. Then she reached up, pulling the hat off her head to tuck under her arm. He gulped, nearly choking on the bubble of desire in his throat.

Looking up to see Solomon filling the doorway, Monique stumbled, and the heel of her shoe caught in the gravel and broke. "Damn," she said, flustered more by his presence than the shoe. It was after seven, and she expected him to be gone.

She knew she should have changed back into her tennis shoes. She grumbled under her breath, trying to balance herself, briefcase and hat as she picked up the pieces of the broken shoe.

"Where's your car?" Solomon asked, walking across the lot towards her.

While trying to salvage her dignity and dislodge her foot from the other shoe, Monique looked behind her frowning, then up at him. He was upon her, taking the briefcase from her hand.

"There it is," she said, pointing to the car with a shoe dangling off the end of her finger.

"No," he said. "I mean the sporty little red thing."

An emotion she couldn't define cracked through his usual poker-faced expression. She wondered with fleet interest what that look was all about. "That was a loaner from my mechanic," she explained, walking off. "Ouch," she exclaimed as she stepped on a sharp gravel protruding from the ground.

"What was wrong with it?" he asked, taking her arm at the elbow.

Monique steeled herself against her body's traitorous reaction to the gentlemanly, innocent touch. She clamped her mouth shut to keep from snapping at him, knowing all her frustration was self-directed.

"I noticed fluid leaking, so I took it in to be checked," she replied, with forced concentration on walking, as she tiptoed across the rocky ground. "There was a small hole in the brake line. He said it was a good thing I noticed it when I did. It was almost out of brake fluid."

Solomon deposited her inside the back door, the cement floor smooth and safe to her feet. She sighed with double-meaning, missing the warm strength of his touch. Chiding herself, she recalled she had dashed out after his meeting to attend another one. But even if she hadn't anywhere pressing to go, she would have left. She needed to get away.

"What are you still doing here?" she asked with irritation fringing her tone.

"Somebody had to be here to sign for your piano," he replied, his back to her as he locked the door.

"Oh, it came!" Walking off, she said with afterthought, "I thought Ralph said tomorrow morning."

"He was in the area," Solomon explained in reply.

In the main room of the club, Monique set her possessions on one of the front tables near the stage and hurried to the piano. She sat on the bench and ran her fingers across the keys, expecting Solomon to appear any second. She wondered where he was when he didn't.

If spending less than a full work day in his presence upset her equilibrium, how was she ever going to make this arrangement work, she asked herself. It was the question that sent her scurrying out to the meeting with Black Women In Business, one of the several organizations to which she belonged.

But even there, he dominated her thoughts. Inattentive to a decision on the floor, she was volunteered to coordinate the next Monday meeting. Pulling the lid down over the keyboard, she leaned across the top of the piano, resting her chin on folded arms. Her gaze was riveted on the door to the offices.

While begrudging the staff's alliance switching to Solomon for his ideas, she found herself admiring other things that didn't have dah-dot—as her mother used to say—to do with managing *T's Place*. She simply had to get her perspective in order. She was a business owner who realized she couldn't do it all by herself. She wanted—no, make that needed, she amended silently—*T's Place* to become a success. Money, energy and pride were tied up in that one goal.

And there was something else, too, she mused, with a bitter piece of history casting a shadow over her eyes. "A promise to keep," she whispered, sealing her lips shut with determination outlining her expression.

She'd better reconcile herself that Solomon Thomas was

the person who could help her achieve her goal. *A means to an end. That's all he was. A means to an end whom she found disturbingly attractive,* she groaned deep in her throat.

"I didn't expect you to return."

Startled, Monique's head snapped in Solomon's direction. He was standing at the corner of the bar, a clipboard in his hands, shirtsleeves buttoned at his wrists. She'd seen that confident pose before, but couldn't halt her roving gaze from the dark eyes framed by his handsome square face down to the wide set of his muscular chest. The shirt neatly tucked in at his narrow waist, the pants, with just the proper snugness to hint at powerful thighs underneath. Though the ensemble was dull in color, the fit was perfect.

Monique wet her lips with her tongue as she pushed herself upright on the bench. Her eyes followed his easy gait until he lowered himself into a chair at a front table across from her.

"I thought you'd be home having dinner by now," he added. "Why aren't you, by the way?"

He sat perfectly still, yet, looked so comfortable, she thought, feeling restless. Uncomfortable in her own club. How utterly foolish she was behaving. "I have some unfinished business to take care of," she replied.

"Oh? Like what?"

"Well," she said with forced patience, smacking her lips, "A new band is coming in for an audition and I need to get their paper work done tonight."

"I thought the club already had a band," he said. "What do you do? Interview a different band every week?"

"Depends on whether or not we have entertainment coming in from the outside," she said, pushing herself up. She had work to do, she reminded herself. Besides, she was starting to feel like an insect under glass on stage and strode to the table where she'd left her possessions.

"Outside? What does that mean?"

Opening her briefcase, she explained, "Take Juneteenth

for example. That weekend, Koko Taylor will perform, so . . ."

He interrupted asking excitedly, "Koko Taylor's coming here?"

"Yeah, you got a problem with that?" she asked defensively.

"No," he denied, "I love the blues. I'm impressed . . . again."

And she was surprised, again, she thought. "I wish we could bring in a big name more often. But the local bands provide excellent entertainment, and most of them are easy to work with. Right now, we contract them for at least two weeks. If they do exceptionally well during the run, we re-negotiate for a longer period."

"You have a contract with them?"

Clasping a brown envelope in her hand, she stared across the tables at him with a bemused look in her bright eyes. "Why do you sound so surprised?"

"I don't know," he replied, shrugging.

"You think I'm stupid?" she asked, in a hands-on-her-hips tone.

With amusement lurking in the depths of his eyes, he raised his hands in mock surrender replying, "You're putting words in my mouth."

"Then put your own words there," she quipped.

"Monique," he said, sighing wearily, "I don't want to fight with you. I don't plan to, now or ever. I suggest that if you feel so strongly against working with me and not against me, then maybe you'd better take that up with Mr. Redmon."

Indeed, she would talk to Mr. Redmon. She had some blue words for him. She had been doing bad enough on her own before he got her into the mess, she thought.

"Why do you want this job?" she asked in a soft, even tone, dropping the envelope back into the briefcase to face him headlong.

"I need to work," he replied, crossing his legs at the knee.

There was something so simple about his answer that it disturbed Monique. She couldn't say what it was exactly, except she had a feeling that he didn't mean he "needed" to work, implying he was in dire financial straits. "That doesn't answer the question," she said.

"It's the only offer I received," he said matter-of-factly, tugging at the pleat in his pants leg.

"You've been out of your last job less than two weeks," she said. "Other offers would have come."

"I wanted this one."

Monique felt a shiver run up her spine. The tone of his voice seemed to dip a little lower in his bass registry, and for a flicker of a second, no longer than a heartbeat, she thought she detected a strange gleam in his eyes. Maybe she imagined it, was looking at him through her own befuddled eyes, noticing the stamp of his usual taciturn countenance. And there they were, back to square one.

"Are you finished?" he asked.

"Yes," accompanied by a nod. Conscious of a dull throb in her head, she pulled a chair from the table and dropped into it wearily.

"Okay," he said, as if it were a summation.

She noticed the slight movement of his jaw, as if a question were on his tongue, but he never asked it. Instead, he looked at her with furrowed brow and pensive inquiry. "Say it, ask it or do something," she said, unable to bear the silence any longer.

"Who owns the club?" he asked.

Monique didn't expect the question, but knew it was coming sooner or later, "I don't know," she replied without even batting an eye.

A brow raised in disbelief, he stared at her. She met his look with her same steady gaze.

"Okay," he said, uncrossing his legs, "we need to talk about some things."

"I thought everything was said in the meeting," she replied.

"No. Not all. There are some things you and I need to get straight without the staff present or even finding out about."

There were indeed a couple of business-related matters they needed to discuss. More for her own peace of mind than anything else, she suspected. But she'd planned keeping some information to herself, giving herself a little more time to get used to her male manager. Breathing space, she told herself, time to analyze what was cueing her sensibilities.

No memory of any man ever garnering her attention so thoroughly as Solomon came to her. Particularly in so short a time span, she thought perplexed. Her reactionary responses suggested that an alien had inhabited her body, making her excessively aware of Solomon T. Thomas.

Meanwhile, she guessed she should listen to what he felt was so important to discuss with her now. "Like what?" she asked, rubbing the back of her neck.

"Your spending for one," he said. "There's nothing I can do about the piano," pointing at the stage, "but before you make any more major purchases like that, we need to discuss it. That money could have best been used for something else we really need at the club."

Too tired to speak aloud, Monique's expression asked for an example. She folded her arms across her bosom and stretched her legs out in front of her, crossing them at the ankle.

She noticed the downward cast of his gaze and followed the favorable appraisal in his eyes upwards and into hers. Approval vanished like a light being turning off and he averted his head. He fumbled with the clipboard, then began flipping through the pages as if looking for notes.

"Well, uh, more liquor," he said, letting the clipboard drop to the table with a clatter.

"Okay. Anything else?"

"Yes, it might be a good idea if I can see what you're planning to spend," he said. "The piano caught me off-guard. I almost didn't accept it. So, if I could see a list or whatever you prepare for your promotions and stuff, I'd appreciate it."

A smug smile twitched on Monique's lips. The unflappable Solomon Thomas was rattled by her, she thought, with pleased delight. It was good to see the shoe on the other foot.

"You'll have it before the week is out," she replied. "Anything else."

"Uh, no," he started, then caught himself. "There is. I almost forgot," shaking his head as if embarrassed. "Six bottles of liquor, rum to be exact, are missing from the stockroom."

"Lights out!"

The command echoed up and down the corridor, in sync with doors sliding closed. From both sides of the cement hallway, heavy steel doors locked into place with a loud clatter, then darkness descended upon the dormitory-like rooms. Two mates to a cell were sealed in for the night.

On the top bunk, the man lay on his back, hands folded behind his head and smiled in the dark. He'd been rehabilitated, a good little boy, earning brownie points for *good time,* he chuckled derisively to himself. But, it had all been worth it. Soon, he would be free.

"Hey man, you sleep?" asked the cell-mate in the bottom bunk.

"Yeah," he replied.

"Heard you up for parole soon. Is that right?"

"Uh-huh." Yeah, he thought. He had a score to settle with a meddling, busybody. If it weren't for her, he wouldn't be here now. Almost five years of his life wasted in this joint for being a man. Well, it was going to change.

"Your boy come see you today?"

"Yeah." His son. He emitted a little sarcastic laugh. Though a wimp, the boy had been a godsend. He still couldn't believe his good fortune when the young man showed up two years ago, claiming to be his son. He had run away from home in Oklahoma and tracked him down to Houston. Looking for his daddy, he thought proudly. It just went to prove that boys knew what they needed . . . knew they could only find it in their fathers, regardless of how old they were.

"What those other people come for? The Center people or whatever they're called?" the bottom cellmate asked puzzled.

"Part of my rehabilitation," he replied dryly. He didn't want to talk about the project. It made him feel like a traitor to his own manhood. "Go to sleep." His cellmate was a 'khaki', a newly arrived con to the joint. If he didn't toughen up, he was going to be a dead one, if he didn't become a victim of the *booty bandits* first, he thought amused.

"Yeah, them," the cellmate continued.

"Aw," he sighed exasperated. "All right. They come to help me get my aggression under control and learn to be sensitive," he said, recalling it was originally his son's idea. Even though the boy wasn't all a father hoped for, he wasn't stupid. It was a good ploy. "My lawyer said if I agree to participate in their program, then it would weigh in my favor with the Parole Board."

"You go do it?"

"What do you think, stupid?"

The prison neophyte fell silent for a second. "I wish somebody would come see me," he said, wistfully.

"You'll get used to it," he replied. "Now, go to sleep," he commanded, rolling to his side as he closed his eyes to dream of freedom.

Four

"Beep. Beep. Beep. Beep." Like a metronome set for whole notes in a slow beat, the measured bells announced calls on the answering machine.

For Monique's Monday schedule, it was late, after ten p.m., and she was starving. Just arriving home upon leaving the club where she and Solomon searched high and low for the missing bottles of rum, she would rather shower and call it a night. She phoned the twins who could offer no explanation, she recalled. The band that was supposed to show up for the audition didn't; nor did they call.

It had been a helluva day. Maybe she'd pass on the shower, she mused, sauntering to the desk in her home office, a windowless, pale yellow room with blue baseboards. It was complete with computer and printer stand that held the fax machine, two metal cabinets, an old model exercise bike and some plastic hand weights. It used to be a bedroom; the only remnant was a day-bed with a gold flower print comforter.

Guided by age-old habit, she pressed the PLAY button on the combination telephone-answering machine. She knew that if she didn't check the messages now, they would remain until tomorrow which might be too late. She could always reheat the stir-fried vegetables, but she had a feeling tonight's take-out dinner would be tomorrow morning's breakfast.

Waiting for the whirling sound to end as the tape prepared to deliver the messages, she dropped into the chair behind the desk as the first caller recorded began to speak.

"I know I can count on you; even though this is a last minute request."

Monique identified the male voice as belonging to her minister, Pastor Julius Franks of Third Ward Baptist Church. Making his long-winded request he rang off, saying, "You don't have to call me back. See you tomorrow evening."

With a click, the tape whirled, rewinding to deliver another message. Monique scribbled "6 dz.-Church cookies."

"Money, this is your old man calling," the next message began.

Monique smiled. The affectionate tone and use of the nickname identified the caller as her father. He accused her of always coming to him with her hands out. Though it wasn't true, she was used to it.

"I have not so good news for you," he continued.

Monique pouted, recalling she contacted her father months ago about bringing Al Jarreau to the club. As usual, the request was accompanied by a prospectus—something she learned years ago was the only thing her father responded to when money was involved.

"In the first place, A. J. is taking his act to Europe, and in the second place, he wants too much money. Well, not too much," he amended, and she chuckled, "but more than you allowed for in your budget. Now, I have a list of some other singers you might be interested in who are available and not over-priced for you. Got a pencil handy? Here goes."

Monique jotted down the names of artists he called off. Each name was accompanied by his personal opinion, which was usually on the mark.

A former record promoter, her father was the impetus for her decision to open a nightclub as a business venture. Though now an executive with a major record company in California, he used to pitch music to radio stations in several states and sometimes, squired entertainers around town. During the summer, she often accompanied him on out-of-town trips. She got the bug to work in the entertainment industry. But, basically a homebody, she didn't care for all the traveling. The club fulfilled her needs of owning a business and providing entertainment without having to leave home.

"That's it," he said. "I'll be in touch. Your old man signing off."

She stared at the names absently, a fond expression on her face. Though she sometimes found her father infuriating—questioning and commenting on every business decision she made—he had been invaluable and very supportive. Which was more than she could say about her mother, she mused as the tape reset to deliver more messages.

Barely listening to the following solicitation messages, Monique recalled her parents dissolved their marriage over two decades ago. Each had gone a separate way, taking on a different partner. Marlon Robbins was married to Cecelia, a businesswoman twenty years his junior, who made him happy.

Her mother, Kathreen, returned to her native hometown in Louisiana to marry a Baptist preacher, the Reverend Hubert Lee. As far as they knew, Monique was a high school substitute teacher who taught full-time and sold a line of women's cosmetics part-time. She never told her mother she owned a club.

Close to her father, she could expect a visit or a plane ticket from him anytime. From her mother, she was expected to perform a daughterly duty with an annual Thanksgiving visit. They succeeded in making it a happy, festive affair on the surface, as long as Monique censored herself. Questions to the effect of what she had done to contribute to their strained relationship was a surefire way to kill the occasion. Kathreen had told her that Monique imagined the barrier that prohibited the kind of close relationship she wanted.

A secret for a secret, Monique thought with a hearty sigh as the messages seemed unending. Doodling on a pad, she debated shutting down the machine altogether.

"One more," she said, covering a yawn behind her hand. "Monique . . . it's me."

She straightened in the chair, alert, recognizing that soothing voice. With her heart beating crazily with apprehension, a look of half-startled wariness shadowed her expression. Her gaze shot across the room as if expecting Dr. Anthony Ward to walk through the door. Assured of her safety, her heart rate slowed to normal and she sagged in the chair. She was neither expecting nor desirous of hearing more, but curiosity won out.

"I know you must be surprised. It's been a long time," the message continued.

"I am and it has," she said over the recording. Three and a half-years to be exact.

"I got professional help, and I just wanted you to know that," he continued, speaking slowly, as if she could respond to the tape. "The therapist helped me put things into perspective and I'm better."

"Good for you," she said dryly.

"I was hoping that maybe you and I, uh, that maybe we, uh, could have dinner sometimes. In a very public place of course. Call me. Anthony."

"Beep-beep-beep," the recorder cried, sounding the end of the messages.

"Not in a million years," she said.

The machine reset itself to await further calls. Monique shut it down completely and strode from the room to another at the end of the lighted hall.

Her hand slid up the wall as she turned the control knob. The master suite lit up. Light blue in color, it was a spacious room that revealed the fun, care, and love she had put into decorating her most private abode. A combination of two rooms, the wall to a third smaller bedroom had been knocked out, to accommodate a dual setting of sitting and sleeping area.

A built-in bookshelf spanned the wall behind the sitting area. It was simple, sparse and invited lounging. A Chiavari chair, its long padded back and low seat in navy velvet and a cherry stained rocker sat on either side of the L-shaped sofa under an adinkra cloth. A gold porcelain statue of the feline resemblance of Bastet, the goddess of music and love, with hieroglyphic writings etched around the black base sat proudly on the glass-topped drum table trimmed in imitation gold.

A miscellany of exotic cushions on a raffia rug fronted the red-brick fireplace in the center of the room, splitting it in half. Potted plants grew healthily at each end of the skirt.

The sleeping area bore a minimalist touch in furnishings—brass queen bed, oak dresser with wall mirror, TV on a stand near the French doors leading out to the patio, with burglar bars visible.

But for all the simple elegance of the decor, a gang of seven photographs on the wall above the plant stand with a fresh bunch of assorted flowers in a crystal vase and bur-gundy-leather-bound African American Bible provided more insight into the character of the room's owner.

Bearing an invisible title of *friends forever,* the color pictures were preserved in a rainbow of wooden frames. The moments captured graduation, a beach outing, a professional pose. Monique and Patricia were in some of the shots, but one face gleamed from every photo—that of a berry-brown complexioned woman with wide, sensitive eyes and an infectious smile. She was Tevis Theresa Haven, Monique's childhood friend since high school. Tevis was to have been her partner in *T's Place.*

"Well, girlfriend," Monique said, dropping to the foot of the bed, "I hope you're satisfied. I did it," she said, removing her tennis shoe. "I hired that man I told you about. Solomon T. Thomas. The T. stands for Taliaferro; I think I forgot to mention that the other day.

"But anyway . . ." she said, her voice trailing off. An unconscious smile tilted up the corners of her mouth as she continued, ". . . we officially met today, and it was not a good beginning for a long-lasting professional relationship."

She chuckled lightly, and the smile lingered quietly on her face, a dreamy cast shadowed her eyes.

"I guess you could say he's handsome," she said grudgingly, then as if caught in a lie, threw back her head and burst out laughing. "All right, he is handsome." Exhaling deeply, with a far off gaze, "No doubt about it.

"But I think he would fire me if he could—that is when he's not looking at my legs," she giggled. Stiffening her legs, she held them up, straight out in front of her, then let them fall. "I seem to have the strangest reaction to him," she said, folding her lips in her mouth. "It must be some emotional aberration or something.

"Lust," she declared, bobbing her head. "The old hormones are in an uproar. It's been a long time," she said, her eyes darkening like a black tunnel; even the hint of a smile completely vanished from her lips.

Since Anthony, she hadn't wanted a man. He had killed the desire for male companionship. Too late, she recalled, she realized she had overlooked all the warning signs—aggression masked as play, the teeth-gritting strains exerted in order to maintain calm, and suggestions about how she should dress, comb her hair, or even, sit in a chair. All were explained away as indications of how deeply he cared for her.

Monique shook her head. She felt mystified and suffused anew with humiliation. She sighed heavily in her bosom, pinching her bottom lip between her teeth. How could two intelligent women, successful in their own right, have allowed themselves to become casualties of so-called love?

Only, Monique mused, she had been far luckier than Tevis. She lived to do something about it.

But all men were not like the ones she and Tevis had the misfortune of choosing, she told herself. It was important that she remembered that. As she did, the image of Solomon appeared like a life-size color canvas in her mind. A mesmerized look forming across her face and softening her features, she recalled his chivalrous stand against Joseph Simpson.

Questions about him that didn't appear in the report popped in her head. She wondered whether he lived up to the reputation of his biblical namesake—Solomon, the wise, judicious king of Israel with a poet's tongue. The mere thought of the original Solomon's magnificence brought a smile on top of her expression. Her desires for the contemporary Solomon superimposed over her respect for the old, and her pulse quickened.

Shaking her head, ridding the image and the thought from her mind, she recalled soberly that pride and self-indulgence paved the way to the ancient ruler's downfall. Still, she speculated, wondering what would have been her friend's reaction to Solomon.

It didn't matter what he was like, she told herself. Though the raw essence of him manipulated her fancies, she wasn't interested in him beyond how he managed her club.

But as she stared headlong into the center photo of Tevis, she felt the laughter on her friend's face was one of mocking. She returned the broad smile with a stern, determined face.

"I'll make it work," she vowed softly. "Somehow or another, I'll make it work. I don't have any choice do I?"

"Monique's not gonna like that," Michael said.

Doesn't matter, Solomon thought, as he quietly continued rearranging chairs and tables in the club.

The inventory check complete, Solomon had begun inspecting the club for other possible improvements. His second day on the job, and he was pleased to note it promised to be as challenging as he had hoped. There was more to managing a club than counting liquor and scheduling employees after all.

Today, he was testing an idea of increasing the number of patrons the club could hold. Monique should have caught it herself, he thought. More chairs meant more money. If for some reason the arrangement didn't work, it didn't work. Monique's feelings didn't factor in the decision at all.

Aloud, Solomon said, "Who knows? She may surprise you."

"I doubt that," Michael replied skeptically, helping Solomon shove a table closer to the wall.

Though Michael was a thoroughly likable young man, Solomon mused, he was a bit protective of what he perceived as Monique's domain. He had to be careful as not to appear unyielding, while at the same time, making sure he laid a solid foundation of his authority.

"Let's get those chairs over here," Solomon said. Grabbing two chairs as Michael picked up the other two, he said, "What are you doing here today anyway? I thought Dennis was on the schedule."

"Dennis asked me to switch with him," Michael replied, setting a chair next to the table. "He had to talk to his department chairman about a grant."

"I didn't realize he was in summer school," Solomon said absently. Looking around, he instructed, "Now, let's move that one closer to the banister."

"He won't be much longer," Michael replied, picking up a small table, "if he can't get his hands on some money. He's on the verge of getting kicked out."

Relocating the chairs to the accompanying table, Solomon said, "What about you? Don't you want to go to college?"

"I've got all I can handle right now," Michael said with a chuckle.

"Well, I think I can take care of the rest," Solomon said. "Thanks, Michael."

"I'll run and get the tablecloths."

As Michael walked off, Solomon turned to survey their handiwork. Several chairs were unaligned with their tables, but overall he was satisfied.

"What are you doing?"

Solomon heard the note of a battle cry in her voice from

across the room. A hint of a smile tilted up one corner of his mouth. Steeling himself for her wrath, he calculated the potential additional earnings the new arrangement would bring.

"I said what are you doing?"

Adjusting the table just so, Solomon wondered what it would be like to fight with her on another level, a raw sexual plane. He felt his body rise like a sparring partner, stepping into the ring.

But he was snapped back to reality, recalling she was a kept woman. Inexplicably, the thought angered him. A little known feeling, jealousy, stirred his blood.

By the time he finished, his impervious mask in place, Monique stood inches from him. She wore a contentious frown on her lovely face and that wonderful sweet scent that aroused his senses.

She was dressed modestly today, he noted, a white cotton shirt that flared from her bodice over·black jeans, a black-and-white checkered pattern in her tennis shoes. But her attitude wasn't any better.

"I asked what are you doing," she repeated, her hands as expressive as her eyes, flashing at him impertinently.

"When I realized that we were not fully utilizing the space we have, I thought I'd try this," he said.

"Why? I thought you liked the arrangement."

"We have enough room. I haven't checked for certain, but I'm fairly confident that if we bought some more tables and chairs, the expense would pay for itself in no time. Are you aware of the number on our occupancy license?"

"Yes, I am," she replied in a 'so-what?' tone of voice.

"Then you know we can legally and safely seat another fifty people," he said.

"But look at what you're doing," she said. "You add more tables and chairs and you ruin not only the atmosphere, but you cut off passageway."

Solomon looked at what he had done by squeezing chairs

and tables closer together. "Well," he shrugged, "there's still enough walking space. Let's just try it and see how it works."

"I can tell you how it will work," she snapped. "The waiters will be bumping into patrons. That's how it will work, so let's not try it," she said between gritted teeth.

At club closing, it was one for Solomon, zero for Monique.

The full moon hovering high in the deep black space shone down on the gently rippling chlorinated blue water in the pool. It was aided by lampposts blanketing the fenced-in backyard with gas-powered light.

The next best thing to being there, Solomon mused.

"Well, not quite that satisfactory," he chuckled lightly. He jigged his fishing pole in the kidney-shaped pool, circling it slowly.

The night was quiet except for the occasional passing car, and the keening wail of a distant ambulance. The siren was a frequent sound in this predominantly African American community in southeast Houston.

Reaching base—the white, wrought-iron patio furniture near the sliding door of his corner-lot brick home—Solomon reeled in the weightless line. An impulsive question popped into his head as he leaned the dark red graphite pole across the back of a chair. He wondered if Monique knew how to fish.

He shook the thought away and lowered himself to a chair at the table. It was covered with fishing gear—rods of different lengths and weights, a spinning and closed-face reel, tan fishing vest with multiple pockets and a large, plastic tackle box the size of a small suitcase.

His neighbor across the street invited him to join a group of them on a fishing trip. They planned to leave at midnight and return by ten in the morning. But he knew the pull of the water was often stronger than plans to leave it, whether or not the fish were biting.

It was tempting, he mused, arranging the assortment of weights in the tray provided. He could certainly use some calming activity to combat the restlessness that followed him home from the club. Fishing could very well become a necessity instead of his hobby, he thought, thinking about his contentious co-manager, Monique Robbins.

Never before had he met a woman who evoked such strong emotions in him. Any and all kinds. Not even Elaine had come close to almost making him lose patience so powerfully. He blew out his cheeks in a whistle as he shook his head, confusion joining his restive feeling.

He'd won one battle, recalling the decorating for dollars fight he had with her. Though she had a good point, he believed her ego suffered more than her decoration scheme.

But he was hired to manage a club, not second-guess his decisions because they offended the sensibilities of its hostess, he reminded himself. Though he didn't care for the arrangement, he would deal with it. For now. In time, he would have enough proof to convince the owner that when it came to management, one head was better than two.

The war between them was far from over. But this was one he intended to win, he thought, recalling the one he had lost.

Fourteen years ago, he was 22, and the world was right with him. He had a job, a wife, and a darling new baby girl. Elaine was working as a chemist, and he was an Assistant Store Manager for a large pharmaceutical company by day, while in his third year of night school. They had both wanted the same things—a good life for themselves, an even brighter future for their daughter. They worked hard, saved their earnings and slowly, climbed rung by rung into middle-classdom.

Knowing her family background—a father who spent his paycheck faster than he could earn it—he succumbed to her obsession to control the money. Though he didn't appreciate the comparison, he believed the day would come and cut the thread holding her mistrust.

That day never came. Instead, she mistook his consent as a sign of weakness and coupled with the fact that she earned more than he, attempted to control him.

Would they still be married today if he had earned more money than she did? It was possible. But then again, what kind of marriage would it have been in the absence of love?

He felt the strains of an old debate—which came first, the chicken or the egg? If he had money, he reasoned, then there would have been no need for her mistrust. But if they had married for money, then he was back at the top of the circle, questioning the quality of the relationship.

The safest thing for him to do was stay away from women with money, he reiterated to himself. If it were likely— which it wasn't, he told himself confidently—that was one question that would never come up with Monique.

"Come on, come on," Jason urged, rubbing his hands together excitedly.

"Smells good," Monique said, twirling the shot glass half-filled with a thick, dark drink under her nose. She was about to test one of the new drinks he had concocted. They were standing behind the bar, near a section where several liqueurs, mixers and assortment of glasses were assembled.

She took a small sip, and her brows rose approvingly, before she took a full swallow. "Hmm," she said, licking the sweet chocolate foam from her lip. "I like it," she said. She flashed a winking smile at him.

"I wanted to do that," Dennis said feigning a pout as he popped into the bar as if out of nowhere.

"You wanted to do what?" Monique asked distracted.

"Lick the chocolate off your mouth," he said provocatively, leaning his face towards hers.

Monique raised her hand to halt his advance while simultaneously stepping back from him. "Dennis," she said with chiding. "You know I don't play that."

"I'm just joking," he said.

Dennis was too playful sometimes, Monique thought, watching Jason mix another drink. At one time, she suspected he had a crush on her, but he had proved too self-centered to hold that theory. Although he could irritate her with his teasing, basically, he was harmless.

"What are you doing here today anyway?" she asked, a thawing in her tone. "I thought you were off."

"I switched with Michael," he replied, filling a glass with Jason's brew. "He had an errand to run."

"Okay, now try this one," Jason said, picking up a glass already filled with a beer colored drink to pass to her.

"When did you get these?"

Monique heard Solomon before she saw him. She held her breath, feeling a tingle of anticipation at his impending nearness. Pretending to ignore him, she accepted the glass from Jason. As she began the taste-testing procedures—first sniffing the drink before actually tasting it—she was attuned to Solomon's manly fragrance. It tickled her senses to livelier heights. She cleared her throat, feeling his eyes on her as she took that first sip. Even without saying it, she knew what he was upset about. The nature of his peeve was always the same.

From the corner of her eye, she saw him gripping one of the new glasses she had bought. He sat it on the bar, staring at them with an unreadable expression. Looking intrinsically self-possessed as ever, she wondered if he ever lost his cool, undaunted poise.

"What are you doing?" he demanded at last.

"We're testing a new drink," Monique said, smacking her lips together. "Not bad," she said to Jason. "Want to . . . ? she started to ask Dennis, but he was gone. He had snuck out the other end of the bar, and she saw him heading up the stairs. She shrugged and faced Solomon. "Jason calls this one the Buffalo Highball. Want to try it?"

"No," he said succinctly. "I want to know why you bought a whole case of these glasses? Do you realize you spent a hundred bucks for twenty of these?

"It's a beer pilsner," she said. "We're going to put Jason's new Muddy Waters drink in that one."

"I don't care what you're going to put in it," he replied. He extracted the clipped tone of impatience from his voice before he spoke again. "You could have gotten a cheaper brand of this same glass," he said matter-of-factly.

He gave her a look as if dealing with a temperamental child. Monique called it condescension, and her temper flared. But she cooled it, knowing she gained no advantage arguing with him. "Well, I only bought one case," she said sweetly. You catch more flies with honey than vinegar, she reminded herself. *And a healthy dose of financial reasoning.* In that respect, Solomon was a lot like her father, she realized amazed, staring at him as if seeing him for the first time.

"If the drink goes over well," she said, "the glasses, as well as the liqueur will pay for themselves."

"How much will the drink cost?"

"Six-fifty a glass," she replied. Seeing calculations conducted in his analytical mind, she felt an uncanny sense of pride.

"Have you done a cost analysis on it?"

"Yes, I have."

"Then, make sure I get a copy," he said walking off.

The score was tied.

Five

"Hmm."

Monique sighed munificently, squired deeper in the downy softness of her bed. A smile crept into her sleep and emerging, transformed her expression into a look of pure pleasure.

"Yes," she whispered in a charmed voice. She floated into the arms of the bronze mirage behind her closed lids and was enveloped in its manly strength. A head lowered, and cool, firm lips touched hers. The breezy touch sent shivers of delight through her.

The bell of the alarm rang in one long strident scream, and Monique bolted up in bed. She looked around her bedroom, spied the morning's white sun peeping through the curtains covering the French door, then reached for the cartoon alarm clock at the head of the bed.

She didn't need to look at the time. She remembered setting the alarm last night to go off at six.

Still, she felt like ripping the bell out as she turned it off. She didn't know if she was miffed because she didn't want to get up or because the bell interrupted a pleasant dream.

The silence restored, she lay back in the drowsy warmth of her bed and stared at the ceiling absently. She knew she should get up, shower, dress and get the day started, even though she'd had a very late night. She was hesitant to leave the lingering sense of satisfaction she felt.

The details were fading from her memory, but not the

essence or the very desirous apparition of Solomon Thomas who'd invaded her sleep and awakened her womanly sensibilities.

In your dreams, she thought sarcastically. Grumpily, she flung back the covers to rise. The phone rang before she planted her feet on the floor.

"Hello," she said, answering the start of the second ring. The girlish voice on the other end brought a kind of maternal smile to her expression. "Hi, Joye, what's up?" she said. Listening to a tale of woe, her smile began to fade. "Oh, no," she said with empathy.

The Redmons were called home to Barbados for an emergency. Their oldest child and her god-daughter, Joye, didn't want to go. Godmother was called upon to offer a sympathetic ear, because both she and Joye knew that when Aurelius made up his mind, he seldom changed it.

"Listen," she said with patient reasoning, "since you're going to be there, why don't you do some shopping for me? I could really use some new items for *T's Place*. . . . I don't know. I'll leave it up to you. Is that a deal? . . . Have your Mom bring you to the club. I'll be there definitely no later than eight-thirty. Maybe by then, I'll have some specific ideas about what you can get. . . . All right, see you later."

Ringing off, Monique sat awhile on the side of the bed, feeling proud of herself. She enjoyed her role as the indulgent godmother. It was as close to motherhood she was likely to get, she thought laughingly, as she pushed herself up to dress.

She took no more than two steps before the phone rang again. Thinking is was Joye calling back, she answered before the first bell ended.

"I'm still thinking about it," she said upon answering.

"I'm glad to know that," came a masculine reply.

Monique stood stock still, gripping the receiver. "Anthony," she said, her voice void of emotion. All of it—annoyance, disgust, and wariness—shone on her face.

* * *

In . . . Out . . . In . . . Out.

Though his body glistened with perspiration, Solomon's controlled breathing was barely audible as he lifted the barbell—round weights totaling a hundred pounds attached to the end of a long, metal bar—over his head. He usually stopped lifting at fifty.

Counting off the numbers silently—sixty-nine—he lowered the weighted bar shoulder-level just above his naked chest, then back up again. Eighty. Ninety.

He performed his morning exercise to the chatter emanating from the portable, color TV on a stand in his bedroom. *Today Show* hosts were gabbing about one-hundred-degree-plus, record-breaking temperatures all over the country.

The bedroom was cool. Strictly utilitarian in style, it was comprised of a heavy wooden, king-size bed; square bedside table for the clock radio and telephone, dresser and hutch in Swedish pine. A long, rectangular mirror hung inside the door of the closet containing his wardrobe; a second closet was used to store his exercise equipment.

The chirping of early risers penetrated the sheer brown curtain over the picture window, set high in the fourth white wall. With a tan carpet on the floor, the only splash of color in the room to be found was in the comforter, a blend of earth tones in a southwest geometric design.

One hundred.

Even with the low noise, it seemed quieter in the house than it was in his head. Re-adjusting his grip on the bar, he held it out in front of him, then pulled it into his chest, starting the count at one.

He had turned on the TV to drown out the thoughts spinning in his head like a spider's web. Monique, Elaine, *T's Place*—round and round, introspection, perceptions, and images crisscrossed, twisting his thoughts in knots.

"Eleven," he said aloud as not to lose count as he continued, pushing and pulling the bar to and from his body.

He had thought about his failed marriage and ex-wife more in the past few days, than in the past five years, he thought. Even though they communicated via long distance calls, their teenage daughter Ariana was the topic and extent of their brief exchanges. Once they said their goodbyes, he never thought about her—good, bad or indifferent.

Though his exchanges with Monique had at some point resulted in all three, he failed to see what the past had to do with the present. Were there similarities between the two women—Elaine and Monique—that accounted for his mental forays into an old history and the new fantasies that plagued him?

None on the surface that he could see. A connection—if there was one, he thought, breaking count to shake his head—would unfold itself in due time. Still, he pressured himself for an explanation.

Was it possible he subconsciously was looking to fill the void in his life with a special person?

No, he answered himself, shaking his head. He was used to his solitary life now. It had been difficult adjusting to the divorce initially, but that was normal. After all, he had been a family man for nearly ten years. Remarrying never crossed his mind. Although a series of brief and meaningless affairs assuaged his physical longing for female contact, he wondered why the suggestion even popped into his head.

Not even the very desirable Monique Robbins could change that, he boasted silently. While she was pleasing to look at and just being in her presence did things to his blood, he was a devout bachelor. If, he chuckled to himself, the term was appropriate to divorcés.

As for his reactions to her, his body had only been reacting normally. After all he was no monk. It was time to go through his personal phone book. Maybe he'd give Tracy Chatham a call.

Setting the weighted-bar on the floor, he stretched his muscular arms, twisting them behind his back. He rolled the bar under the bed, then turned to head for the shower.

The phone on the bedside table rang. His gaze flew to the radio clock next to the telephone. It showed a few minutes past six. He wondered who was calling at this hour.

"Hello."

Yawning, Monique meandered into her office shortly after eight. Every day since Solomon was hired, she arrived at the club earlier and earlier, hoping to get as much of her work done as possible without having him in her shadows. But the long days of late nights and early mornings were starting to catch up with her.

She dropped her purse and briefcase on the desk. The first order of business was something she should have taken care of days ago, she chided herself. JuJu, the new band who was to start playing at the club this week failed to show for their scheduled meeting. She found it odd that they didn't call to cancel or try to make other arrangements. Not very professional, she thought.

Sitting behind the desk, she flipped through the rolodex and pulled the phone in front of her. She dialed the band leader's number. "Good-morning. May I speak to Brother Malik, please? . . . Hotep, Brother Malik, this is Sister Taifa," she said, using the African name given her, her voice animated in the Afrocentric greeting. "What happened . . . you didn't show up?" she asked, getting straight to the heart of her call.

"Who did you talk to?" she asked, easing back in the chair, her face pinched in a frown. "Did you recognize the voice? . . . Okay," she said, confusion still on her face. "I tell you what. Show up tonight and I'll consider your performance the audition." Making notes on the calendar as she spoke, she said, "If it works for us, I'll pay you for the night, then we pull out the contract. If it doesn't, you still collect."

While reviewing the contract with the leader of the six-member band, Monique turned on the computer, pulling up a graphics program. She decided to draft a press release and flyer, promoting the band's appearance at *T's Place*, in the event that they performed to her satisfaction. By the time she ended the call, the release was written.

Waiting for the print job to finish, she pulled out a black-and-white photo of the band from a file folder in the drawer and set it on the desk. She stared at it pensively, replaying the conversation with Brother Malik in her head.

He'd phoned days ago to re-confirm their pre-arranged meeting and was told she had to cancel, he had told her. He was certain he had the right number and was waiting for her return call. He had no idea to whom he had spoken; it could have been a man or a woman with a big, deep voice—which could have been anyone of three people on the staff, she thought. Or, her brows drawing into an affronted frown, it could have been Solomon.

Aside from being a mystery man, there was an air of efficiency about him that fascinated her, she thought. Though he had showed the staff he could smile and laugh and joke around he didn't do those things nearly enough. It was probably a good thing for her that he didn't, she mused, considering she seemed to have an unduly sense of aware-ness of him. He was unlike any man she noticed in a long time.

Maybe when she got to know him better, she wouldn't think so. But the onslaught of a flutter in her bosom opened a crevice of doubt in her mind.

Disconcerted that she'd gotten off track, she remembered the way he was always carrying on about her spending. It was quite possible he made what he would consider an ex-ecutive decision and canceled the meeting with JuJu, believ-ing he was saving the club some money. While a laudable concern for the budget, he had no business delving into the entertainment aspects of the club whatsoever, she thought, peeved. She was going to have to set him straight once and for all!

Just as she turned to pull the release off the printer behind her, the buzzer to the back door rang through the phone. Depressing the bar on the bottom of the phone, she asked, "Who is it?"

"Me."

Recognizing the voice, Monique chuckled. It was Patricia Redmon. "Okay, me," she replied smilingly as she rose from her seat. "I'll be right there."

Moments later, Monique was looking out across the parking lot. "Where's Joye?" she asked.

"She wasn't ready," Patricia replied. "I had to leave her."

"Shame on you," Monique chided. "Now I'm not going to get a chance to see my goddaughter before you leave."

"Hey, I told her to hurry," Patricia said in defense of her actions. "Our flight departs at three. Aurelius had to file some papers down at the court house, so when I leave here, I'm going back to pick him up," she rattled off. She paused to take a deep breath, and when she spoke again, she whispered, "Where's Solomon?"

"Mr. Punctuality is not here yet," Monique replied saucily, locking the door. "I haven't heard from him this morning." Not in person anyway, she said to herself.

"So, how has it been going?"

"Let's just say it's probably a good thing the police department is not far away," Monique replied over her shoulder as she led the way back to her office.

"You better postpone murder until we get back from Barbados," Patricia replied.

"I have my doubts that this arrangement is going to work."

"Oh? Why?" Patricia asked. "He's certainly qualified, a

business degree with accounting and supervisory experience."

She suspected he was qualified for more than managing her club, but she certainly wasn't going to tell that to Patricia. "It's not that," she replied as they turned into the office. She walked behind her desk and opened her briefcase.

"So, what's the problem?" Patricia asked. She dropped into a chair in front of the desk and folded her hands across her midriff.

Rifling through the briefcase, Monique replied, "The man has hegemonistic tendencies."

Patricia's brows arched to the roof of her forehead as she echoed, "Hegemonistic?" Flicking her fingers in the air, she said, "Ooh," with incredulity joining the humor in her voice. "Are you sure that's not your disease, instead of his?"

"I'm not . . . ," Monique started in reply, but cut the denial off herself. Hadn't she cheered her power over whomever was hired?

Patricia laughed. "You can negate a power struggle between you and Solomon anytime you want, you know," she reminded Monique. "Just tell him who's the boss. I'm not so sure why you insist on keeping that quiet anyway."

"You know why," Monique insisted stubbornly. Though she knew Patricia never bought her 'youthful looks' explanation, her friend let her keep the reason she was too embarrassed to admit openly. For all her determined and fighting spirit, she feared she inherited her mother's precarious self-esteem. There were times, usually during moments of stress, she suffered an inexplicable fear of passivity. Although her secret—ownership of *T's Place*—was a source of psychological power to her, it was also a form of self-protection.

"Okay," Patricia sighed, "if it works for you, don't change it."

"I know you," Monique said. Though generally subtle

and tactful, she could tell Patricia had more on her mind. "Say it," she commanded.

"Well," Patricia said hesitantly, "if his front looks as good as his back, maybe you should just sit back and enjoy the view and the leadership. Sorta like a two for one. Chalk it up to another one of your bargain purchases," she chuckled.

Monique's mouth fell open, as she scooted with her back pressed into the chair. Muttering a tsk, she said with scolding, "I don't believe you, of all people, could sit there and say something as, as . . ." she stammered, unable to find the words to express herself.

"My, my, I do believe my sister does protest too much."

Monique stared at the suggestive smile on Patricia's face with frustration lining hers. "It's not the view that bothers me," she said snappishly, pulling a bank envelope from a pocket in the briefcase. "And anyway, what happened to your theory that if I hired a man, maybe I will be more on guard?"

"That part seems to be working just fine," Patricia quipped. "You are definitely on guard, my friend. But I wonder whom you're guarding."

"What is that supposed to mean?"

"I heard about the sparks," Patricia replied, pausing to let the taunt settle in.

Monique muttered another disgusted tsk.

"Aurelius said he considered calling the fire department to put you two out."

"Huh," Monique uttered sarcastically. "He was hired to run my club, not complicate my life." Switching subjects, she said off-handedly, "Anthony has been calling." She spoke as if she'd kept the matter at a safe remove, confident it was a sure fire way to wipe that smirk of a smile off Patricia's face. But the ruse backfired as her face suddenly went grim recalling, "He called again this morning."

Unmasking a forbidding expression, Patricia sat upright

and stiff in the chair. "What did he want?" she asked in a tight voice that nearly growled with disapproval.

"To tell me he'd undergone therapy and that he understands his problem better and that he wants to take me out," Monique replied in a falsely sweet tone.

"Don't you dare," Patricia warned.

"Save your advice this time," Monique replied as she rose from her seat. "I have no intentions of going anyplace with him." She walked around the desk to put the envelope in Patricia's hands.

"If I even hear of it while we're gone, I'll call your daddy," Patricia said, shaking the envelope at Monique in warning.

They both knew there was no love lost between Monique's father and Anthony.

"If he becomes a problem," Patricia continued, "call James Tyler. He'll be handling all of Aurelius's cases while we're gone."

"How long will you be gone?" Monique asked, propping her hips on the edge of the desk and folding her arms across her bosom.

"Don't know yet. Aurelius's grandfather had a heart attack, and his dad called all the kids home." Fingering the crisp dollar bills, she fell silent and wetted her lips with her tongue. "Uh, Monique," she said, deep concern etched in her expression, "do you realize how much money you have in here?"

"Don't quibble with me about money," Monique said defensively, flinging her arms open.

"But, Monique," Patricia countered.

Monique cut her off. "Joye was crying her little heart out when she called me this morning. I can understand why Aurelius is insistent about her going, but that doesn't change the fact that she didn't want to go. I couldn't come up with anything else at this last minute to appease her. At least you won't have to travel with a miserable child."

"An argument like that can only come from a non-parent," Patricia countered laughingly. "What is a thirteen-year-old girl going to do with this much money?" she asked, waving the envelope.

"She and I have already discussed it," Monique said, deliberately evasive. "She knows what to do."

"Aurelius is going to have a fit," Patricia said, smiling as she shook her head.

A broad grin of revenge split Monique's face in half. "I hope so. You just be sure to give my baby that money," she threatened. "And," she emphasized, "let her spend it."

"It's your money," Patricia replied with resignation as she pushed herself up. "I hope you know you're wasting it."

"It will be a lesson learned by us all," Monique replied cryptically.

The purple scent he whiffed was his active memory on the loose again, Solomon told himself.

From the doorway, he looked over the big room. Except for music playing from an unseen source, the inner sanctum of the club was deserted. The tables were covered with a different pattern, a kente design in beige and red. There was no sign of Monique, but he knew she was here.

"I guess your assistant hasn't made it, either."

Teenagers believed they knew everything, Solomon thought, looking not far down to the girl edging womanhood at his side with paternal tolerance. Tall, pretty and healthy, he was still amazed over how much his daughter, Ariana, had grown since he last saw her seven months ago. She was brown-sugar complexioned with a ripening figure and baby-face innocence in her delicate features. Her short dark hair looked like a mass of starched curls with bangs on her forehead. It seemed to him that she was continually pulling them back from her eyes.

Despite the long drive from the airport, he hadn't been

able to erase the call from Elaine. He was still upset that she had put their daughter on a plane without first confirming he was available to pick her up.

Now, not only was he late for work, he was going to have to take some time off to get Ariana situated. He had no idea what he was going to do with her while he was at the club late at night. She definitely needed supervision; three teenage boys lived right next door to him.

He flashed her a quarter-smile and wordlessly, walked off towards the office corridor. Stopping at the door to make sure he was being followed, he said, "This way, Ariana."

At the office door, he ushered Ariana in as his gaze strayed to the companion room. It was deserted, and he wondered where was Monique. It was after ten, and even though she wasn't scheduled to arrive until later, he was grateful she had come in.

"Have a seat," he instructed, then walked off in search of Monique. Noticing the door to the stock room slightly ajar, he walked in. Here, the lilac smell was real, and he sniffed it quietly, its scent imbuing his senses with sweet familiarity as he stared with arduous candor at Monique.

Feeling a hunger rip through him, he wanted to pull her out of that box and . . . What? a silent voice of reason demanded tauntingly. As a male manager, he had to remain above reproach with female employees and shelve personal feelings, he reminded himself. So cautioned, he contented himself by indulging his insatiable desire to simply look at her. She was nearly doubled over the box containing the toilet paper as she talked to herself.

"I need some more pink ones," she mumbled disgruntled. "I guess the white will have to do for now."

Smiling to himself, he now understood why she dressed the way she did: she was always bending over. The navy and white lycra pants hugged her fine hips and round bottom attractively while allowing her freedom of movement. She wore a matching shirt tied at her waist, with blue and white Keds on her feet.

Not wanting to startle her, he cleared his throat with a light harrumph. She jumped anyway, juggling the rolls of toilet paper while trying to brace herself from following their fall back into the box.

Springing into action, he caught her at the waist with both hands and pulled her upright against him. Then, he froze. His big hands splayed around her small waist, her skin was firm, yet soft, and inviting to his touch. Sensations that were new and compelling coalesced inside him. They made him hold onto her, though no more than a second, longer than necessary and caused him to question whether he'd ever felt passion in his life. Ariana was proof that he had once felt desire, but he was hard pressed to make a comparison, he thought.

After sensing she was as affected as he, finally, Monique spun from his light possession and turned to glower up at him. He thought how adorable she looked. Her face was flushed, and her bright eyes were squinted up at him in an annoyed look, but he couldn't return her irritated sentiment.

"Will you please learn to make some noise before you sneak up on people?" she snapped.

Goaded into mobility by her sharp tone, Solomon suddenly felt embarrassed at having rational thought wrestled from his control. He quickly dug into the box, mumbling, "I'm sorry," to retrieve the rolls of paper she'd dropped. Straightening with four rolls of paper clutched against his chest, he felt like an idiot and passed them to her. "Here you go."

"Thank you," she said grudgingly.

"I'm glad you came in this morning," he managed to get out in clear tone.

He noticed her gaze moving to the door, then back on him as if in a haste to make her escape. He didn't blame her, felt the same way. But she didn't move, and neither did he. She just stood there, staring at him with her strangely veiled eyes, holding the paper against her bosom like a protective shield. Finally, after wetting her lips, she spoke.

"You're late."

"I know," he replied. "I called, but the answering machine wasn't on."

A thoughtful look crossed Monique's face. "I must have forgotten to turn it on when we left last night," she said. "So, why are you late?"

Though he'd had enough interrogation for one day, recalling Elaine's attempt to grill him about his new job, Monique deserved an explanation. Had it been the other way around, he would have asked the same thing. "My daughter Ariana is here. My ex-wife quite unexpectedly put her on a plane to Houston and didn't notify me until an hour before her flight was scheduled to arrive. I had to get her from the airport."

"Oh," Monique replied with tempered amazement.

"Yes, oh," he replied, his eyes slightly stirring to anger. He promptly reined in his feelings before continuing. "And I'm afraid I'm going to have to run out again to get her settled."

"She's here . . . at the club?"

"In my office," he said, nodding his head. He knew he should obey the command in his head to move, but his feet seemed planted where he stood, his eyes fastened on her face, as if seeing her for the first time. He felt the first time feeling, as well, only the jolt lingered, promising to occupy a place of permanence in him.

"I really hate this," he said, passing a hand across his head. "Not that I mind my daughter coming, but this is a bad time." He dropped his hand to his side. "We need to talk about that missing liquor. I haven't been able to get it out of my mind," he said. *Or you.*

Even in the privacy of his own head, the acknowledgment made him uncomfortable. He felt exposed and not at all pleased about it. It was going to make working together that much more difficult, he thought.

Silence made itself at home. A sensual static clung to the air. With her gaze taking in the magnificent expanse of him, Monique felt suspended in a lust-zone, breathing desire instead of oxygen. It mixed with his scent, a natural brand simply named clean soap and virile man.

Solomon wore his standard professional attire—white shirt with a wide paisley tie, the mundane colors complementing his navy slacks. She wondered what he would do if she removed the tie and undid the top button on his stiffly-starched white shirt. The daring muse fled as she realized his intense stare was a prompt for her to respond.

"I know," she said at last upon clearing her throat. "That's all I've been thinking about, too," she answered.

"It doesn't speak well for the staff," he replied.

"I've thought the same thing. What are we going to do?" she asked, struggling to adopt a business face to match his.

"We're going to have to tighten up even more," he said. "We've let the matter linger too long. I want to take action before something else happens."

"Okay, what do you propose?"

"I'm going to look into having security cameras installed. It will mean cutting back in other areas, but right now, I don't see any other choice. After I get some prices, I'll contact Aurelius."

"Aurelius won't be here," she said hastily. "He had to leave town for an emergency."

"Is there a number where he can be reached?"

Startled by his hard tone, she answered slowly. "Yes, but. . . ." She fell silent, her gaze sliding down his arms to his hands. They were slowly balling into fists at his sides. Her eyes returned to his; they were flat and as unreadable as stone.

"But what?" he demanded impatiently.

"I think he would rather not be disturbed," she replied frowning, puzzled by the sudden change in him.

"Then you can call him with the figures," he said tersely.

In stunned rebuff, Monique dropped the rolls of paper: most made it to the box; one didn't. His temper sparked her own. Staring after him as he walked away, she quelled the urge to scream, gritting her teeth. She felt as if she'd gone through an encyclopedia of emotions this morning and was starting over with the A's.

"Did you cancel the meeting with JuJu?" she demanded with undertones of accusation in her voice.

He stopped at the door, turned facing her with a distracted frown. "Who?"

"JuJu," she repeated, pushing the name across to him in exasperation. "The band I planned to audition the other night. I talked to the leader this morning. He called and somebody here told him I wanted to cancel the audition," she said, glaring at him accusingly. "He has been waiting for a call from me, but I never got his message in the first place."

His expression grew hard and resentful. "I don't know anything about it. And it might not be a bad idea to ask instead of accusing," he said, with reproach in his tone.

"I did ask," she replied bitingly.

"You better learn to ask a little more politely," he replied in a tense, clipped voice.

"Don't you tell me how to communicate," she retorted, scowling up at him fiercely. Somewhere in the back of her mind, a voice of reason advised her to be silent, lest she say something she would regret. But the message was lost in the gamut of perplexing emotions. "You just be sure not to overstep your bounds. I handle entertainment and promotions. Not you."

"Or you'll do what . . . ," he retorted, his voice hardening ruthlessly, "go running off to tell Aurelius?" He took a menacing step towards her. The law of self-preservation rose naturally, and Monique stepped backwards from the implied threat of his advance. She stumbled on the round roll of toilet paper. She cried out, feeling herself going down, arms flailing with nothing solid to hold on to.

She was snatched from the air, wrapped in a steel band and held against a warm wall. For a long moment, she felt as if she were floating. It all happened so fast, her head was still spinning even after she felt the ground under her feet.

Then awareness came: the relieved rushes of his warm breath fanning her neck, the gentle pressure of his taut body pressed against hers, and a heart pounding next to her bosom. Her arms were wrapped tightly around the soft flesh of Solomon's neck. She needed the support, for her knees were weakened by the quivering of her limbs.

"Don't you ever, ever jump from me again," he whispered breathlessly, his voice firmly lined. "I've never struck a woman before in my life, and I'm not about to start."

Feeling caught in the vortex of wonderful sensations swirling around her, Monique nodded her forehead against his, not trusting herself to speak. Her heart was pounding erratically, but it beat with inspired hope, not fear. Never fear, she thought, reveling in the sweet embrace.

Peeling her hands gently from their tight grasp around his neck, Solomon implored her to look at him. "Monique?"

Slowly, she lifted her eyes to his. They were filled with warmth and concern and a curious deep longing. When she did open her mouth to reply, she spoke in a weak and tremulous whisper. "Yes, Solomon."

Monique recognized the sound from her dream, a tone of need in her voice. She had no idea what he saw in her eyes. She was staring as if hypnotized by the look of scorching intent in his. It filled her with anticipation and sent a stream of warmth rippling along her pulses.

In slow motion, he lowered his head towards her until his features blurred out of sight and the only thing on her mind was his mouth on hers. In a feather-light brush of his lips over hers, he sampled her taste. Delicate, yet potent enough to send a shock wave through her entire body. The tantalizing touch put the dream into perspective, paling in comparison. Eyes closed and lips parted invitingly, she hungered for more. Partly of her own volition and in part propelled by Solomon's tightened clasp around her waist, she swayed closer to him.

Suddenly, his lips were no longer on hers, and the warmth of his arms around her was gone. She whimpered in protest.

"Ariana, what are you doing here?"

Disoriented, Monique knew she would have fallen had Solomon not steadied her as he set her away from him. She saw his eyes gazing over her shoulder, and she turned, following the direction of his look. Standing in the doorway, a young woman was eyeing them back and forth with slightly tilted brows. Solomon's daughter, she assumed, flushing miserably.

"I thought I told you to stay in my office," Solomon said.

Trying to still the wild pounding of her heart, Monique heard the hint of hollow mirth in his voice. Nervous laughter? she wondered, risking a sidelong glance up at him. His expression was unreadable. While his coloring didn't lend itself to a show of embarrassment, she knew he felt it as sanguinely as she. There was nothing either could do to alleviate their shame but make the best of it.

"Hi. I'm Monique," she said, extending the hand to the young girl. "You must be Ariana."

Ariana eyed the hand proffered skeptically, then accepted it in a limp handshake. "A Miss Caldwell from the bank wants to talk to a Monique," she announced, then spun and walked out as quietly as she had entered.

Six

Monique hurried into her office and set the armload of items—dress bag, tote and brown grocery bag—on the desk with a sigh. It was 6:30, and she had thirty minutes to dress and get to her station by seven.

With the toe of one foot pressed against the heel of the other, she stepped out of her tennis shoes, then tossed them on the chair as she returned to lock the door. As she was closing it, Michael jammed it open with his foot.

"Hold it," he said, barging in. He wore the club uniform, black slacks and a pink shirt with *'T's Place'* stitched in small black lettering on the right pocket.

"What's up, Michael?" she asked indulgently, forgetting she was running late. Her door was always open to Michael, not only the newest, but the youngest employee on the staff. His inexperience caused him to almost blow a $200 tab one night! If she didn't like him and admire his tenacity to succeed, he wouldn't have lasted even the short time he'd been employed at the club.

"Jake asked me to see if you got the B & B?" he replied, abbreviating and joining the names of two popular bourbons.

"Over there," she replied, pointing to the bag on the desk.

Walking across the room to retrieve the bag, he said chuckling, "You should have seen Solomon's expression when JuJu arrived to set up. Boy, did you miss it!"

At the mention of his name, the humiliating escapade of this morning leapt sharply into focus. Monique couldn't believe what she had done. Just remembering it caused her to blush anew, but she masked it chortling amusedly.

"No, he would not take to JuJu," she said lightly. Rastafarian-looking musicians were sporting dreadlocks and colorfully-costumed; the percussionist's face was painted like an African warrior's. They were a far cry from what Solomon was used to in his former banker's business world.

So that made them even, she thought soberly. Her swift reaction to the feel of his mouth on hers was also a far cry from what she was used to in her life, as well.

"He's looking for you, by the way," Michael said, the bag held next to his chest.

Instinctively, her gaze shot to the wall of mini-blinds that separated their offices. Unable to see through, she remembered his were similarly drawn and the door closed when she passed his office.

"What does he want now?" she asked more to herself, though she felt she knew the answer to that. He left before she finished speaking with Mona Caldwell who called to inform her that the last payroll check issued to Adrienne Simpson had come through from a bank in Norman, Oklahoma. Now, she wished she hadn't asked the banker to let her know if and when the check was cashed. With the ability to trace Adrienne, Solomon would insist on pressing criminal charges. She was still against taking legal action—even more so since Joe Simpson came looking for his wife.

She was inclined to believe that Adrienne had made a hasty getaway, as well as a serious error in judgment. "I would have given her the money to escape and a place to hide out," she said softly to herself.

"What was that?" Michael asked.

Monique didn't realize she'd spoken aloud. Adjusting her focus, she looked at Michael with a feeble smile on her face. "Nothing," she replied, shaking her head. "You better get out of here and let me get dressed."

"Okay," he replied. He took an exiting step towards the

door, then stopped, smiling at her thoughtfully. "Mr. Thomas is a little stuffy, isn't he?" he half-asked tactfully.

Stuffy? her mind echoed, as her eyebrows rose in amused contemplation. Stuffy wasn't exactly the word she'd use to describe Solomon. Sexy. Intoxicating. Lethal. The list of descriptions was building as she recalled the breach of discretion in the stockroom. But Michael wouldn't know about that, and it was prudent to leave the young man with his impressions for reasons not altogether altruistic.

Diplomatically, Monique replied, "Yes, I would say that."

"Well, if anybody can loosen him up, it's you. See ya' at seven," he added, taking his leave.

I don't know about that, Monique thought. In fact, she didn't know too much about anything, except that if Solomon were any looser, with all the potency he possessed, somebody would be in danger. Right now, that somebody was her. If she wasn't careful, she reminded herself.

She locked the door, then pulled the cord of the blinds. They rattled to a close.

She sauntered to the desk and began undressing to change clothes. Though she'd had a very busy day taking care of club business, her thoughts were stuck on this morning when she'd discovered just how susceptible she was to the quiet, charismatic charm of Solomon T. Thomas.

He had fooled them all, masquerading as a straight-laced, impassive, penny-pincher. While he could no doubt make a penny scream, money wasn't the only thing he was capable of eliciting startling effects from, she thought, her pants joining her blouse across the back of the chair.

She never would have believed it possible, still couldn't explain to her satisfaction her involuntary, rambunctious reactions to him. Just thinking about the feel of his persuasive mouth on hers caused her lips to tingle.

Unconsciously, Monique raised her hand to touch her mouth, to linger against the smile slowly crossing her expression and setting in a dreamy cast on her face. Just as slowly, the smile faded, and a look of pained confusion darkened her countenance.

It wasn't even a full kiss. Just an appetizer. Even if it were prelude to a 16-course meal, it meant nothing, she recited firmly as she unzipped the dress bag to pull out tonight's outfit.

Their anger had simply risen to such a feverish pitch that the only recourse left them was either to kill each other or kiss each other. He had looked as if he wanted to do both, she recalled, a somber chuckle in her throat. In hindsight, she didn't know which scared her the most.

It lasted only a flicker of an instant, but long enough to open her memory of a peccant atrocity. It was the impression of power to either kiss or kill her that frightened her, she now knew with certainty. Not Solomon, the man. She felt safe with him.

Despite her reassurances, her subconscious surfacing, Monique shivered, recalling the first time she'd come close to becoming a victim of a man's violence. She was usually able to stop the history from repeating in her head, but the strain of the past hours had weakened her. To minimize the pain the memory wrought, the muscles in her body huddled together in one tight knot and a dispassionate look came to her eyes as she stared at her past like a voyeur.

She was near the point of submitting her business proposal to the bank, she recalled. Only her father and the Redmons knew what she was up to. There had been no reason to tell Anthony because she neither wanted nor needed him to help complete the deal. As far as he knew, she was teaching by day and selling women's cosmetics nights and weekends.

He had planned a party at his Woodland's home and expected her to help entertain the six couples he'd invited. It was also the day her father was flying in to look over her proposal and offer his business insights and personal opinions.

Her father's plane was delayed, so she arrived late at the gathering. It was in full swing and going well by all outward indications. But Anthony had been drinking and was beside himself because of her tardiness. He called her into his bedroom to scold her in private.

"Women like you don't know how to appreciate a good man. Try to treat you nice and you throw it back in my face," he ranted, the liquor slurring his words. "No lousy high school teacher is going to walk all over me. If it weren't for me, you'd be at home grading papers."

She tried to apologize, but he went on and on, accusing her of ruining everything. Though his reaction prompted her second thought about becoming his wife, it never occurred to her that the mix of anger and alcohol would result in violence.

The strike, an open palm slap across the face, had caught her by surprise. Too stunned to do anything, she'd simply stood there, staring at him with utter disbelief. He was a doctor, an educated, outstanding pillar of the community: those irrelevant phrases had passed through her mind as she rubbed her stinging cheek. When her wits did return, she retaliated verbally, then spun on heels and left the room.

With Tevis's death still on her conscience, she got out of that house as fast as she could. The worst came later when she faced her father at home with tear-stained eyes: she couldn't seem to stop crying. After comforting her, he loaded the gun he always carried and demanded Anthony's address. She refused to give it to him.

Dr. Anthony Ward had the nerve to show up at her house two days after she pressed assault charges. Her father greeted him with a .38, and nearly pistol-whipped him to death. She had to call for help to pull her father off Anthony who was lucky she had hidden the bullets in fear that her father would sneak off to carry out his death threat against the good doctor.

The twist of the doorknob, followed by a short knock on the door, jolted Monique back to the present. As if she were released from a terrible nightmare, her insides breathed a collective sigh of relief, and her muscles unfurled from the tense hold she maintained during the run of the memory.

Staring at the door with residual uneasiness, she knew who it was without guessing. Her heart started back up again, thudding like a kettle drum in her chest. She was not ready for the disruption Solomon brought to her recovering life, she mused abstractively, snatches of the violent episode sneaking back into her mind. While she knew some women never fully healed, she had no intentions of being counted among them.

Still, she wasn't ready, she thought, staring transfixed at the door.

"Monique, are you in there?"

Solomon's voice, though soft and deep penetrated the barrier of the door easily. She felt little protection from the separation. Unbidden memory of the kiss that left her wanting for more leveled the disgraceful one like a steamroller. Now, she wasn't so sure which was the least dangerous option as she pulled her blouse tightly around her.

"I'm dressing," she said, making the words true. She was emotionally unprepared to face him. Sensually disturbed compounded by exhaustion from a late last night catching up to her, she had a feeling it was going to be *another* long night.

"I want to talk to you," he said.

She arched a brow at the note of command in his voice. "It will have to wait," she replied, injecting a sweetness she didn't feel to her tone.

She didn't know why she was making such a big deal out of a stupid kiss. The incident was over and would never happen again. She intended making sure of that, a plan incorporating Patricia's advice forming in her head.

"I really need to talk to you," he said.

That was better, more like a request. "I thought we already did," she said.

She pulled the long red blouse resembling a cheong-sam

with high slits at the sides, over her shoulders. If JuJu worked out tonight, which she was ninety percent certain they would, she thought, her day time responsibilities to the club could be done from her home. She would come in only to greet the customers, then leave at closing time. Solomon could manage the rest on his own.

"We only skimmed the surface."

Monique's hands stilled, one holding the button, the other opening the hole. The words, the velvet rumbling quality in his voice sounded like an appealing offer, like his kiss, a promise of something wonderful. The man was unnerving with his persistence. She drew in a deep, cleansing breath, determined not to yield to temptation.

"I have to be at the door by seven," she said firmly. With her ear keenly attuned to the door, she held her breath, waiting and wondering what he would come up with next.

When silence instead of a rejoinder followed, she assumed Solomon was gone. "Good," she declared.

She buttoned the blouse from the waist up, then slipped into the embroidered, black vest with fringe. Satisfied with the strategy, she stepped into black pumps, then sat at the desk and began applying make-up she pulled from the tote.

She wasn't about to alter her practice which began quite accidentally when *T's Place* first opened, she thought boldly. Without fail, last minute details had prevented her from personally greeting customers at the door any earlier.

Today, it had been running out to purchase some very expensive bourbon that they stocked in limited supply. Chip Yamauchi, one of their most valued customers, was bringing a party of twelve, mostly friends visiting from Japan to the club tonight. On a whim, she also picked up a couple of miniature bonsai trees and added several orders of egg rolls to the mixed vegetable and dip trays the club typically provided its customers.

"Now that I have this folder of activities, I don't think we can postpone a serious discussion any longer."

Monique's hand slipped, and the lipstick smeared un-evenly across her lips. Her eyes did a slow slide to the door in a narrowed gaze, and she cursed under her breath. The man never quit.

"Why is that?" she asked, an edge to her voice.

"What I have to say will affect some of the things you plan to do," he replied.

Blowing out her cheeks, she resealed the lipstick, wiped her mouth clean, then strode to the door and snatched it open with a flourish. The scent of his woodsy cologne spilled into the room as he entered, and she felt her temper scatter into the corner along with her resolve.

"I thought that would get you to open up," Solomon said, walking into the room. He closed the door behind him before he spoke again. "I wanted to see how you were. I heard you sneaked in."

"I did not sneak in," she said defiantly.

"Well," he said, looking at her with a half-grin, musing look, "I heard you had arrived."

She had backed herself against the desk before realizing he had advanced no further than the door at his back. Even at the distance—at least seven steps for her to reach him—he seemed too close. All she did was give herself a better vantage point from which to fully observe him and refreshed her senses of his imposing presence. She claimed no control over her reaction to him, her heart skipping beats in her chest.

Her gaze roved the length of him, in addition to noticing his change of clothes—a yellow dress shirt under navy sports coat over brown slacks—she also saw his hands were empty. It didn't matter what he wore—blue, brown, beige or black—he was both the figurative and literal manifestation of virility.

"So, if you don't want to talk about any of the items in the folder, what do you want to discuss?" she asked, her inner turmoil injecting some of the disgust she felt in her voice as she folded her arms across her bosom. "Or did you come to complain about JuJu? I'd have you know . . ."

"Good gracious woman, will you let me get a word in?" he said, a trace of laughter in his voice. "I've never met a woman so willing to give me a piece of her mind before."

"At least you'll never have to wonder what I'm thinking," she quipped. 'Liar, liar, burn in fire'—the kiddy taunt sang in her head.

"That's true," he said, with an approving nod, smiling quietly to himself. He felt the repartee with her lighten the burden of what he'd come to do. "I want to apologize for my behavior this morning," he said. "I'm afraid that I took my anger with my ex-wife out on you. I never meant to frighten you, and certainly had no intentions of hitting you. I want you to believe that."

She returned his headlong stare, his dark brown eyes soft and watchful. She had nothing to fear from Solomon but herself, she thought, a wave of warmth coursing through her.

"I believe you," she replied.

"Thank you," he said.

"You're welcome."

He sighed heartily, brought his hands from behind his back to cross them in front of him.

"Is that it?"

"Not quite," he said. "As for the other thing . . ."

"Skip it," she replied, pushing herself from the front of the desk to walk behind it. She didn't want an apology for the "other thing."

"No, I don't want to skip it," he said with his usual tenacity. "It's too important. I want to get it out in the open and make sure that we understand each other. I don't go around sexually harassing female employees."

Is that what he thought? Monique asked herself, a bovine expression on her face as she looked across the way at him.

A charge of sexual harassment never entered her mind. If he knew who she was, she thought, he could certainly make a case of the reverse against her.

"Anyway," he said, "I really hope we can be friends."

She wished it were possible also, she thought, looking into his face where a plea for friendship shone in his eyes. She felt assailed by a bout of loneliness welling in her bosom. Right now, more than anything else, she longed for someone she could talk to, lean on and share things with. Even though the Redmons were a call away, she wished for someone who belonged to her, and her alone.

"Have coffee with me after we close."

Monique stared at him startled, her eyes zeroing in on his. Nothing had changed about his expression; it was just as serious and sensual as usual. Still, she was wary. "Why?"

"Don't trust me?"

"I told you I did," she replied. "Isn't that enough?"

"Are you afraid of me then?"

"No," she exclaimed.

"Then prove it," he said. "Have coffee with me."

With her face frowned in deep thought, Monique weighed the offer. She didn't believe she was ready to test her resolve so soon after making it. It had already proved vincible.

"Hey, Monique." Jake's voice, as well as snatches of song and the raucous sounds of laughter from the bar cut into her silent debate.

"Yeah?" she asked, a sidelong glance at the intercom on the desk.

"Chip is here with his party," Jake replied.

"Okay. I'll be right out," she replied. She stared up at Solomon, a thought on her tongue, but she couldn't for the life of her remember what it was.

"Well?" Solomon said. "Are we on for coffee and conversation?"

"All right," she said, with a heavy sigh.

He opened the door and stepped aside. "Better not keep the customers waiting."

From her station, with Francine at her side, Monique said, "Chip, it's good to see you as usual. Who do we have here?"

Chip was third generation Japanese-American and the cross cultural mix was evident in his dress and mannerisms.

"Too many to introduce," Chip replied, his hand extended to encompass his large party, some still piling in. He spoke to them in Japanese, then turned to Monique. "Monique," he said, introducing her.

"Good evening, welcome to *T's Place,*" Monique said in fluent Japanese. "I'm Monique, your hostess, and your waitress for the evening is Francine. If there's anything I can do to make your evening a more pleasurable one, just whistle," she added with a wink.

She also had that speech memorized in Spanish, French and Swahili. As long as no one interrupted her, she could get through it like a pro.

"If you'll follow me," Francine said.

Monique bowed obsequiously as the dozen or so visitors followed Francine to a far corner nearest the stage to four tables shoved together along the wall. Taking position under the stairway in the shadows, she scanned the room pleased by the size of the crowd and the busy staff. They would earn good tips tonight, she thought.

The first floor was divided in half, with Dennis working alongside Francine. The red hair smoothed back and clasped with a rubber band at the nape of his neck in a ponytail identified the bartender as Jake. That left Michael and Cynthia to work the upstairs crowd. Though she would have preferred Michael to work with Francine, he and Cynthia seemed to have hit it off, she mused.

In an hour, Malik who was now performing alone on stage at the piano would break for fifteen minutes, then return with the full ensemble, and the noise level would triple the present jovial din. Leon was in his customary station opposite the stage, guarding the back of the room.

The only person unaccounted for was Solomon, she thought, wondering where he had gone to. An imperceptible shiver coursing through her, recalling his request for coffee and conversation. There was still time to back out, she told herself. As if expecting him to sneak upon her like in that stalking tiger way about him, she looked over her shoulder.

Michael was walking her way purposefully. She wondered if he had fouled up an order again. Though he had improved considerably in the short time he worked at the club, waiting tables was clearly not his talent. But he worked so hard to please that both she and the patrons indulged him. He was a nice young man, and probably her lone good personnel decision, she thought amused.

"What's up?" she asked.

"Joe Simpson is here," Michael replied.

"Joe Simpson, here? Where?" she asked anxiously, her head whipping around to scan the room.

"He's at the upstairs bar," he replied, a thumb pointed upwards.

"I want him kicked out of here," she said succinctly with hostility in her voice. "We're not going to miss the few bucks he spends on drinks. Probably can't afford anymore than one anyway," she added spitefully.

"I already notified Mr. Thomas, and he said that Joe hasn't done anything illegal, so we can't kick him out. He's going to alert Leon to keep an eye on him."

Staring into Michael's youthful face, Monique wondered at the inexplicable irritation she felt that he went to Solomon first. Solomon was likely an authority figure to him, she mused. But it wasn't just Michael: the entire staff deferred to him on many matters that they would have come to her with before. She should feel pleased. If not pleased, she told herself, then she'd better get used to it.

"He probably just came to see if Adrienne shows up," Michael said, cutting into her thoughts. "Mr. Thomas said once he's satisfied that she's no longer here, he'll leave."

Monique conceded silently that Solomon was likely right about Joe's motives. Maybe her paranoia about him stalking his wife was unfounded, she thought. Still. "I don't feel comfortable having him here," she said, drawing a deep breath of reluctant resignation.

"We got it covered," Michael said with uncharacteristic confidence.

Monique smiled, thinking he was going to make some young woman a lucky catch. "Is that what you think, or is that what Mr. Thomas told you?" she asked.

"Both," Michael replied, smiling at her sheepishly. "With all of us on alert, nothing will happen."

The club was closed and most of the staff left for the night. The light over the back door of *T's Place* beamed across the nearly deserted parking lot, spreading to encompass a sporty red car. Within it, a quiet conversation was taking place.

"How has she been acting?"

"Same as usual."

Rays from the light outlined Dennis's profile in the passenger seat. The man behind the wheel was cast in the shadow, only the shadow of his big man's frame was visible.

"Are you sure she hasn't been worried about something?"

"I'm sure," Dennis replied, more interested in the bills he fingered as if they were gold. "There's not that much for her to do since Mr. Thomas started."

"Who is he, this Mr. Thomas, a boyfriend?"

"Nah," Dennis replied. "Just a guy the owner hired a couple of weeks ago. He's not her type," he chuckled. "They're supposed to be co-managers, but it's no secret who's really in charge. I think she may be on her way out altogether."

"Oh, really?" the man behind the wheel asked with decided interest. "That may be the key," he said absently, as if speaking to himself.

Dennis cut him a sidelong pensive look, wondering what his benefactor was up to. The man thought he was smart, insisting on being called *Imhotep*. Few were aware that the ancient Egyptian who lived during the Third Dynasty was considered the real Father of Medicine. But he knew three things, Dennis mused. One, that the man was actually Dr. Anthony Ward—the pseudonym gave him away. Two, he was a prominent physician who inherited his father's successful practice. Lastly, Monique would have nothing to do with him.

"Man, I tried to tell you Monique does not mess with customers or employees," Dennis said. "It's almost a written policy to her. Maybe you should try running into her somewhere in public and make like you never heard of *T's Place*."

"It's too late for that."

"Has she seen you at the club?"

The man ignored the question. "I need you to do another favor."

Close to getting kicked out of school because he'd skated by on paying his fees, the bursar's office caught up with him, Dennis thought. If he couldn't come up with a significant portion of his two-thousand dollar debt, he would have to drop out with just one year left. He wasn't above spying on Monique and reporting it to Imhotep in order to save his academic life. He did have two major stipulations, however, he thought.

"Long as it's not illegal and you paying for it," Dennis said.

"That goes without saying. Now listen up, this is what I want you to do."

"How much you paying?"

"A grand," the man replied.

"I'm all ears," Dennis said. What did he care that the lovesick doctor wasn't especially bright? His money was good.

"How long have you been working at the club?"

"Since it opened."

"You like it."

It wasn't a question, and Monique nodded affirmative in reply. She didn't know what she was doing here in this all-night donut shop, she thought staring out the window at the flow of traffic on Kirby Street. What had she been thinking to accept such a foolish challenge? She didn't fall for that line when she was 15 and Kenneth Berry demanded that she prove her love to him in bed, she recalled, so why was she so at ends now?

"The turnover rate is lower than I expected it would be," he said.

She just wouldn't look at him. *You can't covet what you can't see,* she told herself. "No, it's not bad."

"The pay could be better," he said.

Monique shrugged her shoulders indifferently, then took a sip of her lukewarm coffee. All she had to do was leave, she told herself, irritated that she didn't move. He was hired to manage her club, not her.

Hearing the soft laughter on his lips, her head popped up to look at him. The laughter faded, leaving a boyishly affectionate smile on his face. It took years off his age, presenting the picture of a Solomon who was not always so stern and solemn, and even more attractive. A sigh respired in her bosom, and she felt a crevice open in the wall of her resolve. She zipped that tear back up. "What's so funny?" she demanded.

"I was just thinking that talking to you is like talking to my daughter," he said, mirth in his voice. "I was hoping that in a relaxed environment we could talk. Really talk. But you're more guarded now than ever."

She knew what he was trying to do when she accepted the olive branch, Monique thought. But with mixed feelings surging through her, she was having a difficult time accommodating him. Too relaxed, she feared her senseless emotions would get in the way. With forced agitation, she could remain focused. She stilled her bouncing foot under the table, planting both on the concrete floor. "I am relaxed," she said.

"No, you're not. You're moving so fast, you're almost a blur in that seat. If you're not afraid of me, what are you running from?"

"I'm not running from anything," she replied, and instantaneously felt a sharp twinge in her stomach. She never liked introspection, she thought ignoring the pain. She crossed her arms over her midriff and pointedly looked out the window.

"What's important to you, Monique?"

Monique frowned at Solomon headlong, trying to read motivation in his face. His stare was bold, assessing her frankly. She felt as if he were looking into her soul. No man had ever asked her that, and certainly not with sincere interest in her reply.

"All right," Solomon said, clasping his hands together tightly on top of the table, "what's a Haven House?"

The bear claw pastry and coffee were good, but he hardly touched them. The violaceous scent of the fragrance her lovely skin carried crossed the small table, corrupting his attention. It was a struggle to keep his eyes from straying to the curve of her exceptionally pretty neck, the cleft and gentle swell of her breasts against the shirt she'd changed back into from this morning.

Speaking of which, he still suffered from guilt. There was no logical explanation for his behavior. It was as if some amorous ghost had taken over his body and soul. Coupled with the prohibition of touching, the temptation proved too great to ignore or pass up. Like now, feeling in the throes of temptation to run a finger across her long, thin, elegant brows, down her slender nose and beyond. He folded his hands in his lap under the table.

Deep down inside, the saner part of him stirred irascibly. She belonged to another man. Prudence demanded he cease the untethered thoughts riding his mind like a wild horse on an open plain. Nothing could come of the way she made him feel.

"I would have answered the first question," she said, a note of pique in her tone. "I was just caught off-guard, that's all. But as it happens, Haven House is important to me." After all, this was safe ground, and she was happy to illuminate him.

"I hope so," he said chuckling, "since I recall reading that name in the entertainment package you gave me in conjunction with the KoKo Taylor concert. So, what is it?"

"It's a milestone in the black community," she replied. "Founded and largely supported by a Black woman's organization, Haven House is a shelter for abused women and their children."

"Black Women In Business," he said, recalling his reading.

"Yes," she replied, her features becoming more animated. "Along with the Juneteenth Blues Festival Committee, the organization is another co-sponsor for the Koko Taylor concert."

"The shelter is the reason we're splitting the proceeds," he said. "What was not clear, is what will that money be used for."

"It goes without saying that the shelter is a non-profit organization," she replied. "It provides all kinds of programs and support. But the most important thing is the protection it offers women from violent spouses. The money will go toward continuing the programs and paying the security guards who work around the clock."

"How long has Haven House been around? I've never heard of it."

"It's only been open since the beginning of the year," she replied. "It took so long because the group wanted to purchase a property outright, as well as set up operating capital for a year. With help from the Houston Area Women's Center, a full time staff is in place."

"Where is it located?"

"I can't tell you," she replied. "All of the shelters' locations are guarded secrets to protect the women from husbands and significant others who refuse to accept their decisions to end their relationships."

"That's understandable," he replied.

"Unfortunately, space is already at a premium. It should have been able to house about twelve women. So, it was really small to start with. Right now about nine women with an average of two children reside there. The needs seemed to have exceeded the group's initial expectations."

"Well, aren't there other places in the city?"

"Not nearly enough," she said. "But wishing we didn't need any in the first place is not solving the problem. I have a meeting coming up with the manager of the hotel in the area to see if arrangements can be worked out to house some women and their children."

Pleased and surprised, he never would have imagined Monique as the socially conscious type who volunteered. She was a lot more intelligent than he gave her credit for.

"Why is this so important to you?" he asked.

"Why?" she echoed surprised. "In Houston alone, according to the latest figures documented, more than 30,000 calls were placed to the Women's Center hotline. Nearly three thousand women were abused, and another twenty-two were homicide victims. Nationally, that figure is more than thirteen-hundred. Call it what you want, wife-beating, spousal abuse, domestic violence, but it's not new," she continued. "It's an old crisis, that in our community, dates back to slavery. I would think the answer is obvious. Somebody has to do something."

Wondering why he was attracted to a woman who belonged to another man, he felt less than the honorable man he always believed himself to be. Strong in character, grounded in reality, never wanting what wasn't his. Until now, teased a voice in the back of his mind. He blamed Monique, for the more she talked about a subject of which she was quite knowledgeable, the more passionate she became. It teased him with want to know just how deep her passions ran.

"Thanks for the education," he said. "I wasn't aware the problem was at a crisis level." That wasn't the extent of his ignorance, he mused, feeling a hint of what was missing from his life, what his marriage had lacked. Once, he mistakenly believed he and Elaine could never have more than they had. Looking at Monique, he felt certain that was no longer true.

"Unfortunately, yes," she said wistfully. "If only . . ."

Only once did she use the singular pronoun, he recalled, wondering if she underplayed her role in establishing Haven House. More assumptions about her filling his head, he wondered if she had been a victim of male abuse.

"If only what?" he asked.

With a bittersweet cast to her expression, Monique shook her head. "I was thinking about my friend, Tevis. I miss her," she replied.

Staring into the wispy gleam shining from the honey circle of her gray-rimmed, feline eyes, Solomon wanted to slay her dragons. He couldn't shake the feeling that she was meant for him.

"Okay," he said, "what do you think we should do about security at the club?"

Seven

"Oh yea! Oh yea! Everything gon' be all right this morning' ", Muddy Waters declared in his raspy voice from a nearby boom box.

Edging summer, the street teemed with children playing hide-and-seek, while adults sat on cracked porches to escape the heat inside.

"Give me ten!"

"I'll take some of that!"

A serious domino game ensued in front of a run-down, rickety house, a model for the others on the dead-end neighborhood street. Four men of ages that ranged from twenty-something to mid-life, were assembled at a wobbly table. A fifth stood in the shadows on the sidelines watching. A high wattage bulb on a thick, yellow electric cord hooked to a nail on the porch aided their vision of the black dotted, white ivory dominoes, also known affectionately as *bones*.

"Domino," a gamesman exclaimed as he slapped a bone down on the table almost humbling it.

The move precipitated different reactions, disgusted "aahs" and a high-five hand-slap between partners.

"Next up? Who got the hot seat?"

"It's your turn," the youngest man seated said to the man standing behind him.

"That's all right, son, you go 'head," the odd-man out replied graciously. He had no intention of sitting down to play. Something more important weighed on his mind. "I want to see you win a game. You ain't won nothing since you sat down," he added, barely veiling his disappointment.

The boy was an embarrassment, he thought, staring intently at the board. The dominoes were raked to the center of the table and shuffled round and round, until they were thoroughly mixed up. That was what had happened to his son. Raised by a bunch of women, they had mixed him up and turned him into a wimp. He almost regretted not keeping tabs on his son. Almost.

As each man selected his six bones, the master player seated asked, "How does it feel to be free?"

"Aw man, I can't explain what it's like," he replied. "I could sing. You just don't know. Freedom," he said out loud with a musing smile on his face.

"You never miss your water 'til your well runs dry, huh?"

"You right 'bout that, old man," he replied chuckling.

"Oh-oh, there it is," one of the players said of the lead play as big six hit the board.

"That's right. Play on it," the lead player said, rocking from side to side in his seat. While following the next play, he asked the sidelined player, "Well, what you go do with yourself? Got a place to stay, a job?"

"I'm staying right here with my boy until I get my own place," he replied, patting the young man at his side on the back. "As for job, I don't know yet. I got an interview with an auto shop. They got a computer, but can't seem to keep nobody who knows how to work it."

He spoke with confidence as if the job had already been assured him, but he knew. Once they found out about his record, that job would take wings and fly away.

It was another reason to hate Monique Robbins, he thought embittered. Every time he remembered her testifying against him in court, he wanted to wrap his hands around her neck and just squeeze. He had had to listen to her demean his manhood, labeling him a thing that didn't deserve to walk the earth with the likes of her. Nobody wanted to hear about *her* faults. *She* wasn't perfect either. But he loved her anyway.

"When did you learn how to work a computer?" the eldest of the players asked.

"Aw man, they teach you all kinds of things in the big house," he replied. They teach you how to hate, how not to make the same mistakes and land back there. Now, if he could get hold of those keys, he relished with a grin, rubbing his hands together.

"Well, I don't know nothing about no computers except they replace people who need jobs," the elder griped.

"The computer is a sweet little toy," he said. "It can give you access to all kinds of information. Ain't that right, son?"

"Yes, sir," the younger man replied as he scanned the board mulling his play. The bones rattled in his hand like marbles as he rubbed them together.

"You study long, you study wrong," the lead player chided the neophyte of the group.

"Can I have some of that what y'all drinking?" the standing player asked.

"It's your boy's, ask him."

"Hey, son, how 'bout it?"

"Sure thing," he replied, making a play on the board. Rising from his seat, he said, "I'll run and get it."

"Ain't your girlfriend inside?" he replied. He shoved the young man hard back into his seat. "Let her bring it. She ain't doing nothing but watching TV," he said hotly.

"Hey, Angie, bring that bottle of rum out here," the young man called towards the house.

"Come git it yourself," she replied. "I ain't your maid."

"Boy, you ain't tightened up that broad, yet? I thought I taught you better than that."

The men around the table grew uncomfortably still, hearing the venom in his voice. The host was grateful for the dark that hid his embarrassment.

"Ain't you heard nothing I been saying to you for the

past two years?" he said, slapping his son across the head. The young man flinched wordlessly. "You can't let no woman run your life. You the one who supposed to be controlling her, not the other way around. My mama never would have talked to my old man like that. He'd go upside her head."

"Things ain't like they used to be," said the eldest of the group. "Things have changed. You can't go round beating up on women and children. It'll land you in a whole heap of trouble. But, I guess you already know that," he said with a sly aside.

"Yeah man," another player chimed, "it ain't worth it."

They were all wimps, the whole lot of them, he thought snidely. If his daddy had ever heard him sounding all defeated by a woman, he would have beat the black off him. Though he did on many occasions for other reasons, he recalled, his look in his eyes matching the dark of the night. But it made him tough. His daddy showed him how to be a man, and he was grateful, too, because it saved his life in the joint.

"Man, you just got out of jail for that. You ain't learned your lesson yet?"

The final taunt distracted his thoughts to *Her.* Face frowning, he pressed his lips together tightly as if afraid to speak her name. Saying her name gave her humanity and denied him his. The dead didn't have humanity. "It wasn't my fault," he snapped defensively, then caught himself. "Aw man, you know me," he said with macho laughter. "I'm just talking. Freedom done gone to my head. Ain't that right, boy?" he said, squeezing the young man's shoulders.

The ping-zing battle of video game characters penetrated the walls. Solomon wished he could draw that kind of attention as he knocked on the door of Ariana's room and waited for permission to enter.

"Are you sleeping with her?"

Solomon froze between almost sitting and still standing, with one of the twin beds at the back of his legs. He didn't need clarification of whom she referred. Monique plagued his thoughts the entire drive home from the donut shop. He desperately needed a break from them, but apparently was not going to get it. *She belongs to another man,* he thought, but bit the reply on his tongue before the words poured out.

"You've been waiting up all this time to ask me that?" he replied casually. He sat to her left of the desk that held the portable color TV and Nintendo game system. "It's after four in the morning. I expected you to be asleep. What are you still doing up?"

Ariana was sitting Indian-style in a chair before the video game, which provided the only source of light in the room.

"Are you?" she pressed, cutting him a sidelong glance.

"Typically, I would answer that with 'none of your business,' " he replied, amusement in his voice. Because Ariana didn't bring up the matter earlier, he foolishly believed that the unguarded and unexpected incident had passed unmemorable and would eventually be forgotten altogether. "But this time," he said drawing a deep breath, "I'll forfeit parental rights on this matter, if you promise to answer some questions for me." If she took him up on this challenge, he would be in trouble, he thought, wondering what would he tell her.

"What kind of questions?" she asked warily.

There had been no time earlier for anything more than a cursory conversation, he recalled. "Did you have a good flight? . . . Yes . . . How are you? . . . Fine." Ariana's dry responses, even more than her mother's impulsive decision to send her, indicated that he was caught in the middle of a mother-daughter squabble. Without even knowing the nature of the conflict, he blamed Elaine.

"What's going on with you and your mother?" he asked.

"Nothing," she replied, averting her attention back to the game.

Solomon respired heavily. He was relieved. Yet, still none the wiser, he thought. "Okay. Then none of your business."

When Ariana was young, he took her fishing with him, he remembered fondly. She was such a daddy's girl then. He had to bait her hook, constantly repair the back lashes in her line, and on rare occasions, remove the fish from her hook. Despite her ineptitude at fishing, she hung in there like a trooper.

He used to believe those outings had been significant toward forging and cementing their relationship. Then when she moved away with her mother to Michigan, it seemed their times together had been meaningless.

Returning the first year after the divorce, Ariana spent the entire summer vacation mad at him. The second, three month-visit was cut to one, in which she was indifferent. The third year, she was demanding and belligerent for two weeks.

She didn't come at all last summer, he recalled. It was only at his insistence that she come last fall—the choice was hers—either at Thanksgiving or Christmas. She chose the former, refusing to give up Christmas with her mother who promised her not only a new wardrobe, but her very own charge card over his objections.

"You never tell me anything," she said accusingly, tossing the controller on the desk disgusted. "I didn't even know you'd been fired from the bank until Mom told me." She sprang from her seat and pounced across the room to turn on the light.

Under the glare of the light, he took in the very grown up personage of his daughter glaring down at him. She wore a short pink and white pajama ensemble with a kitten knitted across the front of the top. With her long, slender brown legs protruding the pants and two full points protruding the top, he felt struck anew by a fact that he suspected many fathers didn't want to think about.

A cursory glance about the room showed that the decor

was no longer suitable to its new occupant who had outgrown the frilly yellow curtains on the windows, the Donald
Duck comforters on the beds, the white furniture with gold
trim. Wondering where had the years gone, he realized de-
finitively that his daughter was no longer a baby. Fighting
the inevitable was useless, he mused.

"I wasn't fired," he replied. "I simply wasn't hired by
the new owner."

"There's no difference. You still didn't tell me!" she said,
a pout in her voice.

"I was saving that information until I found another job,"
he replied. In truth, he was too embarrassed to admit he lost
his job and feared losing her respect. Part of a father's role
was to impart a sense of security in his child. Unemployment
implied just the opposite. "You know about it . . . the new
job."

"Yeah, I know now," she said sulkily. "And a new woman
to go with the new job." She dropped onto the twin bed
facing him.

With her legs folded Indian-style and arms across her
bosom, she stared at him with a doleful, pensive expression.
He returned her look with a patient smile, mulling his new
perception of her. Her soft-hued, skintone was a complemen-
tary blend between his deep brown coloring and the mocha
complexion of her mother. She had his button eyes; although
smaller and softer, they were dark, piercing and naturally lined
as if penciled in black. From her mother, she took the straight
nose and small mouth. Standing 5′6″ already, she inherited
his height. She was lovely now, but one day in the very near
future, she would be beautiful.

He hadn't realized how much he missed having his child
around until she was gone and the tug-of-war game he
fought with Elaine to ensure his visitation rights began. But
all his life, he'd fought for everything he'd ever gotten. No
one was going to deny him his child. Still, he wanted his
daughter to know him not as the man she visited infre-

quently, but as her father, her protector and hero. The distance made it difficult, doubled by the material inducements her mother offered to further complicate the relationship. But he refused to buy Ariana's love, and likewise, wouldn't stop trying to earn it.

Noting her sour expression, he asked, "Jealous?" He couldn't help the smile on his lips, realizing that the shoe was going to change feet one day.

"You're teasing me," she pouted, cracking a small smile. "So, if you're not sleeping with her, why were you kissing her?" she asked.

He recognized the questioning scowl, the beetle brow arched in an upside-down V from his mirror reflection, along with the eminently reasonable tone of voice. They served to inject obedience into the receiver of his message, making her feel foolish if she elected to argue with him. The ploy usually worked. But not on him.

"Your mama got a new boyfriend?" he replied.

"Is Monique your new girlfriend?" Ariana quipped.

She was stubborn, his daughter, he thought, proudly to himself. "No," he replied, his boss's name ringing in the back of his head. Money and looks aside, he had believed the lawyer and the hostess were not suited to each other. What an idiot he'd been, discounting the prime factors of their gender. He almost wished Aurelius was his competition instead of his employer. "You got a boyfriend?"

"In Midland, Michigan?" she replied sarcastically, dropping her hands to the bed at her sides. "Get real. There are hardly fifty Black people in that town. I hate that place."

Solomon blurted out the comment on the edge of his thoughts. "What brought that on? Scenic, wealthy, and close to Detroit and Chicago, which if I recall, you used to think was the most happening place in the universe."

"Well, I don't anymore," she replied in a clipped, acid tone. "I want to stay with you."

Solomon opened his mouth to press her further about the

nature of the problem, but decided it could wait. Besides, he knew not to take any stock in her declarative request; by tomorrow she would have changed her mind. But for the moment, it pleased him to believe the possibility existed. At the very least, it would give him an opportunity to become reacquainted with his daughter.

"Fine," he replied.

"You mean it?" she asked incredulously.

"What do you mean do I mean it? Of course, I mean it."

"You've never asked me to," she accused.

"If I would have known it was that simple, I would have done it a long time ago," he said thoughtfully. Was it that simple? he wondered in one of those short bouts of disconnected thoughts. He wasn't as smart as his namesake, he was sad to say, shaking his head ruefully. "I'm sorry."

Muffled, the sound was light, barely perceptible, like someone pounding padded metal. "Monique, open the door!" The voice was feeble, but desperate.

Inside the cool room, Monique squirmed in bed, but otherwise did not awaken. The dream state dominated. It was dark in her sleep, her body was coiled tightly, hands pressed against her lips, as if to stifle the girlish whimper in her throat.

The banging grew louder, more frantic, penetrating her subconscious, but her body rebelled against movement. As the cry became more urgent, more distinct, Monique mumbled an unintelligible protest as her sleepy brain struggled to decipher the intrusion.

"Monique, please open the door!"

Slowly emerging from dream to reality, Monique whispered, "Tevis?"

"Monique, please," the cry implored her softly. "Open the door."

Disoriented, Monique slowly sat up on her haunches in

bed. With her face contorted in a wary frown and uneasiness pumping the blood through her body, she adjusted her eyes to the dark. Her gaze instinctively shot to her most vulnerable position, the left of the bed, where the moon was shining through the thin curtains over the French door. Unaware that she was holding her breath, she squinted, staring hard to see, fearing she would, but hoping she saw nothing.

No shadows lurked at the burglar-barred door. Quiet roared in her ears. Slowly, the breath oozed from her tightly held body as she scanned the other side of the room.

She must have been dreaming. It was 4:20 in the morning. She'd come to bed less than an hour ago. She had thought she was too tired to dream, she mused, squirming back into a comfortable position.

No sooner than she closed her eyes, the phone rang. Her lids popped open, but she lay still, an irascible expression forming on her face in the dark. She let the phone ring, mentally counting off seven bells. Unable to stand the harsh noise any longer, she rolled over and snatched up the receiver.

"This better be an emergency," she said.

"How you doing?" the caller replied in a sweet, affectionate male voice. "You doing okay?"

Monique rose to her haunches and clicked on the bedside lamp light. "Who is this?" she asked impatiently.

"Aw, you don't recognize my voice," he said, his tone crestfallen. "You hurt my feelings."

Monique frowned, searching her mind for recollection of the caller. "Dennis?" she said uncertainly. "Is this you, playing games this time of morning?"

The caller fell momentarily silent; only his breathing indicated he was still on the line.

"That's all right," he said at last. "You'll get plenty opportunity to get used to my voice again."

Angry and in frustration, she demanded, "Who is this?"

"I'm your lover. I'm the man you've been waiting for all your life."

A prank call, Monique thought, emitted a disgusted tsk. "Well, good-night lover, I've got to go," she said, deliberately dropped the receiver in its bed with a clatter. Reaching up to turn off the light, she couldn't believe she'd spent all that time talking to a nut. The room dark again, the phone rang.

She snatched up the receiver. "Listen here you," she said, her temper at a breaking point.

"If you go be my woman, Monique," he said, interrupting her tirade, "you got to learn how to act. I see I'm going to have to teach you a lesson." He ended the call abruptly, slamming the phone in her ear.

She was definitely not going to work in the morning, she thought, replacing the receiver.

Monique made her second trip from her Jeep in the parking lot next to the fenced in pool at MacGregor Park. Her arms were loaded with six boxes of pizza stacked to her nose. She carried them to one of the two wooden picnic tables shaded by an expansive oak tree. Before she finished dividing them between the two tables, a gang of squealing black and brown children converged on the scene with delightful cheers.

The African American children came from Haven House. The Hispanic youths came from the Casa de Amigos Community Center. All were being "treated to lunch" today by Monique, who moved out of their way in a hurry as they claimed sodas from the big cooler, slices of pizza and a seat on the hard wooden benches.

It was two in the afternoon. Though the sun was burning up the sky and anything under its scorching path, the park was teeming with kids of all ages. Monique was mildly envious of their reprieve from worries. Albeit brief for some of them, she thought, thinking of her young guests.

She remembered a time in her youthful life, her biggest worry was when was her daddy coming home. Her mother was a joyless woman with a constant dour attitude. She did her motherly duties, providing physical needs, but not much more. It led Monique into believing she was adopted. She scoured the house one time looking for papers to prove her hypothesis, Monique recalled amused.

Admittedly, Monique chuckled, she was a handful as a child. Energetic, curious, always into something. Kathreen called her hyperactive, a trait unfounded by a doctor's examination. He declared her normal with an overactive imagination and too much television watching as an explanation for her dream.

Looking over her shoulder, Monique spotted the official guardians, Sylvia Flores and Amber Williams meandering toward the gathering from the swings across the parking lot. They acknowledged each other with a wave, then Monique sauntered to the passenger side of the Jeep. She climbed in and propped her feet on the dashboard and lay her head against the back of the seat. She was tempted to run the air conditioner.

She sighed at length, fanning herself with her hand in a futile attempt to combat the heat. But too tired to sustain the motion, she propped both hands behind her head and stared through the windshield at the cackling children.

Arrangements had been made earlier when she called to see how she could help out at the shelter. Her timing was declared most opportune by Amber, the college-aged volunteer, as well as a survivor, responsible for Youth Programs. A call to Sylvia Flores, a guidance counselor at de Amigos, whom she'd met two years ago at a Houston Area Women's Center fund-raiser, was met with equal gratitude.

Seeing the children's happy faces as they stuffed their mouths, she was glad for her self-serving decision. Volunteering to help watch them today meant she couldn't very well go to work, she thought satisfied, closing her eyes.

As soon as she did, the familiar image of Solomon appeared behind her lids.

Not even a full day from the club, and she was thinking non-business thoughts about her manager, she chided herself silently. She couldn't seem to get him out of her mind and keep him out. Even more amazing was her growing feeling for a man she barely knew. She had no idea where they were taking her, or if they were going anywhere beyond her head.

She hadn't felt this confused about anything since college, trying to decide what major to declare. Though she wasn't one to ponder an idea to death, she did like to have a plan mapping out her destination. Besides, she wasn't ready for an emotional entanglement, and her career agenda was already full. There was no mention of a man in her five-year plan.

Maybe it was all right to think about him at a distance, as long as she maintained it, she rationalized, wondering what dull uniform he donned today.

Before she realized where her thoughts were heading, she was undressing Solomon in her head. She stripped him down to his white Fruit of the Looms. With a moan whistling in the hollow of her throat, she rested her gaze on his mahogany physique, roving down the smooth, hard contours of wide shoulders, firm chest and narrow waist. Her mouth watered, and she swallowed, skipping to the business in mind.

Instead of the 100% cotton, store-brand shirts, she'd put him in a designer brand that blended polyester and cotton with an athletic cut. Slacks would contain dacron and pleats with cuffs at the ankles, falling in permanent creases atop hand-sewn leather loafers, maybe with a tassel.

Though she pictured him balking at royal purple, light fuchsia, kiwi and coral, she knew his creamy chocolate complexion would respond aesthetically to colors that integrated earth tones with the dynamic ones of a tropical island.

"Somebody was up all night."

Just as she was about to replace his regulation, wide ties, too, Monique thought, smiling to herself. At least she had clothes on his back as not to give herself away, though she was drooling on the inside.

She cocked open one eye to glance at Sylvia who was standing inside the opened car door. The Hispanic woman was coolly dressed in a plaid short ensemble and sandals, her long dark hair twisted in a ball at the top of her head. She held a can of soda in her hand.

"Does it show?" Monique replied chuckling as she sat up straight.

"Let's just say you haven't been your usual energetic self today," Sylvia replied. "Any other time, you'd be right in there with the children." She pulled the lid off the can, then took a long, thirst-quenching swallow of the cold soda. "Everything going okay at the job?"

"I certainly hope so," Monique replied. Sylvia didn't know she owned her job. "I haven't checked in." She had started to call, but changed her mind. Instead, she faxed a message to Solomon. Needing as much time away from him to marshal up her resolve as she could get, she didn't even want to hear his voice. She would see him soon enough.

"That's a sure sign that all is not right," Sylvia said laughingly. "Maybe you need to take a vacation."

"I wish," she retorted dryly. "How are things going at the Center?"

"Same as usual," Sylvia replied. "Everybody is lobbying to get more money for one program or another, and the board is dragging its feet until the mayor announces the cuts in community services. What we couldn't do with that sixty-thousand dollars the city had to return to the federal government," she said wistfully. "I'll never understand how some people get these cushy jobs designed to create programs to improve the community, then act as if the money is their own personal little fund."

"It's called politics," Monique replied dryly. "We submitted a proposal to expand the services at Haven, but we're in competition against Project Center."

"Oh yeah, the batterers' intervention program," Sylvia said. "Men are rehabilitated and learn strategies of self-control. It's not an easy program, but an attempt is better than the status quo practice of ignoring battering as a social ill."

"But remember," Monique said, "most of the intervention programs attempted around the country have had very limited success. Recruitment has been difficult, and both the drop out and recidivism rates have been high." Monique took a deep calming breath. "I really would like to embrace the goals of intervention programs," she said, wishing a place like the Project Center had existed five years ago, then maybe Tevis would still be alive.

Averting her head to stare at the children, Sylvia said in a soft, pensive tone, "What we really need is money for programs to counsel children who live and grow up with batterers, then turn around later in life and perpetuate violence, or who grow up too afraid to live and eventually destroy themselves."

Monique nodded her head absently, knowing full well the statistics of the circular perpetuation of violence. When boys who just witnessed adult domestic violence become adults, they were seven hundred times more likely to beat their female partners. The number was one thousand times more likely to repeat when physical abuse was involved.

Staring studiously silent at the girls, Monique prayed that they would survive the current crisis and not be eternally victimized by the negative example of manhood. She hoped they would meet a strong man, confident and secure in his masculine power, with tender affections, where they would learn the real meaning of love. She prayed for these of things for them and herself, as well.

"I know," she said regretfully. "I wish there was a way to make them forget." If it hadn't been for her father's example of a decent and kind man, she wouldn't have been willing or able to wish at all.

"No," Sylvia said hastily, staring pointedly at Monique, "not forget. Forgetting is impossible. Hopefully, they will be able to put the experience behind them, but use that memory to keep from repeating history."

"You're right," Monique replied.

The two women shared a silent message, then wordlessly, joined Amber who was sitting at one of the tables with several children.

Standing in front of the desk in his office, Solomon replaced the receiver in the cradle of the telephone. He stared absently at the door, a frown in his expression. Two questions dominated his thoughts—the reason for the phone call and Monique's whereabouts.

The woman who called for Monique refused to leave a message, he recalled. He wondered if the call had something to do with the fact that Monique had yet to arrive. It was 6:48 P.M.

When she'd faxed in a message this morning saying she would be late, he didn't give it a second thought. In fact, he'd taken it as a godsend. Now, the closer it got to the time for her to really start to work and assume her position at the door, he was beginning to feel uncomfortable. She was really cutting it close.

Well, he didn't have time to stand around, wondering and waiting for Monique to arrive. There were other matters to attend to that didn't have anything to do with her job.

With a final rap of his knuckles on top the desk, he strode out the room, pulling the door locked behind him. As he headed for the bar in the club, he heard voices coming from the employees room. He stopped short of making himself visible, amusedly intrigued by the conversation that bore every trace of male bragging rights.

"She does?" Dennis asked incredulously. "Man, you don't know what you're talking about."

"I'm telling you, it's the truth, man," Michael replied. "She does. The woman is rolling in dough. Her old man is some kind of hot-shot record producer or something. That's partly how she got it."

"I wish I could get my hands on some of it," Dennis said enviously. "I'm still a little short on my loan repayment."

"You're too late, home-boy," Michael laughed in reply. "She already owes somebody else. Big time," he said smugly.

"Well, who knows, maybe she wants something better than what she got," Dennis replied with braggadocio. "And I know where she can get it from."

"You wish, man," Michael quipped laughingly.

"We'll see," Dennis said confidently.

After Dennis and Michael left the area, returning to the bar, Solomon walked into the area. So they'd stumble on some woman with money, he thought chuckling and shaking his head. They'd better be careful. Women with money can be more trouble than they were worth.

But they were young with time to learn, he told himself, heading toward the main room of the club.

The last one out after closing, Solomon walked out the back door of the club, with keys jangling in his hand. He noticed a sporty car, a red Corvette, tearing off the parking lot and stared after it with a pensive frown.

He wondered if Monique were having trouble with her Cherokee Jeep and was driving another loaner from her mechanic. But she had strolled in seconds before seven o'clock and was the first one out the back door after ushering the last customer out the front door.

But it was after three in the morning now, why would she have been sitting in the parking lot all this time? Solomon muttered pensively.

Yet, he remembered, the loaner Monique had used from her mechanic was a Camaro, not a Vet. Despite the color similarity, he knew the difference.

Maybe one of the staff was driving a '90 Vet or simply being picked up in one, he mused as he headed for his car. He wondered if Monique was coming to work early tomorrow.

Solomon had a feeling he'd better not raise his hopes. Or jinx them, he chuckled.

Eight

One day turned into two, then two into three. Monique discovered it was not all right to think about Solomon at a distance.

But if nothing else, she did begin to feel as if she had mastered the art of delegation. Her daytime hours consisted of the center and her nights spent being hostess at *T's Place*. Scheduling time for the children where her help was sorely needed, important messages and reminders were faxed to Solomon. She didn't step foot in the club until a minute to seven o'clock, leaving promptly upon saying her final good-night to the last patron just minutes past two. In between times, she played her role as hostess to the hilt.

The tactic prevented Solomon's attempts to detain her with questions. It did not prevent her from thinking about him.

The few hours she did see him were torturous. He seemed to grow better looking, more virile, and disturbingly more attractive to her than ever. The parcel of warmth spurred by his presence enlarged. There were times she felt holistically consumed by her want for him.

Each night she fell into bed, her last waking thoughts were of Solomon. When she fell asleep, Solomon was prominent in her dreams. Solomon T. Thomas was still on her mind upon awakening each morning.

Still, she was relentless, set on proving that she was immune to the dynamic vitality he exuded. And to his credit, after the first day, he acted as if she weren't missed at all. In fact, he even seemed to relish her absences. His casual indifference to her absences irked her to no end. She wanted to strike him out of her mind and make him want her at the same time.

She began to hate the self-imposed schedule. It went against her nature and made her feel as if she were alone in the world. But endowed with a sense of conviction that was part of her character, she maintained that schedule.

The intermittent calls from Anthony helped, serving to remind her about the dangers of succumbing to romantic notions—a belief that physical sensations represented and accompanied a deeper and lasting feeling.

However, she did not entirely relinquish communication with her business, staying in contact with her most trusted employees who informed her routinely of what transpired at the club during her absence.

But by Friday, all of her loneliness and confusion welded together in one upsurge of devouring yearning which created an ache in her chest. She didn't know how much longer she could keep this up.

Monique was standing at the back of her vehicle, waving back at the pink palms of little brown and black hands waving at her as the 18-passenger van that had brought the children to the park drove off.

Something positive that gave her a sense of satisfaction had been accomplished this week. But today, she had stayed longer than she intended. It was four-thirty, and now, she had to hurry home to get ready for work.

Returning to the wooden tables, she lifted the cooler—the only remains of their presence—from the bench. The thought of seeing Solomon surfaced and sent butterflies scudding in her stomach.

Unexpectedly, she remembered another time when she'd

been late for an appointment. The thought made her freeze in mid-stride. "Solomon was not Anthony," she reminded herself out loud, scorning the memory as she lugged the cooler to the back of the Jeep. Besides, Solomon was accustomed to her schedule now and probably wished she didn't come in at all.

Still, Monique quickened her pace. Nearly out of breath after shoving the cooler in the back of the vehicle, she hurried even faster toward the driver's door, pulling her keys out of the pocket of her shorts. Getting them snagged in the fabric, she became conscious of her fast pace, the calamitous beat of her heart.

Drawing a deep calming breath, she forced herself to stop, stand still. What's the rush? she asked herself, untangling the key chain.

She knew being in the constant company of children and workers from the shelter—where the destructive evidence of domestic violence was prevalent—explained her maudlin jaunt into the past. But she refused to stop going to the shelter, though it was as much a curse as it was therapeutic for her. And try as she did to forget her tainted history, she knew it was unlikely. Because on top of everything else, Anthony was still calling her.

"One who forgets the past is destined to repeat her mistakes," she whispered, recalling she had heard those sage words even before Sylvia had spoken them the other day. Although they had been issued in a different context, the application was the same. She simply couldn't let it overwhelm her.

The self-talk, injected with a note of bravura, allowed Monique to regain her composure. She proceeded to the driver's door at *her* pleasure, twirling the key chain on her finger. Just as she opened the door, a familiar blue Olds inched into the parking space adjacent to the Jeep.

Gripping the handle, she gasped and her heart slammed against her ribs like a mallet striking a gong. She stared with shock stuck in her throat as the car rolled to a stop. The driver's door opened, and a female head of stiff curls emerged. Monique realized she had been holding her breath.

Breathing deeply, she sagged against her vehicle. Solomon was not the only man in the world who drove a blue Cutlass Olds, she chastised herself.

As she pulled open the door of her own vehicle, her gaze strayed to the back of the driver sauntering toward the benches they'd just vacated. She felt a sense of familiarity. When the woman, a teenage girl really, sat on the bench, Monique saw her face.

No wonder she looked so familiar: it was Solomon's daughter Ariana. By the droop of her shoulders and forlorn expression on her face, she appeared upset about something. Though full of questions, Monique curtailed her curiosity as she pushed the car door shut and casually strolled toward the bench. "Ariana?" she called out with friendly surprise in her tone.

Ariana looked up at Monique, her gaze at first wary, then with recognition. "Ms. Robbins," she said, her tone and look laced with anxiety, "what are you doing here?"

"I guess I could ask you the same thing," Monique said, sitting on the bench across from Ariana.

"I was just riding around," Ariana replied.

"I didn't think you were old enough to drive," Monique said.

"Neither does my dad," Ariana replied, her lips twisted ruefully. "He may have been right."

"Oh? What's the matter?" Monique asked.

Waiting for a reply, she saw the familiar poker-faced look form Ariana's expression, followed by the lifting of her brows that wrinkled in debate over piercing eyes. She would recognize that look anywhere, Monique thought, feeling an uncanny affinity to the young girl whom she'd only met for a very brief moment.

Then, the look metamorphosed into one of abject defeat,

and Monique's expression revealed deep concern. As she opened her mouth to press for an explanation, Ariana sprang to her feet and stomped over the driver's side of the Olds.

Pointing, the teenager said, "Look."

More curious than ever, Monique followed. Reaching the side of the car where Ariana stood, her expression evolved into a knowing one. "I see." A long scratch, like the single claw of a giant eagle, extended the length of the car from the front tire to half-a-foot beyond the driver's door.

"He's gonna kill me," Ariana said sadly.

Monique recalled a similar incident in which she was hit while driving her father's Jaguar. The damage was worst than this, and she too had felt what Ariana must be feeling. Her father was furious, but he didn't kill her. She doubted Solomon would, either. "When did this happen?" she asked.

"About an hour ago," Ariana said with a moaning keen in her throat. "I was on my way home. I had been driving around, going from place to place all day long and nothing happened until this," her voice rising in hysteria. "I stopped at the Post Office over on Griggs. I went in to buy some stamps and came back out and this," she said, both hands opened toward the scratch.

"It wasn't your fault," Monique said.

"Okay, you tell my dad it wasn't my fault," Ariana replied. "He just bought this stupid car last year. You think he's gonna want to hear this damage wasn't my fault?"

"No," Monique replied weakly. "I guess not. But it's really not that bad. Trust me, I know," she said with emphasis and a chuckle in her voice.

"He's never gonna let me use his car again," Ariana whined in unabashed self-interest.

"Well, maybe you can get it fixed," Monique said speculatively, running her hand along the damage. "It's just the paint that's missing. No dents."

"You really think I can get it fixed before he gets off from work tonight?" Ariana asked hopefully.

Monique hedged, not wanting to raise Ariana's hopes in case the plan in her head didn't work. "We can try. Follow me in the car. Let's see if we can catch my mechanic," she said, walking away. Consulting the time on her wristwatch, she frowned. "His shop is not far from here." George, please still be there, she prayed silently as she climbed in her Jeep.

The back door of *T's Place* opened, and Michael emerged into the bright evening. The need to smoke overrode concerns about the temperature, hot, sticky and windless. One of the new club rules for employees was no smoking inside.

He lit a cigarette, then inhaled deeply, like a nicotine-craved mendicant. With the cigarette hanging from the corner of his mouth, he replaced the pack and lighter in his front pocket, then leaned against the wall and scanned his surroundings with passing interest. About a dozen cars were parked in the lot. It was a slow night inside.

As he took a second drag off the cigarette, the back door opened and Cynthia appeared. Her face was thin, narrow and serious. She was on the skinny side of slender. With her sable complexion, the pink uniform shirt stood out like a neon sign on a skeleton frame, and the pants fit loosely on her small hips.

"Don't you know smoking will stunt your growth?" she said, eyeing him through the flame of the lighter as she lit her cigarette.

"Are you proof of that?" Michael retorted laughingly.

Standing inches from him, one arm crossed under her bosom, Cynthia blew a puff of smoke in his face. Without comment, Michael waved it aside.

"Don't be a smart-mouth, runt," she replied. "How old are you anyway?"

Michael was used to comments about his physical stature, so he was hardly disturbed by Cynthia's snide references to his height. In his estimation, it wasn't a man's height that made him a man. Besides, he made up for it in other ways.

"Old enough," he replied.

"I got a nephew your age, and he's only sixteen. You don't look any older than he is."

Michael shrugged carelessly before he replied. "Looks are deceiving."

She examined him from head to toe, then emitted a harrumph that caused her chest to heave. "Yeah, right," she said, disbelief in her tone. She dragged on her cigarette as though sucking in oxygen. "Where is Miss Thang tonight?" she asked.

"Put your claws away, Cynthia," he replied, flicking ash to the side. "Why people think you're so quiet and shy, I'll never know," he said, shaking his head slightly amused.

"Well, it's after seven and she's not here. He comes asking me if she called?"

They both knew who He was.

"So?" Michael replied, eyeing her sidelong as he took another puff off the cigarette.

"So, I ain't her keeper," she replied sharply, the smoke sneering across her face.

"You sure in a bad mood today. What's wrong with you?" he asked.

"Nothing," she replied belligerently, then fell silent.

Smashing out the cigarette against the wall, he said, "Well, I better get back inside if I want to make some money tonight."

"You made money last night," she said snippily, taking the cigarette out of her mouth. She held it pinched between the first two fingers of her left hand and created a trail of smoke using her hand as she talked. "She knew I wanted some overtime. I told her last Monday that my car was in the shop. It's going to cost me $500 to get it fixed."

"So what does that have to do with her? She doesn't make the schedule; Mr. Thomas does."

"She could have talked to him for me," Cynthia said, unyielding in her position. "She would have done it for you or Dennis."

Ignoring her foul mood, Michael said, "I'm going back on duty."

"Ain't hardly nobody here. Except Joe. He keeps coming here every night looking for Adrienne, and he certainly doesn't tip. He would sit in my station," she spat out angrily.

"Mr. Thomas said ignore him," Michael said.

"Right," Cynthia replied with a disgusted tsk.

"What's really wrong with you, Cynthia?"

She looked at him, a hint of anxiety in her contrite expression. "Michael, I'm sorry. It's just that . . ." Her voice drifted into silence. She looked away, then back. "You have to pro . . ."

The door was pushed open from the inside, and they both jumped startled. Solomon poked his head out, then emerged. Wordlessly, he looked back and forth between Cynthia and Michael. He couldn't believe nor understand the desperation of smokers. "It's a little hot out here," he said.

Michael looked at Cynthia and read the keep-your-mouth-shut look in her eyes. "Yeah, I was just coming back in," he said. "Excuse me," turning sideways to pass Solomon and enter the building.

"Me, too," Cynthia chimed, tossing the cigarette to the ground. She stepped on it, then returned inside.

Solomon stared after Cynthia curiously. He wondered if something happened between those two that he ought to know about. But concern for them was fleeting as he looked from one side of the parking lot to the other. There was still no sign of Monique. He pulled the cuff of his shirt to look at his watch. It was eighteen minutes after seven. He hadn't heard from her or his daughter. He didn't know whether to get scared or mad.

He felt both, for each of the females on his mind.

Frustration his only outlet, Solomon returned inside to

his office. He slammed the door shut and strode to his desk. Snatching up the receiver, he punched out a number.

All day long he kept thinking *today* was going to be the day Monique would make her grand entrance. At any moment, he recalled saying to himself as the extension rang in his ear. He half-expected her to show up with some major purchase in tow, resuming the cat-and-dog fight that began the first day they formally met.

There was no answer at his house, and he set the receiver back in its cradle, still holding the handle. He flipped through his personal black leather-back phone book lying on the desk to the R's, and scanned the page of names, addresses and phone numbers until he found Monique's.

Forget it, he told himself. It was time to face reality. She wasn't coming, and he was going to have to play host tonight.

Solomon relinquished the phone altogether, then drummed his fingers on the desk. He must admit that he was surprised and a little disappointed that Monique had neither phoned in or showed up by now.

Her paycheck would reflect her short hours this week. But it was her rope, he thought disgruntled.

Unbuttoning his shirt, he realized how much he'd missed her. His memory had played havoc with his senses, imagining her charming presence, smelling the flowery fragrance of her perfume, hearing her sassy tongue. The past few days had been quiet and boring without her to fight with over some insignificant matter.

But wasn't that what he wanted . . . to be left alone to put his own management stamp on the club . . . without her interference?

"Yes, but . . ." he replied out loud, then clamped his mouth shut. He wondered if Monique had been out looking for another job.

He never figured her for a quitter, but you just couldn't tell about some people, he told himself, pulling a fresh shirt from his briefcase and removing it from the laundry bag. *If she wanted to quit, fine; all the better for me.* He had better things to do than concern himself with an inconsiderate, selfish, highly unprofessional woman. He didn't need her . . . could probably do her job better than she did anyway, he thought confidently.

"Good evening, welcome to *T's Place,*" he said, practicing the greeting he suspected Monique had said a million times as he put on his shirt. Even to his own ears, the greeting on his lips sounded like a death sentence. He cleared his throat and started again. "Good evening," he said, trying to lighten his tone. This time he sounded like a boy in puberty.

He was never going to be able to say it the way Monique did, he realized hopelessly as he buttoned the fresh shirt. She had a wonderful low voice, soft and clear. It resonated with velvet warmth, lulling the listener into thinking he was the most important person in the world. Just hearing it in his mind sent waves of excitement through him, and he visibly shuddered, as if struck by a chill.

His feelings toward her surpassed confusion. His attraction to her had been instant, and to his consternation, showed no signs of changing except to increase.

Recovering from the war of emotions raging in him, Solomon looked in the small wall mirror he'd brought to put on his tie. Adjusting it snugly at the neck of his shirt collar, he appraised his appearance. He could hear his daughter accusing him of being old-fashioned. Though her motive had been to get the keys to his car, he recalled chuckling, he conceded she had a point.

He pulled off the tie and undid the top two buttons, revealing a sprinkle of crinkly black hairs on his chest. "You're no Harry Belafonte," he said to his reflection laughingly. He re-did the lower of the two, then splashed cologne at his neck.

"This will have to do," he said, opening the door to leave.

Walking toward the belly of the club, he wondered what Monique would think of his new look.

Brother Malik, whom he'd learned was a classically trained musician, played a mellow jazz composition on the piano. The soulful music underscored the subdued din of conversations.

Business was slow tonight, Solomon thought, looking over the room. He was surprised, considering it was Friday. There must be something else going on in the city. The downstairs was only half-full with customers attended by Michael. Chris wasn't scheduled tonight, which worked to Cynthia's favor, for the upstairs was virtually empty, except for two or three smoking patrons. Jason had wiped the bar so many times he felt sure he could see his own reflection, he noticed, passing the bar towards the entrance of the club.

He debated splitting the downstairs between Michael and Cynthia. Recalling the hint of an altercation he'd stumbled upon earlier, it might be better just to send Cynthia home. She wasn't in the most cordial of moods to earn tips anyway.

Reaching the station Monique usually commanded, Solomon poised himself to greet customers. With his hands crossed behind his back and rocking back and forth on his heels, he was uncomfortable in the role of host.

He flexed his stiff shoulders to loosen up, then from an over-the-shoulder glance spotted the approach of a much needed patron. A distinguished-looking gentleman in his early forties sauntered into the club. A big man, he was over six feet and carried his 200-plus pounds well. He figured this customer could not only hold several glasses of liquor without becoming a problem, but could afford it.

"Good evening, welcome to *T's Place,*" Solomon said. "Your waiter for . . ."

The patron interrupted him, demanding, "Where's Monique?"

Solomon was slightly taken back by the somewhat belligerent tone in the man's voice. He stared at him with an extra curious beat, noting the curly black hair and butterscotch complexion. Reminded of a polished version of Joe Simpson, he took an instant dislike to the man bedecked in a pearl gray Armani suit, with a peacock-colored, silk handkerchief tucked in the coat pocket. Personally, he would never spend that kind of money for a suit. It was the man who made the clothes, not the other way around.

But it wasn't the suit that offended Solomon. The guy seemed full of himself. He looked as if he'd spent hours preening in the mirror. He had definitely put on way too much cologne. No doubt some over-priced brand that promised a bevy of women swooning at his feet clad in equally expensive Stacey Adams.

"Monique is not in tonight, sir," Solomon said, struggling to maintain his gracious facade, "but I'm . . ."

"Where is she?" the man asked, looking down his nose at Solomon.

"She's off tonight," Solomon said, trying to unloosen his tightening vocal chords. His hands twitched at his sides. It was all he could do to keep from tugging at his tie. "May I show you to a table or would you . . . ?"

"Tell Monique that I came by," the patron said.

"And you are?" Solomon replied, barely attempting to conceal the insolence in his voice.

"Anthony Ward. Dr. Anthony Ward," he repeated with haughty emphasis.

"Okay, Dr. Ward," Solomon began in an unimpressed tone, but before he could finish the sentence, the doctor abruptly spun around and walked off into the direction in which he'd come. Good riddance, Solomon thought.

So it seemed that Miss Monique Robbins had more than one suitor, this one completely opposite in character from Aurelius. At least in Aurelius, she showed good taste. With disdain carved in his features, he was baffled by what she saw in this guy. But that wasn't his problem; it was Aurelius's, he told himself, simmering with contempt.

He couldn't explain the sick sensation that suddenly filled his soul. Neither did he see Jason approach until the bartender was nearly upon him.

"Mr. Thomas," Jason said whispering, a hint of disgust in his tone.

Solomon doused the conflicting emotions before he spoke. "Yeah, what is it, Jason?" he asked with a patience he didn't feel.

"A whole case of glasses has been destroyed," Jason replied.

"What?" Solomon asked, his brows pulled into a disgusted frown.

"I pulled down a new case because the last load I put in the dishwasher wasn't ready. I got called back to the bar, and after I fixed a couple of drinks, I went back to get the glasses. I opened the box and every last one of them was broken. It's like somebody dropped the box on the floor."

Struggling to keep his anger concealed, Solomon sought out his staff, his gaze swinging across the room. He spotted Michael waiting on a table of four near the stage. Stepping from under the stair railing, he looked upstairs to spot Cynthia leaning against a post. "Where's Leon?" he asked.

"Outside," Jason replied. "He thought he saw Adrienne's husband leave the club and went out to make sure."

Angling his body slightly towards the front entrance of the club, Solomon half-stated and asked, "Dennis still at the door."

"I reckon so," Jason replied. "What do you want me to do about the glasses?"

"Nothing," Solomon said. "I'll handle it. You get back to the bar."

"Oh, I forgot to tell you," Jason said, slapping himself upside the head. "Monique called earlier. She had an emergency and said she was going to try and make it, but she'd be late. She's going to call back."

Dressed in a white terry cloth robe with a towel wrapped around her head, Monique was sitting on the side of the bed in her room, with the phone in her hand, dialing a number. After leaving the mechanic, she and Ariana had come to her home where she immediately jumped in the shower, unable to stand the dirt and grime of the day any longer.

"I really like your place," Ariana was saying as she sauntered into Monique's bedroom. "Oops," she said covering her mouth with her hand seeing that Monique was on the phone.

"Jake?" Monique said into the mouthpiece. "Sorry, Jason. This is Monique. Is Mr. Thomas available now? . . . Okay, then tell him I called back. . . . No, I'm all right, but I definitely won't be able to make it in tonight. . . . How are things? . . . It will pick up," she said confidently, though her face twitched briefly in a sign of dismay. "Did JuJu show up?" She laughed in reply to his response. "Okay. I'll see you tomorrow," she said, ending the call.

"You called my dad?" Ariana asked as Monique hung up.

"No," Monique replied chuckling. "I called the manager. But he was unavailable to come to the phone."

Each time she looked at Ariana, Monique felt she was looking in Solomon's eyes. Though she would hazard a guess that Ariana looked more like her mother, for the featural resemblance lay mainly from the nose up, Ariana inherited his deep-set, beautifully-lined eyes. Along with the same piercing look, as if she could see right through to her soul. Monique shuddered imperceptibly as she rose to her feet, patting her hair dry with the towel. She sauntered into the sitting area of the room.

"Think I should call my dad?" Ariana asked, her facial features bunched in an indecisive frown.

"I don't know," Monique said. "You know him better than I do. What do you think?"

"Well, I haven't talked to him since lunch time," Ariana said hesitantly, mulling the decision.

"It may be a good idea then to let him know you're all right," Monique suggested lightly, hoping Ariana would come to the same conclusion. It was totally up to the young lady to decide what, if anything to tell her father about the car.

"I really appreciate your helping me out," Ariana said. "I don't know how I'm going to pay you back."

Though the painter normally charged two-hundred-fifty dollars for such a job, she had to offer him a substantial bonus to get it done tonight and deliver the car to her home by one-thirty. "I'll think of something," Monique replied. "What can you do?" she asked, setting the towel aside as she began unbraiding her hair.

"Huh?" Ariana replied.

"Can you type, do you know how to use a computer, do you draw?" Monique replied, clarifying the inquiry. "What talents do you have?"

"I can type and use a computer," Ariana replied, "but that's it. Unless you need a swimmer."

"Maybe you can help me out with some correspondence. I've got to get out a pretty big mail out before next week. On top of that, there are flyers to be distributed, tickets printed and a press release written for Koko Taylor who's coming for the Juneteenth festivities."

"I know what Juneteenth is," Ariana said. "The day black people in Texas received news of the Emancipation Proclamation in 1865," she added, showing off. "My dad celebrates it like a religious holiday. But I've never heard of Koko whatever you said."

"Koko Taylor," Monique enunciated distinctly, "just happens to be one of the biggest blues singers in the world, my dear," in a proud tone, as if she played a part in the singer's fame.

Making a face, Ariana said, "Ugh."

"I'll excuse your lack of respect because you're young, and you don't know better," Monique said smiling indulgently.

"You think I ought to tell my dad the truth?" Ariana asked.

Monique's fingers paused in her hair to look at Ariana headlong. She never would have guessed that the young woman was still worried about her father's reaction to the car. She didn't know if that were good or bad. "Ariana," she said, "if you want to call him, the phone is right there on the table."

"I don't know what to do," Ariana said with a weary sigh. She got up to meander about the room, ending up in front of the gang of photographs on the wall.

"She must be somebody important," Ariana said, glancing across the room at Monique.

Monique didn't look up. She knew to whom Ariana referred. "Yes, she is," she replied.

"Who is she?" Ariana asked.

This time, Monique did look up. Watching Ariana, a girl on the precipice of womanhood, she felt as if she were looking at her former self, as Tevis had looked at her on so many occasions. In the teenagers' curiously bright eyes, she saw her own thirst for life and a sense of invincibility that had infused her determination to survive and succeed. More from Tevis than her mother, she had gotten her endless insatiability for approval fed. Tevis was not so much older than she, yet Monique saw her as her guide as well as her friend. Tevis taught her that she had to define herself and that she was responsible for determining her path.

"Was," Monique corrected, a wistful quality to her voice. She never thought to wonder before now, finding herself in a reversal of roles with the teenage Ariana, whether she gave back to Tevis just half the gift of sisterhood Tevis had given her. Clearing her throat, she said, "Her name was Tevis. Tevis Theresa Haven. We were closer than sisters."

"She was pretty," Ariana said.

"She was beautiful," Monique said to herself.

As Ariana introduced herself to the two-room setting, Monique's mind flew into a tandem of introspection as she continued taking the braids out of her hair. With Solomon's daughter meandering about and examining her home, she couldn't help thinking about him. Not that she needed a hint of his presence to blame, she told herself. She had been able to think of little else, even before they met officially.

Feeling a sudden prurient curiosity, she looked up just as Ariana kneeled in front of the fireplace to examine the colorful African print pillows. It was on the tip of her tongue to ask whether Solomon had said anything about her to Ariana. Of course, she squashed the desire and the question. Ariana was too smart not to see through the ruse, regardless of how subtle she could mask her inquiry.

She wished Tevis were here now to help her make sense of things. It seemed so much was happening to her all at once. Before Solomon, she had been content with her life. Though it was dominated and divided between school, the club and volunteering at the shelter, it was uncomplicated. Now, he occupied her thoughts and a warm place in her heart with alarming frequency.

Monique was pulled from her muse as Ariana made her way back to the sitting area. She sat Indian-style on the floor by the drum table and picked up the statue of Bastet. As she examined it, she said, "How long have you known my dad?"

Oh-oh, here we go, Monique thought. She should have seen it coming. She drew a deep breath before she replied. "Just since he started working at the club."

"Is he a good manager?"

"It's too soon to tell," Monique replied, then could have

bitten her tongue at the sudden silence that roared in the room. Ariana replaced the statue on the table, then pushed herself up to sit in the chair across the sofa. "What I mean is that his credentials are impeccable in banking, but managing a club is different from anything he's done before. He has to learn a new system and . . ."

"Do you go with my dad?"

"I haven't heard that phrase in a long time," Monique replied with a slight smile. She stared headlong into Ariana's face. "Would you mind?" The question was out before she interpreted what she was asking.

Ariana rolled her eyes and sighed, exasperated. "Why is that all adults answer questions with a question?" she asked.

Monique laughed softly. "What did your dad say when you asked him?" Her heart was racing with eagerness to learn Solomon's reply to his daughter's inquiry about them.

"In essence, that it was none of my business," Ariana replied.

Monique chuckled in spite of the very unsatisfactory answer. It was typical Solomon, she thought. Thinking about how guilty her equally evasive response would seem to Ariana, she decided to say nothing.

"Then, he asked me if I was jealous," Ariana said. Looking at Monique pointedly, she asked, "Do I have reason to be?"

Either way she answered, Monique thought, there was always that very telling kiss Ariana witnessed. A guilty blush spread across her face. "Are you hungry?" she asked in a small voice.

Nine

Monique was working herself into a sweat, pacing around the coffee table in her living room. Occasionally, she peeked out the window. Despite the hour, nearly four o'clock in the morning, she was wide awake. Solomon was on his way.

The decision to tell him the truth about his car had been taken out of Ariana's hands over five hours ago when the painter called. Underestimating the number of coats required to match the color, he'd run short of blue paint and couldn't finish the job. Ariana had called her father to confess.

Plopping down on the couch, Monique folded her arms across her bosom and crossed her legs at the knee. She had a feeling Solomon wasn't too pleased by Ariana's announcement. After speaking with him, Ariana had simply passed her the phone. He expressed his gratitude to Monique for helping his daughter. It seemed as if he wanted to say more, but didn't—except to inquire whether Ariana could stay until he got off from work.

She wanted to slap his face, she recalled grimacing. What did he think she was going to do? Throw his daughter out on the street?

Instead, she offered to pick him up. He refused, insisting on taking a cab. The implication was that he didn't want to be anymore beholden to her than he already felt.

"Ingrate," Monique whispered, pushing herself up to resume pacing.

Ariana didn't want to discuss what her father had said

about the car, or much of anything else, Monique recalled. They watched a little more television, then Ariana fell asleep. Monique had worked on the promotion material for the upcoming concert at the club. The time had gotten away from her as she had become completely engrossed in her work. Then the phone rang, and she hadn't been able to think about anything else since.

Monique groaned. She couldn't believe what she had done. At Solomon's call to announce he was on his way, she promptly performed her beautification ritual. After a quick shower, she tended her skin with her favorite body oil, then dressed in the silk lavender lounging pajamas she'd bought months ago for an unnamed special occasion. She'd brushed her formerly braided hair until it glistened and fell in gentle waves over her shoulders and down her back like a hand-held fan.

And if she didn't slow her innards down, she would be all sweaty by the time he arrived, she mused, willing her heartbeat to slow.

She forced herself to sit the couch, and grabbed a pillow, clutching it to her bosom. Before long, she was fanning the air with a nervous foot, the white slipper flopping against her heel. She couldn't understand why she felt so anxious, as if anticipating some momentous occurrence.

The only thing that was going to happen was Solomon would pick up his daughter, then they would be on their way, she told herself. *If* he could wake up Ariana.

But the plausible scenario created an odd twinge of disappointment in her. So, what did she expect to happen? she asked herself, folding her leg under her.

Quietly pensive, her thoughts filtered back to the day Solomon had kissed her. The answer came in the form of the dreamy look on her face and the wild palpitations beating in her chest. Hungering from mere memory of his mouth on hers sent the air expelling from her lungs in a soft gasp.

She was amazed by her sharp memory of that one, brief

encounter. Tossing the innocent pillow aside, she was up on her feet and ambling about before finding herself back at the bay window, the heavy green curtains parted. She gave it her back and scanned the double-cube room setting dominated by various shades of green against dark peach walls.

Six high back chairs with green and white striped cushions sat around a smoky glass-topped, rectangular table in the dining area. In the living room, free-standing lamps guarded luxuriously overstuffed sofas and chairs in celedon that formed a circle around the ebony coffee table.

The movers, her father and Aurelius aside, Solomon would be the first man to see the inside of her home, the ground level of a duplex. After the fiasco with Anthony, she completely redecorated. The self-prescribed therapy dictated that she remove every reminder of his presence in her life. The emotional ones were unpreventable, but he had touched nothing present. Except her.

Monique shook her head and the memory from her thoughts.

Everything was in its place, except for the two place settings on the corner of the dining room table. She had pulled out the fine, Kente pattern china when the Chinese take-out dinner she and Ariana ordered arrived. After washing the dishes, she had stacked them on the table, intending to replace them later in a box kept in the hall closet.

Right now would be a good time, she mused, but didn't move except to pivot on her heel and face the window. A cab was pulling into her narrow driveway behind the Jeep. Her heart went into overdrive.

By the time Solomon reached the porch, Monique had already unlocked the bolts and gate of the burglar bars on the outer door. She was waiting for him with the door open. He seemed surprised, but not unpleasantly so, to see her standing there.

Breathless, trembling with unrestrained excitement, she

felt her stomach drop and her knees go weak. She leaned against the door and waited.

The quiescent silence between them simmered with a dulcet tension as Monique feasted her eyes on him. His slumberous gaze glittered in the dim light of the inner hallway of the duplex and roamed her figure with languid approval. Gratified by his admiring look, her heart rate sped up another notch, and she could barely breathe. But her other senses operated at pink perfection.

She noticed the absent tie and opened collar at his neck, revealing curly tendrils of hair on his chest. She could smell his cologne, mixed with his own heady scent. She could even feel his heat crossing the chasm to her, inflaming her with his essence.

Neither the look of fatigue on his face nor the fact that he was attired more casually than she'd ever seen him before, in any way diminished his magnificence, or her reaction to it. Wonderful fragments of sensations fused together in one knot of want in her. With that tiny piece of her mind functioning rationally, she wondered if the look of enthrallment on his face mirrored hers.

Solomon cleared his throat. "Is Ariana ready?" he asked.

Monique's fervor waned, and her heart dropped down next to her stomach. "Aren't you going to come in?" she asked, tempering the disappointment in her voice.

Pointing his thumb over his shoulder, he replied, "The cab is waiting. Tell Ariana to hurry, please."

"That might not be so easy," she replied. At the curious look on his face, she explained, "She's knocked out. I don't think anything can wake her."

Solomon's expression contorted in a frown, and he made a dry sound deep in his throat. "I'll wake her," he said, crossing the threshold into the living room.

Pride kept her from trying to reason with him further. It was obvious Solomon was intent on leaving with his daughter. It was probably for the best, she told herself, for she hadn't

the vaguest idea what she wanted. Whether true or not, justi-
fying didn't mollify her spirits which sank a little lower.

"Which way?" he asked after she'd locked the door.

"This way," she said, leading him to the back of the house
to her bedroom. Reaching the door, she turned up the light
to a visible level. She saw determination to awaken Ariana
leave Solomon's expression, replaced by a benign look as
he stared at his daughter. Snoring softly, Ariana was curled
in a fetal position, a hand snuggled under her chin. In a
gesture of indecision, he passed a hand down his face.

"Why don't you just let her spend the night? I don't see
the point of waking her," Monique asked.

Debate ensued on Solomon's face as he considered the
offer. "Are you sure it's all right?" he asked with emphasis.

"I'm positive," she replied.

He sighed, but she didn't know if it were in relief or
frustration.

"Okay," he said at last.

Darkening the room, Monique lead the way back into the
front of the house. She stopped at the head chair of the
dining table, but Solomon strode past her like a man on a
mission. With regret wedged in her bosom, she watched him
reach the door, telling herself again it was for the best.

"Tell her I'll pick her up early, around six, so be ready,"
he instructed, his hand on the doorknob.

Suddenly, he released the knob, lowered his head and
shook it from side to side. He faced Monique with a sheepish grin on his face. She smiled into it, thinking he was so
tired he couldn't think straight.

"Any idea what time my car will be ready?" he asked.

"The man who's doing the work, Javier Peña, said he'd
get the paint first thing in the morning and have it done by
eleven," Monique replied.

Satisfied, Solomon nodded his head, turned again to take
his leave. Again, he froze, then looked across the way at
her. She saw him wrestle with the fine details of how he

was going to pick up Ariana without a car, then he smiled at her with his exhausted eyes.

Suppressing the chuckle tickling her throat, she asked before he could speak, "Hungry? We have plenty of leftover rice and vegetables."

This time, Solomon didn't pause to think. "Let me tell the cabby to leave," he said with a pleased look of resignation.

A cry of relief nearly broke from Monique's lips as her mood spiraled upwards.

Moments later, she and Solomon were sitting at the dining room table. He was in the head chair, polishing off the remains of dinner, a large glass of tea on the side of his plate. She sat in a side chair within touching distance. But her hands were folded primly in her lap.

"How did you happen to run into Ariana?" he asked.

To answer that meant to disclose where she had been, which could open another whole line of questions she didn't want to discuss. "It was just her luck," Monique replied.

Solomon stopped chewing as his handsome face froze, betraying a certain tension. "She must have been somewhere she didn't have anyplace being," he said, a suspicious edge to his voice.

Monique did not hesitate to allay his parental fears. Just knowing Solomon was concerned endeared him to her a little more. "No," she said, "Ariana had every right to be where she was. You don't have to concern yourself about that."

"That's good to know," he said, letting out a long breath of relief. "I don't know her as well as I should. Sometimes, I feel I don't know her at all, then. . . ." He fell silent, halting the flow of words hinting at his insecurity and guilt.

Seemingly with a volition of its own, Monique's hand reached out to cover his resting on the table. The light contact intended to soothe his conscience, instead, unfurled streams of sensations. Caught up in the pleasure pulsing through her, she forgot the words of her comforting speech. Solomon's take charge nature resumed control and rescued her.

A smile found its way through his mask of embarrassment. He said softly, "Forgive me for boring you with . . ."

"Oh, forget it," she said, at last finding her voice. Her tingling hand was safely back in her lap.

"What made you think you could pull this off without my finding out in the first place?" he asked, lifting the glass to his lips.

"It was worth a try," Monique shrugged.

He set the glass back on the table and resumed eating. "She still should have called me," he said.

"Why? If it weren't for the fact that the painter ran out of paint, you would have been none the wiser," she said smugly. "I think she ought to be commended for taking a little initiative, don't you? Or is it that you don't like that she went to someone else for help?"

"That's not it," he said. "It's just that I want Ariana to feel she can come to me anytime with her problems, regardless what they are."

"She was afraid you wouldn't let her use the car again," Monique explained in Ariana's defense. It was an easy role for her to assume.

Bobbing his head up and down for emphasis, Solomon replied, "She was right," with a dry and cynical chuckle.

"You aren't going to hold this one incident against her, are you?" Monique said, her tone rising incredulously.

"Maybe," he said dryly.

All the while he was chewing, his eyes twinkled at her flabbergasted expression. "I can't believe you're so, so . . ," she said fussily, staring at him in astonishment.

"What?" he said, cutting her off. "Old-fashioned . . . narrow-minded . . . chauvinistic? Which one, or all of the above?"

He was laughing at her, Monique realized. She could not quell the smile that tugged at the corners of her mouth. Two could play, too, she thought, feeling giddy and carefree. "I could throw in a few more if you'd like," she said with sensual impertinence, thrusting forward her shoulder as she leaned toward him, her arms folded on the table.

His eyebrows shot up in surprise. "You mean my daughter missed some?" he replied, staring at her with laughter rumbling in his chest.

His laugh faded, and a beguiling light radiated from the dark depths of his eyes like a beacon lighting her path to him. Engulfed in the melodramatic silence that surrounded them, Monique felt the giveaway heat in her face. She was helpless to stop its betrayal of her, and she covered it as best she could with a smile. But even it beamed, transforming her face into pure sunlight.

"No," she said softly. The smile was still in her voice, a companion to the enchantment residing pleasantly in her chest. "Your daughter thinks the world of you."

For an instant, a wistfulness stole into his expression, then was gone. As if amused, but unmoved by her reply, he retorted with quiet mirth in his tone, "Did she pay you to say that?"

Mere banter or more proof of insecurity in her usually unflappable, stoical manager? Recalling what little Ariana did say about Solomon, she knew Ariana cared deeply for her dad. Probably more than the teenager was willing to admit, she thought, mindful of her own adolescent relationship with her father. Had Solomon been equally silent when it came to verbalizing his love?

"As far as Ariana is concerned, you're better than apple pie."

"And you?" he replied, the tenderness of his smile echoing in the warmth of his voice. "What do you think?"

Staring into his face, the mystery in his eyes beckoned to her irresistibly. Monique gulped, incapable of speech. Astonishment coating her already bright amber eyes, she wondered what he was really asking her. On the tip of her tongue was a second emotion that paralleled his daughter's sentiments, doubled by a woman's desire. Whether by fear or sanity, she abstained her heart's vote and finally, found her bantering tongue.

"You haven't tasted my cookies yet," she quipped lightly, rising from her seat. Eager to escape, she felt certain he could hear the pounding of her heart. "I'll take that since you're finished," she said, removing the plate and fork he'd used. "More tea or would you like something else?" she asked, vanishing through the swinging doors into the kitchen.

Solomon sighed extensively as if emerging from an airless space. "No, this is fine, thank you," he replied absently, staring at the glass in his hand. He knew he should have gone straight home. He couldn't believe he'd almost made a complete and utter fool of himself.

He hadn't wanted to come in. Ever since he saw her at the door, he recalled, his smoldering gaze resting on the after-image of her enchanted vision. She reminded him of the Black porcelain angels his mother displayed on the dresser in her bedroom in a place of reverence under the print of the *Last Supper*. Though fiery, Monique wasn't made of baked clay, he sighed, his thoughts warming him.

He growled silently in his throat. Exhaustion was getting the better of him. Blowing out his cheeks, he reared back in his chair and rolled his head around his neck. Stiff muscles popped.

"You say something?" Monique called from the kitchen.

Solomon chuckled to himself. "You have a nice place here," he said, standing to stretch his arms behind his back. He hated to eat and run, but just as soon as the cab arrived, he was leaving.

"Thank you," she replied.

"Been here long?" he asked, sauntering into the living room.

Standing with his back to the window, he examined the

rooms laid out before him. The decor was elegant and taste-
ful, with a color scheme that signaled new life, a rebirth. It
was not the kind of pampered luxury he expected. Rather,
the room showed the owner's Afrocentric dignity, her forti-
tude and an epiphanic appreciation for nature.

The evidence of his interpretation brought a puzzling
frown to his expression. He sensed his addition was all
wrong about her; somehow, the numbers didn't add up. Just
when he thought he had her minutely penned down to an
ultra-extravagant, limited, yet perennially gorgeous woman
with a mercurial quick tongue, she flipped sides, showing a
different face, a toasty warm inner core.

One foolhardy belief per night, he cautioned his runaway
innards. A professional could have decorated the rooms.

"Five years," she replied, reappearing from the kitchen,
carrying a saucer of cookies.

Staring out with confidence that she couldn't see the truth
behind his blank look, Solomon tracked her approach. She
was so incredibly lovely in the pale purple outfit that com-
plied with her gracile movement that his breath caught in
his throat. He could hear his pulse hammering in his ears.
She passed him to the coffee table, and her flowery scent
teased him with the possibility that he was wrong about
other things, as well; namely, her and Aurelius's relationship.

"I'm finally pleased with it," she said.

"You have a good taste," he said to her back as she bent
to set the saucer on the coffee table.

With her hands folded primly in front of her, Monique
smiled at him shyly, then sat on the couch. "Have a seat,"
she said.

Solomon obeyed, sitting at the opposite end of the couch.
He had to extend his arm to reach the cookies. "It looks
like a cookie." He sniffed it. "Smells like a cookie." He bit
into the cookie. "It tastes like a cookie," he declared, "and
it's good."

Laughing, Monique replied, "Surprised?"

"Well, let's just say I never figured you for the baking type."

I'm not going to touch that, Monique thought. "How was it tonight?" she asked, resting her arm along the top of the couch.

The movement readjusted the longing top to reveal more of the creamy expanse of her neck. Solomon felt his gaze descend the opening like a Geiger counter searching for treasures. Caught swooning, he tore his gaze from her, reached for another cookie and popped two in his mouth. He chewed like a kid who feared the sweet snack would be taken away from him if he didn't hurry and eat it.

"Let's just say," he replied with a mouthful, "that you missed it and count your lucky stars."

Monique scooted to the edge of the couch. "What happened?"

"You really don't want to know," he replied, his hands rubbing down his face.

"Oh, yes I do," she replied with laughter hinting at an uneasiness. "I'll have nightmares if you don't."

"Well, since you were so nice to my daughter, I guess I'll give you this one chance to gloat. You'll probably hear it from one of the guys anyway." He pushed himself up to his feet, walked behind the chair and clutched the top with both hands. He still didn't look at her, and it had nothing to do with fearing her pleasure at his expense. "Where shall I start, the good news or the bad news?" he asked, his face collapsing into a complex set of wrinkles.

"The bad," she said dryly.

For some reason, even he wasn't sure why he wanted to protect her from the worst of the news, but he decided to withhold the situation regarding the broken glasses. There was plenty enough other evidence to satisfy her ego with his inability to carry on without her, he thought.

"I sent Cynthia home," he said in a deadpan tone of voice.

A second of silence passed before either said another word.

"You sent her home?" she repeated, her expression revealed disbelief.

Solomon inhaled deeply, his cheeks ballooning with the breath he took, then released it. "She and Michael must have gotten into some kind of argument that put her in a bad mood. I don't know. I asked her to do something since she was the least busy of everybody," he said, recalling he'd asked her to take care of the broken glasses. "The place was almost empty," he added like an aside. "Well, she took offense to my request, so I ended up sending her home."

Monique moaned and covered her face in her hands.

"I know," he said. "I felt the same way when people started pouring in about ten o'clock. I couldn't believe it. They seemed to come from everywhere," he said, feeling overwhelmed anew.

"The Alley Theater," she said knowingly.

"Yeah, the theater crowd." He whistled. "We got so busy," he said, shaking his head amazed, "I almost called Cynthia back to work. I replaced Dennis at the front so he could work the upstairs." He dropped back to his place on the couch and clasped his hands between his thighs. "I figured I couldn't mess up collecting money," clapping his hands. "Jason had to work the cash register and the bar by himself."

With a slow bob of her head, Monique said, "He's capable of doing that," as if talking to herself.

"Yeah well," Solomon said, "I worried the whole time until closing. All I got to do tonight was a cash count, stack the receipts in a rubber band and dump everything in the safe. I'll go through it tomorrow with a fine tooth comb to make sure everything matches up," he said summarily, dropping his head to the back of the couch. He had never felt so inadequate in his entire professional life, he thought. This was one night he wanted to forget. Closing his eyes, he said,

"Don't let me fall asleep. May I prey on your hospitality one more time and get you to call me a cab?"

"Oh, you don't have to . . ."

That was as far as Monique got. The doorbell rang.

Solomon sat up with a jolt. "Expecting company?" he asked. He looked at Monique who was staring curiously at the door, then down at the time on his watch.

Monique shrugged her shoulders puzzled before she replied. "No."

"Sure?" he pressed. A bout of disconcertion came over him. He had a sneaking suspicion it was her lover calling.

Monique rose slowly and walked toward the door hesitantly. "Who is it?"

"Monique, it's me, Anthony."

Monique spun to face Solomon with her mouth hanging open. "I don't believe this," she mouthed, a scowl of marring her features. She turned back toward the door. "Anthony, go away," she commanded impatiently.

"Come on, Monique," Anthony replied. "You didn't return any of my calls. I just want to talk," he said with pleading.

"No. I don't want to see you or talk to you or anything, Anthony," she said accenting her firm intention by pounding the air with her balled fists.

"If you don't open up, I'll come back again and again until you hear me out," he said.

What a mess he'd gotten into, Solomon thought disgusted. And with his daughter in the bedroom no less!

Monique implored him for help with her look. "I don't want to see him," she whispered vehemently.

"Want me to send him away?" Solomon asked, his lips pressed together in a sign of pique.

"Please," she replied with unwavering conviction.

Grudgingly, Solomon pushed up to his feet. He hated involving himself in a lovers' quarrel. But he didn't particularly care for Dr. Anthony Ward and would take pleasure in sending the good doctor on his way. It was a hapless victory, he thought, remembering Aurelius was still in the picture. He opened the door a crack.

"Monique is not interested in seeing you," he said matter-of-factly. Tacking on, "Anthony," with a smug grin on his face.

"You!" Dr. Ward snarled accusingly. "What are you doing here?"

"You don't have the right to ask me that," Solomon replied casually. "Monique and I," he said with intimate emphasis, "would both appreciate it if you'd be on your way."

"Monique," Dr. Ward whined with frustration lining his tone, "will you please come to this door?"

"Don't make a scene, Anthony," Solomon said in a deathly quiet tone. "It's over. She doesn't want you anymore. Now, why don't you just go away and we won't have any trouble."

Dr. Ward backed from the door, his hands held up in show of surrender. "I know. You're right. I'm sorry. Tell Monique . . . Monique," he yelled over Solomon's head, "I'm sorry, okay? Okay, Monique?"

"Goodnight, Anthony," Solomon said, closing the door shut and bolting the locks. With his face pinched tight, he stared at Monique who sat huddled on the couch. She was tugging at the folds of her lounging top. He had a feeling she wasn't conscious of what she was doing. But he had no sympathy for her. His gender peers seemed to be tripping over each other for her attention, he thought. Jealousy and frustration fused in a bitter outpouring.

"That happens sometimes when you dangle a carrot in front of too many men," he said. "They show up to collect."

Monique's head snapped up to look at him. Her eyes blinked in baffled silence before she spoke. "What are you talking about?"

"Dr. Ward came by the club tonight, asking, no," he amended, "make that *demanding* to see you."

A shock of breath rushed from Monique. "He knows I

work at the club?" she asked surprised, her eyes wide with anxiety.

"Was it supposed to be a secret?" Solomon replied sarcastically, staring down his broad nose at her.

"Well," she said, biting down on her bottom lip, a thoughtful expression, "I guess he was bound to find out sooner or later." She spoke so softly he could barely hear what she was saying. "But he didn't know," she said, shaking her head as she looked up again at Solomon. "I never told him."

"Wait," Solomon said, pulling his hands out his pockets, "I'm missing something here. He's not one of your uh, how shall I say it, boyfriends?"

"Boyfriends?" she chortled offended.

"Well, I admit the term doesn't seem appropriate," Solomon replied, with a casual shrug of his shoulders, "but it will do."

"Solomon," she said testily, "Anthony and I broke up three years ago. I had to get a court order to keep him from coming within 25 feet of me. I'll do it again if I have to," propping her hands on her hips to glower at him. "And *no*, I'm not too old for a boyfriend, if that's what you're implying. And *no*, I don't have any. And *anyway*, what's it to you?"

Solomon blinked, shook his head with a jerk as if he'd been slapped. "But, I thought you and . . ." Assailed by an humiliating dread, he clamped his mouth shut. "Never mind."

"What?" she pressed.

Solomon squirmed and unconsciously, lifted a hand to the collar of his shirt. He realized he wasn't even wearing a tie; hence, had no excuse for the constricting feeling, like a noose tightening around his neck. "I, uh, I thought you and Aurelius were, uh . . ." he said, his feeble voice fading into silence.

Monique picked up on what Solomon didn't finish. His guilty look said it all.

"Oh, that's disgusting!" she said hotly. "How could you

think something like that? Aurelius is married to my best friend. I'm their daughter's godmother, for pete's sake. Where on earth did you get such a crazy idea?"

"I'm sorry," he whispered contritely. His innards danced a jig of joy in his chest. *She's not the boss's woman. She's not Dr. Ward's woman. She's nobody's woman.*

"Maybe I better call you that cab now," she said contentiously.

"Aw, come on, Monique," he cajoled, "you don't have to get so mad about it. It was an honest mistake."

"Mistake?" she echoed hotly, her delicate features flaring. "That's the kind of talk that gets out and ruins reputations and destroys friendships. There's nothing honest about it. What other little falsities are running around in that thick, chauvinistic head of yours?" she demanded.

Since her temper showed no signs of evaporating, he might as well get all of his curiosity satisfied at once, Solomon thought. "Aurelius," he said, "does he own the club or not?"

Monique's expression slightly softened, but only from anger to exasperation. She gave him an unladylike dustup, then wordlessly, spun to walk off.

"Oh, no you don't," he said, charging after her. "Where do you think you're going?" intercepting her at the pass, the invisible divider between the living and dining rooms.

"To call you a cab," she spat out at him.

"You didn't answer my question," he replied.

A gaze of warning, her eyes did a slow slide down to his hand clasping her wrist, then back up to his face. Solomon knew he should release her. The message tumbled in his head right next to the side of his brain that controlled emotions. With his heart banging against his ribs, he felt forces at work in him. They compelled him to consider he didn't know her at all, to correct the wrong assumptions he had, to make some new discoveries.

Ten

Contracting and expanding with an hypnotic lull, the room mimicked the qualities of its human occupants. The temperature was warm and soft as tension rose and silence stretched like a slow drag, accentuating forte heartbeats. It viewed with twin gazes, amber ardor locked into caressive chocolate and reeked with the scent of arousal.

"Solomon . . . ?"

Warning or plea? Monique didn't know what thought prompted her to speak. She didn't recognize the sound of her own voice over the din of her heart galloping in her chest. She perceived the fervency swelling in her as she stared spellbound by Solomon's expression. His deep brown gaze roved her face methodically, lingering on each feature—her high forehead, long lashes curled over almond-shaped, funny-colored eyes, her straight nose, dropping to her mouth, well-formed and wide—satisfying his eyes. She could feel his thoughts in the passionate fluttering at the back of her neck.

Hesitantly, he lifted a hand towards her face, as if afraid to touch her. Her flesh prickled, anxious for his touch. She didn't know what he was waiting on—protest or invitation. She held her breath.

Finally, his left hand reached its target, her hair. She closed her eyes and felt a familiar shiver of awareness, as he gently stroked her thick, wavy mane.

"You took your hair down," he said quietly.

Admiration inscribed his tone. Monique opened her eyes to look into his face; his eyes were glazed in awe. "Yes." She sounded a little breathless.

"It's real. So soft and fine. Like satin. A good grade of hair as my mama used to say," he said in soft musing chortle. "Smells good, too," he said, lifting a fistful of strands to his nose. His eyes closed, and he inhaled deeply, declaring, "I like it." Lids popping open, he added hastily, "I liked the other way, too." A wee smile teased the corners of his mouth.

Only because she felt she had to say something, Monique said, "I'm glad," but even then, the words felt inadequate.

He re-arranged her hair around her shoulders, brushing every strand back in place. Then, as if in one motion, his hands found his pants pockets and he moved an inch back from her. She felt no cause for alarm. The warmth of his nearness remained in place.

His stance was relaxed, customarily still. A pensive gleam shone in his eyes; the soft, overhead lighting painted them black sparklers. She wondered fleetingly what he was thinking, her attention elsewhere. She took in his tempting, attractive, male physique. The crisp hairs peeking from the open collar offered up a temptation. Her fingers itched to play there, and explore the firm, malted-chocolate bed of his chest. Her mouth watering, she forced her gaze upwards to catch the look, a flicker of passion crossing his eyes. Then it was gone, replaced by a look of serene contentment, and she wondered if she saw it or imagined it.

"You didn't answer my question," he said smoothly.

She knew exactly the question of his interest. But teetering on the edge of desire, she could barely swallow, let alone speak.

"And in case you've forgotten," Solomon said, "I'm referring to the one about your feelings for me."

Impaled by his gaze, Monique felt an eminent tension coming solely from him. It filled her with a strange inner excitement. Solomon was looking at her with something more profound than masculine interest, and she couldn't help thinking the moment of truth had arrived. A breath trembled in her bosom. She knew her frame of mind leaned toward lust as far as he was concerned, but sex was not what he was asking from her. His eyes didn't blaze with mere carnal want. He could get sex from any woman. What he desired was something far more intimate, soul deep. And to that, she didn't have an answer. Yet. Caution held her back.

She waited until her quickened pulse subsided before she spoke. "I . . . I don't know," she said honestly.

"He hurt you, didn't he? Anthony. Dr. Ward," he said in a somewhat gruff tone, his eyes slightly stirring to anger.

Monique's eyebrows shot up. She was stunned by the accuracy of his guess and equally uncomfortable with his insight. She averted her gaze from his to stare absently across the room. Her eyes dulled briefly with memory. "That was a long time ago," she said in a distant voice.

"Don't be afraid of me, Monique," he said.

His voice was like a plea, and her head whipped to stare at him. He was looking at her with compassion and understanding. She wondered if there were a hole in her protective shield that hid her victimization—a weakness she'd fought hard to conceal.

"I'll never hit you," he said.

She paused before she spoke. "How did you know?" she asked resigned.

"Sometimes my guesses are better than my arithmetic," he replied.

"I'm not," she replied in an affirmable tone. She looked at him squarely, her eyes riveted on his mouth. His firm mouth relaxed in his handsome face. She felt a sudden, awful desire for a kiss. Like a child who begged her mother to kiss away the pain, she wanted Solomon to help her forget. "I'm not afraid of you."

"That's a start," he replied relieved.

"And you? How do you feel about me?" she asked in a

rush of breath as if in fear of losing her courage. She felt her flesh color.

"I'd have thought the answer to that was very obvious," he replied. "My conscience gave me a hard time about it. I wrestled over it, debating the pros and cons until I didn't know which columns to put them into. Before I knew it, nature was taking my wish for granted," he added cryptically as if speaking to himself. With a lopsided little grin on his face, he asked, "Are you going to get mad again?" Before she could form a reply, he said, "Would it help if I told you I was jealous?"

Even with time to think of a suitable reply, Monique's voice was misplaced. She felt her head spinning from all the revelations. Her mind couldn't process them fast enough for the pandemonium they wrought among her innards. Her heart sang with delight at each analysis unfolding in her head. She knew this charming, but quiet-tempered man did not give his trust easily. Yet, he had laid himself open to her freely. Frightening, and at the same time enormously sating, she felt an humbling crevice open inside her at the most precious gift she'd ever received. Rays of joy pierced her soul and rose to her face like a summer sunrise.

"Say something," he implored her. His deep voice simmered with barely checked passion.

With a smile trembling on her lips and a secretive light dancing in her eyes, she said, "You're mighty talkative tonight."

His lips parted in a dazzling display of pearly white teeth, and he gave her a look that sent her pulses off to the races again. The smile in his eyes contained a sensuous flame, and all her senses congealed into one passionate receptacle of want. She felt, then saw him subtracting the distance between them.

He advanced cautiously. The anticipation was almost unbearable. Monique's feet seemed to be drifting along on a cloud. With her eyes open, she moved into his approach, filling the minuscule space that remained. His warm strength descending over her, he gathered in his arms as she put her arms around his neck and lifted her face to his. His mouth pressed against hers and swallowed the soft sigh that escaped her lips.

All hesitation fled. Shadows befelled to a bright light spilling over them. Monique felt as if a door had opened to welcome her inside.

Solomon treated her mouth like a fine delicacy. His tongue traced the soft fullness of her lips, sending the pit of her stomach into a wild swirl. Slowly, the pressure of his lips increased, and his mouth moved over hers with exquisite tenderness. She felt a breathless wonder, and parted her lips fully, like a flower to receive a drop of dew. Their tongues danced together in a silent melody before the temper of his ardor intensified, and he devoured her mouth, pushing her toward new sensations. She followed his lead greedily, kissing him back with zeal. The kiss was everything she'd wished it would be, and then some.

At last, reluctantly, their lips parted. A breathless whistle, Solomon inhaled deeply, refilling his lungs with new air. He rested his forehead against hers.

"I better go," he said, his voice impaired. It wasn't the only thing in need of repair as he struggled to resume control of his desire-laden aggression. Now, before it was too late, he thought, his mouth open still taking in oxygen.

Monique whined her displeasure and tightened her arms around him in reply.

"My daughter is sleeping in your bedroom." His voice echoed both their longings.

Monique nodded tacitly. She stepped away from him, a bittersweet smile on her face. Unwilling to sever contact completely, his hands instinctively found hers.

"I better get my car keys, otherwise you won't be going any place," she said, regret and resignation in her soft voice.

"Yes, I would imagine so," he chuckled.

Their hands touched until she was out of reach. His immensely fond gaze followed her from the room. What a night, he thought. Powered by a wonderful new energy, he no longer felt tired.

If Monique had been shocked by the depths of his disclosure, then so had he. Even more so. It was as if he were a dam that could no longer contain its weight, and burst loose, freeing emotions in one giant spill. He couldn't say exactly what had come over him. Everything seemed new, and now, brighter. He would analyze it tomorrow.

Monique returned with a single key on a chain. He took the key and the hand it was offered in.

"Did I say thank-you for being there for my daughter?"

"Grudgingly, if I recall," she replied with gentle laughter in her tone.

"Well, let me make amends," he said, pulling her hand up to his mouth. His eyes riveted on her glowing face, he planted a kiss in her palm. He saw the breath waver at her throat. "Thank you. For everything."

"You're welcome," she replied, returning his warm gaze.

Wordlessly, they strolled to the door. "I'll see you tomorrow," he said, unbolting the door.

"Not too early," she replied, a little chuckle in her voice.

"I don't think you have to worry." He faced her with his lips parted to speak, but froze unable to mutter a word or think beyond the sweet dreamy look on her face. A caution to leave eased its way to the surface of his mind. He leaned down to peck her on the cheek, then vanished.

With a whistle on his lips, Solomon walked jauntily to the Cherokee Jeep parked in the driveway. He saw nothing in the black night except her face. Since he couldn't stay, he was anxious to get home.

He jumped in the vehicle, adjusted the seat and steering

column to his height and started the engine. Rock music blared from the radio. Ariana had definitely been in the car, he thought laughingly. He changed the dial to the all-news station.

"Nine year old killer causes uproar in Baytown, and the Harris County prosecutor's office is contemplating criminal charges against a prominent Houston doctor.

"Details on these and more stories right after this message," the reporter promised as Solomon backed out the driveway. By the time he reached the corner, soft music to match his mood played from the radio. He turned off the block, unaware of another set of car lights popping on and another car engine revving up in his disappearing wake.

It was ten-thirty Saturday morning. There was no air current, just blazing hot sun in clear blue skies.

Held suspended in the air over the steering wheel, big, thick brown hands trembled fiercely. It was humiliating to the owner of the limbs.

As if gripped by a spasm, Byron knotted his hands into fists. A spit of disgust rose all the way from his gut and respired in a guttural growl.

He was sitting in his car, a red, 1990 Vet, the engine still running. The car idled on a quiet neighborhood street outside a one-story, gray wood building. It was really a house converted into Project Center's headquarters located in the Montrose area, a replica of New York's Greenwich Village.

A white sign promoting *Project Center* in bold black letters was stuck in the grassy front yard. Three cement steps led up to the porch that expanded from one side of the house to the other. A wood framed glass door was in the center.

The people inside were expecting him. If it hadn't been a condition of his release, he wouldn't be here, he thought sourly. He glanced at the building with debate raging a war

on his seamy brown face. A fear he refused to admit immo-
bilized him.

There was to be twelve of them, he recalled his parole
officer telling him. Among other things, mostly warnings,
if he threatened any of the facilitators of the program, they
were free to boot him out.

Do not collect $200, go directly to jail, he mused sarcas-
tically.

Thirty-six hours. One hundred-twenty minutes. Eighteen
Saturdays. He had thought he could do that time blind-
folded. But just thinking about those people picking his
brain caused a strange alarm in him.

Of course, they had said this was an education program
and not therapy. He didn't believe them. He knew what they
wanted. They wanted to get him to open up and bare his
soul in front of them.

He didn't want to talk about his feelings. Feelings were
for women and children. Neither did he want to talk about
his past. It was over.

"Hey, Byron!"

He looked toward the house where a middle-aged, balding
white man was standing on the porch. The facilitator, he
thought. What was this old man who had been given every
advantage society offered going to teach him?

"Coming in?"

Monique awakened slowly and stretched with languish, a
wake-up sigh on her lips. Rolling over on her stomach to
glance at the clock, her head did a double-take seeing the
hour. It was two in the afternoon! She had slept half the day
away.

She fell back in bed on her back with a groan in her
throat, to stare absently at the ceiling. Memory of her last
waking hours ruffled through her mind like wind on water.

Her last glimpse of Solomon—leaving, but clearly not wanting to—was the most precious.

He was too good to be true, she thought, a surf of warmth surging across her bosom. She hadn't been looking for anything but a manager to run her club. *Didn't even want a man in that position,* she recalled. Then she got one who on the surface seemed callus and distant, far from the kind of man she'd be attracted to—even if she were in the market. But beneath that managerial stoicism of his, she sighed dreamily, Solomon T. Thomas was a keenly sensitive and insightful man.

Each time she saw him, an argument to keep away was lost. He was stripping down barriers she had erected as if they were soft banana peels, exposing her to a cabal of sensibilities she never believed existed in the first place.

Monique didn't want to worry herself with reasons, but a moth of doubt lighted on her pleasant muse. *Remember what happened the last time you rushed into an affair looking for a way to fill the emptiness inside.* The caustic reminder topped her thoughts and bobbed there like a float on water until she nearly protested aloud.

Solomon wasn't like Anthony! the romanticist in her defended.

How do you know for sure? the frightened skeptic demanded in reply.

Monique felt a chill shiver down her spine. Her eyes darkened pensively. Maybe she should stop and analyze what was happening to her, she told herself. She sat up, folding her legs Indian-style. She faced the pictures of Tevis facing her, but she was only partially aware of them.

Her healing had been progressing satisfactorily. She was regaining her shattered confidence and learning to step back a little farther from the humiliation and pain she permitted Anthony to inflict on her. Her attraction to Solomon was different. Though he swept the ground from under her feet as Anthony had, she felt a need for Solomon more compelling than sexual fulfillment.

"It's time to get up sleepy-head."

The thought forgotten, the mental foray for explanation faded into oblivion. Monique recognized his voice instantly, and instantly, her heart reacted to his facile tongue.

"I've got to go."

Solomon added, no doubt to hurry her along, she thought laughingly. "I'll be there shortly," she promised in a rhythmic reply as she bounced out of bed.

Shortly was a record-breaking fifteen minutes. Monique sauntered into the dining room of her home, plaiting a small braid she'd put in her hair. She was dressed in a short, button front, black rayon jacket with full medallion skirt, the colorful head bust of King Tutankhamen in the design. The ensemble was capped by dangling gold and onyx earrings and black pumps. No one was in sight, and she opened her mouth to inquire.

"I see you finally decided to get up."

Monique pivoted in the direction of the sound. Solomon was coming from the kitchen. Each froze—Solomon between the swinging doors and Monique with her hands on the braided strand—as his darkly eyes met her bright ones. A surge of electrical awareness sizzled between them.

Monique felt her pulse beat with that same kinetic energy, returning his enchanted stare. He showered her with his look, his eyes glowing from within with a mix of approval and desire. The blood rushed to the highly sensitive nerve endings in her body, filling her bosom and creating a needful ache in her loins.

Then his earnest eyes sought hers, and his lips spread slowly in a warm spontaneous smile. She lost the battle controlling her smile, or its friend, the blush that crept into her cheeks.

"Hi," Monique said softly.

"Hi, back," Solomon replied. "Do you dress like that every Saturday or did you dress that way for me?"

With a retort on her tongue, Monique's brows rose in jest as her eyes roamed the expanse of his beautifully propor- tioned body. She settled for admiring; her chest rose and fell with a silent sigh. His shoulders level, long brown arms protruded the short sleeve, cream-colored pullover that stretched across his wide chest. It was tucked in at the slim waist of starched blue jeans that molded and emphasized his powerful thighs and long legs. White socks and Nike's on his feet rounded out the look, which for Solomon, she thought, was ultra-casual. She was surprised, but not disap- pointed, completely captivated by his compelling personage. Then in one of those short bouts of disconnected thoughts, she wondered whether he was changing or was she reading him all wrong?

"Which is it?"

Solomon's velvet voice cut into her thoughts and made Monique's heart beat more rapidly. Hunger replaced second- guesses.

"I have a bunch of errands to run," she said, with nervous laughter in her voice. "Flyers and tickets need to be picked up from the printers, and on top of that, an appointment to keep." She knew she was babbling, but was helpless to stop the irrelevant chatter. Solomon was advancing upon her, the message in his eyes uncannily matched the sensation cours- ing through her. "It's a good thing you woke me up. I'm supposed to be there at 4:30," she finished breathlessly.

Her voice faded into silence, leaving a small parting be- tween her lips as she gazed up into his face. She couldn't miss the musky smell of him or the feel of his excitement. Arousal flared in his eyes, the last thing she saw before he drew her against his entire length. Her arms snaked around his waist as she settled in his embrace. She lay her head there against his chest, listening to the music of his heart thudding in her ears and felt the muscles straining against the tight control he held over himself.

"Mm," he sighed, the whisper of his breath on her cheek. "You feel better than I remember," he said. "How is that possible?"

Her thoughts echoed his inquiry. The answer was supplied in the way he made her feel. She smiled against his chest and moaned pleasurably in reply.

"Maybe I just want you more," he said.

Lifting her face upwards by the chin, he lowered his head to brush his lips over hers ever so gently, and her hunger poured forth in a heated gush. Whimpers of her desire escaped her lips. The sweet throbbing of his lips made her nestle closer against his supple strength. His deliberately slow advance increased her yearning. She took his face between her hands and pulled his head down to hers. Forcing his lips open with her thrusting tongue, she took his mouth in a kiss that released pent-up passions and created hotter ones. It shattered his outward calm, and he assumed command of her mouth, surrendering to the crush of feelings that drew them together.

"Is it safe to come in?"

Ariana's voice called out to them from the kitchen. Solomon and Monique sprang apart, laughing softly at themselves.

"Yeah, it's safe," Solomon replied, his arm draped around her shoulders.

Ariana walked in, a teasing look in her expression. But she said nothing other than, "I got the mail," dropping the stack of envelopes on the table. "Do you smoke?"

"Not anymore," Monique replied, then squinted embarrassed amending, "Well, occasionally, if I'm driven to one. Why?"

"There's a whole bunch of butts on your patio deck. Like somebody was chain smoking and just dropped them on the floor."

"What?" Monique replied peeved. "Where? Come show me," she said leading the way through the kitchen, out the back door and onto the raised patio deck of redwood enclosing a small portion of her back yard. She couldn't believe it. As hard as she worked to keep her property clean, she fumed silently.

"Right over here," Ariana said, walking toward the French door.

"I'll be damned." Monique said, her hands on her hips as she looked down at the butts.

Solomon stood across from her examining the black burglar bars on the door. "Have you been having break-ins in this neighborhood?"

"I'm sure we have," she replied, "but nothing out of the ordinary. Why?"

"Looks like something was used, maybe a crowbar, to pry this lock from the wood here," he said speculatively, running his hand along the small opening between the lock and its embedded in the wood bar.

"Let me see," she said, inspecting the door.

"See the scratches right here on the metal part here, and over here the wood is chipped," he said.

Monique sighed as if exhausted. "That's all I need," she said.

"When was the last time you've been out here?" he asked. "This could be recent or it could be old. There's just no way to tell. Unfortunately, if someone wants to break in, there's very little you can do. The best thing is to make sure your insurance is paid up and hope that if they come back, you're not here," he said, draping an arm across her shoulder. Leading her back inside, he said, "I was hoping we could have lunch together."

"I'm sorry," she replied. "I wish I could cancel this appointment, but I can't. It's something I volunteered to do for Haven House. I have an appointment with the hotel manager about providing some rooms at no cost," she said.

"Don't worry about it," he said. "There'll be other times. But we do need to get together and discuss some things about the club."

"Anything in particular?" she asked, eyeing him sidelong, a teasing look on her face. She recalled his near catastrophic decision that caught him by surprise when the late-night crowd rushed in, leaving him shorthanded.

He chuckled with memory before he replied. "That was just half of it," he replied, suddenly unsmiling. "I'm afraid there's more. I didn't want to tell you about it last night."

"Oh, no," she exclaimed, her shoulders sagging from the weight of unknown problem.

"It'll keep," he said lightly, pulling her into the circle of his arms. "Coming to work tonight?"

Monique noticed a different question alight in his eyes. Aware that they were under the watchful gaze of Ariana, she replied, "Yes."

"Good. I'll see you at seven," he replied. Still looking at Monique, he said, "Ariana, are you ready?"

"I'm not the one you need to ask," Ariana replied laughingly.

"Smart aleck," Solomon quipped. To Monique, "I'll see you tonight."

"It's a date," she winked at him.

It was much needed, and Mother Nature granted it generously. Sheets of rain poured from the evening sky. There was still no relief from the heat.

Solomon hoped it wasn't a bad sign. Standing at the opened door at the back of the club, he tugged his shirt sleeve in place. It was six-fifty-five, and Monique was no where in sight.

He had neither seen nor heard from her since leaving her home earlier today, arriving shortly before the painter returned his car. The man refused to tell him what the job cost. He'd meant to ask Monique, but he got sidetracked, Solomon recalled, a suggestive grin splitting his face in half.

Learning she belonged to no other, he was so eager to claim her his that he never stopped to think that he really didn't know her. Something inside him told him he knew all he needed to know. The answer was in how she made him feel, and that was as if he'd found his rightful place in the universe.

Still, he found it hard to believe that she was unattached, in spite of an obvious painful experience with Dr. Ward. They had been separated over three years. That was a long time to get over a lot of things, he thought. He wondered what caused the break-up, not so much out of idle curiosity, but as not to make the same mistakes.

Solomon laughed out loud. Here he was, standing in the door getting wet, thinking about Monique in terms of permanence, he chided himself amazed. And why not?

His daughter wanted to live with him. He shared a mutual attraction with a beautiful woman. Maybe it's time for him to start thinking about his personal future, he thought, closing the door on the rain.

Eleven

Solomon returned to his office. The top button on his shirt was undone by the time he closed the door behind him. He was changing—just in case.

He didn't feel a sense of déjà vu, having done this before, he mused. Because this time was different, he told himself, peeling the shirt off his back. He didn't feel like a manager put in a precarious position because an employee failed to keep her commitment. Instead, he felt like a . . . a what? he asked himself, a smile spreading across his face.

"A boyfriend?" he asked himself aloud, and laughed. Yeah, he mused, that's exactly how he felt.

While he was tucking the fresh shirt in his pants, someone knocked on the door. "Yeah?" he called out.

"It's me, Francine."

"Just a sec," Solomon replied. The shirt tucked, he splashed on some cologne, then opened the door to Francine dressed in the club uniform. "What can I do for you, Miss Francine?" he asked, feeling especially generous.

Winking at him, she said, "Hm. Somebody been back here getting all dolled up. Guess she's not coming?"

"She's just running late," Solomon replied chuckling.

"Well, you look good anyway," she said, looking at him suggestively.

"You wanted to see me about something?" Solomon replied, ignoring her come-on, knowing she was just playing a game.

"Jake is short on Jack Daniels," she replied. "He asked me to tell you."

"Okay, thanks," he replied. "I'll take care of it."

"Okay," she said in a singsong, starting to sashay off.

"Oh, Francine," Solomon called, halting her exit.

She stopped abruptly, then slowly pivoted as she faced him. "Yes, Solomon," she said, batting her big brown eyes at him.

Laughing at her antics, he said, "I noticed Cynthia hasn't come in. She hasn't called either. Have you heard from her?"

The smile dropped from Francine's face, replaced by a pout. "Shoot," she said, "I thought you wanted to ask me out."

"There's no room in your life for another man, Francine," he replied amused. "Now, what about Cynthia?"

"I don't think she's coming back," Francine said, shrugging indifferently.

"That's what I think, too," Solomon said, his lips pressed together thoughtfully. "Okay, thanks, Francine."

"Is that all?" she asked.

"That's all," he replied. "Tell Jake I'll bring that liquor right away."

As Francine sauntered off, Solomon locked his door, then headed for the stockroom. He was a little upset with himself for having lost an employee so soon on the heels of his arrival at the club. In hindsight, he wished he'd handled the situation a little differently. Or maybe even called Cynthia today and try to talk to her. He had a feeling she wasn't a very forgiving woman and resigned himself to keeping the situation locked in his memory for future reference.

He got the bottle of liquor from the stockroom, then secured the door, heading for the bar. Saturday night, and the place was filling up fast. All of the employees were busy, and Brother Malik's entire band was on stage, playing a reggae number.

"Here you go, Jake," Solomon said, setting the fifth on the counter of the bar.

"Thanks," Jake replied absently, mixing drinks for Chris who was waiting, his hands on a round serving tray.

"I thought you were on the door tonight?" Solomon asked in a louder than normal voice to be heard.

"Dennis wanted the door," Chris replied. "That's fine by me. I need the tips."

"Here you go, two gin and tonics, a Muddy Waters and a Lite," Jake said, placing the various drinks on the tray.

"I'll be back," Chris said as he hurried back to his patrons awaiting drinks.

"Did Monique call?" Solomon asked Jake who had already begun mixing another drink.

"Got my bourbon and coke?" Michael interrupted, appearing suddenly at the bar.

"Right here," Jake replied, setting the drink on the counter.

Michael stuck a stirrer in the drink, then dashed off.

"No," Jake said, wiping the bar. "I haven't heard from Monique. She better show up tonight. We're already short-handed. Francine and Jason are going to have to work upstairs by themselves."

"I'll pull Dennis off the door," Solomon said before sauntering to the foyer of the club, where a line of patrons were piled in and dripping from the rain. Dennis was sitting at the table collecting money, while Leon stood guard.

Solomon bent to whisper in Dennis's ear. "You're needed upstairs," Solomon said. "I'll take over here."

Taking over from Dennis, Solomon collected money until the flow of patrons stopped. He whistled.

"It's going to be a good night even though it's raining," Leon said.

"I'm not complaining," Solomon said, looking at his watch. It was seven-thirty, and as far as he knew, Monique still hadn't arrived. His concern grew. "Leon, will you run inside and see if Monique has gotten here yet?"

"Sure thing, Mr. Thomas," Leon replied, then disappeared inside the club.

As Solomon began separating and bundling the bills in neat stacks, the door opened and a single patron walked in, closing an umbrella. It dropped water on the floor, and Solomon made a mental note to have it wiped up before it became a hazard. He formed no impressions of the man, merely noted he was a working-class-looking brother. Not tall, but a neatly dressed, compact man of copper complexion.

"Good evening, sir," he said, "welcome to *T's Place.*"

"Yeah," the man replied, "how much is it?"

"That'll be ten dollars," Solomon replied.

The man pulled his wallet from his back pocket, then laid a fifty on the table. As Solomon counted out his change, he asked, "Taylor here?"

"Who?" Solomon asked, looking up into the man's face.

"I mean Monique," the man replied.

"Uh," Solomon said looking towards the main door, "I'm not sure."

"All right, thanks," the man replied, pocketing his change before strolling into the darkness of the club.

Leon returned. "She's not here, yet," he said.

"All right," Solomon said, a decision on his face. "Leon, I need to make a call. See who's the least busy who can come out here for a few minutes."

As Leon disappeared through one door, two more patrons, a couple rushed inside. With their backs to Solomon, they brushed the raindrops from themselves that the umbrella failed to catch, laughing like young lovers. As they turned to approach the table, Solomon stiffened, recognizing the man instantly.

What was Ward was up to? he asked himself. Though the willowy woman at his side was lavishly attractive, she looked like a prize. He wondered suspiciously whether she was a shield to mask another reason for the doctor's presence. Ward recognized him, as well, he noted. The doctor faltered for a brief second, then regained his composure.

"Good evening, welcome to *T's Place*," Solomon said by rote, forcing a politeness in his voice. "That'll be twenty dollars, please."

Wordlessly, Ward cut an eye at him as he flung a bill on the table. Placing his hand in the small of his date's back, he said, "This way, baby."

With raindrops dripping from her face, hands and raincoat, Monique bolted into her office at the club and locked the door behind her. Head pressed against the door, she closed her eyes and sucked in long, deep breaths of air to settle her nerves and still her pounding heart.

I'm safe.

She forced the image to her thoughts, murmuring it to herself over and over, until she felt calm come and soothe her. At the three-knuckle knock on the door, all semblance of inner peace scampered. She jumped away from the door and faced it with wide anxious eyes. Both hands were clutched to her bosom where calm cowered behind the ferocious beat of her heart.

"Monique?"

"Solomon," Monique exclaimed relieved, dropping her hands to her sides. She scolded herself laughingly for her irrational bout of fear as she opened the door. Just knowing he was on the other side gave her a sense of protection she couldn't give herself. Physical proof of that fact was confirmed as she looked at him filling the doorway with his steady presence that inspired a thesaurus of emotions in her. She coveted him with her gaze. Her heart beat a different melody, in harmony with the dulcet expression on her face. Wordlessly, she walked into his arms knowing she would be welcomed.

"Not that I mind getting such a greeting," he said amused, "but something tells me it's not for the reason I would like." He moved them inside the privacy of her office in order to close the door. Stroking her back, he asked, "Where have you been? I've been going out of my mind wondering what happened to you."

"I'm sorry," she said, her words muffled against his chest. She didn't want to leave this place. The shelter of his arms and gentle touches were a comforting balm to her senses.

Finally, he pushed her away from him to look in her face, his hands draping across her shoulders. Staring into his inquiring gaze, she took a steady breath and cleared her head.

"Solomon, he's out. They let him out and nobody warned me," she said with a wounded look on her face.

Solomon's face frowned in puzzlement. "Who's out?" he asked.

"Byron. Byron Henderson." Staring at his blank look, she realized he hadn't the faintest idea who she was talking about. "Of course you don't know." She backed from his light possession, clearing her thoughts of fear and the sexual affinity she felt under his nearness. A cold, hard-pinched expression clouded her face. Her hands fluttered in the air indecisively before she folded them across her midriff.

"Byron Henderson is a convicted wife killer. He murdered my best friend five years ago. I testified against him." Bewildered, she grabbed a handful of her hair. "He served a lousy five years on a twenty year sentence." As if speaking to herself, "Obviously time was cut because of good behavior, or jail overcrowding, whatever," she said, throwing her hands up in the air with disgust. "They let him out early. I just found out today. A letter was in my mail. I didn't notice it until I got back home from the meeting to get ready to come here." Opening the folds of her raincoat, she said, "As you can see, I didn't even change clothes. I was in such a panic," she said, a hint of self-derision in her expression, "that I didn't stop to think."

"Has he contacted you?" Solomon asked.

"No. Yes. Well, I think so," she said, another look of self-loathing on her face. "At the time, I just thought it was a prank call." His expression requested an explanation. "Over a week ago, maybe longer, I got this strange call. At first I thought it was Dennis. It's not unlike him to do something silly," a weak, self-mocking smile wobbled on her face. In hindsight, it no longer made sense; Dennis was occasionally thoughtless, but not mean and spiteful as the caller seemed to be, she recalled. "Anyway," with a heavy sigh, "the man said he was the lover I've been waiting on or some such nonsense, so I hung up the phone. He called right back and said I needed to be taught a lesson."

"When did he get out?"

"That's just it, I don't know," she replied, her hands splayed before her.

"Who sent the letter?"

Chuckling with disbelief, she replied, "Anonymous. Somebody just stuck it in the mailbox along with the rest of the mail. There was no stamp and no return address on the envelope." Again, she rubbed her hand across her face, trying to make sense of the series of coincidences. "I tried to track down the prosecutor who handled the case, but she's no longer with the D.A.'s office. That's why I'm so late."

"What could she do anyway?" he asked.

"Probably nothing," she replied frustrated. "I just wanted to vent to somebody. Nothing's happened to me. I have no proof that he called. Or that it was even him. I can't even prove that the car that followed me early today was his."

"He followed you?" Solomon asked amazed.

"Yes," she said. "I think so. I didn't notice until after I picked up the tickets from the printer's. And then again, it could have been anybody. I mean, who knows how many red, 1990 Vets are still on the road."

"A red Vet?" he asked, his gaze narrowed suspiciously.

"Yes," she said, her eyes dull with memory. "The same

car he used to run Tevis down in." She looked at Solomon aware of his expression for the first time. It was dark, brooding and knowing. "Why? Do you know something?" she asked apprehensively.

"I saw a '90 Vet in the parking lot several nights ago," he said, staring pensively toward the door. "At first, I thought you borrowed your mechanic's car again, then I remembered the car you got from him was a Camaro."

"Here?" she asked, pointing a finger for emphasis. Her heartbeat began to speed up, like a locomotive gaining steam. A troubled look settled on her face.

"Yeah. I thought it belonged to one of the staff," he said.

"So now, he not only knows where I live, but where I work," she whispered in despair. The facts whirling in her head, she recalled Byron's threats to her.

"Monique . . ."

Seeped in memory, Monique didn't hear Solomon. All she could see was Byron's ravaged face in the courtroom after hearing his sentence, then his gnarly gaze pointed at her with a murderous gleam promising revenge.

"Monique," Solomon said, more forcefully this time.

A somber, dazed look on her face, she said, "I'm no good tonight. There's no way I can work. I'd be jumping each time somebody walked through the door." She looked at him, waiting for soothing words.

"You're right," Solomon replied. In her present state of mind, he certainly wasn't going to tell her that Dr. Ward was in the house. "Why don't you stay at my house tonight, and tomorrow we can put our heads together to try and figure out what to do."

"Oh, I can't do that," she said half-heartedly. She didn't want to be alone, but neither did she want to impose. She hated her fear. Letting some man run her out of her home, she railed herself silently. "I'll just go back home and lock myself in."

"No," he said insistently. "Then I won't be able to work

tonight, worrying whether you're okay. Just go to my house," he said walking behind her desk. "I'll call Ariana and tell her you're coming."

"Are you sure it's okay?" she asked. Brave and dead didn't appeal to her, either, she thought.

"I'm sure," he said, lifting the receiver from the phone. "I'm calling her right now, then I'll walk you out to the car."

Monique dosed, flitting in and out of sleep. She was partially aware of the movie showing on the portable television. Actors's voices droned on low volume in her ears.

Her lids were heavy, but she just couldn't seem to let go altogether. She had a sense of an unknown thing nudging the edge of her mind. She felt it was something she should know or remember. But it was obscured by events that led her to Solomon's home, his daughter's bedroom. She was lying on a bunk bed in a very girlish room, in very girlish pajamas.

She gave a thought to turning off the television. But she didn't rouse herself. She felt she had needed the company of noise. Like last night when Ariana stayed with her, the teenager was fast asleep in the other bed.

A commercial potted at a loud volume roused her full attention. Her lids popped open, and she stared at the screen absently, wondering what time it was. When would Solomon arrive?

She had no idea why sleep was eluding her. She felt as safe in Solomon's home as she had in his presence. Maybe because it was an extension of him—all brown and somber, salient and strong, she mused drowsily. She snuggled next to the pillow and closed her eyes, trying to enforce sleep.

The noise from the TV seemed uncannily loud, the glare suddenly too bright. She got up to turn off the television, then was amazed by the roar of silence in the house.

And something else.

Everything silent in her, Monique froze, listening keenly. A faint though distant sound somewhere in or near the house, and she felt a flutter of apprehension.

As quietly as possible, she picked up the short robe Ariana loaned her from the foot of the bed and traipsed from the room into the hall. She looked both ways in the dark corridor, then tiptoed to the other side of the house into the family room. The curtains over the sliding door were gently swaying to and fro.

They'd forgotten to lock the back door, her brain screamed! With her heart pounding in her chest, she inched toward the door. She heard it again, more distinct this time, like something solid slapping water.

It was seconds before she realized that someone was in the pool, and several more before she ruled out a burglar, thinking no one would be so bold. It had to be Solomon. Relief respired from her in a wild rush of air, and she walked out onto the patio.

The air had taken on a clean smell after the rain. It left a dulcet wind and sleepy-faced, quarter moon yawning in the black skies. And there, in the water, under the hazy glow of lampposts guarding the back yard, Solomon was swimming laps. He touched the bank on the opposite side of the pool, then enacted a smooth underwater turn and continued.

She debated returning inside. With proof that Solomon and not some thief had stolen into the house, sleep should come easily, she told herself. But she didn't move, couldn't tear her eyes off him. The sleepy sexuality of her body was fully awakened.

He swam hard, fast, as if in a race against time. Then he altered his tempo, swimming slow and leisurely, the motion of his arms graceful as slightly cupped hands dove in, then out of the water.

A quiver surged through her veins. She stared after his long, lean body gliding through the water cleanly, entranced by the play of muscles rippling in his arms as he swam effortlessly from one end of the pool to the other.

Then he reached the end closest to the patio area and propped his elbows on the bank. He stayed there for several moments, just staring across the water. She wondered what he was thinking, why didn't he wake her when he arrived.

Then, he turned and hauled himself out in one swift movement, and his smooth, strong wet body was standing on the bank. If she'd thought him big with clothes on, he was even bigger now, wearing only brief black trunks that clung wetly to the fine contour of his hips, a splattering of hair on his chest and thighs.

He froze mid-stride upon seeing her, then flashed one of his rare smiles, and she felt her lungs laboring in her chest.

"I thought you were asleep," he said.

He continued in her direction with his long, easy strides, emphasizing his power. Teeming with sexual wariness, she watched his approach with a look she hoped was non-revealing. He came to the patio table where a dark, terry robe and towel were strung across the back of a chair.

"I thought I heard something," she said around the lump lodged in her throat. She tried to ignore the aching in her loins.

He picked up the towel. "I thought I was being quiet."

"You were," she said, "I didn't even hear you come in."

He began toweling his neck, his chest, arms, thighs and legs. With her heart thumping erratically, she watched as he dried all the places she longed to touch. Hungering for his touch in return, but knowing she didn't dare reveal such, she averted her head to stare absently at the pool.

"I know Ariana doesn't hear anything once she falls asleep," he said, with a hint of amusement in his voice.

Monique cleared her throat before she spoke. "No, uh, she's knocked out," she said. She wetted her lips with her tongue and cast her eyes downwards. A pair of beige, thick-soled plastic slippers were under the table. "How long have you been home?" She heard her voice, stilted and unnatural.

"I haven't been here long," he said.

As he tossed the towel back onto the chair, his gaze lowered over her. With a pinched guarded look, his eyes roved her face and down her figure. Self-consciously, she pulled the folds of the robe together. He tried to hide his excitement from her, but her femininity felt it, and her body reacted to it.

She hid a thick swallow in her throat, then asked, "You swim every night when you get off?"

"It helps me unwind," he replied. His voice was edged in gruffness. "Sometimes."

She understood well what he meant. Right now, she could use a cool dip to douse the flame of desire burning inside her. He tossed the towel aside as if disgusted. She looked up into his face and saw the solemn gravity of his look. But also in the depths of his eyes were glimmers of desire and need—and even regret. Everything she was feeling, a war between flesh and reason. She became more uncomfortable as her yearning grew and reminders of Ariana's presence waned.

"Monique."

He spoke in a tight voice, a whisper, straining with sensual affectation. The timbre of her name on his tongue echoed in her ear, sending a warming shiver through her. She floundered before his smoldering gaze, watched like a voyeur watches as he severed the distance separating them and lowered his head towards hers. She held herself still, hands knotted into fists at her sides and insides trembling with desire.

His mouth brushed her cheek, then stole across her mouth as gently as the wind. She sighed deep and low, an ancient articulation of excitement, pleasure. Powerless to resist, she closed her eyes to reason and moved toward him, impelled by her own passion. She wrapped her arms around his neck. The bottoms of her feet lifted off the ground. Their mouths came together in an infinitely sweet caress. It was a kiss to lie down with and curl up next to for hours.

The kiss went on, deepened, and was joined by hands. Big, lightly textured with roughness, his hands stole inside her robe and under the girlish top. One at her back, held her in place; the other, tenderly, caressed the soft mound of her bosom, teasing an already taut nipple to an erection, immense and hard, similar to the one pressing into her. She gasped, and he stemmed the rapturous cry, covering her mouth greedily, devouring its softness. Standing was impossible: she sagged into him and was lifted higher as his hands and mouth sought her essence with an intense eruption of his masculine need.

She was on fire for him, from him. Her hands dropped from around his neck, to touch those places—kneading the corded muscles of his shoulders, rubbing up and down his back, her fingers skimming the fine hairs on his firm chest. It was not enough.

"Solomon," she begged, her body crying for more.

"Monique," he groaned raggedly, tearing his mouth from hers reluctantly. He caught her incited hands and pinned them behind her back. "I'm sorry," he said gulping for air. "I didn't mean to start this. I know we can't finish."

"No," she agreed breathlessly, resting her forehead against him. They remained that way for a while, until their breathing slow and limbs steadied enough to stand alone.

"I better get back inside," she said, risking a glance up at him. His expression showed the same pained look she was sure in hers. Wordlessly, she walked back inside the house, with the ache of her unsatiated hunger. Closing the door behind her, she heard a loud splash.

Twelve

"Money, this is your old man calling."

With a smile tugging at the corners of her mouth, Monique listened to her father's voice replaying on the answering machine. She was standing behind the desk in her home office. Dressed in a simple, yet elegant dress with a low flaring skirt in inky blue silk and high-heeled shoes, she held a black choir robe with a kente collar across her arm.

"I haven't heard back from you, and I'm starting to get a little worried," he continued. "You've got until midnight to call and let me know that you're all right, or I'll see you tomorrow, or Tuesday at the latest. What I would rather hear is that you've been out enjoying the company of a real nice man. In either case, call me."

With that command, he rang off, and the bells beeped, signaling the end of the messages.

"Oh daddy," Monique said wistfully. "If only you knew."

She was tempted to call him right now, but knew she didn't dare. She was ripe with a bittersweet sensation and felt like crying. Tears of confusion threatened to fall from her eyes.

Despite the long cold shower she had taken upon arriving home, she couldn't wash away the longings, or something else she'd had time to analyze since leaving Solomon's home at the crack of dawn. He had branded her in more ways than physical, more than she had believed was humanly possible.

Sleep had been out of the question, she thought, recalling the brief paradise she'd felt in his arms, especially following the unfulfilled aftermath. Lying there in the dark, staring up at the ceiling, it suddenly came to her—the something that had been gnawing at her mind.

She was in love with Solomon Taliaferro Thomas the manager of *T's Place.*

She tried telling herself it just wasn't so. She had been— and still was—horny. As if one precluded the other, she humored herself.

But there was no rationalizing or laughing away truth. The indisputable idea stuck, and she knew it. Deep down in her soul, the seed of love had been planted. Without her knowing or consent, it had sprouted. Even without the magical powers of prediction, she knew it would continue to grow and blossom.

She had wanted to be alone with her discovery, away from his all-pervasive influence. Maybe with distance, she would have felt differently and realized it was lust after all. Or so, she had told herself as she sneaked out of his house, leaving a note of gratitude on the refrigerator door.

Arriving home with her breath suspended in her throat, she checked every door, window and any other space opportune for hiding in the place thoroughly. Under the cool sprays of the shower, she resumed examining her feelings— turning them over, taking them apart and putting them back together again. She'd known the love of a parent and the love of true friends. But not that of a man.

It was an alien feeling that left her in a hopeless quandary. It highlighted the shortcomings of what she thought she had felt for Anthony, illuminating her naiveté about love. She never really understood what Tevis meant, she now realized in musing. Her friend had tried to explain it to her, but woman-to-man love wasn't something that could be learned from a discussion.

One had to feel it, taste it, touch it, submit to its awesome power. Now, gleaning insight into its wonders, she was afraid.

Was love a paradox? she wondered, recalling that even while she was being pummeled by Byron's fist, Tevis continued to love him. After Byron killed her, he proclaimed he loved her throughout the trial.

Deciding she needed a good dose of religion to help put her mind at ease, she dressed for church. She checked her calendar and saw that the choir to which she belonged at the church was supposed to sing today anyway. She considered it fate.

And if she didn't hurry, she would be late for the march in, she told herself.

The sun and the clouds battled for control in the skies. Heat poured through the light overcast. Bare-chested and wearing shorts, Solomon followed Ariana out to the patio. He was not in the best of moods, but he couldn't decline to eat the lunch she had prepared for him. It was a little after one Sunday afternoon. But both his thoughts and his appetite were elsewhere.

A lunch of chicken sandwiches and chips was laid out in a two-place setting on the patio table. Silverware lay atop cloth napkins next to the best dishes he owned. Next to the table was the portable serving tray with coffee, cream and sugar. A can of soda was on the table where Ariana had sat. The coffee cup atop the saucer sat next to his plate.

"What's the occasion?" he asked, sitting at the table after filling his cup with coffee.

"No occasion," she replied with a shrug.

He lifted the bun to peek into the sandwich. "Hm," he muttered, impressed, looking at the thinly sliced white meat and mozzarella cheese with lettuce and tomato on thick slices of Texas bread. "Grilled chicken. You fixed this?" he said, cocking a surprised brow at her.

"No. Well, I helped. We did it last night. Monique showed me how to de-bone a chicken," she explained before biting into her sandwich.

"Hm," he replied, bobbing his head. It was nice to know Monique could cook, but that didn't explain her disappearing act.

"I talked to mama last night."

"Oh? What did she have to say?" Solomon asked absently. He didn't notice Ariana's leg bobbing under the table, and he could care less about Elaine right now. Ever since he'd awakened to find Monique gone, he wondered why she left. Her departure didn't make sense to him. He knew she was genuinely scared of that Byron Henderson person and distinctly remembered that they were supposed to have talked about it and looked into her options. *Together.* Instead, she sneaked out at heaven knows what time, without saying where she was going. He'd tried her home and got the answering machine.

"She's doing okay," Ariana said.

Solomon grunted in reply. He was also teeming with leftover desire, which didn't improve his mood. She could have stayed to say good-bye. "That's good," he said, some of the exasperation he felt in his voice.

"She apologized," Ariana said.

Solomon muttered absently. Monique's behavior was cause for concern because it wasn't just the two of them whose feelings had to be considered, he thought, chewing a bite of sandwich. He had an impressionable teenage daughter whose relationship with her own mother was unstable. He wouldn't subject Ariana to anymore confusion and chaos in her life. If Monique were too immature to see that, then . . .

"She said she wants me to come back," Ariana said.

A pregnant silence sat on the table between them. Solomon stopped chewing to stare at his daughter. She wasn't looking at him, but down at her food, crumbling the chips in her plate.

"And what did you say?" he asked.

"I told her I'd think about it," she replied, looking up at him from a sidelong glance. "She seems kind of lonely, you know. And I was thinking maybe that I'd go back and check on her."

All of this was said as if Ariana were testing her ideas out on him, Solomon thought. He didn't know what to think. He swallowed the food down in a uneasy gulp, then wiped his mouth with the napkin, apprehension coursing through him. Ariana returned his look with a timid one.

"I thought you wanted to stay with me."

"I did," she said, then added hastily, "I still do."

Solomon concealed the tad of guilt that surfaced inside him. There was no denying he had wished Ariana wasn't around when he lost his head to Monique, he recalled, grim-faced. But that was just passion talking.

"What did Elaine promise to buy you this time?" his voice harsh with disgust. It was Elaine's way of flexing her muscles, he mused bitterly. Flash money in Ariana's face and make him look like a weakling in his daughter's eyes. Oh, he could play the game, could buy Ariana whatever her teenage eyes wished for, but that wasn't the parenting route he took or would ever take.

Wasn't that always the way? he thought angrily. Elaine could give things, but was stingy with warm emotions. Monique on the other hand, had plenty of emotions to share, but she didn't have any money. *Well, I guess I should be grateful for small favors.*

"Nothing," Ariana denied. "She didn't offer to buy me anything."

Hearing the unvoiced conjunction, he pressed, "But?"

"I'm . . . I don't feel . . . uh . . ." she stammered.

"Ariana, tell me what's on your mind," he commanded, frustration getting the best of him. "I don't stand a chance in a guessing game with you." He'd hardly gotten any sleep and spent what was left of the night awake, staring at the ceiling and gritting his teeth over the ache in his loins, he bemoaned silently. Now, this. Damn, Elaine!

"You have Monique," she blurted.

Solomon's mouth dropped open. "I beg your pardon?" He gripped her with a profound look of bewilderment. "I don't understand. Please elaborate."

"I feel like I'm in the way here," she said softly with hesitation.

Shaking his head with disbelief, Solomon blew out his cheeks. "Women," he declared. "I swear I don't understand how you can go from point A straight to Z, skipping all the other letters in between," he said, gesturing with his hands. "First she runs out of here, leaving some stupid little note on the door," he said to himself, then frowned at Ariana. "Then here you come, uttering some nonsense. Where did you get such an idea from, Ariana? In the first place, there's nothing definite between me and Monique," he said flustered, yet rationale enough to think, *except the hots for each other.* "What did you and Monique talk about last night?"

"Things," she said, wiggling like a shy girl in her seat.

"Ariana, look at me," he said in a tone of voice as if he'd had this discussion before and didn't plan to have it again. "No one can replace, remove, or interfere with my feelings for you in any shape, fashion or form." He reached a hand across the table to cover hers. "No one," he said with emphasis.

"But aren't you in love with her?"

"If I am or I'm not doesn't make any difference!" he said, throwing up his hands. In a calmer tone, he said emphatically, "It doesn't change how I feel about you. Give your old man a little credit. Okay?" he asked, his eyes holding her warmly. "I love you, Ariana."

A blush of pure happiness broke out across her face, and Solomon wanted to kick himself. He couldn't remember the last time he had assured Ariana with the words all humans longed to hear from someone. He couldn't believe he had denied his own child that brand of security.

Ariana took a big bite from her sandwich as if suddenly ravenous. Solomon felt a wonderful sense of victory, as if he'd won a major battle in the parenthood war. He was amazed by how easy it was to accomplish.

"She likes you," Ariana said with a mouth full. "A *whole* lot."

Solomon laughed for the heck of it. "And I like her, too," he said, biting into his sandwich. It wasn't a lie, just not the whole truth, he thought.

"You need to spend some time together," Ariana said, popping a chip in her mouth.

"Thank you, Dr. Ruth," he quipped.

"Well, couples need to spend some time together to see if they're compatible," she argued, washing her food down with a swallow of her soda. "You and mom didn't do that and look what happened to your marriage."

"Who said anything about marriage? We hardly know each other," he said with protest in his voice. But the idea was not unappealing to him. It would certainly solve dilemmas such as last night.

"She's thirty years old," Ariana began and continued to rattle off. "She's a high school English substitute teacher. She also has an associate degree in business. She's one of the founders of Haven House, a shelter for abused women and their children. She belongs to the Third Ward Baptist Church and sings in the choir. She's never been married. She doesn't have any children, but she wants some . . ."

Solomon stared incredulous at his child. He could just imagine her grilling Monique as if she were applying for a job. He was equally amazed and impressed by the personal details she unearthed. He never would have guessed half of those things about Monique, he thought, shaking his head. Still, none of it changed the fact that he felt he knew all he needed to know about the enigmatic Ms. Robbins. Chuckling, he halted Ariana's flow of words asking, "Did you leave the woman with any secrets?"

The doorbell rang before Ariana could reply.

The weather battle continued at an impasse. A light rain fell from the hot, sunny skies. Neither hampered Solomon. He sped along Highway 288, and took the Binz/Calumet exit, doing sixty, instead of the regulated 35 mph. Heading for Monique's, he was governed by an incipient desperation. Everything felt hurried inside him.

He hadn't called, but figured if she weren't home, he'd go straight to the club. Even though it was early yet, not quite two o'clock, he knew there was work he could busy himself with. He didn't want to stay home alone.

That little sneak, he chuckled to himself, recalling his conversation with his daughter. He couldn't get over it. All Ariana wanted was affirmation that she wasn't being displaced in his life.

After the doorbell rang, he recalled, the truth came out. Ariana and Monique entertained some of the kids in the neighborhood last night, when an outing to the beach in Galveston had come up.

It accounted for the scrumptious lunch and a fact that wasn't obvious until daylight explaining why the house looked as if it had been treated to a thorough cleaning. Now, he knew not only what they talked about, but did together in his absence.

He was satisfied with the arrangements after speaking with the lone adult—his neighbor three houses down—accompanying the kids on the trip. He doled out some money, then lectured about sex as Ariana loaded her beach bag. It seemed she and Monique had discussed that, as well. He recalled Ariana telling him point blank, "I'm not ready for a physical relationship. As I understand it, adults have a hard enough time with it as it is."

He felt double-ganged, but this time being trapped in the middle wasn't half bad. If Monique had imparted that bit of sagacity, he was truly impressed with her insight, he thought as he pulled into her driveway behind the Jeep.

Cutting the engine, he sprinted across the way to the front porch; the burglar bar door was already opened. Standing in the covered entry, he pressed the buzzer. Within seconds, the door opened, and Monique consumed his gaze.

When Solomon saw her, his muscles relaxed and went soft. He was open to absorb her ambrosial aura, as he embraced her with his eyes, his want, his essence. She was expecting him, but not quite sure he would come. He saw and felt her anticipation, and fed from it.

Her face was clean and bright, her eyes especially so, a natural gloss on her pleasantly pursed lips. Her hair was pulled back in a single braid that fell somewhere down her back. She wore a lavender pullover in a soft fabric and cut off jeans that revealed her slender thighs and long straight legs. Diamond studded earrings pierced her ears. She held a slipper in her hand, the other on her foot.

He gulped once. Disinclined to break the affettuso-like mood, wordlessly, he entered to take the slipper from her hand. He kneeled at her feet and slid the shoe on the narrow bare foot with clear polished toenails. He returned to his height, his stare, and his one thought: she was more beautiful than any woman he had ever seen.

No words were exchanged between them, save the voiceless longing that languished in their eyes. She moved only to lock the door, then offered him her hand. He followed her lead to the bedroom where strawberries scented the air. A bowl of them rested on a tray next to the bed where the newspaper was strewn. The television was playing softly in the background.

She vanished from the room, then reappeared with a mint

green towel. He was still standing where she'd left him, and she returned to him. Gently, she toweled his face, his bare arms, hands, then disappeared again. He began to walk around, the invitation extended by the room itself. Though more intimate, the rooms reflected a cozy continuation he'd picked up in the living room.

It was unpretentious; no trophies, certificates or plaques donned a wall or table as he guessed there surely must have been based on what Ariana had told him. Rather, it was rich in colors of life, bold art and ancient artifacts. And just below the smell of strawberries another scent, myrrh-like, made the ambient air fragrant, with light entering from the east. Everything and every color had its place, but seemed interdependent, a oneness about their placement and selection, transforming the combined areas into an African Paradise.

From the corner of his eyes, he saw Monique return to clear the papers from the bed. After which, she picked up the bowl of strawberries and sauntered across the room to sit on the couch, tucking her leg under her.

There was something different about her, a calm that never registered before. Comforted in knowing she was near and unafraid, he turned from her a moment. His examination took him lastly to the gang of pictures on the wall near the television. He guessed the identity of the main subject, but another woman appeared in several of the pictures and he inquired. "Who is the third woman?"

"Patricia Redmon," she replied. "Aurelius's wife."

As he angled his body to look over his shoulder, his eyes did a slow slide to her face. A teasing look gleamed in her eyes, and he knew what she was thinking. He let it pass as she did, for another question surfaced as he faced the pictures again. But he didn't ask. He decided he would wait until she volunteered to explain the significance attached to the prominently displayed photos of a dead woman in a setting that proclaimed an appreciation for and of life.

Again, facing her, his hands clasped together in front of

him, he simply stared at her because it made him feel good—proud and possessive—to do so. She caused a spark to light in him—several in fact—until a flame now burned steadily inside him. He never felt attractive before, never thought he needed the vain quality, but the way she was looking at him, the sense of awe she transmitted gave him a generous and pleased perception of himself. Not just as a sexual object, but as something more divine and omnipotent than his shell of mortality.

He strode leisurely across the room and sat next to her. His mouth opened to receive the strawberry she offered. He saw the sharp breath she inhaled, then trapped in her bosom when he captured and held her hand at his lips as he chewed. Her tongue snaked out from her mouth to slide across her mouth, then retreated. He felt an esurient urge to follow her tongue, to taste the strawberries and other delights beyond her lips. Instead, he remained still, his eyes affixed to her face, the emotions that crossed her visage. All expressed prurience simmering just below the surface of her outwardly serene demeanor.

He took the bowl from her hand and set it on the drum table. His eyes never left her face, which he touched with the back of his hand. It turned to feel the silky softness of her flesh next to his palm. Her cheek, jaw and down her slender neck to rest on her bosom and caress the unrestricted breast beneath. A mellow moan escaped his throat, and for the first time, he closed his eyes, imagining the fullness he felt through the fabric.

But he need not see, for his senses were keenly attuned to her reactions—the soft gasps that respired from her, the increase in her pulse and heart rate, her almond eyes dilated with passion—to each feel he took. To each response she gave, he received tenfold. His craving grew so intense, he feared he would explode from it.

"I want to see you," he said. His voice was rough, urgent, need resonating through his chest.

Monique didn't rush to his bidding. Neither did she stall. She uncurled herself from the couch with languid grace. Standing before him, she pulled the shirt over her head, then let it fall to the floor.

A whisper of a whistle escaped his lips as he sucked in an astonished breath. His imagination fell comparatively short as he caressed her breasts bared before his eyes. They were high and round and full, the nipple slightly darker than the spring-tanned bosom. Her waist was tiny and stomach flat; the promise of shapely hips were still hidden from him. But he knew the perfection of her continued.

He saw the instant she grew uncomfortable before his ravenous gaze, and stood to capture the hands she would have crossed to cover her lovely nakedness. "Don't," he whispered beseechingly, taking her hands in his. "You're so beautiful." He admired her a moment more, then said quietly, "I never imagined in all my life . . ."

She relaxed, a soft sough seeped past her mouth. He kissed her lips in a feathery touch, and felt the tremor course through her body. Lowering his head, he tasted the side of her neck, felt the hard swallow in her throat. His head, his lips dipped lower.

"Solomon," Monique cried. She held him steadfastly, gripping his shoulders. A nipple, protruding at attention, saluted his firm, hot tongue. He treated it gingerly, nipping it carefully between his teeth, lavishing it with his tongue and sucking it into his mouth.

His hands spanned her waist as he descended further the smooth planes of her body. She felt his tongue dip into the small indentation that was her belly-button, and her nails dug into his shoulders. She knew the pain reached him, felt her own sweet ache about to humble her, but he didn't stop his divine torment as if he'd read into her thoughts.

Monique closed her eyes and coached herself to breathe,

taking short, shallow breaths and reveled in the sensations, wishing they were never-ending.

His hands moved to the waist of her jeans. She heard the snap open, the zipper sliding down, felt the guttural moan from his mouth in the soft flesh of her flat stomach. It vibrated through her as he peeled the shorts from her hips.

He rose to look at her as if he had created her and was immeasurably pleased, a possessive gleam in his eyes. He found the end of the braid behind her back and freed it, then spread her hair about her shoulders, and again, stood back to assess his creation.

She felt cherished under his reverent gaze. It imbued her with confidence to reveal herself. She caressed the touch and look on his face, the love she felt for him brimming in her eyes. Surprise, then sublime happiness stole across his visage as he stared at her with glory in his dark eyes.

"Monique," he said.

There was worship in his tone, love in his look. He took her mouth in a kiss that was long, deep and wet, but so much more than a simple touch of lips. In a statement of affiance, he kissed her soul.

She made a sound in her throat, a plea for him to take her, to satisfy the awesome ache. He trapped her wanton hands behind her back as he kneeled before her and buried his head in the center of her thighs and kissed her lips. His hands gripped the back of her thighs to steady her as he feasted from her inner core.

He sent her to the edge, then pulled back. Muses and shadows fled, leaving Monique a mass of pining sensations, an entity sensitive to Solomon and his tender torture of her. Feelings too potent to resist intensified. She thought she would die.

She cried out as he swept her in his arms and carried her to bed where he lay her near the edge. Before his hands reached the first button on his shirt, she was up, helping him get rid of the offending clothes.

They fell across the bed, consumed by their need, greed for each other. Her hands touched him, defined him muscle by muscle, seeking and satisfying the points of delight in his needful flesh. When her reach fell short, she gave him a message with a pleading whimper in her throat and was given access. Lying atop him, she did as she wanted, returned the loving treatment, venting her needs on his body. He was strong bones and firm flesh of creamy chocolate virility. Long, wide, big, and beautiful.

Nothing of him was left untouched, unkissed. She branded every inch of him, until he was the one writhing uncontrollably on the bed under the onslaught of her hot ministrations. He reached down to her face, cupped it between his hands and tugged gently. She crawled up his body with hers pressing seductively into his, eliciting passionate groans from his gut. Coming face-to-face with him, he captured her mouth in a kiss that was like the soldering heat that joins metals. In one fluid motion, they rolled over. Lips fused together, she lay beneath him in willing surrender, body and soul.

Acquiescing to his man's lead, her thighs parted. He lifted her hips slightly off the bed, then found her in one painstakingly sweet, slow penetration into her body. She cried out during the languid act of his possession, and his hoarse cry mingled with hers as she possessed him.

He was a physical, inventive man who moved with power and grace, taking her to the point of release and beyond. She was a woman who was assertive in her needs, nimble enough to communicate them and driven to deliver in kind.

Her breath caught again and again, his name a litany on her lips. But he never left her, each bold thrust was accented with a kiss, a caress, a cherishing word or complimentary groan. As his passion grew, he drove her higher and higher. She drove him higher still.

Reaching the heavens, she cried out as her love poured

from her in a long, heated gush. His expression changed, and he filled her with his warm beauty.

The day progressed with the sun shining through the lone opening. The room was cool and quiet; the bed warm-scented by lazy bodies wearing nothing but the shadows of lovemaking. Satiated and pleasantly exhausted, Solomon stared fascinated at the photos on the wall across the way, while Monique lay half-sprawled atop him.

"Okay, my curiosity has gotten the best of me," he said.

"About what?" she asked, her breath fanning his neck.

"The woman whose face appears in all those pictures," he replied. "I assume it's Tevis."

"Yes," she said. "Tevis Theresa Haven."

"As in Haven House?" he said, arching a decidedly pointed brow. Monique confirmed his good guess with a nod. "How long have you had her pictures up there?"

"Three years there or about," she replied. The question spurred a taunt that had the pictures been up longer, she never would have forgotten, nor repeated the serious error in judgment. She shook it off before it could infect her good feelings.

"Tell me." Looking at her with questions in his beseeching gaze, he added, "Unless you have a problem talking about it."

Ironically, she didn't feel the usual bout of emotional upheaval associated with conversations about Tevis. Rather, she felt suffused by a deep sense of peace. "No," she replied, looking at him with a beautiful soft smile. "I think she would have liked you, Solomon T. Thomas."

Solomon lifted her hand to his lips, kissed it, then held it snuggled over his chest.

"She and I met in grade school. She was in the sixth grade, and I was in the second. We went to this private school that paired students together. You've heard the philosophy, 'each one, teach one'?"

"Yes."

"Well, she was assigned to me," Monique replied. "And pest that I was back then," she said laughingly, recalling how desperate she sought friendship and attention as a child, "she couldn't get rid of me. I followed her academic footsteps from elementary school to college. Though by then, I had developed some identity of my own, she was still my role model, so to speak."

"Then she must have been something," he said sincerely.

"Tevis loved everybody and was loved by everybody," she continued, a fond musing look touching her face. "Too much by one person who didn't know what love was." Her expression soured with a frown stripe across her forehead.

"Byron Henderson," Solomon supplied when she remained silent and still. "Her husband?" he asked surprised.

Nodding her head, Monique said, "Byron had a temper. The full range of it wasn't visible during the courtship." Her voice grew distant, tremulous as she sank into her memory. "He fooled all three of us—me, Patricia and Tevis. Always a gentleman, always in control of himself. After he got the ring on her finger, he revealed his true self. Controlling, possessive and jealous of any time Tevis spent away from him."

Feeling the memory pulling her under, Monique changed positions. Rolling over to lie on her back, she stared absently at the ceiling. Angling her head sideways to look at him, she could see the questions in his hard pinched expression.

"Couldn't you get her to leave him?" Solomon asked.

As if with a volition of its own, a hand reached out to take hold of Solomon's. She held it over her chest as she spoke. "Battering is a silent crime," she said. "Tevis fit the mold almost to a tee."

Releasing his hand, she sat up, folded her legs Indian-style, gazing absently towards the gang of photos. "She denied it, believed the violence would end if she were just more supportive, hid it from her friends because she was too embarrassed, and forgave it. Then one night he beat her so badly that she couldn't hide the bruises."

Solomon began rubbing her stiff back, stroking away the tension the recounting of the story wrought. She relaxed into the soothing touches.

"Of course, she fell for the old apology and promise that it would never happen again," she said. "But twice after that, she was forced to report it because he sent her to the hospital."

Monique fell silent; she wanted to stop. Respiring deeply, she forced herself to continue. "By the time she realized he wasn't going to change, it was too late. He followed her to my house. The driveway was blocked with cars, so she had to park on the street. When she got out of her car, he ran her down like an animal." She shuddered in remembered agony.

Solomon pulled her back in his arms, cradling her next to him gently. Monique didn't realize she was crying until he kissed her eyes and wiped the tears from her face. His gentleness cushioned the pain from ripping out her heart.

"She couldn't have been too much older than you," he said softly, bathing her with tenderness in his eyes.

Restored, she spoke with happy memories in her voice. "Four years. But she was everything I wanted to be. She was strong and assertive and outgoing . . . the most charming person you'd ever want to meet."

"What did your mother think of that?"

"My mother," she said with an odd humor underlining her voice, as if to cover sarcasm. "My mother and I didn't communicate."

"Oh?"

"We were as different as night and day. She used to tell me all the time I was just like my father. Always going, always striving, never satisfied, never stopping long enough to take a look at what was going on around me," she said laughingly.

"Was she right?" he asked, looking down in her face. "Were you just like your father?"

Monique thought about it as she had never thought about it before. Searching her memory, she could only recall hearing the comment as if it were an indictment, but she could find no reason for it until she became a teenager and she accompanied her dad on occasions. "Yeah, I guess so. I did want a lot. My dad calls me Money."

Laughing with her, he asked, "And have you stopped running from whatever was chasing you?"

"I wasn't running from anything," she denied hastily. "What makes you say that?"

"I don't know. It just seemed like you must have been trying to escape someone or something . . . reality maybe?" he said speculatively.

"No, I just never wanted to be like my mother," she said dryly. "For as long as I can remember, she acted like a victim who never recovered from her trauma."

"Victim," he said thoughtfully. "That's an interesting choice of words."

"My mother, God bless her, was a very distant woman. We get along a lot better now, but when I was growing up, sometimes, well, a lot of times I felt as if she blamed me for some horrible crime," she said pensively. Then abruptly, her mood lightened. "I think she was glad when I met Tevis. It's hard entertaining an only child."

"You say Tevis has been dead for five years?" he said, looking over his shoulder at the photographs.

"Yes," she replied, looking at him curiously, wondering where he was headed.

"Yet, you keep her alive," he said.

"I never wanted to forget," she said.

"So, the pictures went up after the break-up with Anthony," he said, voicing his thoughts.

Staring into his face, his eyes had moved back into hers and glowed with a savage inner fire. He was too perceptive for her own good.

During the pregnant silence, his hard expression softened. Squeezing her gently to him, a possessive gleam came to his eyes. Monique felt a spurt of hungry desire to spiral through her body. She cupped his face between her hands. "Anthony who?" she asked, her lips meeting his.

Over the next several days, endless seconds of supreme happiness and joy rose and set with each passing minute. There wasn't a cloud in Monique and Solomon's sky that burned hourly like the hottest sun.

Monique wore a perpetual bloom. Solomon smiled . . . a lot. As if they had all the time in the world, they began to discover, starting with the seemingly insignificant, things about the other—her talents for cooking, his pleasure for fishing.

And Monique finally got near Solomon's closet.

"How about this one?" Ariana asked.

Standing in front of a full length mirror in a fashionable men's store, Solomon scrutinized himself, then frowned at the tie his daughter was bringing their way. He was outfitted in a soft lavender shirt with French cuffs and a pair of pearl gray dress pants with pleats and cuffs: only the socks on his feet belonged to him.

"Oh, it's perfect," Monique exclaimed, taking the tie from Ariana.

Lifting a brow of dispute, Solomon said, "I think not."

"Oh, come on, try it," Monique cajoled, as she looped the tie around the collar of the shirt.

"It's getting late," he said, squirming at his reflection. "If you two still plan to have lunch, we'd better hurry."

"Oh, Daddy, it's Saturday and you don't have to be at the

club until four," Ariana said. "It's only noon, so we have plenty of time."

Monique was not about to be put off by his squeamish concern over what he considered loud colors. "You're not going to get out of this so easily," she said laughingly. "Be still so I can get this right."

"How did you learn to tie a tie anyway?" he asked.

"My daddy taught me. There," she said, flattening the collar.

Looking in the mirror with a bitter look as if he tasted something bitter, Solomon said, "It's a bit much."

"Nonsense," Monique replied. She turned him around to face Ariana and the salesman who was attending them. "What do you think?" she asked.

"Oh, Daddy, it looks great on you."

"Help me out here," Solomon said sheepishly to the salesman.

The suited salesman shrugged. "I happen to agree with your wife and daughter. This purple print tie goes fabulously with that lavender shirt."

From a sidelong look, Solomon saw the Cheshire cat grin on Monique's face. Another look in the mirror, he had to agree. "Ring it up along with everything else," he said with pleased resignation to the salesman.

"See, that wasn't so bad," Monique said, leaning into Solomon to kiss him on the mouth.

"Cut it out you two," Ariana said. "I'll have you home in a few minutes, so you can carry on in private."

Everyone around them benefitted from their love. It was like an invitation to shared happiness. The staff of *T's Place* had something new to gossip about, and Ariana couldn't have been more happy. In his new expansive mood, Solomon's generosity was emotionally, as well as financially rewarding: she got everything she asked for, except her own car. Monique's father was equally delighted and wanted to meet the man who put the bliss of heaven in his daughter's voice.

The lights were low, and the band on stage loud. *T's Place* was packed. Sitting at an upstairs, corner table in the shadows, Byron scanned the crowd seated in the low lighted club. He was impressed and envious.

Watching the band, he thought they looked like a bunch of weirdoes. But they sure knew how to play. They were performing an old 'War' song that was popular when he was young. It brought back some fond, poignant memories and made him wish.

Monique got herself a fine place, he mused, sipping his gin and tonic. He remembered his late wife—he still couldn't say her name—had envied Monique's ability to entertain . . . said that if she ever decided to open a business, she would be her own best product. He hadn't known what *She* was talking about then, but seeing Monique in action, it made sense to him.

He had sneaked in while Monique was leading another party to a table and came upstairs. It was easy to follow her movements below. She was flitting around like a dainty little butterfly from table to table, chatting and charming strangers like they were her best friends.

She looked gentle and soft, approachable. Like a real woman supposed to be. But it was all an act. She wasn't like that in private. In private, she was mean and unforgiving, recalling all the horrible things she had said about him in court.

If it weren't for him, she wouldn't have gotten this place. With him in jail, there was no one to contest the will in which she had inherited everything—a hefty life insurance policy, savings, and some property. She made off like a widower who married well, he thought bitterly.

And he was supposed to forget it, he recalled, snorting

sarcastically in his drink. Leaving the session at the Center, he had to attend another meeting with the counselor whose job was to help ex-offenders adjust to the outside again. His temper had surfaced during the session, and he was advised to reconcile himself to what he couldn't change.

His son had been preaching the same thing, begging him not to do anything foolish. He made no promises.

Seeing all she had gained which confirmed all he had lost, he couldn't let it go. How could he forget? he asked himself, with a scowl on his face as he sought her out in the dark below.

With his gaze reflecting her movements, he recalled he had been following her for the past couple of days, peeping into her lady-of-leisure life discreetly from a distance. She was her usual arrogant self, going about her business, confident of her safety when he could have put an end to her life anytime he wanted. Wouldn't it be ironic if he caught her at that shelter for battered women where she did volunteer work? he chuckled amused.

So why hadn't he made a move?

Byron squirmed under the question, but only momentarily as a cocksure expression settled on his shadowed face. One thing prison had taught him was patience. "It wasn't time," he whispered into his drink as he took a swallow.

He needed to know everything about her habits at the club, as well as away from it. She had gone to church this morning, sang in the choir, then left after the service. He watched her from a back pew. He'd forgotten just how lovely she was; he never knew she could sing.

Boy! he thought, if she could ever be taught to learn her place, she'd be an asset to any man. Still, she could never be the woman . . .

Byron halted the thought before completion. He swallowed it in a sip of liquor and forced his thoughts elsewhere. He wondered who was the guy? He noticed his car at her place the other night. As not to reveal his presence, he'd parked his car on the block behind her street, then walked back. Hidden behind the big palm tree in the yard of the corner house on her street, he'd seen the man enter her home. He couldn't make him out in the dark, but the outline of his silhouette was big.

He didn't wait around for the guy to come out. Didn't believe he would, he snorted lewdly. Besides, it didn't matter to him. He'd seen what he had gone to see.

His features bunched in a frown, his eyes blazing with hatred and envy. He spotted her at a customer's table, slightly bent over in conversation. The candlelight beaming from the table caught her face in a piquant glow.

Byron gasped. His insides hushed. He saw Monique laugh, and in that instant, that particular smile on her face reminded him of her—of Tevis.

The breath in his chest ached like a wound. He felt the threat of tears stinging his eyes. He gulped down the remains of his drink, dropped several bills on the table, then headed for the stairs to sneak out as unobtrusively as he had come in *T's Place*.

Loathing had infested his blood by the time he ducked out the front door among the patrons who were still entering.

The giddy laughter of a tired crew permeated the club at closing. Dennis and Michael were wiping tables, while Jason was behind the bar, checking supplies. Jake was in the corner of the stage which had been cleared of all instruments except the piano.

"I need the key to lock up the sound system," he said to no one in particular.

"Mr. Thomas has the keys," Michael yelled back.

"Hey, Mr. Thomas!" Jake called out in a Dennis the Menace voice.

Francine bounded into the downstairs area from the front of the club. She was carrying a large, square tray filled with bottles of liquor. "Why you making all that racket? You know if he's in the back he can't hear you." She set the tray on the bar and began conferring with Jason.

"Will somebody go get the keys so I can lock up?" Jake asked exasperated.

"Don't be so lazy," Jason replied. "Go get them yourself."

"I'll get them."

Moments later, Jake caught the large set of keys on a steel ring from the air. As he kneeled to lock up the system, Jason and Francine left the room, each carrying a tray. Michael and Dennis were still cleaning up.

"Can I get a ride with you?" Michael asked Dennis.

"What happened to your ride?" Dennis replied.

Michael looked around and waited until Jake left the room, twirling the keys on his fingers, before he replied. "He called and said he got a hot date."

"Damn, he works fast," Dennis replied chuckling. "Yeah man, I'll take you home."

"He was here tonight," Michael said in a conspiratorial tone.

"You're kidding?" Dennis whispered astonished.

"I saw him," Michael replied.

"He was taking a mighty big chance," Dennis said. "You better tell him to be careful."

"I'm been trying," Michael said with pensive concern. "He's just so . . ." he fell silent, a frown on his face. "I don't know if it's going to work."

"Hey man, don't sweat it," Dennis said. "Let me show you something," he said, looking around to make sure they were still alone. He pulled out a wad of money from his pocket. Michael whistled. "And it ain't from no tips, either," he bragged.

"Where do you get all that money from?"

Dennis winked at him slyly, shoving the money back in

his pocket. "I guess you could say my man came through, too."

Michael stared at him with a sidelong suspicious look. "I hope you're not doing anything illegal, man."

"Moi?" Dennis replied guilelessly. He clapped his hands together and threw back his head with laughter.

Thirteen

Monique checked her rearview mirror. There was hardly any traffic on the streets at three in the morning, but the Cutlass was right behind her. She was heading home, and Solomon was coming with her.

If it weren't for him, she would be riding in his car, instead of driving, she pouted to herself. Even though the staff knew something existed between them, he insisted on maintaining an air of propriety.

Even the patrons had begun to comment on how well she looked, asking what was it that was different about her. She had merely smiled as she was doing now, gave some innocuous reply, while harboring the warm, potent feeling in her heart like an invaluable secret. She hadn't done anything, she thought, except submit to her love.

Monique broke out laughing, a cheerful sound induced by the champagne giddiness bubbling inside her. She still didn't know whether or not love was a paradox, she mused. But she wondered whether Tevis's explanation of love lacked a crucial component.

Though neither she nor Solomon had committed the emotion to words, she couldn't fathom anything that could possibly change her mind or her feelings for him. It helped knowing he was unlike any man she had ever met before or was likely to meet again.

When Monique turned onto her street, she found it lit up like a Las Vegas night. Red and blue lights whirled atop police cars that blocked the street off at the corner. Just beyond them were two, spit-polished fire engines. Men in yellow slickers and black helmets were lugging a giant fire hose to one of the trucks. Neighbors and curious on-lookers were everywhere.

With a creeping uneasiness rising from the bottom of her heart, she wondered what was going on. A police officer standing in the street directing traffic stopped her. Her gaze stole to the center of activity where a gathering of firemen stood in conference, and she gasped in a shiver of panic.

Monique jumped from her vehicle, leaving the keys in the ignition and engine still running. The acrid scent of smoke filled her lungs; her eyes widened and filled with tears and disbelief.

She didn't need to ask any questions, for the evidence was clear that her house, her home no longer existed. Only the detached garage still stood. She broke out in a fast run toward the water-logged remains. A fireman caught her mid-air, halting her advance for the charred ruins.

"Damn you, Byron!" The accusation that laid dormant in her mind tore from her in a scream as she lunged to break free.

"Are you Ms. Robbins, the owner?"

"Damn you," she cried, sliding to the wet ground in a pitiful heap. "Goddamn you, Byron!"

He looked at her sorrowfully, "Wait right here, ma'am. The arson investigator will want to speak with you."

Byron Henderson had made good on his promise.

The thought echoed in Monique's head. She was numb of feelings when she drove into the circular driveway in front of the Four Seasons Hotel on the south side of downtown.

Several young men were standing in front of the smooth, red brick building in uniforms of white shirts and black slacks. She stopped midway the drive next to the inside curve, and a black man in his fifties, obviously the captain because of his attire in a gray and black uniform, came out to the car.

"Good morning, ma'am," he said, as cheerfully as if it were eight o'clock in the morning as he opened the door.

"Good morning," she replied woodenly.

"Shall I take care of your vehicle, ma'am?" he asked.

"Yes, please," she said. With just enough wherewithal to realize she needed clothes, she said, "I need to get something from the back first." She opened the back of the jeep and pulled out a gym bag, then dropped the keys in his hands.

"Enjoy your stay," he said, as she walked off.

By the time she reached the doors, Solomon was driving up. She waited for him. He left his keys and raced to meet her at the door. It was opened by another uniformed attendant of Hispanic nationality, and they walked inside.

The massive lobby was quiet and stately, but not somber, with plenty of greenery in a wonderfully extravagant decor of understated elegance. A gleaming wood, spiral staircase opened to two separate directions under a crystal chandelier in the high ceiling. A hotel official greeted them.

"May I be of service?" he inquired.

"I'd like to check in," she replied. Still, she was as animated as a robot, operating on remote control.

"Yes, ma'am," he replied. He directed her with his hand. "Right this way, then turn left."

Responding to the friendly manner more than anything, she said, "Thank you," walking off with Solomon at her side.

"Enjoy your stay," the official called after her.

Reaching the front desk hidden in a enclave off the foyer, Monique babbled incoherently, trying to explain her needs to the clerk: Solomon had to help her. She imposed a tighter rein on her emotions, blanking her thoughts and fighting back tears.

The clerk, a very polite and patient young Asian-American woman with a cute oval face and bob haircut set a white registration card on the high marble counter for her to sign.

Peeking over her shoulders, Solomon said, "Don't worry. I'll figure out a way for the club to pick up the tab."

Monique didn't register the comment, barely paid attention to the $230 a night cost for a Junior Executive Suite that was printed on the registration card. By rote, she gave the young woman her gold credit card.

"You'll be in room 918, Ms. Robbins," the clerk explained. "Here's your room key and a key to the wet bar. Will you need a bellman to take your luggage up?" she inquired.

Monique looked at her befuddled as if she didn't understand the words. Her mind had blanked out again.

"It won't be necessary," Solomon replied, placing a soothing hand in the small of Monique's back.

"The elevators are right to your left. Enjoy your stay at the Four Seasons."

On the quiet ride up, Monique heard nothing, saw nothing, except the destruction of her home. She wasn't aware of the tears streaming down her face until she was pulled into Solomon's embrace. He said nothing, simply hugged her endearingly and kissed her on the head. Then the elevator doors opened with a silent swish.

As if they were attached, he guided her the short walk down the corridors, other guests fast asleep behind wooden doors, to the room. At the door, she fumbled the key in the lock before Solomon took it from her trembling hands. He unlocked the door, clicked on the lights, then stood aside to let her enter. She entered, stood in the entryway facing a set of double-doors and stopped. She didn't have the heart or the energy to get excited about the room which, at any other time with Solomon at her side, would have been a high point in her life.

She heard the door close, turned to look up at him, gulped

hard, then yielded to the convulsive sobs she had been suppressing. Solomon took her possessions and dropped them on the tabouret, then pulled her in his arms.

"Why don't you take a nice hot bath and I'll call room service to see what they can rustle up?" he suggested.

"I don't want anything," she blubbered in his chest, soaking his shirt with her tears.

"I know," he crooned, leading her toward the bath across from the closet. He pushed her inside the room, then turned on the faucets.

The bathroom was steamy. Monique was one tight knot when she first stepped into the low tub filled with water in the corner of the bathroom. Stretching out to rest her head against the back, before and after visions of her home appeared behind her closed lids.

She recalled the interview with the fire official. She named the perpetrator who had committed the willful and malicious burning of her home, and in the next breath, gave him one of the best motives on record—revenge—even before he asked his first question. Finally, he got a word in.

"Ms. Robbins, some of your neighbors noticed a red Vet parked in front of your home about a half hour before the fire was noticeable. Do you know anyone who drives a red Vet?"

Angry and hurt tears slipped through her tightly shut eyes. An old image of Byron Henderson came to her mind. She remembered Tevis had been more impressed with his attitude than his looks. He moved like a tall man—confident, a little cocky—though he was of average height with a compact, muscular build and bow legs. He wasn't particularly handsome, but his wide smile was attractive, his teeth strikingly white in his coffee brown face. She envisioned him as she last saw him in court. Everyday he wore a conservative dark suit, with a cold, congested expression stamped on his face.

Solomon interrupted her memory, bringing a glass of wine. He set it on the side of the tub, then slipped quietly from the room.

The long hot soak, the wine, helped relieve some of the tension in her body and her thoughts gravitated toward practical matters. She would find out just how good her insurance company was tomorrow. She had to call the arson investigator to give him a number where he could reach her. Then there was the follow-up preparations for Koko Taylor's appearance at the club this weekend.

The water got cold, and she got out. Standing in front of the mirror over the sink, she dried herself with one of the large white towels.

It was the first time she noticed her surroundings. She managed a smile seeing a bidet across from the commode. She had never seen one in person before, but remembered it from the "Crocodile Dundee" movie.

Wrapped in the towel, she tucked it at her bosom, then picked up the empty wine glass. "Solomon," she called, walking out the bathroom into the sitting area.

The lights were dimmed. She took in the secretary-looking cabinet stocked with miniature bottles of liquor and assorted snacks, and a television on a slab atop three wide drawers. Perched in a L-nook of the wall were the couch and chair in front of an oval coffee table in glass and wood. In front of the picture window, with the drapes slightly open, was a round dining table and chairs, adjacent to the writing desk. It was an executive's delight.

She padded deeper into the suite, passing the invisible divider that separated the sitting area from the bedroom. There, she found Solomon sitting on the side of the queen-sized bed. He was just getting off the phone.

"Calling Ariana?" she asked.

"No," he replied, rising to walk towards her. "The front desk. How do you feel?"

"May I have some more wine?" she answered, holding out her glass to him.

As he returned to the living room, she sauntered to the picture window in the bedroom. The drapes were drawn, and she stared at the bright lights flickering over the city's south side of town and beyond.

It was spectacular. She didn't have this view from her home. But of course, she reminded herself, she didn't have a home at all anymore.

Fighting the painful lump in her throat, she said, "Talk to me, Solomon. Tell me about your marriage." The topic didn't matter; she just said the first thing that popped into her mind.

"There's not much to tell," he said, a shrug in his voice. He put the glass of wine in her hand. "It was a bust from the onset. That's it."

She turned to stare at his back as he sauntered to sit in the chair next to the window and propped his feet on the ottoman. He stared into her sad expression, trying to force a smile to his face and failed.

"We married for the wrong reasons," he relented at last. "When Elaine and I were dating, it was comfortable, you know. Safe." He unlaced his shoes, then set them on the side of the chair.

When he spoke again, his tone and demeanor were mechanical as if he were detached from the experience, she noticed. She understood the distance he imposed on his painful history, as well.

"I was working during the day and going to school at night. She was already working as a chemist for a plastics company. We both came from poor backgrounds, so we had a lot in common. Even though her father stayed, he wasn't very good managing the money. It was a sore spot with her."

Monique smiled at that, thinking about her nickname. "So she controlled the money when you got married."

"Mistake number one," he said ruefully. "Not that women can't control the purse strings," he added hastily, "but when money is used as a leverage in a personal relationship, it's not as beneficial as it is in business. Anyway, she earned more money than I did. It seemed she got a promotion every nine months. Her field was rising faster than mine. Besides, even after I earned a degree, I still had to get experience."

"Which meant low paying jobs in the interim."

He nodded before continuing. "Pretty soon, I think she more than I did, resented the fact that the man who was supposed to take care of her didn't make as much money as she did." He fell silent, pensive for a moment. "Maybe I began to resent it a little myself; I don't know. Anyway," he sighed wearily, "the marriage began to disintegrate when Ariana was about five, but I didn't see it. I just thought we were a couple going through the normal routines of living in America—struggling to save, working hard to make a better life for our family and hardly having time for each other. I ignored the arguments we had. I thought they were petty; usually, about money. While I was getting experience, she was traveling all over the country for her company. By the time I was in a comfortable and upwardly mobile position, she had already outgrown me."

"I'm sorry," she said.

"Oh, you don't have to apologize," he said. "Like I said, it was as much my fault as it was hers. But it hasn't turned me sour on women, as you already know," he smiled.

"Then why haven't you found someone before now?" she asked.

He chuckled softly. "I don't know. A bunch of reasons. The game was tiring. I was examining women as thoroughly as they were examining me."

"You were being cautious," she said, offering him a defense.

"Yeah, I guess you could say that," he replied amused. "I put so much emphasis on making sure the woman was not like Elaine, didn't make more money than I did and had a sane family background," he enumerated on his fingers, "that it became more like work when I was checking into people's backgrounds when they applied for a loan."

Listening to the qualities he identified, she recalled Tevis reminding her not to judge a book by its cover. *You might pass up a good black man.* But Byron hadn't been one of them, Monique thought, her morose feelings returning full bloom.

She felt Solomon walk up behind her. He took the wine from her hand and set the glass on the table. Then he was back, strong and supportive, wrapping his arms around her as if knowing what she needed before she did. He turned her in the circle of his arms, unwrapped the towel knotted at her bosom from her body.

He took her lips in a kiss so sweet, so tender, a hot exultant tear slipped from her eyes. It was a tear that contained her contradictory feelings of supreme joy, and yet, hurt from the violence perpetrated against her home.

Suddenly, she didn't want to think of the past, wanted to lose herself in the present. With strong and vivid desires coursing through her mind and body, she stripped him as naked as she. Desperately needing to lose herself in the euphoric sensations that destroyed thinking, she pressed her body closer to his, fastened her mouth harder against his lips. She didn't want tame, tender caresses. Her ardor was aggressive, sensually forceful, exacting his swift surrender.

Matching her urgency with his own lusty, unsated needs, he carried her to bed, and there, the hot, energetic pace intensified. They loved each other hard and furious because Monique demanded it, and Solomon was compelled by it. With the city lights twinkling at their feet, they created purely physical memories in the path toward ecstasy.

* * *

Just at that time of new day before official sunrise—when the dark of night and the light of day first meet—Monique stirred in bed. Even in sleep, instinctively, she reached for Solomon. Her eyes blinked open not finding him in the warm spot next to her.

He was at the window looking out. His splendid, naked profile against the promise of morning, he never looked more powerful, more virile, more strikingly male. God must have been exceptionally pleased with his creation, she thought, an exclamation of approval in her throat.

She slipped quietly from bed, sidled behind him and splayed her hands up over his chest. He felt like a balm to her soul. The scent of their lovemaking teased her drowsy senses to a heightened awakening. Pressing her cheek against his back, she held him close. She felt the quivering that shot down his spine and the lazy smile in his voice when he spoke.

"Couldn't sleep?" he asked, clasping his hands over hers.

"I missed you," she said simply.

"I'm right here."

His tone said more than three words, and Monique held her breath. A strange and new, but ancient sensation came over her. She was shocked by the sudden depth of her need. Nothing in her life could have prepared her for this timbre of yearning she felt, an eloquent hunger in her heart to possess him wholly.

In a tremulous voice, she asked, "Worried about Ariana?" It was not what she wanted to know.

"No," he replied. Peeling her hands away, he turned in the invisible circle she made to face her. "I'm concerned about your safety," he said, taking her hands in his to hold against his mouth.

Staring up into his eyes bathing her gently, the sad smile on his serious face, she wanted to protect him. "Don't worry," she said, assuring him in a soft voice.

"Oh, I'm not worried." He kissed the tangle of hands. "Because I'll never let anything happen to you."

"My hero," she said in a half-joking manner. All her innards were seething with wants, both physical and emotional.

"Yes, I'll be that, too," he promised with conviction. "Whatever you want or need," his eyes soft, his look intense with deep affection. "I don't know what I did to deserve you, but I'll do everything in my power to deserve this rare gift you've given me."

A startled gasp escaped her lips. Her eyes sought his, narrowed fleetingly with disbelief, then widened to read the truth shining in his dark-eyed gaze. "Solomon," she exclaimed in a whisper.

Her eyes locked into his, and was an exact copy of the single emotion that expressed their love.

"Monique," he said plainly, "I love you."

After the words, the declaration was sealed in a kiss. And right there, with sunrise creeping in, Solomon treasured Monique, cherished her body, and made true his confession in deed.

It was hot enough to fry an egg on the sidewalk, Byron thought, wiping the sweat from his brow. He was walking along a long avenue in Houston's Fifth Ward community with his jacket thrown over his shoulder and a section of newspaper bunched under his arm.

The community had changed greatly since he lived here as a youngster. Once a thriving area of businesses and religious activity, it now looked like any other run-down, inner-city community of abandoned buildings, stray dogs, unattended children, and goal-less men hanging on street corners. Nearly as many Hispanics as blacks, who once dominated, lived in the area, seemingly untouched by economic development of any sort.

He'd blown this dump once, he thought, determined he wouldn't fall back in its trap again. Despite this new setback, he mused somewhat anxiously.

On his way to his son's residence, the small A-frame house with a cracked cement porch his girlfriend inherited from her grandmother, he recalled he had had a busy morning. The car was in the shop as of two hours ago getting a new paint job. Hearing the news about the house burning down, he had raced from the dingy little hotel room where he'd spent the night with a nameless woman to buy a newspaper. A small article was buried on a back page, but the essentials were disclosed. A fire inspector suspected arson. Though no suspects were named, the finger pointed at him, as someone noticed a red Vet in the area.

The truth didn't matter, he thought resigned. He couldn't yell bum rap: he had a record. *Shoot first, ask questions later.*

Turning on a side street, Byron pulled up. The house was the third from the corner on the right hand side of a dead end street. He noticed an official-looking car parked in front of it. He watched as a tall, brown-skinned man got out and walked up to the porch, pulling something from his inside coat pocket. He also noticed the gun bulging from his waist. The heat in plain clothes, he guessed.

Byron ducked in between two houses and loped hurriedly across backyards, passing a group of small children in a kiddy pool. They were oblivious to him, probably used to people making a shortcut of their yard. Reaching the house of his destination, he tiptoed along the side of the house, plastered himself against the chipped wood.

"Why are you looking for him?"

Byron recognized his son's voice, a note of anxiety in his tone. *Be cool,* he warned silently. *Just answer the man's questions.*

"Sir, is he here?"

Byron guessed by the cop's forceful, impatient tone that it wasn't the first time he had inquired of his whereabouts.

"No, he's not."

"This is his address," the officer confirmed with emphasis.

"Yes, he lives here, sometimes."

"Do you know where he is?"

"No, I don't."

"Sir, if Mr. Henderson shows up, please give him my card and a message that it would be in his best interest to call me right away."

"Yes, sir," Michael replied.

Best interest hell, Byron thought.

"Yes, I'll tell her you called."

Solomon ended the call, then placed the pink message slip on top of the stack of them on his desk. The phone had been ringing off the hook ever since he arrived at the club three hours ago, he mused, fingering the stack of messages. All were for Monique, representing everyone from the media to a city council-woman. Reading about the fire, they called requesting an interview or simply to offer their support.

He had no idea she was so popular, or that her personal crisis would bring such a outpouring of concern. The more he learned about her, the more he loved her. He felt extremely proud to be associated with a woman whose generosity was as great in the community as it was towards him. He already knew how unpretentious she was and wondered if she had an inkling of the community's concern for her.

The memory of staring at her formerly beautiful home that had been decorated with care and attention filled him with a sudden anger. He was angry because of the sense of helplessness that stole into his being even now, after the fact. He hadn't felt that degree of powerlessness since accepting the inevitability of his divorce. He had wanted to lash out at the unknown perpetrator of such destruction with a violence he never felt before.

But Monique didn't need those embittered emotions from him, he told himself. She needed him to be clear-headed, rational and supportive.

Reluctantly, he had left her sleeping this morning, he recalled, his thoughts of her pure and clear and loving. Even in sleep she was delectable. With the image of her focused in his memory, he felt a duplicate sensation of the ecstasy he'd found in her arms, the glory she favored upon him with her love. Walking away had been so hard to do.

Though the matter hadn't come up yet, he wasn't all that keen about her looking to replace the house the fire took. He would rather they look for a house in which to build a new life together. He felt confident that this time, he'd found his soulmate. Monique was all the woman he wanted, all he would ever need. He had no fears that she would turn out to be another Elaine and cause him to resent her. He felt as if the thread of an ancient pleasure stretched endlessly into the future for them—he, Monique and Ariana.

The unconscious smile on his face vanished, replaced by a scowl. He had to concern himself with a very present and potentially life-threatening matter, he reminded himself. On top of all the other unknowns about the fire starter, they didn't know his exact intentions. Obviously, he—or she, Solomon mused—knew Monique was not home when he set the fire. Was the act committed in a fit of rage, or would a subsequent and direct attempt on her life be made?

With time to consider that the incident involving her vehicle leaking oil was not a coincidence, he now believed it was part of everything that had happened to her the late-night phone call and evidence of an attempted break-in.

Monique pointed an accusing finger at Byron Henderson, he recalled. It was not surprising that she would suspect the man who served time for killing her best friend, and it was not uncommon for offenders to commit crimes on the heels of parole. But unless Henderson was incredibly stupid, he seemed too obvious a culprit for his liking.

But he didn't like his suspect either, Solomon thought, his brows drawn downward in a pensive frown. It disturbed him greatly that his best guess was someone who worked, or who used to work at the club. The only proof he had were the acts of vandalism, little things he deliberately kept from Monique, like the stolen liquor, the broken glasses, the destroyed origami art and some missing plants. Right now, even though she was no longer employed at the club, Cynthia was at the top of his list.

The staff were still coming in for the meeting which had been originally called to discuss the details of the upcoming concert. He was curious to see their reaction to the news about the fire.

Checking the time on his wrist watch; it was twelve-thirty, he picked up a manila folder from the desk and strode from the room. He pondered how to play his hand as he walked into the club where the staff was assembled. Jake and Francine were sitting at the bar, while Chris and Dennis each occupied a table. They were whispering among themselves and fell silent upon noticing him. Leon was just walking in from the back of the club.

"Mr. Thomas, what's this I heard on the radio news about Monique's house burning down?"

"Yeah, I heard about that, too," Francine said, a curious frown on her face.

"I didn't believe it when I heard it," Jake said.

"That's cause you're stupid," Jason retorted.

"Who's stupid?" Jake replied.

"All right," Solomon said, raising his hands as if addressing a chorus of singers. "Let's settle down." Reaching their silent attention, he said, "It's true. Monique's home was burned to the ground last night."

With disbelief reigning, a chorus of astonished mutterings reverberated across the room. As the announcement sank in as true, the questions began flying across the room at Solomon. "When did it happen?" "Was she in the house? The paper didn't say." "Do they know who did it?"

"When was after she got home from closing up here," Solomon replied. "All that is known at this point is that it was deliberately set. As for who, we have no ideas."

"Think it could be Joe Simpson?" Francine asked. "He's been coming here quite a bit lately. He ain't no big spender, buys the limit, then leaves after a while."

"He doesn't believe in tipping," Dennis chortled. "I hate waiting on him."

"Besides the infamous and seemingly harmless Mr. Simpson," Solomon said, "have any of you noticed anything out of the ordinary?"

"Like what?" Jake replied.

"Anything, stupid," Jason quipped.

"Who you calling stupid?" Jake retorted. "Go grow some hair."

"I think we're getting sidetracked," Solomon said with a scolding look. "This is serious."

Leon snapped his fingers. "I remember something." With all eyes on him, he said, "Remember that night when Monique was running late, this guy asked me if she were in."

"What did he look like?" Solomon asked.

"Dark, short haircut, average height, nothing that stood out. You were working the front that night," Leon said.

"You know what," Solomon said thoughtfully, "I do remember a guy, average looking, blue collar type worker. He asked me if somebody named Taylor was working, and I must have said or looked at him kind of puzzled, then he asked for Monique."

"Too bad we don't have everybody sign a guest book or something," Francine said.

"Do you remember seeing him again after that?" Solomon asked Leon.

"Yeah, as a matter of fact, I do," Leon said excitedly. "He

was in here last night. Sat upstairs. Didn't stay long though. Left early."

"Who worked upstairs last night?" Solomon asked, catching Leon's excitement.

When the meeting came to an end, Solomon was not as comfortable with his initial belief. He expected that Cynthia's name would have cropped up during the conversation, but when it wasn't, he decided to keep his counsel. He wondered whether his suspicion was based on some quirk in his thinking as a newcomer to the club, for everyone seemed as anxious as he to figure out the puzzle. At least, everyone except Michael who wasn't present.

Monique had worked up an appetite by noon, having spent the entire morning on the phone. In addition to hunger and stiff muscles, the midday brought her a new attitude—a keener appreciation for what she did have. It was only her deep affections for Solomon keeping the fires of her positive emotions lit and holding back the thread of hatred for Byron.

She had lost a house, a physical structure. The most precious thing in it were the memories of friendship, the history of love she had shared with Tevis and Patricia. But the pictures could be replaced, and she still had her memories and her life, she told herself, as she stepped off the elevator, heading for the hotel's Terrace Cafe. A mural depicting swans in a rich red and gold fronted the restaurant. Business execs in power suits and wealthy women of leisure in Christian Dior and diamonds dominated the noon time crowd. She spotted no one as casually attired as she—a blue sweatshirt with the sleeves cut off and a pair of white jogging shorts were all she had.

Feeling under-dressed, she thought about leaving. Right from the restaurant was a walk-way that linked the hotel to the Park Mall Shopping Center. Before she made a decision, the maitre d', a tall, uniformed man in his sixties, with warm friendly dark eyes and thinning blond hair approached.

"Good afternoon, welcome to the Terrace Cafe," he said, tilting his head obsequiously. "Table for one?"

"Yes," she replied to his polite, undaunted manner.

"Right this way, miss. I'll seat you at my favorite table."

His favorite table turned out to be perfect, Monique thought as he pulled the chair from the table for her. She wished Solomon were with her to share in the view. It was a picnic kind of day, the sun high in the stretch of blue sky that a skyscraper had not hidden. Just behind the glass panels was the terrace, the restaurant's namesake that contained huge porcelain pots brimming with greenery and small flowers that produced delicate blooms. Below on the street level was a little park, and in the distance sat the George R. Brown Convention center which looked like a giant steamship.

She had driven that street everyday on her way to and from the club for years, passing both the Four Seasons Hotel, as well as the park. She never stopped to find out the name of the park, taking for granted that it would always be there, she mused.

Suddenly, she felt a horrendous longing for Solomon in her. She didn't know what time he had slipped from her bed, but he'd left a very detailed note on the cold pillow that retained his scent next to her. Because of the concert at the end of the week, a staff meeting was in order to ensure that everyone knew what was expected. Additionally, the club was one of the ticket outlets, so someone needed to be present as early as eleven in the morning.

Though normally a job she would have assumed, she obviously couldn't do it now and was still not sure she would work tonight. Solomon vetoed the idea altogether, she recalled. The arson investigator, Peace Officer Pearce suggested she lay low until he followed up on the lead she had given him. He promised to let her know the instant Byron was picked up for questioning.

A Hispanic waiter came to the table, interrupting her thoughts. "Good afternoon," he said, placing a glass of water on a flower shaped napkin before her. "May I get you something to drink from the bar?"

And from there, the service only got better. Her waiter, whose name tag identified him as Leo, was as friendly as everyone else she had met in the hotel. She accepted his recommendation of drinks, and shortly, a glass of Chardonnay was placed on the table, followed by a basket of oregano and black pepper bread with nuts. After ordering a lunch of lobster and shrimp sandwich with papaya chutney, Monique returned to her private thoughts.

Staring out into the clear, sunny skies, she couldn't help wishing that the reason for her stay at this elegant hotel were different. Had Solomon not been at her side, she mused, she didn't know how she would have coped on her own. It was not so much what he had said, for he was not a man of meaningless words, but his strong, silent presence had restored her wits and confidence to overcome this setback in her life.

Solomon had promised her as much with his loving touches, quiet murmuring in her ear, she recalled with dreamy abstraction. She wondered if she would ever get used to his brand of love-making. A lover for all moods, he could be tender and submissive, or fierce and overwhelming—whatever she needed, wanted.

She knew she would never get enough of it. Each time he made love to her, she responded like a kid facing a limitless supply of gifts to unwrap. She didn't believe there was another man in the world for her. Certainly not one like Solomon who could anticipate and satisfy the mandates of her desires. She had only a wonderful future to look forward to with a man who could manage not only her club.

The joy absorbing her heart shone brightly on her face. She never thought she'd live the day to admit that a man could indeed do something for her that she couldn't do for herself.

One thing she was certain about, a cast iron look of determination on her face. Byron Henderson was not going to destroy another life.

He knew more about her personal life than even Solomon. She had time to rectify that oversight, she mused, with her focus on Byron. She needed an edge, an element of surprise over him. The first order of business was to get her car. Not the Cherokee; she needed something fast that could compete with the deadly Vet he drove, and she owned just the thing.

Leo placed her lunch on the table. He topped off her glass of wine, then left upon ascertaining whether she required anything else.

He couldn't provide what would make her lunch complete, she thought, feeling an onslaught of melancholy as she watched him go. Only one handsome, chauvinistic, loving manager could do that.

Remembering his confession, she found it hard to believe that his caution led him into a habit most commonly practiced by women. It was almost uncharacteristic of him, but one she found adorable because it highlighted his sensitivity and showed he was blessed with a foolhardy side, as well, she mused.

Judging a woman by the size of her pocketbook, Monique thought amused as she took a sip of wine. She nearly chuckled out loud and caught herself. Holding the white cloth napkin to her lips, she wiped her mouth, thinking she was glad he'd gotten over that.

Replete and feeling a hundred percent better than when she walked in, Monique left a generous tip, then took the walk-way to the adjoining shopping center. Competent, gracious service with a smile seemed a mandate here, she thought. She wanted to meet the person responsible for hiring the staff of employees to pick up some pointers for herself.

Fourteen

By six that evening, Monique was stir crazy. Solomon vehemently vetoed her plan to leave the hotel earlier, she recalled, pacing the floor in her room. Impressed by his concern, she relented.

Now, she wished she hadn't promised to stay put. She grabbed the remote control, plopped at the foot of the bed and clicked on the television, just for the company of noise. The screen opened on a typical news set in a wide shot of two news anchors.

"Double troubles for the doctor," the male anchor announced. "Details right after this message from our sponsors."

She didn't want to hear about anybody else's troubles, Monique thought; she had enough of her own. Tossing the remote control on the bed, she was up and ambling about again during the first commercial. Impulsively, she decided that a warm shower would help soothe her. It always worked, she told herself, heading for the bathroom.

With running water in the background, the news returned. "The legal troubles of Dr. Anthony Ward, III, a prominent OB/GYN continues," said the male anchor.

Monique was already in the shower. But an hour later, she was worse. It was seven, the time she was supposed to man her station a the club to greet guests. Cooled from the warm shower, she paced the room, dinner untouched on the table, like an animal held against her will in an alien habitat.

She called Officer Pearce, but he wasn't in. Feeling trapped in her luxuriant surroundings, her mind became a fertile field for questions about Byron's intentions: no one thought stayed longer than a second-hand revolution around a clock.

She wondered if Byron really meant to harm her . . . or, whether he simply wanted to frighten her. Was he satisfied with his vengeful deed . . . or, did he need her death to soothe his insane need of revenge?

Whatever his motivation, she thought, he held the power over her now, by forcing her into hiding. That in itself was a form of abuse.

Then, Solomon arrived with Ariana and a kiss. Elated, Monique began to believe she could live like this forever. The three of them left the room, heading for the patio. Several of the hotel's guests were already poolside, and others were lounging in the chairs under the blue awnings. Ariana immediately took off for the water.

Solomon and Monique found a fairly secluded spot, pulling two chairs side by side, near the well-tended jungle of luscious plants and trees, and ordered drinks. He resumed the conversation that started in the elevator.

"I know you don't want to, but you have to," he said with emphasis.

Sighing from boredom, Monique would rather he change the subject and enjoy the lazy evening, sipping sweet drinks from tall, frosted glasses. She wanted to savor the knowledge of his love, bask in his presence, make plans for their future.

But her remarkably attractive man was in his all-business mood, she thought. Annoyed, she blew bubbles in her drink, recalling the very proper and very dissatisfying kiss they shared before coming down. Cutting a sidelong glance at his fine profile, want fired her gaze. She wanted to comb out the curly hairs on his broad-shouldered chest and sit between his powerful thighs encased in a pair of modest trunks. A trembling thrill raced through her, and she slurped her drink.

"It doesn't take a lot of strength to strike a match," he said in a quiet voice that couldn't have been more emphatic had he screamed.

"I don't believe Cynthia is capable of such viciousness," Monique said, her eyes straight ahead as she absently twirled the straw around in her glass.

"You've said that about everybody," Solomon said flippantly, "but somebody started that fire."

"Byron started that fire," she said unmoved.

"It doesn't make sense for him to come anywhere near you or your property," he replied. "You told me he wasn't stupid."

"Stupidity doesn't have anything to do with wanting revenge," she quipped.

"But why . . . because you testified against him in court?" he asked rhetorically. "From what you've told me, you really didn't have to say much of anything against him since he had been reported to the police at least on two prior occasions."

Churning the straw in the glass, Monique risked a sidelong look at him with a deliberately blank stare. He glared; she smiled. Unable to maintain his peeve with her, he sighed expressively.

"Monique, listen to me," he said with forced patience. "There is no way he could have gotten to the back of the club to break those glasses. He wouldn't have been able to set fire to Leon's little paper designs without one of the waiters or somebody seeing it. Again, that could only have been done by one of the staff. The same thing applies to the missing liquor. He certainly wouldn't have gotten into the stockroom. Even if he had a key, someone would have seen him going into the back room."

Monique didn't pretend not to understand what he was saying. As distasteful as it was accepting that one of her staff stole from the club, she still didn't believe there was a connection. "Well, even if someone on the staff did those things," she said grudgingly, "I can't think of anything I did to cause any of them to set my house on fire."

"Baby, you don't have to do anything to some people," he said in that infinitely reasonable and patient tone of his. "Jealousy is also a motivation for hateful acts."

"I know, but . . ." Monique began, then fell silent. Mulling his irrefutable comment, she remembered something Aurelius had said to her a while back. *You just don't know people.* The reminder stalled her in a quagmire; trust in her own instincts wavered. Yet, she insisted, "You don't know Cynthia like I do."

"And maybe you don't know Cynthia as well as you think," he retorted.

"Cynthia was referred by a friend who works at the Houston Area Women's Center. Do you know what that is?"

"Yes, I'm quite familiar with the Center and Haven House, as well," he said. "But that doesn't . . ."

Cutting him off, she said, "She has a lot of bitter emotions to work through, and sometimes she comes across as mean and spiteful, but she's not," she defended with staunch loyalty. "She's just trying to get her life in order and find her worth."

"A decision must be made soon," Solomon said weary of the discussion. "I'm fairly certain that the incidents at the club have been committed by someone on our staff. We've got to find that person and get rid of her, or him, before none of us has a job." With a soft chuckle in his throat, he said, "You're too kind-hearted for your own good, you know that."

That's why you were hired, Monique almost quipped aloud, but caught herself. As certain as she felt about Solomon, she didn't know how he would respond to finding out she owned *T's Place.* She was equally uncomfortable with her hesitation to simply tell him. *There should be no secrets between them.*

Solomon rose to take her drink and set both glasses on the ground, then sat on the side of her chair. Angling his body to face her headlong, he took her left hand between his. It was the most intimate and affectionate gesture they'd shared since he arrived. Suddenly, the noise of activity seemed to silence around them. Dusk had set, and the hot summery evening took on a paradisiacal atmosphere.

He gazed at her with a roving, languid look—from her face, down the black, one-piece suit, hugging her slimness. A quiet, sensual light glowed in his dark, sultry eyes, articulating want. The dormant sexuality of her body awakened again. A habitual tingling that was as natural as breathing flowed through her. Neither embarrassed nor distressed by her reaction, she returned his look with a message that spoke her reciprocal desires.

"You know," he said in a soft, affected voice, "everybody who called for you yesterday, from reporters to people who hadn't even met you, but knew of your work with Haven House and in the community, had something wonderful to say about you." With a small sheepish grin on his face, "I was embarrassed by my ignorance of the extent your community work."

She stroked his strong jaw with her right hand, smiling at him sheepishly. "I'm sorry."

"Don't apologize," he replied. He turned his face in her hand, planted a kiss in its palm. "It's not your fault; it's mine. It reminded me of what I seem to have forgotten . . . the place I came from," he said with a rueful shake of his head. "I buried my head in my own little individual sandlot and didn't put half of what I'd gotten from the community back into it."

Solomon lowered her hand to his lap, cupping it in his warm grasp, his eyes intent. "It also made me realize how little I know about you," he said. "Every time I think I know all there is to know, or at least, the most essential thing, I learn something else about you to show me how lucky I am. And it makes me love you more."

Touched by his reaffirmation, Monique caught her breath, the threat of tears stinging her eyes. Though he had more than demonstrated his love for her, she felt bolstered by the words nevertheless. She slipped her arms around his neck the same time his arms snaked around her waist.

"I don't plan to lose your love just because you're stubborn and refuse to see reason," he whispered in her hair.

Held tenderly, she felt the strength of him flow into her being. He was as strong in character, as he was in the flesh, she thought. It made her believe he could carry the weight of the world on his shoulders. Certainly her little secret wouldn't weigh so much.

"I won't be able to spend the night," he said wistfully.

"I know," she replied, nodding her head against his chest. What was one night when he offered her tomorrow, went so far as to guarantee it would be bright. There was nothing she didn't trust about him. She was in no threat of losing her identity or anything else to him. Deciding to share her secret, she pulled back from him, her hands splayed palms-flat against his chest, the short hairs between her fingers. "Solomon . . ."

"Shhh," he said, hushing her with a kiss on her lips. "Don't worry. It will be over soon."

"But I . . ."

"No more business tonight," he said. His gaze slid across to the pool where Ariana was sitting on the bank, talking to another young guest of the hotel. "I'm going to take a swim," he said, holding her hand as he stood. "Want to join us?"

The thought to press the issue came and passed. "No, thank-you. I prefer watching," she said, an appreciative sigh in her bosom as she watched him walk off.

* * *

Clinging to her memories of passion and Solomon's promise that it would soon be over, Monique made it through the night.

Tuesday morning, she busied herself returning phone calls that had come to the club the previous day. She even called Cynthia, but had to leave a message. Then, Officer Pearce returned her call with apologies instead of a liberating message: he had yet to locate Byron Henderson. The disappointing news heightened her eagerness to get out in the streets and do something beneficial for herself, or at least, the club.

The anxiety lasted only until Solomon arrived after closing *T's Place*. His presence filled her with other sensations, banishing her quest to vacate the safety and comfort of the Four Seasons. Though a welcome sight, he looked exhausted and drained. There was so much to be done in light of the concert, she felt guilty that he bore the responsibility of running the club alone. She delayed telling him her secret and instead, fortified their relationship with a demonstration of what he had to look forward to in their years to come.

Monique awakened with an unknown fear Wednesday morning. Tears were falling from her eyes, and a nightmarish sensation wavered around the edges of her consciousness. Rubbing her eyes dry, she remembered a small child, a girl in a dark place, afraid and crying.

But before and after that image, she couldn't recall anything except the uneasy feeling. "That's it," she said firmly, tossing aside the comforter.

60. 80. 109. 117.

The small, sporty car sped along the highway like a sleek black panther on the prowl. The scenic country view, neat rows of crops, homes set back miles from the flat paved road of Highway 59 passed in a blur. The speed limit signs along the way were but mere inconveniences and ignored. The driver was unconcerned about the possibility of receiving a speeding ticket: the car needed to be tested.

Straight-ahead jazz filled the cockpit, and behind the wheel, Monique sat comfortably in the low-slung seat, pleased with the horsepower of the Ferrari that responded to her foot commands.

The car was like a gun in her hands: it had been a gift from her father and stepmother three years ago. Her father had actually wanted to buy her a handgun. She had quipped he might as well put a Ferrari in her hands, knowing he was quite familiar with her driving record.

She was completely caught off guard when he and Cecelia put a set of car keys in her hand. She was supposed to become a more cautious driver. But she had hardly put the car on the road because she didn't trust her own sense of daring in the aerodynamically-built-for-speed instrument.

But today, the car fulfilled the need she had to restore power over her life. She recognized the exhilaration she felt was but a mere token of the real thing, but she could no longer cower in her hotel room afraid another day.

After breakfast, she spoke with the general manager of the Four Seasons Hotel and explained her plight. He was a dynamic, energetic man who didn't mind extending himself or his staff to help her out. A driver from the valet parking pool was assigned to accompany her to the Redmon's ranch-style home in Richmond, roughly 40 miles outside of Houston, where the car, christened Nzingha in honor of the famous African warrior queen, was kept. The hotel employee drove the Jeep back to the hotel.

Feeling in control, Monique couldn't help thinking that the next time Byron came after her, she would have a surprise for him. The power was more evenly distributed between them.

The only thing she had to fear now, she mused laughingly,

was Solomon's wrath. She reviewed her defense to him, knowing it would have to be a good one. She could hear him now railing about her disobedience of not only him, but Officer Pearce, by putting her life in jeopardy.

But she had a response. With a cocky laugh erupting from her, she recalled the little spot on the side of his neck that drove him wild. If that didn't work, certainly reason would.

By his own admission, they were still strangers to each other. Byron, regardless of his intentions had severely affected their time together. Not just of them, but Ariana as well, whom she had cautioned Solomon about bringing to the hotel, fearing the off-chance that Byron would follow him. And if all failed, she thought, she'd throw in something about needing to start house-hunting.

Looking in the rear-view mirror, she saw the red and blue lights atop a police car whirling, its siren barely audible inside Nzingha.

Arriving at the club, the parking lot was semi-full with several cars. Monique saw the twin's souped-up canary yellow Chevy and Dennis's purple Mustang, but not Solomon's car. She let herself in the building and locked the door, before venturing into the club proper. Taped music played from a hidden source, and except for the light streaming from the front of the club, the place was empty.

She followed the stream of light to the foyer. The front door was opened, and in the far corner, Dennis was sequestered in the closet-size booth with a window in front of the protruding counter raised. He poked his head out upon seeing her.

"Hey, good-looking," he exclaimed cheerfully. "I thought you weren't coming in."

"I couldn't stay away any longer," she replied laughingly.

"Sorry about your place," he said, looking at her ruefully.

"Yeah, well," she shrugged, "what's done is done."

"But I'm glad you didn't get hurt," he said.

Monique didn't want to linger on the subject. "Which twin is on today?"

"Jake," Dennis replied. "He went with Mr. Thomas to restock some supplies and liquor."

She nodded, even more satisfied with her decision to return. Now Solomon wouldn't have to do everything on his own. "How are sales going?"

"You just missed the lunch time rush," he said jokingly.

"Sorry," she replied chuckling with him. "I had to do some shopping."

"Oh well, that's important," he said in jest. "But we have about two hundred seats left."

"Did Solomon take out fifty?" she asked, recalling her instructions to withhold seats for walk-ins.

"Done," Dennis replied.

"Well, I'm going back to my office to take care of some other details. Buzz me if you need me," she said, walking off to her office. The blinds were drawn, the door locked when she arrived. She opened the door and scanned the room as if re-acquainting herself.

"Miss me?" she asked, entering the room. "I missed you," she said, setting her purse on the corner of the desk.

Getting busy, she was dialing a phone number even before she sat in the chair. Within minutes, she was immersed in work. An hour later with business matters wrapped up, she took time for a personal call to Barbados.

Sitting at the edge of her seat, a bottle of soda in her hand, she chuckled into the mouthpiece. "Yes, I'll have lots to tell when you get back." Giggling, she said, "Neither can I. Just wait until you meet Ariana. She's adorable." She broke out in a fit of laughter. "Can you picture me a stepmother? . . . You think so? That's sweet of you, but don't say anything to my god baby. I don't want her to get any foolish notions that she's being replaced. Does she have . . ."

From the corner of her eye, Monique saw her office door

open and fell silent as Michael burst into the room. The look on his tense drawn face alerted her that something was wrong. "Patricia, let me call you back tonight," she said. "Yeah, I'm fine," she assured her absently. "Okay, bye," then set the receiver in the cradle. "Michael, what's . . ."

"You've got to drop those charges against him. He didn't do it."

"What are you talking about? Drop what charges?"

"Don't play dumb! I don't have time for games," he yelled.

Monique stared at him startled, not afraid, but very concerned. Michael inhaled deeply, drawing calm to himself.

"I'm sorry," he said contritely, his voice barely audible. Running his hands through his hair, he dropped into the chair against wall. "This thing has got me going crazy," he said, as if speaking to himself. He looked up at her with pleading in his expression. "He didn't do it. But they think he did because you must have given them his name. I swear to you, he didn't do. Call them off. Please, Taylor."

Monique gasped as if she had been struck. Her face tightened at the use of a name that hadn't been spoken in years. "What? What did you call me?"

"Taylor," he replied. "That's your name isn't it? Taylor Monique."

A second of silence in which hardly a sound was heard passed. It was her secret, tied up in a frightening dream she could barely remember. A horrified sensation powered her rapid heartbeat. "Ho . . . how did you know?"

"He told me."

"He who?" she demanded.

"Byron. Byron Henderson."

A deeply perplexed frown settled over her glum face. "Byron Henderson?" she said in an astonished whisper. "What is he to you?" she tossed the question across the desk at him.

"He's my father," Michael replied.

Confused, furious, frightened, Monique sprang from her chair, shaking her head in denial. She flipped through her memory file for information about Byron Henderson, things she learned from Tevis. "No. Byron didn't have any children."

"Long before he married your friend," Michael replied. "My mother was fifteen years old when I was born. She never got the benefit of a marriage license from him." His face held a note of mockery.

Monique walked from behind her desk and paced a circle in front of it. Feeling the fool, she snorted. Byron still had one up on her. A spy in her camp, she thought, staring warily at Michael as if he were a condemned criminal. Knowing instinctively from whom he'd learned her name, she wondered what else Tevis had told him, no doubt innocently, in a moment of quiet confidence shared between lovers.

"You knew who I was all along," Monique said. It was part question, part accusation. His guilt-ridden look answered. "So, you're not studying to become a hair stylist; you're not in school at all," she challenged.

"Yes," he said hastily. "That part's true. I am."

Still, Monique felt betrayed. "Why did you come here for a job? Why?"

"I just needed a job," he replied.

"No," she chortled angrily, slamming a fist on the desk.

"It's true," he replied, rising from his seat in one action. He approached her with an imploring look, gesturing with his hands. "At first, it was fun, like a game. That's all, I swear. I never intended anything."

"I don't believe you. You came to spy on me so you could go back and report to your father. A murderer. Who are you?" she asked, glaring at him with the pain of betrayal glittering in her eyes.

"Monique . . ."

"What else did your father tell you about me?" she spat out, contempt blazing in her amber eyes.

Dejected, Michael dropped into the chair, his head bowed. "That you own *T's Place.*"

"Where is your father?"

Solomon's voice, soft, prosaic, and unexpected, slid into the room. Monique's head whipped up to see him standing in the doorway, and her heart leaped at the sight of him. From the corner of her eyes, she saw Michael tense in the seat, gripping the armrests on the chair.

"Solomon," she whispered. She started towards him, her body mimicking the excitement spiraling inside her, but he stilled her with a rapier glance. She swallowed hard and eased back down in her seat.

With a curious, assessing gaze, her breath lodged in her bosom. She tracked his entrance into the room. He stopped at the corner of the desk, staring down at Michael. Confidently calm, he revealed nothing of what he felt.

"Where is he, Michael?" Solomon asked again, his tone unchanged.

"I . . . I don't know," Michael stammered in reply.

"What if I said I don't believe you, Michael?"

Michael showed a face of belligerence. "I don't . . ." he started, springing from his chair.

Solomon shoved him back down so handily and swiftly, Monique wondered if she had missed a movement in his reaction. Michael looked to her with a frightened, wary expression. His Adam's Apple pronounced, he swallowed hard in his throat.

"I don't know where he is," he said, studying Solomon intently.

A decided chill hung in the air. Monique knew it came in with Solomon like a cold front. Though she knew she'd have to face his annoyance with her for disobeying soon, she was grateful she wasn't the target of his present wintry wrath.

"You believe him?"

Solomon angled his head to Monique's face. His eyes

were strangely veiled, and she merely gulped. She felt as if she, instead of Michael, were the victim to his quiet, foul mood. She was unnerved by the sheer power of his control, the menacing aura emanating from him. He turned from her as if she were insignificant.

"What do you know about Adrienne?" Solomon asked.

"Nothing," Michael replied. "Except Cynthia doesn't believe she stole that money. She never told me why. And before you ask, I didn't take it either."

"Who tampered with Monique's car?"

Michael looked at him dumbfounded, shaking his head.

"I guess you wouldn't know about late night calls or an attempted break-in either," Solomon snorted.

"I just know my father didn't have anything to do with setting that house on fire," Michael contended.

"How do you know that?" Solomon asked. He sat on the corner of the desk and folded his arms across his chest as if they were having a casual discussion.

"I just know he didn't do it. He's been going to his counselor and those classes at Project Center."

From a sidelong look, Solomon quirked a brow at Monique. She didn't know how to interpret the look—inquiring or as proof for his belief that matched Michael.

Michael answered, "It's a program designed to work with men who batter."

"He never said anything to you about getting even with Monique?" Solomon asked Michael.

Michael squirmed in his chair, a debate warring in his expression before he replied. "Not lately. Not as much as he used to when I first went to see him two years ago. But since he's been going to his classes," he said eagerly, "he's been getting better. I know he has. I'd stake my life on it."

"And you'd lose it," Monique quipped.

"No, that's not true!" Michael said. He scooted to the edge of the chair as if fearing further movement would land him in trouble. "I know what he did to that woman is unforgivable to you. I know you can't forget it. But he's paid for that. He wants to go on and make a new life for himself."

"Where he is, Michael?" Solomon asked quietly.

"You think I'd tell you even if I knew?" Michael asked, looking back and forth at them suspiciously. "You'll turn him in and I'll be right back where I started. You can't possibly know what it's like." He sagged pathetically in his chair.

"What it's *like?*" Monique said incredulously. "I know what it's like to have my best friend's life taken away."

"And what about my life, huh? What about me? All those years wondering all the time about my daddy? What he was like? Was he really no good like my mama always said he was? And what did that say about me? Huh? I got his breath and blood in my body. Am I like him?"

"Michael," Monique said sympathetically, "you're not a murderer."

"Neither is he!" Michael said, bolting to his feet.

Staring at Michael, Monique was suddenly filled with remembering. She understood the sense of desperation in his tone, his look, even his action begging for his father's life. She could identify with his inherent need for validation of self, an identity transmitted by blood. She had sought it as a child from her mother. Receiving rejection, she behaved as a child seeking affection did: since her name, Taylor, seemed to offend her mother, she stopped answering to it, and soon, no one called her by that name. She became Monique. "Michael," Monique said, "I want to believe because you obviously do, but . . ."

Michael leaned over the desk, facing her headlong. "Will you tell them he didn't do it?"

Monique shook her head amazed that he would ask or that she was even considering his request. "I could tell you anything," she said flippantly as a self-directed jolt.

"No," he replied. "If you say yes, I know you'll keep your word. Will you do it?"

"Michael," Solomon cut in between them, "you want a man for a father. Give this man a chance to be what you want him to be. Tell him to turn himself in."

Michael glowered at them both, then stormed from the room.

Monique dragged her glum face from the after-image of Michael. A wee smile began to form across her visage as she stared up at Solomon, but it suddenly fell short of turning up the corners of her mouth. He was looking at her with an odd look, an expression she had never seen before; but so telling, it filled her with an awful, sinking sensation. The silence loomed between them like a heavy mist.

"Twice I asked you who owned *T's Place,* and twice you denied knowing."

His voice was barely audible; his tone devoid of emotion. Monique felt the dread she'd only sensed earlier, but her mind refused to accept what her heart tried to tell her. She shuddered inwardly. "I was going to tell you," she said with anxiety consuming her whole being.

He stared at her a second longer, his eyes beams of hostility. "Consider me told . . . Boss Taylor," he said in an ice-cold voice. Pushing himself from the desk, he strode from the room.

With the indictment of his tone ringing in her ears, Monique was too stunned to move. She sat there staring after him with her mouth hanging open. Questions that begged to differ from the sudden desolation that swept over her whizzed around in her head. Bolting from her seat, she raced from the room, calling after him.

"Solomon!"

Fifteen

Slammed shut, the door rattled on its hinges.

Solomon stomped in his office. A cold, implacable expression engraved on his face, he stared absently at the desk.

He felt a strange ambivalence, a sensation at odds with his conscience. His pride was angry, his heart still soft with love for her. But he was a man of principles! Truth and trust between people claiming to love each other were essential. He simply couldn't forgive her; even though it hurt. She had made a fool out of him.

He had taken her into his home, shared her with his daughter, and in return, she shoved a sharp blade in his heart. He didn't mind her money. It was the lie he couldn't take, he thought, thinking if she lied about this, more lies would follow, if they hadn't already occurred.

On two separate occasions, he fumed silently, she looked him dead in the face with her alluring amber eyes in a guileless gaze and lied through her perfectly even white teeth.

It wasn't Monique who was too kind-hearted. He had made it easy for her, lapping up the attention she bestowed on him like a lovestruck puppy. He had been all too eager, too accepting and too willing to believe that no such ugliness could come from such a beautiful woman. He should have known: if it looks too good to be true, then it wasn't.

Picking up the small container of paper clips from the desk, Solomon flung the plastic box indiscriminately across the room. Paper clips swarmed against the walls like a bevy of bees, then dropped with just a prickle of sound.

The door opened with a flourish. Solomon spun facing Monique. Though he knew she would come, the shock of her ran through his body. He dreaded the confrontation. Yet, he was perversely gladdened by her presence.

Mouth pursed, his dark, hooded eyes pierced the distance between them. He didn't have far to search in his memory for recollection of what lay beneath the new set of clothes she wore, a black, teal and white checkered pantsuit. She looked like the college student he had once thought she was, he mused. But she was an accomplished lover who had taught him lessons in sensory delights.

He could tell she was wound up. Staring at him indecisively, she was wringing her hands, her eyes lit by anxiety. To his profound consternation, he was aware of her. He felt want threatening to block off his air passage.

Reminding himself of her deceit and betrayal, Solomon forced wayward desires to shut down. His brows descending over cold, brown eyes, he said with barely concealed hostility, "Get out of here, Monique."

"Solomon, will you tell me what's going on?" she asked, gesturing with her hands like a child in trouble.

He snorted, then feinted innocence in reply. "Why, Miss Taylor Monique Robbins, I haven't the faintest idea what you're talking about."

With her eyes squinted in a baffled gaze, she begged an explanation. "Why did you walk away? What's wrong? What did I do?"

He took a menacing step forward, and she backed up, her eyes darting nervously. It increased the timbre of his anger, and he bit off a curse.

"I'm sorry," she said softly. "But you're so mad. I don't know what I did that was so wrong."

"You dare say that to me," he snapped. "You've been lying for months and you don't know what you did that was so wrong? If I had known you were the owner, I never would have . . . Never mind," he said, waving a disgusted hand at her. "Forget it; the past is done."

"Solomon, what are you saying, that because I own the club, that changes things between us?"

He stared at her wordlessly with a hard, narrowed gaze. "Yes," he said shortly.

"Solomon, that doesn't make sense," she said.

"It doesn't matter now."

"It does matter," she argued, stomping her foot. "How can you just turn off your feelings like, like a faucet?"

"The seasons will continue to change, the sun will continue to rise and set, and the world will continue to rotate on its axis," he said, as much in response to his own torment as the pain and disbelief glittering in her eyes. He stared back into her troubled gaze, saw the tremor touched her smooth lips and discounted her agony. Even without her, he would continue to exist, as well. "We're just tiny particles. We'll hardly be missed."

"What are you saying?" she asked as if stunned into breathlessness.

The question aroused a fight between his principles and his emotions. He felt her distress like a tangible substance with many capabilities. It had the taste of guilt, and it soured on his stomach. Suddenly, he was very, very tired. "I'm saying that I'll get over it," he said, dropping into the chair behind the desk.

"Solomon!"

"Don't worry," he said, opening the briefcase on his desk. "You'll get over it, too."

Storming across the room to stand in front of the desk, staring at him from over the top of the briefcase, she sputtered in demand, "How can you be so . . . so . . . ?"

"So what?" he replied, setting a folder on the desk. "Practical." He closed the lid on the briefcase. "Sensible," setting the briefcase on the floor behind the desk. "Honest," cutting her a mocking brow. "Because it's me, and I can only be what I am. Now, it's getting late. Since you're here, you might as well get ready for work. Assuming I'm still in charge . . . Ms. Robbins," he said, cocking a questioning brow at her.

"Solomon!" she yelled, pounding on the desk with her fist.

With the folder in his hands, he looked at her contrarily. In calm summation, he said, "This is not the time nor place for this discussion anyway."

"Are you coming to the hotel after closing?"

"No," he said, his eyes scanning the contents of the folder.

"Solomon, we need to talk about this," she implored him.

"There is no this to talk about, Monique. Or do you prefer Taylor? *T's Place*," he mused aloud mockingly. He recalled snatches of overheard conversations among members of the staff: Dennis and Michael's macho conspiring, the references to *Miss Thang* and knowing smirks when they asked him about her absence. They knew. Everybody knew except him. He felt like an absolute idiot. Shaking his head bemused, his expression tight with hostility, he said in a musing tone, "What a fool I've been." Dropping the folder onto the desk, he added, "The entire staff knows."

"No," she denied, shaking her head emphatically.

He didn't argue. The look on her face supported her truth. Only it wasn't true. They knew in spite of her attempts to hide it. He was the only one of whom she had pulled off the ruse successfully.

"Please, let me . . ."

"I don't want to hear it now," he said, then contradicted himself. "Were you ever going to tell me the truth? Or did the plan call for you to string me along a little longer? Well Ms. Robbins, I've been down this road before, and I'm not traveling it again." He was irrational, knew it, but felt helpless to stop the flow of hurtful words. "Just like Elaine," he said, as if talking to himself. "All nice and sweet and agreeable in the beginning, then when my defeat was certain, here comes the inevitable change," he said mockingly. "The manipulation begins in earnest. But by then, it would be too late; I would be committed, imprisoned in another nightmare."

"Solomon, I wanted to tell you sooner," she said.

He remembered their first night in the hotel, right after the fire. She had been so vulnerable and delicate, so in desperate need of what little he could give her. He was proud that what he offered answered her needs. Relenting to her request, he shared his most vulnerable thoughts with her. His truths, he snorted bitterly. "But you were so thoroughly enjoying watching me make a fool of myself . . ."

She cut him off. "That's not true," she protested excitedly. "You know that's not true."

"No," he said, a slight thaw in his tone, his look. But replacing the scowl on his expression was a grave, empty mask.

"Let me explain," she begged in a tear-smothered soft voice.

Solomon steeled himself against the gentle softness of her voice. He stared at her as if seeing her for the first time. His embittered mind pictured a parade of two women— Elaine and Monique—marching side-by-side, waving a wad of money under his nose as they passed him by. He wasn't jealous, but taunted by the symbolism that challenged his manhood. "How much do I owe you?" he asked, rising in one fluid motion.

Involuntarily, Monique jumped back. He glowered at her, and she swallowed hard. "What are you talking about?" she asked.

"The car," he replied. "How much did it cost to have it repainted?"

"Solomon, please."

"How much?" he demanded, patting his coat as if in search of something. He leaned down to rifle through the briefcase. When he stood, he held a checkbook in his hand. He leaned over the desk, uncapping a pen.

"Solomon, it was no big deal," she replied, shifting from one foot to the other, uneasy.

He stared at her with fierce dignity outlining his face. "Money never is a big deal to those who have it. How much?" his tone echoing harshness.

"Three hundred-seventy-five," she said weakly. "Solomon, how can I make this up to you?"

Tearing the check from the book, he replied, "Don't toss any crumbs my way, Monique." He held out the check to her. At her refusal to extend her hand, he stuffed it down the collar of her jumpsuit.

"Solomon!" she cried, balling the check in her hand, tears forming in her eyes.

"Get out, Monique," he replied.

"No. I won't leave until you talk to me," she said, her hands balled in fists at her sides.

"Well, it's your office. I'll get out."

"Solomon, I'm not Elaine," she said, tears streaming down her face. "I'm nowhere near like her."

Unmoved by her tears, he replied, "No, you're not. At least, I'll give her that much. She has more pride than you do."

"What happened?" Jason asked, mouthing the words.

"It's obvious what happened," Francine whispered in an irascible tone. "Look at her. She didn't produce one genuine smile all night. The love affair is over."

"I bet it was just a misunderstanding," Jason replied.

Francine rolled her eyes at him. "Men," she chortled in disgust.

"What about men?" Jake asked, sliding up to the bar.

Francine snapped up her tray, then vanished to the back room.

"What did I say?"

With a glazed look of despair on her face, Monique was ambling about the downstairs of *T's Place*. The club was as quiet as a tomb, the staff subdued after closing. She heard them whispering behind her back, knew she and Solomon were the topic of their conversation. They were trying to guess what had happened between the co-managers. She wished she knew.

She wrestled with her thoughts, juxtaposing the joyful past to the painful present in her mind. She didn't want to believe things had gone so bad, so fast between them. She expected they would have the occasional disagreement, but nothing with such a devastating end.

Pondering what more could she have done, she wondered if she dare try again to reason with him. That he so callously and abruptly dismissed his feelings was incredible, as was the excruciating sense of loss she felt.

With a trembling sigh in her bosom, she stopped to stare forlornly toward the back exit. Solomon was already gone. He didn't even say goodnight . . . told Leon to tell her to lock up, as if he could no longer bear the sight of her.

This devastation she felt was worse than that which she had undergone after Anthony's violent episode. She felt as if the breath of life had been sucked from her body. Solomon couldn't have hurt her more than had he physically struck her. No pride he had said, she recalled, tears stinging her eyes.

She sniffed, dabbed at her eyes with her fingers. He was right. As far as he was concerned, she was prideless, shameless. Pride was cold and shame unfulfilling. She preferred the warmth and satisfaction she felt from loving him. But unlike before when he left her, he took them with him, leaving her to feel the biting chill of his pride and a wretched emptiness.

He had talked to her as if she were some spoiled, pampered woman who used money as a leverage to get her way—which was so blatantly inconceivable, it was almost laughable. She swallowed the lump of regret lodged in her throat.

Okay, she was wrong to withhold the truth from him for as long as she did, she told herself, a stab of guilt in her bosom. Knowing he was a serious man by nature, she should have never assumed he was changed by loving her and being loved by her. But in her defense, she couldn't have known he still felt so strongly.

Tiredly, she climbed on stage and sat at the piano. She opened the lid and fingered the notes. The acoustics produced clear and distinct notes of melancholy.

Well, she mused sadly, she had the answer to one question that had been plaguing her for quite some time. Love was indeed a paradox. She couldn't think of anything else in the entire world that had the power to bring her as much joy as it had brought pain.

"Monique, you about ready?" Leon asked.

Her hands rested on a discord as she looked up at him dumbfounded. "What?"

"It's three-forty-five," he said. "Everybody's gone."

"Oh," she said. "I'm sorry, Leon. Just let me get my things."

Where the hell was she?

Solomon showed no indication that he was haunted by the question as he passed out checks and assignment schedules to the staff the following afternoon. Despite his outward calm, the passage of time reconfirming Monique's absence, the more his uneasiness grew.

All were assembled in the Employees Room, except Monique. He had a check for her, too, he mused, placing it at the bottom of checks in his hands. It was three in the afternoon, and she had neither called nor had been reachable since seven this morning. Guilt was eating a hole in his stomach.

"Is Michael coming back?"

Snapped back to business at Francine's inquiry, Solomon replied, "I don't know." His mouth twisted wryly, he recalled that Michael didn't return after storming out of Monique's office yesterday. He hoped Michael's absence meant he was trying to persuade his father to turn himself in. He knew the young man had been thus far unsuccessful.

"Well, we're going to need another waiter," Jake said.

The staff erupted into a spit of excitement, talking among themselves about the huge crowd they expected for the rest of the week until Saturday night. The Juneteenth festivities meant more tips. Underlying their comments, however, Solomon sensed an unvoiced question. Curiosity about Monique punctuated their tones and constantly exchanged glances: he shared it elsewhere. He knew he had created speculation after bolting out of the club before closing this morning. Even more uncharacteristic was the fact that he had left her unprotected, he recalled with self-loathing.

Just because he was concerned about her safety didn't mean he had forgiven her, he reminded himself, his composed mask slipping into a grim expression. After all, a man without pride and principles was worthless.

But buried beneath his bruised self-esteem, deep, deep inside, he still burned with his love for her. In time, it would wane and ultimately extinguish itself from his soul, and he would be free to live again. A cynical inner voice promptly cut through his thought, scoffing at the empty years ahead of him. Just imagining it made him feel bereft and desolate.

"Solomon?"

Shaking his head as if to clear the painful, jagged thoughts from his mind, Solomon said, "I'm sorry, Jake. What were you saying?"

"With a sell-out crowd coming Saturday night," Jake continued, "we're really going to be swamped. If we can't get a replacement for Michael . . ."

Solomon cut him off. "I've already interviewed a replacement," he said, passing a check to Dennis. "Francine, I'm counting on you to show her the ropes and get her trained real fast. She's had some experience according to her application, but I haven't had time to double check it."

"What station?" Dennis asked.

A humorless smile broke through Solomon's business facade. He knew full well Dennis's interest. "Don't worry, Dennis, you're working the stage area downstairs."

"So that means I got upstairs?" Francine asked, none too pleased.

"Just tonight for training purposes," Solomon said hastily. He couldn't risk losing another irate employee. "For the concert, you and Dennis will definitely work downstairs."

"That still may not be enough," Jason said.

"Monique may have to help out upstairs," Solomon said. He caught the tail end of the sly look Francine exchanged with the others. He knew what was on their minds: they believed he was unaware of the pool they had started, placing bets on whether or not Monique showed up at all.

He had been calling the hotel ever since he got home last night, or rather, in the wee hours of the morning, he recalled, irritation settling over his expression. Not until he had answered the appropriate questions did the operator ring her room. After several rings, the operator came on the line to take a message. He had even stopped at the hotel on his way to the club and was escorted by Four Seasons Hotel Chief of Security up to her room. She was not in, but had been seen healthy and alive by the maid: it was the only reason he wasn't completely beside himself. The hotel offered excellent security—if only she'd stay put.

"Leon, keep your eyes open tonight," he said absently as he glanced up at the clock on the back wall.

"Right," Leon nodded, accepting the check. "I got two

more guys coming in tonight to work the rest of the weekend. Longer if we need them. They'll be here at seven."

"Good," Solomon replied. "Don't forget what we discussed."

"If she comes in, I'll be at her side at all times," Leon said.

"Are we expecting trouble?" Dennis asked, his eyes darting back and forth between Solomon and Leon.

Solomon looked at him as if weighing the question. Officer Pierce's lack of success locating Byron Henderson could mean just that, he mused. But he didn't want to scare the staff needlessly. "No," he replied evenly. "Just a precautionary measure."

"You think someone's gonna go after Monique because of the fire?" Dennis asked.

Solomon picked up the subtle increase in tension coming from Dennis. Or was it his own anxiety rising, he wondered, eyeing him stealthily. He'd found the pretty-faced waiter to be self-serving. He didn't particularly care for Dennis as a man, though he was faultless as an employee. He concealed his suspicion about this newfound concern of his under a forced half-smile.

"I want everybody to be alert," Solomon said with emphasis, looking at each of them one by one. "Nothing happened last night and I expect nothing to happen tonight." Short of going out looking for Monique himself then locking her up, *if* he could find her, he didn't know what else to do. "But it doesn't pay to relax our guard." If anything happened to her, it would be his fault. Hurt or no hurt, his behavior was unforgivable, he chided himself. "Got it?" he asked.

At the nod of heads, Solomon passed all but one check to the twins. "Okay, that's it. Let's get busy. Oh, the new person is Rebecca Young. Jake, Jason, let's go over the liquor sheet now. If Monique comes in, call me. I'll be in the stockroom," he said to the others dismissing them.

"If, she gets here," Solomon heard someone mutter as he stole another look at the clock.

"She's here."

The strong velvet-edged voice was a deep buzz in Solomon's ear. He would recognize it anywhere. His gaze led the rest, zooming across the room. Anxiety abating and anger renewing itself, he frowned fiercely in a desperate attempt to resist the captivating picture Monique made. She stood poised in the doorway, stylishly dressed and infinitely pleased with herself.

She looked the part of a sharp, high-paid executive, he thought, unable to tear his gaze from her even if he wanted to. Her hair was parted in the center and pulled on top of her head in a braided ball. A red two-piece suit of a shoulder padded jacket and pencil-slim skirt with a slit on the side that showed off her thigh and leg. Three-inch, high heel shoes in black and red capped the ensemble. She looked friendly, yet unapproachable. It didn't negate his awareness of her.

"You missed me?" she said to all, but her eyes were trained on Solomon as she sashayed right up to him.

He could tell she'd been shopping while he was worrying about her needlessly, he thought. "You're late," he said with icicles in his tone.

"Why Mr. Thomas," she said sweetly, "I didn't know you cared."

Standing so close, he smelled her lilac perfume, a passion fragrance on her soft skin, and the warm heat of her disrupted his senses. A rush of feeling that was elemental and cogently familiar coursed through him. Fighting his erogenous excitement, he glared down at her, felt his mouth working in his face, but no words came. He remembered they were not alone and barked, "What are you people standing around for? Get to work."

She arched an elegant brow at him. "Have you told them yet?" she asked.

Solomon noticed from a corner of his gaze the staff lingering, bunched up in a huddle waiting for a showdown. Glaring down at Monique, she smiled broadly up at him. He wondered what game she was playing at.

"No," she said, answering her own question lightly. "Well, I'll leave it up to you, Mr. Thomas," she said walking off, with a deliberate sway of her hips. He followed her exit with a hot ache in his groin and a snarly frown in his expression. He trained that look on the staff, and they hurried from the room.

The high energy of excitement seeped through the intercom in Monique's office Saturday night. *T's Place* was full to capacity. The audience was eagerly awaiting the start of the KoKo Taylor show.

Listening to their enthusiasm, Monique wished just some of that energy would rub off on her as she depressed the bar, ending the sound. She was sitting behind the desk, the mirror from her small suitcase raised, as she began putting on her make-up.

She spread foundation evenly across her face and neck, applied a blush, then selected a colored pencil from a case. She lined her lips, her eyes and darkened her lashes and elongated her brows. Applying lipstick to her mouth, she then tossed her make-up back in the suitcase.

She didn't know how much longer she could wear her phony gay mask, she thought, staring at her dejected reflection. Despite the pampered treat she'd given herself, no facial in the world could bring a lush radiance to her eyes and brilliant polish to her cheeks like one man.

It was amazing the things one remembered when something cherished was lost, she mused, patting and pinching her cheeks. She pushed them up in a smile, but letting them go, the corners of her mouth drooped in a frown, allowing a lachrymose little sigh to escape her lips.

Solomon didn't want her. It was time to face the indisputable truth. All the tricks and seductive taunts had failed, the flip tongue, the devil-may-care attitude, flashy styles of dress and even wearing her hair down at the club, which she never used to do.

She couldn't give up without trying, she rationalized to her somber reflection. Solomon must have uncapped a stubborn well of persistence in her she didn't know she possessed.

Or, maybe it was just the memories of what she was going to miss that drove her to behave so brazenly the past two days.

Her thoughts rolled back on a pure and unsullied image of Solomon, and her eyes glazed with erotic remembrances. She marveled at the sight of him in her mind, poised buck naked at the window staring out over the city. Chocolate-coated, he was strong in body, rich in character, flavored sweet in love.

A lovely, wide, warming smile spread across her face and coursed through her veins. She sighed languidly, envisioning his tall, supple and superb figure, molded of square shoulders and wide chest that tapered into a narrow waist. Beautiful, powerful, yet slim thighs created a flutter in her bosom. Her enraptured gaze paused a second: she gulped desire down her throat, then trailed long legs with muscular calves. Her legs twitched together like crickets under the desk as a poignant ache settled in her loins. "Splendid," she murmured breathlessly.

A knock on the door jolted Monique from her hot, enticing muse.

"Who's there?"

"It's me, Miss Robbins."

Excitement and anticipation mounted, her heart thudded expectantly. He wanted pride. Well, she'd give him pride, Monique vowed silently as she squared her shoulders.

"Just a minute please," she replied sweetly, launching the

game. She cleaned off the desk, stashing her dressing items in a corner behind the desk. She staged herself in front of the desk, pasted a smile of nonchalance on her face, tried to school her heart to a normal beat. Failing, she drew a deep breath. "Come in."

Solomon walked in with his customary purposeful strides, words on his lips. The words stilled on his opened mouth and he froze, his hand still on the doorknob. His astonished gaze melted the distance between them, gobbling her with his eyes.

Watching his eyes dilate with desire, she basked in her power to excite him still. But it was short-lived, for just as quickly, the look metamorphosed into contempt, his brow pulling into an affronted frown.

"That's what you're wearing?"

The slight crack in his voice, though coolly disapproving, pleased her. "Yes," she said, flinging her hair as she pivoted like a model to give him full view of her outfit. Even by her tastes, it was an outrageous costume with a low scooped neck and uneven hemline that revealed her cleavage and left thigh in metallic tangerine that caressed her slender figure. She'd been saving it for tonight.

"Don't you like it?" she asked as she struck a piquant pose, one hand perched on her hip, the other idling gracefully at her side. She lifted her chin a little higher, smiled a little wider. She wanted him to take note of her and remember what he would be missing. He tugged at the tie around his neck, and she saw his Adam's apple bob. A tingling delight coursed through her.

"I'm sure it's fine," he said without inflection, his expression unreadable.

A sense of despair teased her conscience, and her confidence waned. She marshaled a tone that would not betray her humiliating disappointment before she spoke. "What can I do for you, Mr. Thomas?"

"Mr. Bookman wants to collect the cashier's check," he replied. "Miss KoKo Taylor is about to take the stage."

"Oh, yes," she replied, turning sideways to pick up the envelope from her desk, "money up front before the show. Here it is," passing the envelope to Solomon.

"Well, I better get this check to them so the show can get started," he said, turning to leave.

"Are you coming to the after-party at the hotel?" she asked eagerly.

Looking at her over his shoulder, he stared at her with lifeless, iron-brown eyes. In a cold and exact tone, he said, "No."

"Not even for a little while?"

He paused a second, his back to her. "Not even."

She watched his exit with hope submerged under a tide of grief. He left the door open, and the strains of the opening song drifted into her office, as KoKo Taylor sang:

"Don't put your hands on me. You and I may disagree. Don't put your hands on me."

"I'm not the only person who drives a Vet," he said with a irritated growl in his tone.

"Then why did you have yours painted black, Mr. Henderson?"

"You know why," Byron shouted contentiously. Holed up in this standard dull interrogation room with two Peace Officers serving as Arson Investigators for the Houston Fire Department, he was fed up answering the same questions over and over again. One, an Officer Pierce, he recalled seeing at his son's home. The other, whose name was Sharky, he'd met at eight this morning. "Can I get a cigarette?"

Sharky, a slimly built man with a pale complexion and unruly red hair knocked one from a pack and passed to him.

Lighting the cigarette with the lighter he dug out of his shirt pocket, Byron said, "As soon as I heard about the fire and realized whose place it was, I knew she'd put the finger on me. Hell, I just got out. I didn't want back in. Certainly you can understand that."

Pierce and Sharky exchanged glances as he puffed on the cigarette, pulling the ashtray from the far corner of the table near. "We'll be right back," Officer Pierce said.

Left to smoke in silence, Byron stretched in the chair. He had turned himself in at the badgering of Michael, he recalled, blowing smoke rings. His son had gone on an excursion, driving around town until he'd found him at one of his favorite dives. He was safe there with a bunch of ex-cons who could care less that he was wanted for questioning.

All night long, the boy pleaded and begged. He talked and reasoned, trying to convince him that Monique would help, rather than further exacerbate the situation. Snorting, he didn't know which one of them was the bigger idiot. But one thing the boy had said made sense, he mused, leaning over the table.

"In this society, if you run, regardless of your innocence, they'll think you're guilty. Turn yourself in, you at least create doubt in your guilt, and they may start looking elsewhere for the real culprit."

The interrogators returned. "You used that car to run your wife down," Sharky said.

"I paid for that," Byron replied defensively. Stabbing the air with the cigarette, his voice rising, "You can't keep throwing that in my face. I paid for that!"

"Then, who would want to frame you, Mr. Henderson?" Officer Pierce asked. "Your son maybe?"

"Don't be stupid," Byron retorted, angling in the chair. "That boy adores me," he said, a hint of pride in his tone. "If it weren't for him, I'd be out the country by now . . . somewhere in Mexico."

"Right," Officer Pierce replied with a significant lifting of his brow.

"I came in on my own, remember," Byron said disgruntled.

"So what?" Pearce replied unimpressed. "It doesn't prove a thing. If you know something that will help your cause, now is the time to speak up."

"I'm no rat. Go out and do your jobs," Byron shot back.

"He doesn't know anything," Sharky said to Pearce. "Let's just lock him up. He did it. I know you did it, Henderson," he reiterated, leaning into Byron's face.

"You're getting old Byron," Pearce said. "Can you handle another nickel in the joint?"

Intrigued by the taunt, Byron bit down on his lips in a sign of contemplation.

"Come on," Pearce cajoled, "make a liar out of my partner here. Give us something to prove you're not guilty of starting that fire."

Byron stared back and forth at his interrogators intently. He liked freedom, he mused. It was different on the outside, but a far sight better than the Huntsville Hilton. If he went back so soon on the heels of his parole, things would be worse for him. They probably wouldn't let him near the computers. No, he couldn't go back.

"All right," he said irascibly. "Somebody else drives a red Vet. I saw it parked on her street one night." He even tried to trail her, but she lost him, he recalled, suppressing his laughing emotions from showing.

"Yeah, who?" Sharky asked with disbelief.

Sixteen

"I see you're still sitting in the dark."

Solomon squinted and raised his hands to shield his eyes from the wave of light as it filled the family room. "You're back," he said, his voice void of emotion. "What time is it?"

"About five-thirty," Ariana replied.

"Where did you go?" He remembered her saying "good-bye" early this morning, but not much else. He was exhausted, the emotional skirmishes over the past several days had taken their toll. He was contemplating his resignation from *T's Place*.

"I went with Monique to her church, remember?" she said, dropping on the ottoman in front of the chair where he sat.

With his head pressed against the back of the chair and eyes closed, Solomon steeled himself against the incredible longing that welled in him at just the mention of her name. He swallowed it in the suffocating sensation of regret tightening his throat. "I thought I told you to stay away from her," he said.

"You suggested it," she replied, "you didn't say I had to obey you."

"I don't want you to get hurt."

"From Monique?" she replied with typical teenage incredulity. "How?"

"I already told you she has a tendency to lie," he replied.

"She hasn't lied to me," she replied. "She didn't lie to you, either."

"Stop right there," he warned. "You're treading dangerous waters." This was Monday, his day off. He couldn't remember the last time he'd eaten; neither had he gotten much sleep. He didn't want to hear about anything remotely connected to *his boss*. His feelings were still too raw to discuss.

Ariana shrugged. "Okay." In the seconds passing, she tapped a rhythmic beat on the ottoman. "You wouldn't believe the number of hungry people there are," she said. "I think we fed half of them today," with a chuckle in her voice.

"Sounds like you had a good time," he commented. At least, Ariana was doing something positive in the community. But she was with a woman known for her unselfishness. He wondered whether she was forgiving, as well.

"Yea, I did," she replied, a proud smile in her voice. "As fast as we set plates out, they were snatched up. I thought we were going to run out of food, but Monique must have cooked for two armies. When we left the church, we took the rest of the food to that rest home for senior citizens not far from here. I got enough for our dinner, too. You hungry?"

"No, thank you. I'm not hungry."

"Tomorrow I'm going with Monique to Haven House. She's . . ."

Lifting his head, he opened his eyes and flashed her a look of irritation. "I don't want to hear about it," he ground out.

"Dad, why don't you call her?" Ariana said, pleading in her tone.

Don't you understand that I can't? he wanted to shout at Ariana. With his lips pressed together tightly, shame and regret shone keenly in his eyes. He had hurt Monique deeply, flung her apology in her face like a backhanded slap. Monique could never forgive him, he mused, shaking his head unconsciously. She certainly wouldn't forget: the pictures of Tevis were testament to her memory of abusive men. He couldn't blame her. Resigning from *T's Place* was his only recourse, the only apology he could offer.

"I don't understand what you think she did that was so bad," Ariana said with impatient chiding.

He had been asking himself that very question for days now. He'd gotten no comfort whatsoever in pride and principles, twin excuses that held no weight with his heart. All they'd given him was a sense of permanent sorrow.

"You're a child, that's why," he replied to Ariana. With a weary sigh, he rested his head and closed his eyes. "You're too young to understand, Ariana, so just stay out of grown-up business."

"Right, fall back on your safety cushion," she snapped. "Play it safe. Is that how it's done, Daddy?"

"Don't sass me, young lady," he warned, but there was no bite in his voice.

"You think you know everything, but you don't know nothing!" she said, springing up from her seat.

Solomon sat up alert, a suspicious line stretching across his mouth. He stared intently at Ariana, really seeing her. She was fidgety, not just excited by her outing. "What is that supposed to mean?"

"You asked me why mama got rid of me, well, do you really want to know?" she quipped, traipsing from the room.

With a pondering mutter deep in his chest, Solomon scampered up to follow her. "Ariana?" he called, walking through the house. "Answer me, girl." He found Ariana in her room, lying across the bed. "Ariana."

She angled her head facing him. "What?"

"All right," he said in an admonishing tone, "don't use that tone of voice with me." He dropped to the edge of the opposite bunk bed. "Tell me what's going on. Please."

"So you can cut me out of your life like you did Monique?"

Solomon sucked in an astonished breath as the taunt

slashed across his chest. A pained expression shadowed his face. "That's nonsense, Ariana, and you know it," he said softly.

"Is it?"

"Ariana, make sense," he commanded impatiently. "If you have something to say, say it."

She studied him with a fractious look, then rolled over to sit up, her legs folded Indian-style across her thighs. Seconds passed with Ariana looking at Solomon as if trying to read his thoughts in his blank face before she spoke. "You asked me what was going on between me and Mom when I first got here."

"Mom and I," he corrected absently as he ran his hands across his face. At her silence, he said, "Well?"

"I didn't know how to tell you before," she said floundering. "I'm still not sure I can make you understand. Then, when Monique and I talked . . ."

He should have known, Solomon sighed heavily in disgust. "What does she have to do with it?"

Ariana smacked her lips in annoyance. "If it weren't for her, I probably wouldn't be telling you at all. She told me to just tell you how I feel, to give you a chance at least."

Solomon gritted his teeth, then sighed heavily in acquiescence.

"She told me about this dream she has sometimes. She had it again last night," she added as if it were an aside. "She says it doesn't make sense, but when she wakes up from it, she has this bad feeling, you know."

He hadn't heard this story, which was not surprising, he mused. Monique was true to form, afraid to trust her secrets to anyone but the dead. "No, I don't, but I'm sure you'll give me some excuse," he quipped in reply as he slapped his hands together in a sign of impatience.

"It's about a little girl. She's hiding in a dark place and she's afraid of something and she's crying. She thought the little girl must have been her, so she asked her mama about it. Her mom said she didn't know, but Monique doesn't believe her. It's like a secret between them."

"So, what's the point and how does this story relate to you?"

"I feel as if mom's keeping a secret from me."

Perplexed, he tugged at his ear. "What secret?"

"I don't know."

Famous last words, Solomon thought.

"She's always signing me up for something. I don't understand it. It's like she wants to get rid of me for some reason. She's always finding something for me to do. Community Choir, swim team, piano lessons," she enumerated on her fingers. "I don't have a life!"

"Honey," Solomon said patiently, suppressing his laughter, "why don't you just tell her that your plate is already full?"

"Huh?" Ariana replied, looking at Solomon as if he'd spoken a foreign language.

"Tell her you have enough activities and don't want anymore," he explained.

"She won't listen! We never get a chance to sit down and talk to each other. Either I'm on my way to some activity or she has to go to a meeting or out-of-town on business. The only time we do talk is when she's giving me some lecture on the importance of expanding my horizons, or networking with different people and stuff like that. She wants to *raise me right,*" she summed up sarcastically, rolling her eyes.

"Ariana," Solomon said with patience, "your mama is just trying to provide you with different kinds of experiences that will be beneficial later in your life."

"But I don't want to be raised," she declared, adding with mockery, "I'm not some farm animal."

Solomon understood what Elaine was doing. Quite frankly, he was pleased to know that she had not abandoned their dream to give Ariana a better start in life than they had. He did not understand his daughter's rebellion against opportunities that would improve her chances to level the field on which she would one day have to compete.

"Ariana, what do you want? Don't give me 'I don't know.' Tell me exactly what it is you want."

"I want to be loved, Daddy."

There was something so esoterically profound about Ariana's rejoinder, that Solomon paused to think about what he heard from the mouth of his baby. *Tread carefully.* He heard the warning echo in his head, feeling as if he were in a minefield: the wrong step, and a bomb would erupt, wiping out every wish, hope and dream he and Elaine planned for Ariana.

"I feel like she's pushing me away for some reason," Ariana said, her expression sad. "I don't know what I've done to her. All I can figure out is that something is going on she doesn't want me to know about. What," she said, bunching up her shoulders, "I don't know. She's keeping a secret from me. Just like Monique's mother is keeping something from her."

Watching the tears welling in the corners of her eyes, Solomon traded beds and sat next to Ariana. He didn't have an answer, but he could give her this, he thought, draping an arm around her shoulder.

"She's not sick or dying, is she?" Ariana asked through her sniffles.

Solomon's first reaction was to scold Ariana for coming up with yet another nonsensical idea. But he bit back the chiding words on his tongue, realizing Ariana's insecure feelings were not her fault. Rather, Elaine had sent a warped message. He had sent a few himself, he thought, hugging Ariana affectionately. "No, she's not ill."

"Will you call her and get her to see my point?" Ariana asked sniffing, wiping her nose. "She won't listen to me. I know she won't."

"Yea, I'll call her," Solomon promised, kissing Ariana on the top of her head. "I'll try."

"What about Monique?"

Solomon sighed heavily, his hands still enveloping Ariana in his embrace. He never wanted anyone as badly as he wanted Monique who owned his soul. The need nearly shattered his decision to stay away. But he couldn't succumb to his fantasy's desires, he reminded himself. At the very least, he owed Monique a debt of gratitude for helping Ariana. He'd thank her, hand in his resignation, then he and Ariana would take a vacation. "Baby, I know you like Monique, but I think it's best that you stop seeing her."

"But dad!"

"No, buts. That's final."

"You shouldn't have gone back there."

Lines of tear tracks staining her face, Monique sniffled in reply. The Redmons returned to Houston early this morning. Only, she didn't have the energy for Patricia's company. She didn't want to share her misery.

Sitting in bed in her hotel room, pillows propped at her back, she looked vacant and spent, felt as if her whole body was engulfed in tides of weariness and despair. Holding a glass of wine next to her bosom, she chuckled a bittersweet sound at the image reoccurring in her mind.

After dropping Ariana home, she recalled, she'd gone by her old place. She ambled around the remains, everything dried by the sun, and finally, reached the concrete slab section that used to be her bedroom. The first place she and Solomon made love had been the first to go in the fire, leaving her no bedroom, no love, she thought, sighing morosely at the bitter irony.

"The arson investigators are going to question Anthony in connection with the fire," she said in a lifeless voice.

"Anthony?"

"Yeah," she replied. "Byron told them that he saw Anthony hanging round my place, so they called me to confirm that he had come to the house."

"Oh, that's ridiculous!" Patricia said. "Why would Anthony set fire to your place? From what I've heard since we got back, he's got enough troubles of his own."

"Whatever," she dismissed. "I was in another world, so I missed all his hoopla," Monique said feebly in a mocking tone as she imbibed more wine.

"Besides," Patricia said, "how would Byron know that Anthony had gone to your house if he weren't hanging around himself?"

"I asked Officer Pierce," she said, chuckling sadly. "Byron told him he was trying to work up the courage to talk to me. Said I didn't respond to any of his letters from jail and he wanted me to know that he was sorry."

"Right!" Patricia chided sarcastically.

"I don't know," Monique said tiredly. Her mind went absolutely blank, like the future she saw for herself. She leaned over to the lamp table, reaching for the bottle of wine. Refilling her glass, she said, "I don't know anything anymore."

"Why don't you come stay at the house?" Patricia asked, moving from the chair to sit on the side of the bed.

Monique flashed a weak, half-smile. "You told me, didn't you? You told me to tell Solomon from the very beginning. And you didn't even know him then, but you read him right," she said, feeling as if her heart had literally sunk in her chest. "Aurelius was right, too," she said, as if speaking to herself as she stared across the way out the window. She absently noted it had started to rain. "I don't know people. Maybe I went into the wrong business. Maybe I need a place where I'm a staff of one."

"Monique, that's utter nonsense," Patricia scolded mildly. She reached for the glass as Monique raised it to her mouth. "Please, come to the house with me."

"Thanks, but I need to stay close to the club."

"It's Monday," she replied with frustration in her tone, "the club is closed today."

"That's all right," Monique said wearily as she took another swallow of wine. It was the only place she had left, the only tangible sign of her existence, and she wanted to be near it. It was where she could see Solomon, even if he didn't want anything to do with her.

"How much longer are you planning to call Four Seasons home?"

"I don't know," Monique said. "I'm supposed to look at an apartment upstairs next week. Someone is moving out."

"I didn't know they had apartments," Patricia said. She looked around the room with an indecisive expression on her face. "I don't see how you can stand it. I mean, it's nice and all, but when I think about how hard you worked and worked us to fix up the duplex, I can't picture you living in a hotel."

"Yeah, we had fun didn't we, me, you and Tevis," Monique said, a bit of a fond smile in her voice. Staring in the wineglass, she saw the ruin of her bedroom, and wild grief ripped through her. Though she tried not to think about it, inexorably, her mind returned to the painful parallel. "It was like a first love, you know. As if the bedroom had been decorated for him. Solomon was the first man to christen it. You know, it burned down first. Isn't that rich?" She shook her head regretfully as a tear rolled down her face.

"Monique," Patricia said with commiseration, "I hate to see you like this."

"I'll be all right," Monique replied, wiping the tears from her eyes with the back of her hand. "It's just going to take a little time, that's all. But I'll get him out of my system, and in a couple of weeks, you'll forget you even saw me looking like this." She tossed back her head and drained the glass.

"I think you've had enough of this," Patricia said, picking

up the bottle of wine on the lamp table next to the bed. She walked from the bedroom.

Monique heard pounding on the door. She looked toward the opening. "Patricia?"

"I got it," Patricia called back to her.

Seconds later, Ariana burst into the room with a backpack on her shoulder and tears streaming down her face.

"Ariana," Monique said in an astonished whisper. A tad of animation shadowed her face, and her heart reacted immediately. She stared greedily into the dark, keen eyes, so much like Solomon's, despite the glimmer of tears they contained. She moved too quickly, then stopped to get her balance that had been impaired by the wine she had consumed. "What's the matter?"

"He told me to stop seeing you," Ariana cried. "For no reason at all!"

Monique opened her arms, and Ariana dropped her backpack and collapsed on the bed against her. "Shhh," she cooed. "It's going to be all right."

"He's just unreasonable," Ariana cried. "He makes me sick!"

"Where he is now?" Monique asked.

"At home," Ariana said, "sitting in the dark like he's been doing. I know he still loves you, but he won't admit it."

"Your daddy is a proud man, that's all," Monique said softly. She had accepted the words and the truth of them with pain swaying through her heart. Solomon would not change his mind.

"It's stupid," Ariana said with sulky truculence. "Can I stay with you?"

Patricia returned, carrying a towel in her hand. She cleared her throat from the opening. Monique looked up, and she tossed her the towel.

"This is Ariana," Monique said, drying Ariana's face and arms with the towel. "Solomon's daughter."

"I gathered as much," Patricia said, a tone suspiciously

like amusement in her voice. "Look, it's after eight. Since you won't be alone, I'll call you tomorrow. Maybe we can do breakfast."

"Wait a second, I'll walk you down," Monique said. She needed to clear the alcohol buzz from her head.

Ten minutes after Monique left, Ariana became restless with her own company. She meandered about, walking into the living room and peering out the window. The light drizzle had cleared the patio of guests, but she didn't mind the rain. She retrieved her backpack from the floor in the bedroom and began digging through it, pulling out clothes. Locating a one-piece bathing suit, she began shoving the clothes back in the pack. There was a knock on the door, and she dropped everything to open it for Monique.

"Where's Monique?"

Ariana froze, panic filled her eyes. She tried to push the door closed, but the man was stronger.

"Oh, no you don't," he said, shoving the door open in her face.

Ariana screamed.

Biting on a fingernail, Monique returned inside the hotel. Heading for the elevator, she pondered what to do about Ariana. There was no way she could in all good conscience support her running away from home. Solomon would kill them both.

He probably thought she was a bad influence on Ariana and decided they shouldn't see each other anymore. For once, she agreed with him, she thought, absently stepping on the elevator car. Besides, it was hard on her having Ariana around. She was a constant reminder of what she could never have.

"Hold the door please!" someone called out.

Monique hurriedly pressed the appropriate button on the inside panel, and the doors sprang open. A man dressed in full rain gear walked on.

"Thanks," he said.

The doors closed, he punched a button, and the car stopped with a jolt. "Hello Monique," he said, pulling the rain hat from his head. "We finally get a chance to see each other."

It was ten o'clock, his child was not home, and the woman he once believed was his soulmate was nowhere to be found.

Solomon was prowling around his house, both cross and gnawed with anxiety. He was waiting for a call from a member of the security team of the Four Seasons.

He hadn't heard from Ariana since she stormed out of the house. He learned a couple of hours ago that she had hitched a ride to the hotel. One of the boys next door dropped her off.

He intended to let Ariana get her anger with him out of her system, then he'd bring her home. Only, he'd called the hotel several times and had gotten no answer. From the hotel's security chief, he ascertained that Monique was last seen talking to a tall, light-skinned woman with an accent. He guessed it was Patricia Redmon. But that was at eight, and no one had seen her since.

A sense of deja vu sneaked into his uneasiness, recalling once before wondering and worrying the whereabouts of Monique and Ariana. They were safe that time, he thought, but this time, he felt a knife-edged danger lurking in his senses.

A melancholy frown flitted across his features. He was losing the women in his life faster than he could count, he thought, feeling the sickening sensation of having his life plunging downward.

Maybe they had gone out for a ride in Monique's flashy,

expensive car, he mused, grasping for a reason to ease the tension in his body. But he'd seen Monique drive. In her hands, the Ferrari was a death toy.

The phone rang, and he raced to his bedroom to answer before the first ring completed. Snatching up the receiver, he said, "Hello."

Seventeen

The waiter looked inept, not at all suitable to his man's body.

"I swear, Mr. Thomas, I didn't have anything to do with setting that fire. I would never do anything like that. And I didn't touch your little girl. Tell him!" Dennis implored Ariana desperately.

"Shut up," Solomon said with impatient irritation. He locked eyes with Dennis in a visive grip. He felt murderous, his hands clenching and unclenching into fists at his sides.

"Dad, we still don't know where Monique is," Ariana said as she sidled next to Solomon.

The tone of her voice, soft and trembling with concern, held his rage in check. Solomon relaxed his hands, his combat posture.

"I know, baby," he said, absently draping an arm around her shoulders. "But I'll find her," he said, as if speaking to himself with conviction in his tone. He couldn't afford to be distracted by self-flagcllation, he told himself. Pity had no place in the sense of urgency he felt.

"Well, they kept him as long as they could."

Solomon heard the Four Seasons Chief of Security Matthew MacGregor, a sandy, redheaded man before he emerged from the bedroom into the living room of the hotel suite. He looked slightly uncomfortable in a suit, but his built-for-action body and competent manner inspired a sense of security.

When MacGregor came up to the room to check on Monique, he discovered Dennis holding Ariana hostage instead. Upon his arrival, Dennis began spilling his guts, Solomon recalled, staring contentiously at the young man. He confessed to carrying out pranks against Monique, but only after learning from Michael that Byron Henderson had turned himself in and identified Anthony Ward as a potential suspect in the fire.

"While he's still a suspect, they have no proof," MacGregor continued. "They've been trying to track down the lead he gave them. A doctor by the name of Anthony Ward."

Solomon looked at Dennis, his eyes conveying the fury within him. The waiter shriveled under the look: drawing into himself as if he were trying to become invisible on the couch.

"Where's Ward now?" he asked.

"I, I, I don't know," Dennis babbled in frightful reply. "I swear I haven't seen him in a week, not since he paid me after the fire."

MacGregor turned a repugnant, blue-eyed stare on Dennis before he spoke. "They suspect the good doctor has flown the coop. He was to have appeared in court this past Friday on federal charges for welfare fraud, but he didn't show up. There's an APB out on him."

"What are we supposed to do with him?" Solomon asked with bridled anger in his voice, nodding his head toward Dennis.

"Officer Pierce is coming with a sergeant from HPD to collect him," MacGregor replied.

The police action was all good and fine, Solomon thought angrily, but it didn't address his major concern. He felt his *pride* attacking his soul like a malignant cancer, fearful for Monique's safety.

"How did you know where Monique was staying?" he asked Dennis.

"Michael. Michael told me."

"How did Michael know?"

"His old man. He said his old man followed Monique from the club last week after he went in to talk to her. It was his proof."

"Proof of what?" MacGregor asked curiously before Solomon could.

"Proof of his innocence," Dennis replied. "If he intended to harm Monique, he could have done it anytime he wanted to because he knew where she was staying. But since he didn't do nothing . . .", he said realizing the hole he was digging for himself, his voice faded into silence.

"So, you figured Dr. Ward was guilty," Solomon said emitting a tsk of disgust. Dennis was motivated by fear that he would be implicated for setting the fire by his association with Dr. Ward, Solomon thought, staring at the waiter with burning reproachful eyes. Wordlessly, Dennis lowered his eyes back to the floor. "Damn!" he exclaimed, spinning to stare out the window. The rain had stopped, but dark clouds remained in the blue-black, starless night.

None of them knew who was the real criminal, Solomon thought, putting together the pieces of information they'd learned from Dennis. Some time ago, the waiter was hired by Dr. Anthony Ward to spy on Monique and pull some stupid tricks, accounting for the late night phone calls and mock burglary attempts. So Ward had known Monique worked at the club long before he made his appearance, Solomon mused.

Michael's loose tongue to Dennis about his father's history with Monique helped formed the plot concocted by Ward to regain Monique's interest. The scare tactics were done in part to throw suspicion away from Ward and onto Byron Henderson. They were timed to coincide with Byron's release. Monique was to have been sufficiently frightened as to accept Ward as her hero.

"But why? Why was he willing to go so far to get Monique back?" he asked himself out loud.

"Did she have money?" MacGregor asked Solomon.

"According to the news reports I've seen about the doctor, he seems to have squandered his inheritance. And on top of his legal troubles, he could certainly use some cash."

"Dennis?" Solomon prompted the waiter.

"He seemed to know a lot about her," Dennis replied. With self-loathing cloaking his demeanor, he said, "It was like she was some prize he had to own. It didn't make sense to me, you know. A man like him could have any woman. But, he seemed desperate to get her. Had to have been to set her house on fire."

MacGregor and Solomon exchanged a knowing look. "Money," MacGregor said.

Solomon nodded in agreement as he glowered at Dennis. "You stole that liquor and that money, didn't you?" he challenged. He didn't know for sure, but it stood to reason that Dennis was guilty of a lot more than malicious tricks.

He could see denial forming in Dennis's expression, then the waiter experienced a change of mind. With an affirmative nod of his head, he lowered his gaze to the floor.

"Yes," Dennis murmured. "I knew about Adrienne's ex getting out. She was scared all the time. It made her careless."

"When was the last time you saw Michael and his father?"

"I saw Michael earlier today when he told me his old man turned himself in," Dennis replied, still stammering nervously. "I never saw the old man. Michael said he and some guy they call Cactus who just got out of the joint went drinking in celebration last night," he said, his eyes wide and begging trust. "I guess he hadn't come in."

"Is it possible that Ms. Robbins could be riding around?" MacGregor asked, though his tone was speculative.

"She wouldn't have left Ariana to go riding," Solomon said confidently. He ran a frustrated hand across his head, staring unseeingly across the room. He felt as if he were overlooking something that was very obvious. He couldn't get Dr. Ward's face out of his mind. Quite possibly because he'd never seen Byron Henderson, he mused, he had only a monstrous image of what the man looked like. But he knew what he was capable of doing. He'd already murdered one person. Still, he couldn't discount the possibility that Ward had become so desperate that he wouldn't add murder to the crimes he was already facing. Which one burned the house?

"Where are you headed?"

MacGregor's inquiry cut into Solomon's thoughts. He didn't even realize he had started for the door. "Can Ariana stay here?" he asked urgently.

"Sure," MacGregor replied. "I'll take this one downstairs to my office. I can have someone stay with her if you like."

"Yes, thank you," Solomon replied as he headed with long, purposeful strides towards the door. He was praying his gamble paid off.

"Where are you going?" MacGregor asked.

"T's Place," he replied, his hand on the doorknob.

"Why there?"

"One of them, Byron Henderson or Anthony Ward burned down her home," Solomon replied. "Why not the club? It's all he believes she has left." Neither counted on him.

She never learned the name of that park.

Monique counted it among the list of regrets her mind latched on to, with fear carved in merciless lines on her face. Riding in the car with her captor, terror set the quick tempo of her heart beat. She felt trapped in a real nightmare beyond anything she'd ever encountered or could have dreamed.

The car pulled into the parking lot behind the club. It was dark, and the street lamps were too far away to bring more than a shadow to the area. The car pulled parallel to the railroad stumps separating the parking lot from Buffalo Bayou, a thirty some-odd drop below, and stopped.

She risked a sidelong glance at him, at the shiny weapon

clutched in his hand. He was checking the rearview mirror. Then, he got out. Constantly looking to make sure they weren't followed, he walked around to her side of the car and opened the door.

"Don't forget who's in control."

Monique followed the instructions of the gun waved in her face. From across the lot, the flood light over the back door of *T's Place* beamed a path to the door. She headed towards it shakily, feeling as if she were walking a tightrope.

Wondering what he had in store for her, she knew that once they got inside the club, her chances were nil. But she didn't have the keys to open up, she thought with a speck of jubilance.

"Here," he said, tossing her a set of keys, "open up."

"How . . . how did you get these?" Amazement and defeat in her voice, her hands trembled as she inserted the key in the lock.

"That's my secret," he replied. "And don't try anything stupid."

Entering the back way, an amber light popped on automatically. Monique stood in the utility room as though fastened to a wall, her gaze anxiously scanning the area. A mop leaned against the wall from inside an industrial bucket, offering an attractive weapon.

At the thought of making a dash for it, she felt herself careening towards the doorway of the club as he shoved her, then jerked still by the back collar of her shirt. He was enjoying his power over her, and she felt helpless to lessen his power, knowing he could smell her fear.

It was pitch black beyond the door. Seconds, later, lights flicked on, and she was pushed into the club. Only the bar and stage area were lit; the light spread to encompass the five or six front row tables and chairs.

Monique felt the cool, damp end of the gun barrel at her neck. A quick, hot touch of the devil shot through her, and her heart lost its rhythm. She wondered if this were it, her last breath of life. She thought with great shame that she hadn't tried harder to understand the woman who birthed her. She hoped Ariana was all right, recalling she'd left the young girl in the room waiting for her. She prayed Solomon would forgive her.

"Don't forget who's in control. Now walk," he commanded.

Monique led the way, directed by the gun at her neck. Then, it was gone, and she expired out a sharp breath like someone who had plunged into icy water. Hearing the rustle of movement behind her, she angled her head to look over her shoulder. She stared into the treacherous grin splitting his face in half.

"Did you think I was going to disappear?" he asked, dropping the raincoat on the nearest table, the gun still in his right hand.

Wetting her dry lips, she babbled an attempt to reason with him. "Look, why don't—can't we talk?"

He cut her off, yelling, "Shut up. I'm controlling this action. I tried talking to you before, and you refused to listen. What I had to say wasn't important enough for you. You were too busy *living the life* to concern yourself about me. You're a selfish . . ."

"That's not . . ."

"I thought I told you to shut up!" he said enraged, his arm crossing the space between them to slap her across the mouth with the back of his gun hand.

Monique's hands flew to her mouth, lip split and bleeding. She stifled the whimper in her throat.

Waving the gun towards the stage, he said, "Sit down over there." He didn't wait for her to move, shoved her so hard she stumbled and fell onto the stage floor. "Get up goddamnit, before I lift you with my fist!"

Crying silently, tears streaming down her face, Monique struggled to her feet. He stepped up on stage, grabbed her by the back of the neck and marched her to the piano bench.

He shoved her down, and a startled cry escaped her mouth. He popped her on top of the head.

"I told you to shut up. You women just don't know when to be quiet . . . always running your mouths, demanding this and that, ordering people about. You want to wear the dress and the pants."

With pain and fear owning her wits, Monique sat like an obedient puppet at the piano. She followed him with wide, liquid eyes as he walked down to a front row table. He set the gun on the table in full view. She was certain he did it to remind her of his power. He strutted in a small circle, looking with awe at *T's Place.*

"What do you want?" she asked.

"What do I want?" he repeated with sarcastic disbelief as he spun facing her headlong. "I want . . . ," he paused thoughtfully, a wicked gleam in his eyes laughing at her, "I want my life back the way it was before. Can you handle that, Monique? Can you grant me my every wish?"

"Byron," Monique muttered feebly, then lowered her desperate-glazed eyes to the piano. A drop of blood from her lip fell onto an ivory key. She didn't know what to say to him. Escape seemed hopeless.

"You want this place?" she asked, scarcely aware of her own voice. "You can have it."

"You still don't get it, do you? For such a bright young woman, you don't know anything about people. I don't want this building," he said, his dark eyes radiating hatred as he spread his hands expansively towards the club. "What I'm about doesn't have anything to do with tangibles. They're replaceable. A man's love and his honor are not. But you wouldn't know anything about that, would you? You're nothing but a pathetic little piece of female flesh. You don't have any idea what pride to a man is. What I want, Taylor, is for you to pay like I paid."

With her mind blocking the words of her pending demise, she asked desperately, "What about Michael?"

"What about him?"

"He said you changed, that you were being helped by the people at Project Center."

A wild, hyena-like laugh erupted from Byron. The laughter faded and the smile jelled into a vicious set across his lips. "You believe I was going to give up my manhood to those people, put my balls in their healing hands so they could turn me into some sissified creature? You're as stupid as Michael."

"He believes in you," she said, an edge of desperation in her voice. "You owe him something for that."

"Michael is a boy," he spat out with disdain. "He has a woman's view of what a man is. He'll always have it. That's my only regret," he said in a musing tone. "I was away from him too long to make a difference in him now. And part of being a man is knowing when to give up."

She paused for a moment, as if hesitant about saying her next thought. "Does that mean giving up on yourself? It sounds like a cop out."

"That's just like a woman. You think you know everything. But you don't know nothing. Nothing! My old friend Cactus and I were talking last night," he spoke with conversational casualness. "And we both agree that you women have weakened this country. Everything was going along just fine when you knew your place. But ever since we let you out the house, you've been running hog wild."

"Is that what this is all about, Byron, saving face to prove your manhood to Cactus?" she asked in an even tone.

"I don't have to prove anything to Cactus," he snapped.

"Byron, it's not too late to stop this," she said, guessing he had been influenced by his friend. If he were gullible to Cactus's influence, then maybe she stood a chance to persuade him to end his avenging act. "Let me go, and it will be over like it never happened. Don't let Cactus land you back in jail."

Wordlessly, Byron fixed his penetrating gaze on her as if

contemplating her advice. She felt a tiny ray of hope. Then, a fond gleam came into his eyes.

"Cactus reminds me of my old man. He's the only man left I know who understands what it means to be a man," he said in a resolute voice.

"I don't know about Cactus, but it seems to me you're forgetting your history," she said. "African women came over on the same slave ships that brought African men. We lived under the same enslavement, worked side-by-side in the same fields, hung from the same trees, escaped in the same black nights together." Anger dulled the edge of her fear, fueling her boldness. "How dare you hold yourself more grand, more deserving, more worthy than us to enjoy the benefits of our labors together? And to think that you let someone named Cactus define you," she said, a note of loathing in her tone.

"You shut up talking about Cactus! And it's you who forgot our history, not me. As soon as the white man let you out of the kitchen and into the boardroom, you forgot about us. We weren't good enough for you anymore. You made more money, were given more power and enjoyed more freedom than we did. Then you started harping on us to improve ourselves, and when we couldn't live up to your expectations, you demeaned us. It's why I wanted Tevis to quit her job. I knew it was going to happen. She tried to bring the power and control she had at her job home to me. I couldn't have that in my house."

"That's not true and you know it," Monique replied vehemently. In defending her friend's memory, she was fighting for her own life. "Tevis was not like that. You made up that image, and because you were afraid you couldn't live up to it, you murdered her."

"And then you were calling all the time," he said, as if she hadn't spoken at all. His gaze was dark with bitter memories as he shoved the words at her angrily. "Getting her to go to this meeting, and that meeting, one thing after another, always taking her away from me, from us, what we had together. I loved her. I would have given her anything . . . anything in the world," he said beseechingly with a wounded expression on his face.

With her hopes completely doused, Monique realized the futility of trying to reason with him. His twisted concept of manhood had been formed years ago, she thought despondently. He was thoroughly entrenched in his warped views.

"You don't know what love is," she said gently. An absent smile spread across her face, and her eyes softened, filling with precious memories of Solomon. "Love is not about fists and bruises. It's not about body strength; it's strength of character. It's not about domination; it's about sharing. It's about tender caresses and sweet kisses. It's about savoring the differences and respecting them." She and Solomon almost had it all.

"Sing that song," he said. "The one you sang in church."

Startled, Monique looked up to see him standing at the end of the piano. She hadn't been aware when he came on stage. "What?" she asked, gazing at him with a bemused, wary look in her eyes. Noticing the gun back in his hand, her whole body tightened, her heart thumping against her rib cage.

"You know the one," he said, walking towards her. " 'Precious Memories',," he said with a sarcastic chuckle in his voice. "I think it's kind of appropriate, don't you?"

Monique began to sing, her voice at first wavery with fear. Byron was standing at her back. *Precious memories, how they linger. How they ever flood my soul. . . .*

The more she sang, the stronger her voice became. Her mind was filled with the precious memories of Solomon and Ariana. For a brief moment in her lifetime, love had touched her up close. The memory was a balm to her spirits, and it empowered her voice. She sang fearlessly, her soul gladdened. Solomon would be proud of her.

In the stillness, of the midnight. Sacred secrets will unfold. The words on her lips died, as did her consciousness.

Monique slumped over the piano, and a discord echoed through the sanctum of *T's Place*.

Solomon drove as if the devil himself were chasing him. He sped up Commerce St., heading into the parking lot behind the club. Too late, he swiveled to miss the car pulling out. The slippery street sent the car in a wild spin, and the end of his car spun headlong into the front of the black Vet.

Jolted by the impact, Solomon shook his head at the whirring sound of an engine trying to catch. He peered out his window, and recognition screamed from his gut. He jumped out of his car, racing towards the other that was stalled on the edge of the parking lot.

He saw the man reaching for something in the passenger seat just as he pulled open the door. He didn't care who it was, Anthony Ward or Byron Henderson, just grabbed him by the neck and dragged him from the car.

Enraged and fueled by fear, he slammed him into the door, then watched him slide to the ground, groaning. Apprehension pounded in his chest like a kettledrum, fearing that he was too late.

"Where's Monique?" he demanded. He grabbed a handful of hair and pulled the head back to look into his victim's face.

Breathlessly, Byron tried to laugh and choked on his laughter. Solomon slammed a raging fist down into the side of his face. He fell to the ground like a limp nugget.

"Monique," Solomon screamed as he set out in a furious pace, running towards the club. He heard the fire alarm ringing before he reached the door. He pulled up, cursing himself, remembering the keys were back in the car. Infuriated with himself, he kicked the door in angry frustration, and to his utter surprise, it opened.

At the first sound of silence he encountered, a roar of

blood pounded in his ears. Advancing, the smell of smoke greeted him.

"Monique!" he shouted as he bolted into the club, covering his face. It looked as if miniature bonfires had been set atop several of the tables. The fire jumped from one wooden chair or cotton tablecloth of one table to the next. It was spreading fast.

Coughing and sputtering from the smoke, he raced to the offices. Fire was blazing in each one. "Monique, where are you?" Solomon called out desperately.

He hurried to the kitchen and turned on the faucets while pulling tablecloths from a cabinet over the sink. He wetted them, covered his face with one, then left the room with the water running.

With smoke billowing around him and fires burning in earnest, he checked the restrooms . . . double-backed to the employees station, and finally, he hurried to the stockroom.

After several attempts, he unlocked the door and pushed it open. His eyes adjusted to the dark and darted around the room not yet touched by smoke. A body was sprawled lifelessly on the floor between a carton of Charmin and several cases of liquor.

With fear a frozen thing in his heart, Solomon gasped, trapping the breath in his chest. He approached cautiously, each step a dreaded, frightful one. He kneeled beside it, and gingerly, turned it over. The soft sough of Monique's breathing filled him with such relief, tears filled his eyes.

Sirens sang in the distance as he covered her face with a tablecloth, before lifting her in his arms. He raced through the maze of rooms returning to the club proper. The stage area that contained the electronic equipment exploded, nearly knocking him backwards. He stumbled, regained his balance and continued out the back way, just seconds before a blaze of fire burst out into the black night.

Eighteen

Monique didn't have the energy nor the inclination for gratitude, even though she knew she had plenty for which to be grateful. Standing in the bathroom mirror, she applied the final touches of make-up.

She was doing it to at least look alive, even though she didn't feel it. Aurelius was on his way over. Since her home was destroyed, she directed her mail to the Redmon's. He was bringing the check from the insurance company. They would also discuss plans for the club.

It had been seven whole days since the fire at *T's Place,* and four days since her physical recovery from a concussion and cracked ribs. Her face no longer showed evidence of the black eyes and swollen mouth, all of which were compliments of Byron Henderson. He was back in jail awaiting trial.

She'd keep a closer watch on his incarceration this time. Reliving the nightmarish memory, she felt a tightness in her bosom. She could almost smell the suffocating smoke burning her lungs as the fire sucked the breath from her body. She shivered, swallowed and shook the sensations from her mind.

She felt really awful for Michael. He had so desperately wanted Byron to be the father of his dreams. But he was recovering, too. Dennis had been a surprise, she thought, disdain darkening her eyes. Learning he not only stole from her, but conspired with Anthony Ward against her continued to amaze her. It confirmed what she had been told about herself—she didn't know people, she thought, twisting her lips in self-reproach.

It was especially true about her reading of Solomon. She felt a fresh pain of his rejection, a prickling in her chest, like a puncture wound in her heart. Somehow or another, she had to recover her soul.

"This will have to do," she said to her reflection, flipping the single braid over her shoulder. She turned off the light as she left the bathroom, heading for the bedroom.

On every conceivable surface in the living area of the suite was a bright, sweet-smelling flower or decorative plant, sucking up sun that shone through the drawn curtains.

The room looked like a funeral parlor, she thought. The get-well wishes were still pouring in. But not her wish, she mused, absently dropping to the couch.

After pulling her from the burning building, Solomon was with her for the ambulance ride to the hospital, then to the Redmons where she stayed a couple of days. When her parents arrived after a call from Patricia, he disappeared. It was as if his duty to her were complete. She had heard from neither of the Thomases since last Thursday.

With a leap in thoughts, she wondered if Ariana opened up to Solomon. Regardless of how idiotic he might believe her notions to be, it was crucial that he give her a hearing. Though she suspected Ariana's mother kept no secrets from her, it was likely that their relationship was strained by the demands and expectations Elaine put on her daughter. They weren't completely unreasonable, but recalling her own goddaughter's complaints, she knew they felt cumbersome to a teenager. Unfortunately, no one could tell Ariana that she was lucky to receive her mother's attention and interest. Awareness and appreciation would come later, when Ariana matured, and if she were given a positive sense of self from at least one of her parents.

Unaware she had even picked up the black, leather-bound

notebook from the table, Monique thumbed through the pages. It was a reminder of what was important. She had to put Solomon and Ariana out of her mind altogether. It was time to get on with her life, she told herself, replacing the book on the table.

But something positive had come from the horrible events she'd lived through, she thought, trying to console the sense of loneliness she felt. At last, she knew the whole story about the girl in her dreams. Her father Marlon Robbins—or rather, the man she'd known as her father—was actually her stepfather. He forced her mother to tell her the truth.

She, Taylor Monique, was the frightened, little girl hiding in the closet. She always ran there when her real father, for whom she was named, Taylor King became abusive. He was Marlon's best friend, as well as business partner in a record store they owned.

The end of her dream matched the final episode of abuse she witnessed from her safe spot. Taylor beat her mother for the last time when Marlon showed up, and the two men fought. Marlon, the man she called *Daddy,* was the person who rescued her from hiding.

In exchange for her and Kathreen's freedom, Marlon gave up his ownership in the store. Taylor King agreed to give up custody of her and promised never to contact them again.

Severing all connections to him, her mother married Marlon. He admitted to having been in love with her for quite some time, even before he knew about the abuse. But her mother never fully recovered from the battered wife's syndrome. Both she and Marlon were constant reminders of her guilt and shame. Unconsciously, Kathreen blamed them for being a mother who was too frightened to protect her child and a woman who had abandoned her vows. Their marriage dissolved five years later, but by then, she was Marlon's daughter legally and emotionally.

Her real father had been dead now for ten years. An alcoholic, he drove his car into a ditch one night and was killed instantly. She felt nothing for him.

The secret out, the little girl was truly free, Monique mused. But she wondered about her own future—whether she was destined to live with regret for the rest of her life. She had no one to blame but herself, she mused, slipping back into her thoughts of Solomon.

With a bittersweet sigh of longing respiring in her bosom, she remembered their very first meeting. He was forbidden to her right from the start, a patron of whom she couldn't get out of her mind. The next thing she knew, he was the manager of *T's Place*. From there, the attraction persisted. Oh, she'd fought it, she mused with a sad smile on her face: he nor the feelings he created in her appeared in her business plan.

Even before she knew anything about him, she was drawn to him. But the more she came to discover—though sapiently reticent on the outside, he was sensually loquacious in bed, predisposed to speaking words of desire with demonstration—the wishing, the wanting, the knowing ineffably heightened. No resistance in the world could have warded off the inevitable.

Solomon Thomas was the kind of man her daddy wished for her, a man who managed her with a loving hand. He was very different from Byron, she thought with rue for Tevis. She found it impossible to compare the intangible emotion that bound them together with what she and Solomon had, even briefly. In hindsight, she realized that Tevis never knew real love, the kind that brought supreme joy, one that hurt without putting an end to all sensations. But because Tevis had been her role model, she forgot that role models were susceptible to false feelings and prone to make mistakes like everyone else. Like her. Still, she had been the luckier of the two.

A knock on the door jolted Monique from her melancholy muse. With a tired sigh, she pushed herself up and sauntered to the door. "Coming," she said, pushing her cheeks up in a smile with her hands. She opened the door, and the phony smile melted into a look of pure shock that brought with it, streamers of utter delight coursing through her.

Her gaze roamed the length of Solomon. She imbibed her fill of his handsome face and exquisite body clad in a gold Polo shirt and tight-fitting jeans, molding the power of his physique. He was even wearing sandals, she noticed amazed, with mouth-watering hunger in her eyes. She detected something indefinable in his manner—she couldn't say what, but it only enhanced his august presence.

"Solomon," she exclaimed in a breathless whisper. "What are you doing here?" she asked, though she felt rejuvenated. The woodsy fragrance of his cologne crossed the threshold and caused further disruption to her senses. Her heart beat a joyous rhythm in her chest.

He cocked a brow and looked down his broad nose at her. "Has the meeting been canceled?" he asked in a somewhat haughty tone.

With her wits retarded, she replied dumbfounded, "The meeting?" Watching the blank expression on his face, she felt extremely annoyed at the transparency of her feelings and swallowed her disappointment. "Uh, uh," she babbled. Finally, "No, Aurelius should be here shortly."

"Then I'm here for the meeting," he drawled with distinct mockery.

He walked past her nonchalantly into the room. She slammed the door so hard—as if to shut out the swooning desires threatening to carry her away—its rattle reverberated up and down the corridor.

The nerve of him! Monique fumed silently. She hadn't heard from nor seen him in four days, and he comes waltzing in here like, as if he belonged, she thought, her heart palpating furiously in her chest.

* * *

Solomon advised his innards to calm down. The nearly five-day absence from Monique created havoc with his senses. He stood at the side of the dining table for the view the position afforded him. Under the guise of an unaffected stare, he feasted on her as she stormed into the room.

She was beyond mere prosaic beauty, he thought, a sigh expanding his lungs. The healthy glow of her warm brown complexion was unblemished by the scars of Byron Henderson's violent hands. His eyes narrowed and darkened with the memory, and he felt a shiver of fear slide down his spine. With a barely noticeable shake of his head, he banished the reminder with a silent prayer of thanks that he had not been too late.

He watched her with veiled eyes. She flashed him a pout-like tsk, dropped to the couch, and crossed her leg at the knee. As her disposition suggested, she struggled for restraint, fanning the air with her foot. He almost felt guilty for setting her off the second he arrived. But he was still a desperate man in need of desperate measures to reclaim his second half.

In truth, he was enjoying her hot reaction. It infused him with hope: she still felt something for him, though he'd rather set something other than her temper on fire.

But it was too soon for that. They had other matters to work through, he reminded himself. Aurelius, as planned, would be late.

"I guess you're wondering where I've been," he said.

Her foot stilled, and she rolled her eyes up at him. "I could care less," she replied in a chilly voice, before that foot went back to work.

Solomon suppressed a smug smile. "Ariana and I flew up to Michigan to see Elaine," he said. Noticing the pique of interest in her eyes, he took the chair across the couch from her. "We got back late last night."

"And?" she pressed, a hint of impatience in her tone.

"It was the most intense few days we've ever spent together. It was as if we were on a parenting retreat," he said, soft laughter unfurling from his throat. "It's a good thing Elaine has a big house."

"You stayed at her house?" she said with amazed disbelief edging her tone. A none-too-pleased look shone on her face.

Reading the hint of jealousy in her expression, Solomon was immensely gratified. "She insisted, and so did Ariana," he replied, with a casual shrug of his shoulders. "It didn't make sense to waste money on a hotel room. The place has five bedrooms."

Monique smacked her lips with censure. Still, he could tell she was no longer as upset as she let on. Her foot was no longer moving.

"Anyway," he picked up, "I think we made some head way. Part of the problem was what I had begun to suspect, but didn't want to accept. I wasn't the only one. Elaine was guilty, too."

"Guilty of what?"

"Not wanting or ready to accept that our baby is growing up," he replied. "Ariana wants answers for her pain, not a kiss on the cheek or a new toy. Those days are over."

Monique nodded in agreement.

"And then we realized something else," he said, brushing his hands together. "Two things really, but they're interrelated. We were so intent on preparing Ariana for the future, that we forgot to introduce her to her past. We were raising her based on what we experienced growing up, and she didn't understand it. She's never known about our childhoods," he said with rueful mirth.

"Because all her needs have been met and her wants fulfilled," Monique supplied. "The Redmons have voiced similar concerns about their children."

"Yeah," he said. "Needless to say, we couldn't cram generations' old history of struggle and success in a few days. But, at least Elaine and I are aware." He expired lengthily as if exhausted. "The changes in society pose a hell of a problem for parents in many situations. Sometimes," he said with a bemused look, "you just don't know what to tell your child."

Solomon smiled at her indulgently. In the lingering silence, he watched Monique staring into her private space. He knew she was concerned for Ariana's sake, but he also knew she really didn't want to hear the nightmares of parenting.

"Teach her to jump," Monique said. "Encourage her to reach for the stars. If she falls from the sky, catch her, brush her off if need be, then send her back to try again."

A smile turning up a corner of his mouth, he asked, "How did you get to be so smart?"

"That's my secret," she replied.

Staring at her intently, he felt the onslaught of the uninhibited desires she provoked in him: he wanted to take her right then and there. "Yeah, you're good with those." It was something they were going to have to correct.

"Elaine and I got a chance to talk . . . really talk for the first time since the divorce," he continued in a soft, somber voice. "It became clear that the problems we had over money, quite honestly, had nothing to do with money at all.

"Money was the name we used because neither one of us wanted to admit the truth . . . that there was no passion between us. Elaine had realized it even before I did, but she felt in a bigger quandary than I did about what was wrong with our marriage and didn't know how to bring it up. When we married, somewhere in the back of our heads, we resigned ourselves to settle for the comfort and security we could give each other." Only to find out that it wasn't enough, he thought solemnly.

Noticing the look of sad regret in his expression, Monique felt a hazy warning spread through her blood. More fright-

ened than when she believed she was about to die, it chilled
her to the bone. The more she heard, the clearer Solomon's
presence became to her. With pulse-pounding certainty, she
realized he'd come to completely sever ties with her.

The silence in the room stretched and tightened with tension. Assailed by an upheaval on her entire being, Monique
stared at him with an odd mingling of sensations. Her insides softened and ached in ways that made her burn with
more emotional than physical want. Yet, her heart was crying, dissolving into a torrent of bitter tears. She could no
longer feel happy for Ariana and riled herself for suggesting
she involve her father with her mother. Her noble gesture
backfired: Solomon was going back to Elaine.

A painful lump lodged itself in her throat. To her utter
humiliation, the threat of tears stung her eyes. "I uh, I don't
know what to say," she said, pinching at eyes as if something
had caught in them.

"You don't have to say anything," he said, sliding from
the chair to sit next to her on the couch.

Monique sprang up and crossed the room to stare out the
window. She couldn't acknowledge the endless stretch of
clear, sunny skies, feeling dark gray clouds building on her
spirits. She felt Solomon's approach before he was upon her.
She stiffened against his imminent touch, thoroughly familiar with its potency. When it came, she struggled against his
attempts to turn her facing him. She didn't dare look at him,
let him see her anguish, fearing she would start crying and
begging him to stay. She wasn't as principled as he and
Elaine.

Her frozen stand was no match against his dogged determination. With his hands firm on her shoulders, she felt her
bereavement and longing meld together and intensify.

"Monique, what is it?" he asked, staring down at her intently.

When she didn't reply, he lifted her face by the chin.
Forced to look into his compelling gaze, a sense of all she

had lost and all Elaine had gained at her expense loomed monstrously before her. Knowing she had to escape this malignant episode with all the dignity she could muster, she adopted anger.

"What is it?" she replied in a steel-edged voice. "How much deeper are you going to twist the knife?" Solomon tried to speak, but she wasn't finished. "I'm really happy that you and Elaine didn't toss aside Ariana's feelings as unimportant. I'm sure Ariana is relieved to have both of her parents in her corner. But if you've come here to tell me you and Elaine have reconciled and you're moving to Michigan, just say it and get it over with."

Stunned by her interpretation, Solomon ran his hands down his face. The chuckle in his chest blossomed and shortly, his laughter filled the room.

"What's so funny?" she snapped.

With his laughter winding down, Solomon draped his arms around her, pulling her into the circle of his arms. Dignity scattered. She couldn't deny herself this opportunity to bask in his nearness. Elaine would have him forever; certainly she wouldn't begrudge her this final, but brief moment of a tender memory.

"I wasn't going to say that at all," he said.

Over her head, she felt the vibration in his throat as his voice poured over her like a smooth, dulcet liquid. "Oh?"

"No," he replied, shaking his head, stretching the moment.

"Then . . . ," she said over her choking heart, "then what were you going to say?"

"I was going to say that my life didn't begin until the night I walked into *T's Place* and saw you," he said. "From there, the wonders never ceased—even when I accused you of betraying my trust. Please forgive me," he said in a deeply affected voice that trembled. "I made a horrible, horrible mistake because of my own insecurity and punished you for it. Only," he said, pulling back to look down into her face,

"I was punishing myself, by denying the most precious gift two people could give each other."

Monique stared speechless up into his face, the veracious intent in the depths of his eyes. Her heart readily accepted the truth in his expression; her brain trusted it, and the warmth that had been missing from her life surged through her.

"I love you, Monique Robbins," he said in a loving, proud assertion.

With the gray rims of her eyes wide and a felicitous light beaming from her amber gaze, Monique replied in a barely audible voice, "You do?" She just wanted to hear it again.

"I do," he replied, bobbing his head. "Very, very much. Will you marry me?"

All the life support systems in her seemed to concentrate in the region of her heart, brimming to an overflow with her love. And the tears began to fall in earnest, like quiet drops of joy from her eyes. "Yes," she replied, feeling glorious sensations, like rockets going off inside her. Clinging to him, her arms around his neck, she exclaimed, "Oh, yes. I'll . . .

"Always love you," she was about to add before his mouth swooped down on hers for a kiss that stole her breath away.

Locked in the untold delights of each other's arms with lips sealing their pledges of love in a lingering kiss, neither heard the door open.

Aurelius walked in carrying a bottle of champagne. Patricia followed with a cake box in her hands.

"Good," he said. "I'm glad you've already worked out a satisfactory compromise."

ROMANCES ABOUT AFRICAN-AMERICANS!
YOU'LL FALL IN LOVE
WITH ARABESQUE BOOKS FROM PINNACLE

SERENADE   (0024, $4.99)
by Sandra Kitt

Alexandra Morrow was too young and naive when she first
fell in love with musician, Parker Harrison—and vowed
never to be so vulnerable again. Now Parker is back and
although she tries to resist him, he strolls back into her life
as smoothly as the jazz rhapsodies for which he is known.
Though not the dreamy innocent she was before, Alexandra finds her defenses quickly crumbling and her mind,
body and soul slowly opening up to her one and only love,
who shows her that dreams do come true.

FOREVER YOURS   (0025, $4.99)
by Francis Ray

Victoria Chandler must find a husband quickly or her
grandparents will call in the loans that support her chain
of lingerie boutiques. She arranges a mock marriage to
tall, dark and handsome ranch owner Kane Taggart. The
marriage will only last one year, and her business will be
secure, and Kane will be able to walk away with no strings
attached. The only problem is that Kane has other plans
for Victoria. He'll cast a spell that will make her his forever
after.

A SWEET REFRAIN   (0041, $4.99)
by Margie Walker

Fifteen years before, jazz musician Nathaniel Padell walked
out on Jenine to seek fame and fortune in New York City.
But now the handsome widower is back with a baby girl in
tow. Jenine is still irresistibly attracted to Nat and enchanted
by his daughter. Yet even as love is rekindled, an unexpected
danger threatens Nat's child. Now, Jenine must fight for Nat
before someone stops the music forever!

*Available wherever paperbacks are sold, or order direct from the
Publisher. Send cover price plus 50¢ per copy for mailing and
handling to Penguin USA, P.O. Box 999, c/o Dept. 17109,
Bergenfield, NJ 07621. Residents of New York and Tennessee
must include sales tax. DO NOT SEND CASH.*

TIMELESS LOVE

Look for these historical romances in the Arabesque line:

BLACK PEARL by Francine Craft (0236-0, $4.99)

CLARA'S PROMISE by Shirley Hailstock (0147-X, $4.99)

MIDNIGHT MOON by Mildred Riley (0200-X; $4.99)

SUNSHINE AND SHADOWS by Roberta Gayle (0136-4, $4.99)

Available wherever paperbacks are sold, or order direct from the Publisher. Send cover price plus 50¢ per copy for mailing and handling to Penguin USA, P.O. Box 999, c/o Dept. 17109, Bergenfield, NJ 07621. Residents of New York and Tennessee must include sales tax. DO NOT SEND CASH.